A NIGHT IN WITH AUDREY HEPBURN

Actress Libby Lomax has retreated into the world of classic movies, where the immortal lives of her favourite screen goddesses seem to offer so much more in the romance department than her own. After a terrible day on set, where she embarrasses herself in front of the entire cast and — worst of all — its sexy bad-boy star, Dillon O'Hara, she plonks herself down on her battered couch to watch *Breakfast at Tiffany's* for the trillionth time. Suddenly, Libby is astonished to find screen icon Audrey Hepburn — complete with little black dress, trademark sunglasses and vintage cigarette holder — sitting beside her and offering advice. But has Libby got what it takes to turn her life from a turkey into a blockbuster? Perhaps with a little bit of Audrey Hepburn magic, she might just pull it off . . .

SPECIAL MESSAGE TO READERS

THE ULVERSCROFT FOUNDATION
(registered UK charity number 264873)
was established in 1972 to provide funds for
research, diagnosis and treatment of eye diseases.
Examples of major projects funded by
the Ulverscroft Foundation are:-

- The Children's Eye Unit at Moorfields Eye Hospital, London
- The Ulverscroft Children's Eye Unit at Great Ormond Street Hospital for Sick Children
- Funding research into eye diseases and treatment at the Department of Ophthalmology, University of Leicester
- The Ulverscroft Vision Research Group, Institute of Child Health
- Twin operating theatres at the Western Ophthalmic Hospital, London
- The Chair of Ophthalmology at the Royal Australian College of Ophthalmologists

You can help further the work of the Foundation
by making a donation or leaving a legacy.
Every contribution is gratefully received. If you
would like to help support the Foundation or
require further information, please contact:

THE ULVERSCROFT FOUNDATION
The Green, Bradgate Road, Anstey
Leicester LE7 7FU, England
Tel: (0116) 236 4325

website: www.foundation.ulverscroft.com

A NIGHT IN WITH AUDREY HEPBURN

LUCY HOLLIDAY

LARGE
PRINT

First published in Great Britain 2015
by
Harper
an imprint of HarperCollins*Publishers*

First Isis Edition
published 2016
by arrangement with
HarperCollins*Publishers*

A catalogue record for this book is available
from the British Library.

ISBN 978–1–78541–268–4 (hb)
ISBN 978–1–78541–274–5 (pb)

Published by
F. A. Thorpe (Publishing)
Anstey, Leicestershire

Set by Words & Graphics Ltd.
Anstey, Leicestershire
Printed and bound in Great Britain by
T. J. International Ltd., Padstow, Cornwall

This book is printed on acid-free paper

Acknowledgements

Heartfelt thanks to Kate Bradley, Kate Elton and all the team at HarperFiction, without whom this book would simply not exist. Thanks, too, to Clare Alexander for wisdom above and beyond the call of agenting, and to Lana Bonacic for telling me all about working as an extra on a film set. And, if I may be so bold, to Audrey Hepburn, for being Audrey Hepburn.

June 1999

There's no way on earth I'm going to get this part. For starters, the show is called *The Sound of "Music"*, and I'm about as musical as a rusty tin opener. Seriously, I can barely hold a tune. If the director and casting agent suddenly have a drastic change of heart, and decide instead to start auditioning the hundred-odd kids gathered here this afternoon for a brand-new musical called *The Sound of Rusty Tin Openers* . . . well, then I'll be a shoo-in. Until then, though, I'd estimate my chances of winning the role of Louisa Von Trapp at roughly zero.

Oh, and for another thing, all the other girls here at the New Wimbledon Theatre with the label "LOUISA" stuck to their chests are petite, blonde, and cute-as-a-button pretty.

Whereas I'm a bit gangly, my hair is the colour of double espresso, and even though I don't think I should be walking about with a paper bag on my head, cute-as-a-button prettiness isn't really my thing.

In fact, surely the director and casting agent are going to seriously question why I'm here at all.

It's a question with a pretty straightforward answer, though: my mother.

And here she is now, bustling back over towards me and my sister Cass, fresh from five minutes of wrangling with the casting director's assistant.

"Did it!" Mum practically yells, with the sort of triumphant fist-clutch Tim Henman is always doing on Wimbledon's Centre Court, just a mile down the road from here, shortly before he's knocked out of the tournament for another year.

"Mum! Can't you be a bit quieter?"

I mean, it's embarrassing enough that she forced me and Cass to come to the auditions in matching, egg-yolk yellow dirndls (though actually Cass, a cute eight-year-old, looks rather fetching in hers, whereas I, an awkward thirteen-year-old, look like a badly stuffed rag doll, in a much smaller rag doll's dress, after eating an entire deep-pan pizza); but now she's drawing even more attention to the three of us.

"They've agreed to move your audition half an hour earlier, Cass," Mum is going on, ignoring me, "because of the family emergency we have to get to."

"What family emergency?" asks Cass.

"*You* know. The important one," Mum fibs. "Anyway," she adds, lowering her voice so that only Cass and I can hear her, "the point is that it'll get you in to audition ahead of the youngest Walker girl, so I'd be perfectly happy to say your grandparents were on fire if it did the trick."

"The youngest Walker girl" is Mum and Cass's nemesis: a triple-threat nine-year-old (acting, singing and dancing) from an apparently unending line of showbiz Walkers. She has pipped Cass to the post for three big roles lately: Annie in the Aylesbury Waterside production of *Annie*, Cosette in a production of *Les Mis* at the Secombe Theatre in Sutton, and, most gallingly of all, Tevye's youngest daughter Bielke in a nationwide-touring revival of *Fiddler on the Roof*. In fact, she's over in the far corner of the lobby right now, practising some stunning-sounding arpeggios, and occasionally, for no terribly good reason at all, sinking into an impressive splits. (I don't know if the splits are required in *The Sound of Music*, I don't actually *remember* any in the Julie Andrews movie version, but it's certainly doing a good job of psyching out all the other prospective Brigittas.) The last display of the splits caused three of them to burst into simultaneous tears and flee the auditions before their names were even called. Though it did earn the youngest Walker girl a pretty fierce telling-off from her older sister, another of the showbiz Walkers, who's evidently here for the part of Louisa, and looking almost as unenthusiastic about it as I am.

"They just need a chance to see *you* before they see *her*, darling," Mum is telling Cass, "and that part is yours. Now, do you need me to run through the words to the goatherd song again, or do you think you've got it now?"

"I've *got* it, Mum!" Cass may be a full five years younger than me, but she's got roughly five times my chutzpah. "For God's *sake*. Anyway, if I forget any of the main words, I'll just skip as fast as possible to the *Star Wars* bit."

Mum and I both stare at her, in confusion.

"*You* know, the bits where I sing Yoda Yoda Yoda Yoda ... I don't understand, though," Cass adds, plaintively, "what Yoda has to do with *The Sound of Music* at all."

I think I need a breath of fresh air.

"Where are you going?" Mum shrieks, as I reach across to one of the orange plastic chairs for my rucksack. "What about your audition?"

"It's not until ten past three, Mum. That's three and a half hours away. Anyway, I thought I might go and find a quiet place to rehearse."

"Finding a quiet place to rehearse" often means I get left in peace for a while, without Mum coming and nagging me to help Cass learn lines for whatever audition or show is currently on the schedule, or without Cass coming and nagging me to give her a makeover so she looks like Sabrina the Teenage Witch.

Honestly, if I was rehearsing as much as I claim I am, I'd probably be acing it at this audition, exactly like one of the showbiz Walkers.

"That's probably a good idea," Mum agrees, because even if she must know there's no chance of me getting this part, at least if I'm well rehearsed I won't actually embarrass her. "Oh, and Libby . . ." She's reaching into her handbag for her mobile phone, and handing it over to me. "*Please* will you ring your father and remind him he's picking you up from *here* at four o'clock, not home. I've already left him two voicemails, and I'm not calling him again. Why he thinks I've nothing better to do with my time than chase around after him trying to convince him to keep his rare appointments with his only daughter, I don't know."

"He's been busy," I tell her, "with the book."

"And the Pope," Mum replies, "is Catholic."

Which means it's time for me to get out of here, before Mum can start on about Dad's book again. And the one thing this hideous waiting room really needs is Mum working herself up about Dad in a manner that would make you think they'd been divorced for only ten minutes instead of almost ten years.

I mean, she only divorced Cass's father Michael six months ago, but she manages to remain calm — pleasant, even — throughout all her dealings with *him*.

"OK, OK," I say, already backing towards the doors that lead to the main auditorium. "I'll see you a bit later. Break a leg in there, Cass."

But Cass has started to spritz her face with an Evian water spray and isn't paying any attention.

I already know the auditorium at the New Wimbledon Theatre pretty well, from way too many days spent waiting around here last November while Cass was rehearsing *Babes in the Wood*, the festive season pantomime.

It's so massive that it's perfectly easy to squirrel yourself away far up in the upper circle, right at the back, and nobody will know where you are to bother you, even if they felt like it. So that's exactly where I'm heading now, for a bit of peace and quiet. And it's actually really, really nice up here, once you've recovered from the climb up the half-billion stairs, that is. Row F, that's where I always used to hang out: I ended up

5

feeling quite at home there on all those endless cold November days, with a good book, and my Discman, and a posh, weekly-allowance-busting chicken Caesar sandwich from the Pret a Manger opposite the station.

I settle down into seat number 23, perfectly situated halfway along the aisle, and reach back into my rucksack for my book.

Actually, my *books*. Three of them, placed on special order from our local library in Kensal Rise, and just come in yesterday.

Humphrey Bogart: A Biography.

The Man, the Dancer: The Life of Fred Astaire.

Enchantment: The Life of Audrey Hepburn.

Hmmm.

Now that I've actually got them, here in my hands, I'm not looking forward to ploughing into them quite as much as I'd thought.

They look a bit . . .

Well, I don't want to actually think the word *boring*. Because these are all books that Dad recommended I read — books he recommends to his film studies students — and I doubt he'd have suggested them if they were really as dull as they look.

And I'm sure they won't be dull at all, once I actually get into them.

It's just that it's the movies themselves I love, and not (what Mum, rather dismissively, calls) all the pontificating about them.

Which Dad doesn't do. Pontificate, I mean. Even though it's his job to pontificate, so it wouldn't be wrong if he *did*.

I do sometimes think it's just a little bit of a shame, though, that he doesn't seem to be able to really enjoy the movies themselves any more. Especially when it was him who introduced them all to me, on the nights when I used to go and stay at his place. And he picked them carefully as well, starting out with the lighter stuff — *Some Like It Hot, It's a Wonderful Life, Roman Holiday* — when I was seven or eight, and moving on to more grown-up fare — *Casablanca, Sunset Boulevard* — by the time I was ten or eleven. I might not have always understood everything I was watching (in fact, in the case of *Citizen Kane*, for example, I understood precisely *nothing* of what I was watching), but that never stopped me being dazzled. I mean, just the Hollywood *glow* of it all. And Dad would make popcorn — well, he made popcorn a couple of times — and turn off all the lights so that, with his huge TV, it was almost like we were in a proper cinema . . . and these screen legends just seemed to come to life. Marilyn Monroe. Ingrid Bergman. Grace Kelly. Lauren Bacall. Audrey Hepburn — most of all, Audrey Hepburn.

No: I'm quite sure a book about Audrey Hepburn isn't going to be dull. How could it possibly be? My favourite of favourites, the movie star I've worshipped from the moment I first saw her.

I'll make a start on this one first — and leave Bogey and Fred Astaire for another day — so that I can talk about it with Dad when I see him tonight. He's bound to have read them all already: he's writing a book, my Dad is, not just about Audrey Hepburn and Humphrey

Bogart, but a . . . hang on, what did he call it the last time he mentioned it? *A definitive, fully updated, no-holds-barred history of Hollywood's most exciting era.* So it'll be really nice, over dinner tonight, to discuss everything I've been reading, and hopefully —

"Anything good?"

It's a boy.

Sitting two rows behind me, on Row H.

Well, I say "boy"; he sounds — and looks, now I've spun round to stare at him — fourteen or fifteen, so "young man" might be a more accurate description. He's tall, maybe over six foot, if his legs dangling over into Row G are anything to go by, and he's wearing a light brown Stüssy sweatshirt that matches his hair and, because it's too big across his shoulders, makes him look a little bit lanky.

"The book, I mean," he goes on. "Anything good?" Then, probably because I'm just staring at him with a startled-goldfish look on my face, he adds, hastily, "I didn't follow you up here, or anything, by the way. I was just sitting and having a bit of a break when you came in."

"A break from the auditions?" I ask, in the sort of flat, bored-sounding voice you're meant to use with boys (and that I'm not very good at; I always end up sounding like a depressed robot).

"Christ, no! I'm not actually doing an audition. I'm just here with my sisters. My mum had to take one of my other sisters to an audition for the Royal Ballet School today, and she didn't want them travelling all the way to Wimbledon on the buses by themselves."

Sisters — plural — auditioning for this show, and another one trying out for the Royal Ballet School . . .

"You're not one of the Showbiz Walkers, are you?" I ask.

He looks startled for a moment, and then laughs.

"Bloody hell. Is *that* what my family's known as?"

"Sorry . . . I'm really sorry . . . that sounded weird. It's only me who calls you that. And only in my head, I don't say it to anyone else."

"It's all right. Do you want a sandwich?"

It's my turn to look a bit startled, because it's such a non sequitur, but he doesn't seem to notice. He's busily opening a large plastic container on the seat next to him, and taking out a large wedge of something wrapped in waxed paper, some sliced tomatoes and fresh lettuce leaves, and a small penknife.

"I always bring my own stuff when I know I'm going to get stuck waiting about at these stupid auditions," he's saying, reaching down beneath his seat and producing, rather like a magician, an entire baguette in a paper bag. "And this cheddar is amazing. It's Irish. My sisters got it for me for my birthday."

"They gave you *cheese* for your birthday?"

"No, sorry, that sounds weird. They gave me membership of a cheese club. You get sent a different cheese through the post each month." He uses the penknife to hack, enthusiastically, at the cheddar. "So? Would you like a sandwich, or not?"

"Yes, Please. I'd love a sandwich."

"Coming right up. I'm Olly, by the way. Olly Showbiz-Walker."

I grin at him. "I'm Libby. Libby Lomax."

"So are *you* auditioning, then?"

I'm actually surprised he has to ask, thanks to the egg-yolk-yellow dirndl, and all. But it's just possible he thinks I actually dress like this . . . I reach for my rucksack again and hastily drag out the grey hooded top I know is in there, pulling it on to disguise the worst of the faux-Austrian look.

"Yes," I admit. "But only because of *my* little sister. She's the showbiz one in our family. I've just ended up sort of sucked into it because of her."

"Oh? You look quite keen on the whole showbiz thing yourself." When I obviously look a bit confused, he gestures towards the book I'm holding. "Audrey Hepburn," he adds. "Are you a big fan?"

"Isn't everyone?"

He shrugs. "I'm not. I don't get what makes everyone so gaga about her."

I stare at him. "Not even in *Breakfast at Tiffany's?*"

"Never seen it. Never seen a single one of her films, now I come to think of it."

"Well, then, you can't possibly say you don't like her! And you really should see one of her films. There's an Audrey Hepburn —" I have to pause for a moment, because I almost always get this word wrong — "*retrospective*, right now, at the Prince Charles cinema in Leicester Square. A commemorative thing, because she would have been seventy this year. I'm going there with my dad this evening, in fact."

"Hmmm. You do know that *The Matrix* is on in Leicester Square, don't you?"

"*The Matrix*," I say, rather haughtily, "is *not Breakfast at Tiffany's*."

"Right. OK. Well, you're obviously a total Audrey Hepburn nut," Olly Walker says, cheerfully. "I can tell there'll be no reasoning with you."

"I'm not an Audrey Hepburn nut!" I protest.

On the other hand . . .

Well, I don't tell many people this . . . in fact, I've never told anyone this, but I do sometimes have this . . . well, I don't know what you'd call it. A daydream? A fantasy?

In which I imagine that I'm best friends with Audrey Hepburn; that she and I hang out together in amazing locations all over New York and Paris; that we windowshop on Fifth Avenue and take tea at the Ritz; and that, most of all, she's always there to talk to me, to listen to me about stuff that's going wrong in my life, to dispense calm and wise and perfectly judged advice, all the while looking breathtakingly chic in Givenchy couture and radiating her aura of gentle serenity.

Because I don't know if you've noticed by now, but calmness and wisdom and gentle serenity aren't things I have very much of in my real, non-fantasy life.

Or Givenchy couture, come to mention it.

And I know it might sound a bit weird — OK, I know it definitely sounds completely weird — but honestly, who *wouldn't* want a best friend like Audrey Hepburn? Sweet, stylish, and utterly lovely in every imaginable way? Who better to "chat" to, in your idle moments, about anything and everything that's bothering you, from the unfortunate outbreak of zits along the entire length of your jawline the night before the end-of-term disco, to your mother's refusal to accept that you might not be cut out for a career on the stage . . . to worrying, just occasionally, that your dad enjoys spending time in the company of long-dead movie stars more than he enjoys spending time with you . . .

"Libby?"

Olly Walker is looking straight at me, a concerned expression on his face.

It's a pretty good-looking face, now I come to notice it. He's got these really interesting grey-coloured eyes, like pebbles on a Cornish beach, and his smile is sweet, and ever so slightly wonky, and — hang on, what's going on here? — he's reaching over the back of my seat, and taking my hand, and gently splaying out my fingers with his own, and . . .

Wrapping them around a large, freshly made cheese sandwich.

"You look like you need this," he says, kindly.

Ridiculous of me. How could I ever have thought he was going to . . . what? Hold my hand? Kiss me?

"Oh, no, no," I say, shoving the sandwich back in his direction. "You should have the first one!"

"I'm all right. I'll make another."

And then Mum's Nokia starts ringing, right at the bottom of my rucksack.

Annoyingly, I don't get to the phone in time before it stops ringing.

"You've got your own mobile phone?" Olly Walker glances up from his sandwich-making, looking impressed.

12

"God, no. This is my mum's." I glance at the screen, which is displaying Dad's number as the last caller. "I'd better call my dad back, if you don't mind? He's picking me up here after my audition."

"Of course. For your Audrey Hepburn retrospective."

"Yep. And," I add, because I'm getting the ever-so-slight impression that Olly Walker thinks the Audrey Hepburn retrospective is a little bit pompous, "to go for a meal in Chinatown."

"Hey, great, where?" He's looking a lot more interested in the Chinese meal than in the retrospective. "I know a couple of really amazing Chinese restaurants in Soho, if you're interested? I did some work experience in a bistro in Soho last summer — I'm going to catering college when I leave school — and after we'd finished our shifts, all the kitchen staff would always head to this fantastic Chinese on Lisle Street . . ."

"It's OK. My dad's booked his favourite place already. The Jade Dragon, on Gerrard Street. He's a regular there."

"Oh, right." He looks a bit crushed, and it occurs to me, a moment too late, that — maybe? — he was trying to impress me with his work experience story. "Is it good?" he asks me.

I can't say whether it is or it isn't, because I've never actually been to The Jade Dragon before. Dad's planned to take me several times, but it's never actually worked out. He's been really, really busy over the last few months — well, years, I suppose — and a lot of our plans to go and have a nice meal together after a movie end up getting cancelled at the last minute.

Oh, the phone's going again. I get to it quickly this time.

"Marilyn, hi," comes Dad's voice, as soon as I answer. "Look, you're going to have to tell Libby I'm not going to make —"

"Dad! Hi!" (I remember, too late, that he prefers to be called by his first name, Eddie, rather than being boring old *Dad.*) "I mean, Eddie, sorry. It's not Mum, it's me."

"Libby!" He sounds startled. "I didn't expect you."

"No, Mum gave me her phone, I was meant to be calling you, actually, to remind you that you're picking me up outside the theatre in Wimbledon. Not at the house."

"Yeah, that's why I'm calling, sweetheart. I can't make it."

"You can't . . ." I stop. I take a deep breath. "But I thought we were going to celebrate my birthday."

"Mm. That's right. But we'll do it another time, sweetheart, I promise."

You said that, I almost say, *the last time. And the time before that.*

"I'm just pushing really, really hard for this new deadline, and the college isn't giving me any time off teaching like they said they were going to —"

"That's OK." I use my calmest, most mature voice, because I want Dad to know I'm not going to be a baby about this. "Obviously you need time and space to

14

write, Dad. I mean, Eddie. It's perfectly OK. We'll do it another time, like you said."

"Exactly. I can always rely on you to understand, Libby. I'll call with some dates, yeah?"

"Well, I'm pretty free next weekend, and the weekend after that, or . . ."

"Great, So I'll call. And I'll see you really soon, OK?"

"OK, Eddie, just let me know wh —"

"Bye, sweetheart."

He's gone.

I drop the phone, casually, back into my rucksack, and busy myself nibbling the outer edge of my sandwich. "It's really good," I say. I don't meet Olly Walker's eye.

"It's your birthday?" he asks, after a moment, in this weird voice — like, a super-gentle voice, all of a sudden, as if he thinks I might break or something.

"No, no! My birthday was weeks ago. Well, months, actually, back in February."

"But you said, on the phone . . ."

"Oh, that's just because I didn't get to see my dad on my actual birthday He was . . . we were both really busy around then. So today was going to be a belated birthday thing. It's no big deal. We'll do it in a couple of weeks, or whenever."

"Right." He falls silent for a moment, then clears his throat and says, "Hey, you know, if you wanted to see a film and have dinner this evening anyway, I could always take you to *The Matrix* and a Chinese restaurant. If your mum would let you, I mean."

15

"Oh!" I look at him properly now, startled. Is this . . . is a boy asking me *on a date*, for the first time ever?

"I . . . I don't —"

"I'd get my sister Nora to come, too!" he says, hastily, "so it wouldn't just be, like, us two, or anything."

Oh. Right. So it wasn't a date, then. Of course it wasn't.

Suddenly — I don't know why, because it's not like I've never been disappointed by something a boy has said or done before — I feel these awful, sharp tears pricking at the backs of my eyes. Without any further warning, three of them — I can feel each individual one — stop pricking the backs of my eyes and start sliding out of the fronts.

"Oh, Jesus." Olly Walker, who can't have failed to notice the tears, is looking agonized, as if he wishes he'd never mentioned films or Chinese food. As if he'd never *heard* of films or Chinese food. Or — most of all — as if he'd never met me. "I didn't mean to . . . look, it doesn't even have to be *The Matrix*! I'll go and see your Audrey Hepburn retro-whatsit, if you want to. I'm sure Nora would much prefer that, anyway . . . oh, here she is now!" he practically gasps with relief, waving like a drowning man towards the Upper Circle entrance several rows down, where a girl has just appeared.

Nora is, of course, the pretty, blonde, prospective Louisa who told the littlest Showbiz-Walker off for doing showy-off splits downstairs.

"Olly, hi." She starts to make her way up the aisle towards us, squinting through the gloom, while I scrub away the tears with the back of my hand. "I just came to say they've moved Kitty's audition fifteen minutes later — something to do with another girl having a family emergency — so . . . oh," she stops next to row F, noticing me. "Hi."

"Hi," I gulp. "I'm Libby."

"I'm Nora. I'm Olly's . . ." She stops. "Are you *crying?*"

"No! Not at all!" I lie, putting on a huge, bright smile that, along with the tear-stained cheeks and the dribbly nose, probably makes me look a bit deranged, as well as a liar.

"Olly!" She turns to him. "What have you done?"

"I didn't do anything!" Olly protests. "She was meant to be seeing her dad this evening, and he had to cancel."

"It's nothing to do with my dad. Anyway, I'm fine. I'm not crying! In fact, I probably ought to be getting back downstairs, I've got an audition in . . . well, about three hours . . ."

"Oh, God, not you, too." Nora Walker pulls a sympathetic face that makes her look just like her older brother, for a moment. "This is seriously the last one of these godawful things I'm agreeing to come to just to keep my mum happy. And you don't look any keener on it than I am."

I'm torn between sounding like a wuss who can't stand up to my mum, and sounding like the sort of person who actually *wants* to star in *The Sound of Music* at the New Wimbledon Theatre.

"Do you want to go and get a drink, or something?" Nora Showbiz-Walker asks, in a properly mature-sounding voice, rather than the one I was trying to use with Dad earlier. "There's a café just over the Broadway that does these really amazing smoothies."

"Oh, I know the one," Olly chips in. "They do a pretty good lemon drizzle cake, too."

I'm starting to wonder if it shouldn't be the Showbiz Walkers so much as the Food-Obsessed Walkers.

"I can leave my little sister annoying everybody downstairs for a bit," Nora adds. "Or you could go and chaperone her, Olly."

"Oh. I thought I might come and have a smoothie and a bit of cake," Olly says, looking like a Labrador that's just been deprived of a doggy treat. "It's hours until we can get out of here."

"Fine," Nora sighs. "I'll ask one of the mums to keep an eye on her. If you'd like to go and get a drink, Libby, that is?"

"Yes. I'd love to."

"Ace. Why don't you walk Libby over there, Ol, and I'll go and find a random stage mum to watch Kitty."

I don't suggest that she ask *my* mum, unless she wants her little sister to end up suffering a nasty and suspicious accident that takes her out of the running for the part of Brigitta and, potentially, any other role for the rest of her child-acting life.

Olly looks hesitant for a moment — presumably concerned that, if left alone with me, I'll start bawling like a baby again — but then Nora adds, cheerily, "And order me something with lots of pineapple and stuff in it. But not kiwi. I hate kiwi," and starts to head back down the aisle towards the doors. So he doesn't really

18

have much choice about the being-left-alone-with-me part.

Still, he's a trooper, because he just starts to gather up his stuff ready to leave, while I do the same, and then we both start to make our way towards the Upper Circle exit doors too.

"You're wrong about *The Matrix*, by the way," he says, as we reach the doors and he holds one of them open for me. "I mean, it may not be Brunch at Bloomingdales, or whatever your Audrey Hepburn thing is called —"

"It's not called Brunch at Bloomingdales!" I gasp, until I see his grin and realize that he's joking.

"Dinner at Debenhams, then?" he hazards.

"Supper at Selfridges?" I suggest.

"Lunch at Liberty's?"

"Tea at Tesco's?"

"Now, *there's* a movie I'd definitely go and see," he says, with a bark of delighted laughter.

As we start down the half-billion stairs, I zip up my grey hooded top as far as it will go. This is partly to hide my own delighted smile — because I'm not sure I've ever made a boy laugh like that before — and partly because I don't want anyone in the café to choke on their smoothie when a thirteen-year-old girl wanders in wearing an egg-yolk-yellow dirndl.

CHAPTER
ONE

Everyone on set is looking suspiciously gorgeous this morning.

The catering bus is filling up quickly on our location shoot near King's Cross this morning, with crew members already on their second (or third) bacon roll of the morning, and actors and actresses sipping, piously, at large mugs of tea and honey. All over the bus, people are looking as if they're off for a Big Night Out. There are freshly blow-dried hairdos, newly fake-tanned legs, and more layers of mascara than you can shake a stick at. Everybody looks stunning.

And then there's me.

Today is my first day in my brand-new speaking role, after months of being a random, silent extra.

Unfortunately, the role I'm playing is Warty Alien. So this morning I'm wearing the most grotesque costume you've ever seen in all your life.

I give it one last go with Frankie the Wardrobe assistant as she passes by my table now, just to see if there might have been some sort of mistake.

"You're absolutely sure," I say, "that I'm down on your list as *Warty* Alien? I mean, there couldn't have been a spelling mistake? And it isn't meant to be . . . I don't know . . . *Party* Alien?"

See, *that* couldn't be too bad. Especially if I could wear one of the alien costumes like my sister Cass wears, in her starring role as one of the Cat People. They're actually quite sexy — skintight silvery bodysuit, mysterious eye mask, high-heeled knee boots — and even if I had to accessorize it, as Party Alien, with, say, a silly paper hat and a hula skirt, I'd still look halfway decent. *Especially* if I had to wear a hula skirt, in fact, because it would hide whatever horrors the silvery bodysuit would reveal in the bum region. Two birds, one stone!

"Sorry, Libby. There's no spelling mistake. Anyway, the part's not actually *called* Warty Alien, you know. You're down on my list as —" Frankie glances down at the notepad she never lets more than two inches from her sight — "Extra-Terrestrial Spaceship Technician."

(This basically means that I'm playing an alien version of a Kwik Fit mechanic, and explains why my one and only line — my Big Break! On National Television! — is: "But fixing the docking module could take days, Captain, maybe even weeks." Look, I never said it was a *good* line.)

"OK, then," I say, desperately, "are you sure this is definitely the costume the Extra-Terrestrial Spaceship Technician is supposed to wear?"

"Well, you're more than welcome to query that with the Obergruppenführer. Because if there *had* been any kind of an error, it would be *her* mistake."

The Obergruppenführer, otherwise (just not very often) known as Vanessa, is the production manager. It's probably obvious, from her nickname, that she's not the sort of person you want to accuse of making mistakes. Particularly not when you're a lowly extra on a surprise hit TV show, with literally thousands of out-of-work actors ready to kill their own grandmothers to take your job instead.

"Anyway, I don't know why you're complaining," Frankie adds, over her shoulder, as she sashays in impractical four-inch heels to the bus's exit. "In technical terms, that costume is a work of art, you know."

I stare down at the vomit-green latex suit I've been sweating into since seven o'clock this morning and pick up the separate alien head that's sitting on the chair beside me. The head features one particularly giant pustule, right in between the eyes. It doesn't look like a work of art.

"*God*, Libby, is that your costume?"

It's Cass, squeezing into the seat opposite me.

And I mean literally squeezing, because she's somehow managed to inflate her already fulsome cleavage by another couple of cup sizes, and given herself the biggest blow-dry this side of Texas. She's not changed into her Cat Person costume yet, so the eye-popping cleavage is (barely) contained by a teeny pink hoodie with the zip pulled scandalously low, and I'm quite sure she's teamed this, as she always does when she's all out to impress, with either an equally teeny pair of denim cut-offs, or a sassy towelling micro-skirt.

(We're half-sisters, by the way. Different dads. Even though the irony is that actually, my dad is the better looking out of the two: her dad, Michael, is a nice-but-nerdy geologist while my dad is as handsome as he is an utter waste of good oxygen. Anyway, Cass is quite definitely the better-looking out of *us* two: blonde, blue-eyed and curvy while my hair and eyes are from an uninspired palette of browns, my bosom is very nearly non-existent, and the only reason you'd ever call me "curvy" is because I have a sturdy bottom half that's seemingly impervious to all forms of exercise.)

"Yes, it's my costume," I tell Cass, with as much dignity as I can scrape together under the circumstances. "It's a technical work of art, as a matter of fact."

But Cass has already lost interest. "So, do I look OK? Do I look better than Melody? Do you think he's going to notice me?"

Melody is the lead actress on our (sci-fi, if you hadn't already guessed) TV show, *The Time Guardians*.

The *he* that Cass is referring to is Dillon O'Hara, our brand-new star. Whose first day on set it is today and who — in case you were starting to wonder — is the reason that everybody has turned up to work this morning in their Saturday Night Best.

"I'm sure he'll notice you, Cass. You look very eye-catching."

"You're sure? Because you do know, don't you, the kind of girls Dillon normally goes out with?" To back up her point, Cass rifles in her bag for this week's copy of *Grazia* magazine, puts it down on the table next to the script I was given this morning, and jabs a manicured finger at the front cover. "*That's* the competition."

It's a paparazzi shot of a blonde Victoria's Secret model — I can't remember her name, but she's platinum blonde and buxom, with legs roughly a mile high — exiting a nightclub with Mr O'Hara.

I hate myself for thinking it, given that the wretched man is keeping an entire cast and crew waiting for him on location this morning while he decides if he can be bothered to show up or not. But he's annoyingly gorgeous. If you happen to be a fan, that is, of ripped torsos, muscular shoulders and angelic cheekbones. His hair is sooty black, his eyes almost match, and he's stocky and well muscled in a way that implies not so much a life spent pumping iron while gazing into a gym mirror, but long teenage summers spent working on building sites. Shirtless, probably. Getting an all-over tan on that ripped torso . . .

"Rhea Haverstock-Harley," Cass spits, gazing at the Victoria's Secret model with loathing. "You know she won Hottest Woman in the Stratosphere *again* in *Made Man* magazine's Hundred Hottest list this year?"

Oh, well, now Cass has reminded me of the name, I do, vaguely, know this. And I also recall that, in a (deliberate? publicity-seeking?) echo of the whole Naomi-Campbell-throwing episode, this double-barrelled Rhea girl got in pretty big trouble a few years ago for hitting her hairdresser with her phone. Which, now that I've remembered it, has sort of put me off Dillon O'Hara a bit, even though I don't think he was going out with her at the time.

"Oh, *Made Man*," I scoff, with a practised air. (Cass didn't make the top 100 in the most recent poll. I've not quite recovered, yet, from the sobbing 3 a.m. phone calls I received from her last week, four nights in a row.) "What do they know? And anyway, there's more to life than just being leered at in your bra by a bunch of drooling pervs, you know."

"You're *so* right, Lib. I'm going to show them all tomorrow night, by the way."

(Tomorrow night is the *Made Man* party celebrating their pathetic poll, and Cass is attending. She may not be Top 100 material, but she's pert and blonde and on TV, which is evidently quite enough for an invite.)

"That's the spirit, Cass!" I undo one of my Warty Alien gloves, reach across the table and pat her on the hand. "You show them all!"

"That's why I bought the dress I'm going to wear. It's got a massively plunging neckline, and it's totally sheer down the back, so you can sort of see my bum — but through the lace, so it's really classy."

"Cass, no, that isn't what I meant by *show them all* . . ."

"And I'll need you to alter that ruby pendant thingy. It'll look amazing with the dress, but remember I said I'd prefer it longer, so the ruby bit dangles right down into the top of my cleavage."

That ruby pendant thingy is actually a garnet necklace I made for Cass's twenty-fifth birthday; painstakingly crafted, to be more accurate, from a gorgeous garnet cabochon (garnet being her birthstone) and a vintage Swarovski-crystal teardrop charm, both hanging from a gold-plated chain that I customized with teeny-tiny garnet-coloured crystals at intervals along the length. Pendant-making may only be a hobby, but I did put a fair amount of work into this particular one, and the chain was so expensive that I could only afford to make it an eighteen-inch pendant (sitting elegantly against Cass's collarbones) rather than a twenty-four-inch one (nestling brassily between her breasts).

"I can't make it any longer," I tell her. "I don't have a replacement chain."

"Well, bung the ruby bit on the end of a bit of ribbon, or something," Cass says, airily unconcerned about compromising the artistic integrity of my creation. "I just need it to draw maximum attention to my boobs."

"I don't think you'll need a necklace to do that."

"No, Libby." She looks very serious. "I really have to pull out all the stops if I'm going to stand a chance up against Rhea Haverstock-Harley."

"Surely" I say, feeling a bit like whatshisname standing in the sea, telling the tide to go back, "you shouldn't really be in hot pursuit of Dillon O'Hara anyway, Cass. If he has a girlfriend, that is. Not to mention the fact that you have a boyfriend of your own."

His name is David, apparently. I say "apparently" because Cass hasn't introduced him to either me or Mum yet. All I know about him is that he's a "talent manager" for a big showbiz agency, so it's perfectly possible that he's covered from head to toe in huge warts, just like my costume, but oozing real pus — and Cass would still be perfectly happy dating him.

27

"David isn't my *boyfriend*. We're just *seeing each other*." She emits a sigh of exasperation, as she always does when I don't just happily spout whatever it is she wants to hear. "You're no use, Cass. I'm going to text a selfie to Mum, see if she thinks I should change into something a bit sexier."

"Christ, no, don't do that!"

I'm not yelping this because I fear that the only thing "a bit sexier" than Cass's plunging top and micro-shorts is a thong bikini, and I'm trying, as her big sister, to protect her remaining modesty.

I'm yelping this because if Cass texts Mum, Mum will call right back. And after lengthy discussion of Cass's outfit options, she'll finally ask to speak to me. And then she'll ask exactly what part I've been given and what my costume is like.

You see, my lack of enthusiasm for the Warty Alien costume isn't down to the fact that I was secretly thinking *I* might be the one to catch Dillon O'Hara's eye if he ever makes it to the shoot this morning. I mean, even if I wasn't perspiring in puke-coloured latex, I don't think for a minute that he's going to stop dead in his tracks, grab the nearest passing crew member and whisper, "By God, tell me the name of that flat-chested brunette with the pear-shaped bottom, for until I have bedded her I shall go mad with lust! Mad, I tell you."

The reason, in fact, is my mother.

The thing is that she's not only my mother, but also my agent, and the one responsible for badgering *The Time Guardians'* casting director until the poor woman eventually cracked and agreed to promote me — against my will, I might add — from Extra to Bit-Parter. So it's not exactly ideal that the first words I get to speak in an acting role in the last five years are going to be from behind a vomit-green, wart-covered alien head, which renders me not only revolting but also — much more importantly, from my mum/agent's point of view — invisible.

"Well, *you're* not being any help," Cass retorts, ignoring my plea and starting to undertake her very favourite activity — posing for selfies with her mobile phone camera — while I decide that the best way to avoid Mum for a bit longer is to leave Cass to it and go and find myself a bacon roll instead.

After all, I tell myself, as I lumber off the catering bus in my Warty Alien feet, it's not as if I need to worry about tummy bloat while I swelter away inside my layers of concealing latex, is it? And anyway, the bacon rolls are exceptionally delicious, and made to order by lovely Olly Walker, who's been one of my best friends ever since I met him, donkey's years ago, at that godawful *Sound of Music* audition in Wimbledon. He runs the on-location catering van, so I can go and have a chat with him while simultaneously waiting to be called by the assistant director to deliver my line, and — most important of all — avoiding my mother.

Olly is not currently at his catering van. He wasn't there when I fetched my first bacon roll before going to Wardrobe at eight this morning either, so when I reach the head of the queue, I ask his sous chef, Jesse, if he's all right.

"Hasn't he called you?" Jesse asks, squirting ketchup onto three waiting rolls he's just finishing off for Liz, the production assistant (pretty, blonde, and Dillon-ready in a crop top and skin-tight jeans, so I can only assume the bacon rolls are actually for some hungry electricians or cameramen, or something, and not for her to snarf down herself).

"No. Well, he might have done. I've left my phone in my bag." I don't add: *because, although I'm twenty-nine years old, I'm still avoiding my mother.*

"He's gone in his van to the studios. Mentioned something about doing a furniture run. First to Woking and then to you and your new flat?"

This, really, should be making me a bit less stressed about the whole Mum-and-my-Big-Break situation: the fact that I don't have to go back to her house after work this evening and have her harangue me about my career over the kitchen table. Tonight, if she wants to harangue me, she can do it over the phone while I relax at my very own kitchen table in my *very own flat!*

It's not much — it's really, *really* not much, just a tiny one-bed above a parade of shops on Colliers Wood High Street; I've seen hip-hop producers' downstairs loos, on *MTV Cribs*, that are at least three times the size — but I'm going to make it cosy, and homely, and lovely.

Of course, a slight barrier to this, up until a couple of days ago, was that I've managed to reach my ripe old age without actually acquiring the basics you need to *make* a flat look cosy and homely.

I don't mean cashmere throws and Venetian glass lamps and Victorian writing desks. I mean — and this is a bit embarrassing to admit — a sofa, a table, and a double bed.

I was bemoaning this fact to Olly when he came round to Mum's in his van the night before last to pick up my boxes full of clothes, books and other bits and bobs, and that's when he told me about the Pinewood props store. Pinewood Studios, which is where the majority of *The Time Guardians* gets filmed, is home to an enormous treasure trove (well, a giant corrugated-steel warehouse) of old furniture that's been used, over the years, to dress the sets of countless films and TV shows. Lots of it is pretty ropey, some of it is surprisingly lovely, and none of it is really used any more. Olly knows about this treasure trove because his Uncle Brian — not his actual uncle, just an old friend of his former-actress mother's — is the security guard there. Oh, and because Olly's former-actress mother, who now runs an amateur dramatic society in Woking, is always getting him to raid the props storeroom to bring her set dressing for their productions. Anyway, on Olly's advice I popped round there when we were shooting at Pinewood yesterday, and managed to put aside a handful of surprisingly lovely things to furnish my flat.

I thought I was going to head back there tonight, with Olly in his van, and pick up the stuff before heading all the way back to Colliers Wood to collect my keys, but obviously it must fit Olly's schedule better to go to Pinewood himself this morning.

"Thanks, Jesse. Oh, and I'll have one just like those, please," I add, pointing at the row of bacon rolls he's wrapping in greaseproof paper to hand over to Liz.

"You're kidding," Liz says. "You can't seriously be planning on eating a greasy bacon roll."

Which is a bit personal, isn't it? I mean, Liz and I have chatted in the ladies' loos at the studios before, but that's about it. I wouldn't have thought we were anywhere near friendly enough for her to —

"Vanessa," she says, in a hushed, reverential (OK, terrified) tone, "will *literally* kill you if she sees you eating so much as a Polo mint while you're wearing that costume."

"*This* costume?" I ask, glancing down at my alien head, because I can't believe a bit of dripped ketchup is going to make the thing look that much worse.

"It's one of the most expensive costumes we rent," she says, rather piously, as if the money is coming out of her personal bank account and leaving her unable to pay her gas bill. "If Vanessa finds out there's so much as a single, solitary stain on that latex . . ."

"OK, forget the bacon roll," I tell Jesse. "I'll just have a coffee and a muffin."

"*A blueberry* muffin?" gasps Liz. "Filled with sticky, purple-staining berries?"

"Fine! Just the coffee, then."

Which is not going to hit the spot in any way. I mean, I was up at 5 a.m. this morning, in Wardrobe at 7, and I've been sweating out vital calories inside this horrible costume ever since.

I think I've got a half-eaten packet of peanut M&Ms in my bag, though. I can go and retrieve it from where I think I left it, back on the catering bus, and see if there's a message on my phone from Olly at the same time.

The bloody costume slows me right down, though. I don't know if you've ever tried walking anywhere while wearing half a stone's worth of baggy latex, but it's not the most enjoyable way to get about.

Honestly, on days like today, I seriously wonder what the hell I'm doing pursuing a career in acting. Though, to be entirely fair to the Warty Alien costume, there's scarcely a day goes by when that thought *doesn't* occur. I'm only stuck in the bloody job because of a childhood spent following Cass from audition to audition, during which time I utterly failed to gain any decent qualifications — or other career ideas — of my own.

Well, that and the fact that I've always had a bit of a fixation with the movies, and I've spent far too long kidding myself that grunting about as a non-speaking extra on iffy British TV shows is halfway to the Old Hollywood magic I've long been seduced by.

Far too long, because I don't think any of my Hollywood heroines ever had to schlump around the arse-end of King's Cross in latex warts on a boiling June morning . . .

"Cheer up," a fellow alien says, passing me by on its way out of the Wardrobe trailer nearby. "It might never happen."

"Easy for you to say. You've lucked out." I mean this because it — he, I guess, from the voice inside his alien head — is nowhere near as grotesquely attired as I am. His is more like a spacesuit: Guantanamo-orange canvas with a matching orange plastic bubble helmet. No latex, no warts, no problem. "But thanks for the moral support. It's nice when us extras stick together for a change."

"You're welcome. I mean we have to, don't we, with these arsehole lead actors swanning around the place?"

I snort. "When they can even be bothered to turn up, of course."

"Oh?"

"We're all waiting for his Lord Chief Arsehole to decide whether we're worthy of his time or not. Dillon O'Hara, I mean," I add, for clarification of the "Lord Chief Arsehole" bit.

"Really? Because I heard he was only called for eleven a.m. So in fact, if he turns up in the next half-hour or so, he'll actually be early."

"Bollocks," I snort. "He's late because celebrities like him love to be late. It's their favourite way of proving to people what a big shot they are."

"Be fair to the poor guy," the alien extra says. "Maybe he got stuck in traffic."

"If there's anything at all he got stuck in, it's more likely to be some leggy supermodel."

And then I stop talking.

Because the alien extra is taking off his helmet, and it turns out that he's not an extra at all.

It's Dillon O'Hara.

"That was fun," he says, a wide grin spreading over his face. His accent is Irish now, instead of the English one he — I now realize — has been putting on for the last couple of minutes. "I felt a bit like a prince in a fairy tale. You know, the kind who disguises himself as a peasant in order to mingle with the real peasants and find out what they truly think about him."

I'm mortified.

But at the same time, I have to say, I'm outraged. Because not only has he just quite deliberately set me up, he's also — I'm fairly sure — just pretty much called me a peasant.

"I didn't mean to imply," he says, as if he's read my mind, "that I think you're a peasant."

"I should bloody well hope not."

"But then, to be fair to me, you did just call me — now, what was it? — Lord Chief Arsehole."

"That was different . . ."

"That's true. It was behind my back, for one thing."

"It wasn't behind your back!"

"Well, it wasn't to my face."

"You set me up! You . . . *entrapped* me."

"Oh, stop getting your knickers in a twist. If you're wearing any knickers beneath that thing," he adds. "I mean, Jesus, these costumes are like a bloody sauna as they are, without adding extra layers beneath them, aren't they?"

I would say something in reply — I'm not sure *what*, exactly because it's not often that I get asked by strange men if I'm wearing any knickers, let alone strange men like Dillon O'Hara who, now that I come to notice it, is even better looking in real life than he looked on the pages of Cass's *Grazia* — but I'm stunned into silence by the fact that he's starting to take his clothes off.

Seriously: he's undoing the Velcro down the front of his jumpsuit, peeling the fabric off his shoulders and down to his waist and then — oh, dear God — pulling his T-shirt up and over his head to reveal the most perfect torso I've ever seen in my entire life.

I'm not exaggerating: his shoulders are wide and packed tight with lean muscle, he has a smooth, rock-hard chest, and an actual, proper six-pack where most men — my horrible ex-boyfriend Daniel, for example — sport varying sizes of beer gut.

"Ahhhhh." He lets out a sigh of satisfaction. "*That's* better. They told me, the nice Wardrobe girls, that I'd be more comfortable if I took my T-shirt off, but I got all shy." He grins at me, in an extremely not-shy sort of way. "I assumed they were just after my body."

I can't tell, dazzled as I still am by the ridiculous perfection of the body in front of me, whether his cheeky arrogance is attractive or annoying.

I think, probably, it's fifty-fifty.

For now, anyway, I need to concentrate on *not staring* while Dillon swivels round and takes something out of the back pocket of his jeans.

It's an open packet of Benson & Hedges, from which he's pulling a cigarette.

"No!" I yelp, and then, because he looks rather startled, I explain: "I mean, you can't. Vanessa will have your guts for garters if you light up in costume."

"Vanessa . . . Vanessa . . . oh, you mean the scary production lady?

It's reassuring to realize that Dillon is as scared of Vanessa as the rest of us.

"Yes."

"But I'm the big star, right? I should be allowed to do whatever I want, whenever I want?"

I *think* he's joking . . .

"Or," he adds, with another of those grins, "I could just nip round the back of this catering bus and have a sneaky smoke where Vanessa won't catch me. Might be safest all round, hey?"

"I think that would probably be best."

"Join me?"

"Huh?"

"Join me? In a cigarette?"

"Oh . . . I don't smoke."

The moment the words leave my lips, I regret saying them.

I mean, I don't have to go all ga-ga over the man to be able to admit Dillon's attractions. And yet here I've just turned down the opportunity to continue this little chat — while he remains, I should point out, completely shirtless — just because I don't actually smoke cigarettes.

Which is nuts, because it's not like I've *never* smoked. I *used to*. Admittedly only when I was drunk, and not since I was about nineteen, when I went on a trip to Paris with Olly and smoked so many overpowering French cigarettes that it put me off for life.

But is this sort of hair-splitting worth missing out on another few minutes in Dillon's company, when he's never likely to exchange another word with me again?

"What I mean to say is that I *try* not to smoke."

"Oh, well, if you've given up, then all credit to you —"

"No, no, I haven't given up! I've failed completely at it! Love smoking. Love it to death. *Literally* to death, probably, the amount I smoke!"

"Then be my guest." He hands me the cigarette he's holding, takes another for himself and then reaches into his back pocket again for a lighter.

"So you're one of the extras, right?" he asks, flicking the lighter on and holding it out towards me.

"Mnnh-hnngh." This is because I've got the cigarette in my mouth. "I've sort of been promoted, though," I add, once the end is lit. "I mean, I've got my first line to speak today. It's not exactly a proper part, and obviously I get to wear the ugliest costume on set, but . . ."

"Oh, I don't know. I've seen worse." He takes an expert puff on his own cigarette, blowing the smoke in the opposite direction from me (which is courteous of him, seeing as I'm technically smoking too; I just haven't risked actually inhaling yet in case I cough and sputter, unattractively, all over him). "I've an ex or two that looked a bit like that," — he nods at the alien head I'm clutching in my hand — "without their slap on."

This is unlikely. But I appreciate his generosity.

"Anyway, if you're one of the extras, you probably know a thing or two about the way things work around here."

"Work?"

"Yeah, every show I've ever worked on, the extras are always the ones who know how it all works. Who's the biggest diva. Who's got the biggest coke problem. Who's getting it on in the props storeroom. I mean, there's *always* somebody getting it on in the props storeroom, isn't there?"

Given that I'm about to furnish my entire flat from the props storeroom, I can only hope that he's joking about this.

"So?" he asks. "Dish the dirt! Tell me who to avoid, who to cultivate, who I'm going to get a stonking great crush on . . ."

"Don't you have a girlfriend?" I suddenly blurt.

No, I'm not sure what's wrong with me, either.

His black eyes narrow. "That's a very personal question."

"Sorry, I only asked because . . . well, I read things in *Grazia*, obviously . . . not that I read a lot of celebrity gossip! Only when I'm in the waiting room at the dentist, or something. Hardly ever."

"You hardly ever go to the dentist?"

"No! I mean, yes! I go loads!" I say, continuing my apparent quest to make him think I have poor dental management and stinky cheese-breath. "Well, not *loads* . . . a normal amount, I'd say . . . Actually, it's my sister Cass who reads all the gossip magazines —"

"Then tell the silly cow not to believe everything she reads in them."

"Hey!" I don't care how gorgeous he is, standing here with his bare chest, and chivalrously blowing smoke away from me. "That's my sister you're talking about."

"Sorry." He looks, and sounds, instantly contrite. But then he is an actor, I suppose. Still, he repeats it. "Sorry. That was unforgivably rude of me."

"It was, a bit."

"It's just that the girlfriend thing . . . it's private, you know?"

"Yes. Of course. I shouldn't have mentioned it."

"Ah, you're all right . . . Sorry, I've just realized I don't know your name."

"Libby. Libby Lomax."

"Well, you're all right, Libby, Libby Lomax. I'll forgive you for calling me an arsehole. And for lying to me about being a smoker."

Damn it; I've let the bloody thing practically burn itself out in my hand.

"I am a smoker! I just forgot I had one," I say, popping the cigarette back into my mouth and hoping I can look one-tenth as sexy as him when I take a drag on it . . .

"Dillon!"

Shit. It's Vanessa, coming out of Wardrobe and walking towards us.

If she catches me smoking a cigarette, I'll be off this location shoot in even less time than it would take Dillon to talk Cass into bed with him.

Instinctively, I do the first thing that springs to mind, which is to pull on the head I've got squashed under my arm.

It's a nanosecond later that I realize I still have the cigarette between my lips.

But it's OK! It's OK, because all I have to do is walk past Vanessa and go, as fast as I can, round the other side of the catering bus, where I can pull my head off and take the cigarette out.

Or at least, I could, if she weren't blocking my way with her arms folded and a scowl on her face.

"Libby," she hisses, none too quietly, "what the fuck are you bothering Dillon for?"

"She wasn't bothering me, Vanessa, don't stress about it." Dillon taps me on the shoulder from behind, and when I wheel round unsteadily he's holding out one of my latex gloves. "You dropped this."

"Thank you," I mumble, snatching the glove and making to turn away again. But he stops me.

"You're smoking," he says.

Traitor! He's sold me out, and right in front of Vanessa, too.

"I mean, you're really smoking, Libby."

He's staring into my eyes, through the pin-holes in my Warty Alien head, with such intensity that I can't help but think . . . Is he saying he *fancies* me? I mean, nobody's ever called me "smoking" before, and certainly not someone as smoking-hot himself as Dillon is, but I *suppose* weirder things have happened —

"For *fuck's sake*!" Vanessa ruins the moment by screaming, at Obergruppenführer volume, from behind me. "Her fucking *head*'s on fire!"

At the very same time as she screams this, I inhale an extremely unpleasant smell that can only be burning latex.

OK, so I know the Thing To Do in a fire is to stay cool, calm and collected. I know the worst thing you can do is to panic, because you just start to drag other people under with you . . .

Oh, hang on a minute, that's *drowning*.

In a head-on-fire scenario, panic, I suspect, is perfectly acceptable.

"*Shit!*" I almost out-scream Vanessa, pulling at my head in a wild frenzy But it isn't coming off! *It isn't coming off!* "Get it off, get it off, get it off me!"

"For fuck's sake!" Vanessa is yelling, again, as she stampedes away from us toward the catering bus door. "We need the fucking fire extinguisher!"

"There's no time for that." I hear Dillon's voice, and then feel his hand grab my wrists to stop me ineffectually yanking at my head. "Stop," he orders, "and keep still."

Then he grips the alien head, pulls it clear of my actual head, and throws the smouldering latex down onto the ground.

And then everything goes black.

I haven't fainted, by the way. I think Dillon's just thrown his T-shirt over me to put out any lingering sparks.

There's a brief, stunned silence.

"You all right under there?" Dillon asks, a moment later.

I open my mouth to say "Just about" when I'm hit, smack in the middle of the face, with a powerful jet of very cold liquid.

I gasp, which draws a large portion of sodden T-shirt into my mouth. I gag, splutter, and double over.

"Fucking hell!" I hear Dillon say, from my position near his groin. "It was under control. You didn't need to blast the poor girl with the fire extinguisher!"

Ah, so it was very cold *foam*, then. Just in case I didn't look like enough of an idiot with a wet T-shirt over my head . . . no, it has to be a foam-covered T-shirt instead.

But Vanessa clearly isn't in any kind of mood for sympathy.

"Libby! What the *fuck* are you playing at?"

"Hey, leave her alone." I feel a hand on my shoulder, pulling me upright. "Let me get that off you," Dillon says, pulling at the T-shirt.

"I'm fine! Might be better to leave it on for a bit longer, actually!" Like, until the end of time. Or at least until I've regained my composure, and until everyone on the catering bus — whom I can now hear leaning out of the windows, asking each other what's been going on, and having a good old chortle when they hear the answer — has gone home and, ideally, sixty or seventy years down the line, died, without me having to face them again. I grip onto the T-shirt at neck level. "Better not to . . . you know . . . expose burnt skin to the air."

"Shit, did your *skin* burn?" Dillon rips the T-shirt off my head in one smooth movement; he's obviously a man accustomed to removing items of clothing from women. "Oh, don't worry, you're all right. It's only your hair."

"Only my hair what?"

"That's been burnt off."

"My hair's been *burnt off?*"

"God, no, no, no."

I feel weak with relief, until he goes on.

"I mean, not all of it. Only most of the right side. Unless . . ." He studies me for a moment. "I'm sorry, maybe I just didn't notice. Did you have a lopsided haircut when I was talking to you five minutes ago?"

"No!" I yelp, clutching the side of my head. I'm horrified to feel short, crispy, burnt bits where there used to be, if not exactly locks worthy of a Victoria's Secret Angel, at least a perfectly decent amount of hair.

"Oh, for fuck's sake, Libby, it's only fucking hair." Vanessa is snapping her fingers at one of the crew members leaning out of the bus window to come and take the fire extinguisher from her. "It'll grow back. Unlike the chunk you've burnt out of that costume!"

"I'm really sorry, Vanessa. It was an accident."

"Yeah, it was an accident." Dillon backs me up. "I mean, nobody would intentionally set light to themselves like that. Unless they were a Buddhist monk, or something, Which you're not, are you?"

Before I can answer, there's a collective wheeze of mirth from the watching crew members, and one of them starts up — oh, so hilariously — a chant of *Om*.

"Ah, give her a break, guys." Dillon grins up at them and pats me on the shoulder. His hand stays there. I don't breathe in case this alerts him and he decides to move it. "Poor girl's had a nasty shock. You know, one of you baboons could make yourselves useful and get her a nice cup of sweet tea, instead of standing there taking the . . ."

44

His eyes suddenly flicker sideways.

Which is hardly surprising, given that my sister has just teetered into view.

Lord only knows what Mum texted her after seeing the selfie, but Cass has ramped up the sexiness by roughly one hundred degrees centigrade. She's changed into her Cat Person costume, for the show, but with a few little tweaks that only a certifiable man-eater like Cass is truly capable of. She's unzipped the front of the skintight jumpsuit down to a near-pornographic level, replaced the regulation black Dr Martens with — and I can only assume she either brought these with her this morning, or borrowed them from a streetwalker a little closer to King's Cross — a thigh-high pair of stiletto-heeled boots, and coated her mouth in what is surely the entire contents of a tube of Nars Striptease lip gloss.

Part of me wants to applaud her for such brazen, no-holds-barred chutzpah.

A much larger part of me wants to rip off her thigh boots and beat her over the head with them.

Because Dillon's hand has just dropped off my shoulder. And I've just dropped off his radar.

"Oh, my *God*!" Cass squeals, clasping her hands to her mouth and doing a pretty decent performance of Distraught Woman. "Libby! My darling *sister*! What *happened?*"

"Your darling sister set fire to her fucking head," Vanessa snaps. "Costing me six hundred quid for a replacement costume in the process."

"Oh, my *God*!" Cass says, again. (Her performance might be decent, but the script has its limits.) "And your *hair*, Libby! What have you done to your beautiful, beautiful hair!"

Which would be a nice thing for her to have said, if it weren't for the fact that I suspect it's just a vehicle for her next trick, which is to break down in melodramatic sobs and clutch a hand to her (ballooning) chest, as if she's about to swoon.

"Woah, there!" Dillon slips an arm around her waist. "Let's go and get you a hot, sweet cup of tea."

The same hot, sweet cup of tea that he promised me a moment ago. And which, I can't help but notice, the entire leering gang of crew members is practically leap-frogging each other off the bus to fetch for her.

"I'm sorry!" Cass gulps. "It's just such a terrible shock . . ."

"Oh, for crying out loud," Vanessa mutters, which actually makes me feel quite fond of her all of a sudden.

"Of course it is, sweetheart," Dillon is saying, in a melted-dark-chocolate tone quite unlike the one he was using while he was chatting to me. "You just need that tea, and a nice sit-down . . ."

"I do," Cass replies, dabbing prettily at dry cheeks. "I *do* need a lie-down."

You have to give it to her (and Dillon, no doubt, will do exactly that), she's good at this stuff. The Damsel in Distress act (when I'm the only one round here who's got any reason to be in distress); the subtle hint that she'd rather be lying down than sitting . . .

"I'm Dillon, by the way," Dillon is murmuring, putting a hand in the small of her back and steering her in the direction of the leap-frogging crew members on their way to Olly's catering truck.

"And I'm Cassidy . . ."

Vanessa and I watch them go, united — for once — in irritation.

"Your fucking sister," says Vanessa.

To agree would be disloyal; to disagree would be rank hypocrisy. So I don't say anything.

"You're all right?" she asks, gesturing at my burnt hair. "Not actually injured or anything?"

"No, I'm OK." I'm touched that she's concerned. "But thanks, Vanessa, and I'm really sorry again about —"

"Good," she says, briskly. "Then I don't need to get the first-aid guys over before you leave."

"Leave?"

"The shoot. The show, in fact."

I stare at her. "You're . . . firing me?"

"Well, of course I fucking well am. You're lucky I'm not also charging you for the costume you've just wrecked."

"But I . . . this was meant to be my big . . . I mean, I need the money for my rent . . . And my mother is going to . . ."

"None of that is my problem." She turns on her heel. "Sorry, Libby," she adds, in a flat tone of no regret whatsoever. "But can you please just return the costume to Wardrobe and get off my set?"

There's absolutely no point in arguing. All I can do now is do as she says and get out of here while I still have my dignity.

OK, while I still have a *shred* of dignity.

OK, before I annoy her any more and she decides to charge me six hundred quid into the bargain. Because, in all honesty, I think my dignity has pretty much gone the way of my hair. Along with the ability to pay the rent on my flat, and the long-awaited approval of my mother.

Still, at least the *Om*-chanting crew are no longer around to witness my walk of shame. I suppose I have to be grateful for small mercies.

CHAPTER
TWO

I'm due to pick the keys up from my new landlord, Bogdan, at six o'clock this evening, but there are several things I need to get done before then.

The first, and let's face it, most important, being to buy a hat.

This I accomplish by nipping in to the huge TK Maxx near Marble Arch tube, grabbing the largest straw sunhat I can find (thank *God* it's a sunny day, so I have an obvious excuse to be wearing it) and taking off the label to wear it immediately after handing over the fiver it cost me.

And it's a good thing it was reasonably cheap, because my next stop is at the cheese shop on New Quebec Street, where I'm due to collect forty quid's worth of eye-wateringly expensive (and probably just eye-watering, ha-ha) cheese that I ordered a couple of days ago. It's for Olly, as a thank-you gift for all his help with the move and the furniture. I racked my brains for quite a while to come up with something I knew he'd love — a sci-fi movie box-set, a kitchen-y gadget for messing about with when he's cooking (for fun, staggeringly) at home — but in the end I thought some serious cheese was a great gift for someone who's . . . well, as serious about cheese as Olly is.

As we both are, in fact. Cheese was one of the very first things we bonded over, and cheese has continued to play a front-and-centre role in our friendship ever since. We sometimes go to cheese-tasting evenings — right here, at Le Grand Fromage on New Quebec Street, or at Neal's Yard Dairy in Covent Garden; we once went to an entire cheese *festival*, at some Nineties rock star's country farm down in Somerset; when I was nineteen and he was turning twenty-one, we celebrated his significant birthday by taking the Eurostar over to Paris for the day, wandering around the first arrondissement, from *fromagerie* to *fromagerie* (with *l'*occasional stop-off at *le bar* on the way), buying more cheese than we could possibly afford, and eating most of it on the Eurostar on the way back home. Le Marathon de Cheese, we called it, and we've long talked about repeating the performance.

The owner of Le Grand Fromage recognizes me by now, and waves to me from behind the counter as I make my way through the door and into her shop.

"Hi, there! Libby, isn't it?"

"That's right!" I don't know her name; she did mention it to me once, but I've forgotten it and now it's too embarrassing to ask again. In my head I just call her The Big Cheese Woman. Which makes her sound like she's made entirely from wheels of cheddar, with mini Babybels for her eyes and nose, when in fact she's a pleasant-looking forty-something with a petite figure and an enviable choppy haircut. (Enviable even *before* I burnt half my hair off this morning. Right now, I might actually kill to have hair like hers.) "You called to say my cheese order was ready?"

"That's right! All cut and ready to go. The Brie de Meaux, the Fourme d'Ambert, and the aged Comté. Oh, and something else . . ."

"No, no, nothing else," I say, hastily, because I'm not sure my precarious bank balance can take any more posher-than-posh cheese just now.

"No, I was just going to say that I'm popping in a little sample of something for you to try. A goat's cheese. Because don't I remember you asking about a particular goat's cheese the last time you were in? Something rolled in ash, with a cross shape printed in it?"

Oh, my God.

Is it possible that she's found the "mystery cheese" from Le Marathon?

There was this one particular goat's cheese, in all the cheeses we stuffed ourselves with on the way back home on the Eurostar that day, that Olly and I still talk about in mystic, hallowed terms, the way football nuts might talk about a incredible volleyed header that won a cup final. It was light as a soufflé and tangy on the tongue, it was rolled in ashes with a cross shape on the top, and we've never been able to track it down before or since.

"Hold on a sec." The Big Cheese Woman is heading off the shop floor and into the cool, straw-lined room at the back where all the cheeses are kept.

If this really is the mystery cheese, it will be a big moment. I know it sounds silly, but the search for this cheese has been a bit of a thing for me and Olly for the past decade.

Though I suppose, if I'm being entirely honest, that some of our obsession with tracking down the cheese is — for both of us — our unspoken way of detracting attention from the Mistaken Thing that happened on that Paris trip, in a corner booth in a quiet bar somewhere on the Left Bank.

Which is that, just after we ordered a second bottle of white, we suddenly, somehow, found ourselves kissing as if our lives depended on it. An *extremely* Mistaken Thing to do when you've been friends for years and when, thanks to your Best Friendship with his sister, his entire family have sort of unofficially adopted you as one of their own.

I'm still not sure how it happened exactly. All I can really remember is that one minute we were talking about unrequited love, and Olly was telling me about the girl that he'd loved from afar for, well, it sounded like years, but I must have got that bit wrong and then the next minute we were snogging as if the world was about to end. I've no idea which of his friends it was, even all these years later — Alison, probably, the old college friend he eventually went out with for several years. The kiss was finally interrupted by the arrival of that bottle of wine. Realizing what we had just done and in a bit of a panic, I blurted out, "Well, when you get to kiss the real love of your life just make sure you're not as drunk as we are!" and laughed like some sort of crazed lunatic — just to make absolutely sure that Olly knew I understood that he was unrequitedly in love with *another* girl, and that I wasn't going to get all silly and take that kiss as anything other than a Chablis-induced mistake. I think that is what I thought anyway. Now I just remember the look on his face as I spoke the words and the feeling of teetering on the verge of something and of stepping back from the edge.

And thank God we did! Olly must have been as drunk as I was or utterly appalled by the fact he'd just ended up in a drunken clinch with his little sister's best mate. Either way, he didn't have much to say at *all* until we caught our Eurostar a couple of hours later, by which time the mystery cheese had found its way into our lives and we could spend the journey home talking about that instead) because neither of us has ever mentioned the Mistaken Thing since. I've barely even let myself *think* about it, in my case, and I'm certain in Olly's case, too.

"Was this the one you were looking for?"

The Big Cheese Woman has re-emerged, and is holding a cheese out towards me. I stare at it: it's flat, and circular, and ash-covered, with a cross on the top.

"Um . . . I'm pretty sure it *could* be . . . I'd have to taste it to be certain . . ."

"Yep, well, that's why I thought I'd pop one in your order. It's called Cathare, and it's made near Toulouse. You must let me know if it turns out to be the right one or not."

After a morning like the one I've had, I actually feel like I could leap across her counter and kiss her. Blow the fact I'd squash the precious cheese in the process.

"That's so nice of you!"

"Oh, it's nothing! Happy to try to help. Now, the other cheeses will be . . . thirty-seven pounds in total, please."

I can feel myself actually wince as I hand over my debit card.

"Sorry," the Big Cheese Woman says, clearly noticing my wince. "The Comté was a pricey choice, I'm afraid."

"No, it's fine. I mean, it's not your fault. I just . . . well, I lost my job today, that's all."

"Oh, my God! I'm so sorry to hear that!"

"Oh, no, don't worry. It's absolutely fine. Better than fine, in fact."

She gives me a funny look. "Really?"

"Yep. Losing my job," I tell her, "is going to turn out to be the best thing that ever happened to me."

This is the tactic I've decided to take, anyway, since I slunk away from King's Cross this morning with my tail between my legs. Accentuating the positive. Because in all seriousness, what's the *point* of sitting around weeping and wailing and gnashing my teeth? Where will it get me? Nowhere, that's where. And anyway, I've got loads to be cheerful about. I have my health. I have my friends. I will have — when I pick up the keys a couple of hours from now — a brand-new flat.

The trick, for the time being, is just to try and ignore the fact that I haven't told my mother I've lost my job and that I might not be able to pay next month's rent to my slightly scary new landlord.

"Wow. I really admire your attitude!" the Big Cheese Woman tells me, handing over the machine for me to type my PIN into. "Positive thinking will get you a long way in life."

"Exactly!" I say, (also ignoring the fact that, actually, positive thinking hasn't got me all *that* far in life up to this point). "It's just like trying to track down this mystery cheese! Where would we be if we all just gave up at the first hurdle?"

"That's the spirit!" But the Big Cheese Woman can't cheer me on any more, because she's just being asked by another customer if she stocks organic Roquefort. She hands me my Visa and my carrier bag, and I head out into the warm sunshine.

It's only when I peer into the carrier to check that she's put the receipt inside that I realize she's only charged me half what she should have, *and* thrown in a packet of posh shortbread biscuits into the bargain.

Which is lovely of her, and proves that a positive attitude reaps its own rewards.

Oh, and talking of lovely, and positive attitudes, my phone has just pinged with a text from my best friend, Nora.

U in the new flat yet??? Hope my bro is helping you get settled? Nxxxx

Nora's "bro" is Olly, and they've pretty much ended up as surrogate brother and sister to me since that day I met them in the big old Edwardian theatre in Wimbledon. It's weird, actually, now that I think of

Olly as my surrogate brother, to remember that first meeting. Specifically — thanks, teenage hormones — the part where I thought he might be about to kiss me. Anyway, despite them coming from a proper showbiz family (there's not just their mum with her am-dram group in Woking, but also one other sister who's now a dancer with the Royal Ballet, and of course Kitty, the youngest, who's a presenter on a Saturday morning kids' TV show), Nora has the most serious, grown-up job of anybody I know: she's an A&E doctor at a huge teaching hospital in Glasgow.

I miss her like mad.

Though, of course, now that I'm about to get settled in my own flat, it'll be easy as pie for me to invite her and her lovely fiancé Mark down for the weekend. We'll be able to do all the kinds of things you can only do when you've got your own place: brunch on Saturday morning — perhaps with Olly too, if he can make it — and a casual party on Saturday night, with random friends dropping round with bottles of wine while I whip up a delicious stew in the kitchen . . . or maybe Olly could come over again and do the stew bit, come to think of it, because I can't actually cook for toffee. And, seeing as it'll be a rare weekend off work for Nora and Mark, I don't think she'd be too happy if she ended up having to administer emergency medical treatment to the other guests if I've accidentally poisoned them with my Lancashire hotpot.

On way to flat right now!! I text Nora. BTW it's possible have tracked down mystery cheese from Le Marathon.

She must be in a lull between ward rounds, because amazingly she texts straight back: You and Olly and that bloody cheese. V exciting re flat. What is big plan for first night on your own?

Hmm, that's a good question. Because, in all honesty, my plan — once Olly has come and gone, that is — is to put on my pyjamas and curl up in front of one of my favourite old movies on my iPad. Perhaps, for maximum granny-era bliss, with my vintage bead-box and my ribbon bag for a bit of cosy crafting at the same time.

I mean, come on, it's not like it's knitting, or anything.

But I can't tell Nora this. Nora thinks it might as well be knitting. (Though unlike Cass, she at least fully appreciates the results, and I'm hoping she'll love the beautiful, *Breakfast at Tiffany's*-inspired necklace I'm currently working on to give her to wear on her wedding day.) More to the point, Nora worries that I spend far too long not dealing with my problems in the real world by escaping into Hollywood fantasy.

She'd worry even more if I ever admitted that I still, sometimes, allow myself these silly daydreams I used to have when I was about twelve, where Audrey Hepburn is my best friend, and we spend our time hanging out together.

I mean, I don't do it *often* these days, I'd like to point out, if that makes me sound any less weird and sad at all? Only when I feel in need of a bit of comfort.

And we all do weird things for comfort, don't we? Some people eat entire tubs of Phish Food ice cream.

Some people have kinky sex with complete strangers. So it's pretty harmless, surely, that I occasionally like to zone out with an imaginary shopping trip, or afternoon tea, or night out dancing, in the company of the delightful Miss Hepburn?

My phone pings with another text from Nora: Please Libby for love of all that is holy don't tell me you're just going to string beads and watch back-to-back Audrey Hepburn films in your PJs all night. If u wanted to do that u could have stayed living in old bedroom with your mother.

Damn and blast her.

No intention of anything of sort, I text Nora back. Am planning productive evening of unpacking, sorting out, and then might spend five mins on Amazon looking up best cookbook to buy for delicious stew-making.

Which is met with total silence, either because she's been called away to a life-threatening medical emergency or because she just doesn't believe me.

Any way, I need to hop back on the tube now and make my way to Colliers Wood, because it's time for me to pick up the keys to my brand-new, grown-up, *very own* home.

The shops in the little parade beneath my new flat are an eclectic mix, with one unifying theme.

BOGDAN'S TV REPAIRZ
BOGDAN'S DIY SUPPLIEZ
BOGDAN'S CHICKEN 'N' RIBZ

And finally, just in case you started to worry that Bogdan didn't get quite enough of a good deal on the letter Z from his sign-making people:

BOGDAN'S PIZZA PIZZAZZ!

My particular flat, somewhat unfortunately, is right above this final one. But still, this might have its advantages, because I won't even have to change out of those pyjamas Nora is being so negative about if I get a sudden craving for pizza, with pizzazz or otherwise, at ten o'clock at night.

And it's at Pizza Pizzazz that I'm due to collect the keys, where Bogdan the landlord has left them for me.

The keys are handed over to me by a very large, rather frighteningly silent woman (who does not possess, if truth be told, the smallest hint of pizzazz), and I let myself in at the little door outside the pizza parlour before climbing the stairs all the way to the third . . . no, hang on, I forgot, *fourth* floor, where there are three doors arranged around a little landing. Which is odd, because I only remember there being two doors. Anyway, mine, Flat F, is on the side closest to the street.

I try to control the little chill of excitement I get as I turn the key in the lock, and . . .

OK, it's . . . well, it's quite a bit smaller than I remember.

I told you I'd seen rappers' downstairs loos that were bigger, didn't I?

I think, actually that I've also seen public conveniences that are bigger.

I step inside, trying to estimate how big it really is (eight feet by ten?) and offset this against how big I remember it (fifteen feet by ten?).

How can it have shrunk by seventy square feet since I first saw it? And — by the looks of things — lost a window and . . . an entire *shower room* . . . at the same time?

Though it's the very last thing I want to do, I'm going to have to phone the landlord.

He picks up after a couple of rings.

"Is Bogdan."

"Bogdan, hi! It's Libby Lomax . . ."

"You are happy with flat?"

"Well, that's the thing, Bogdan, I —"

"You are liking renovations?"

"Renovations?" It's only now that I notice the smell of fresh paint and the faint hint of sawdust. "Um, Bogdan, have you . . . put up a partition wall, or something?"

"Well observed, Libby. Am turning one flat into two."

As I stare around the place now, it's quite clear that this is exactly what he's done. Turned one small flat into two tiny ones, taking one of my two windows and my only bathroom with it.

"You are liking? Is perfect, yes? Is more compact, is more cosy, is more easy to be keeping clean . . ."

"But Bogdan —"

"And you can be recommending next-door flat to friend, perhaps? I am thinking *girl* friend," he adds, for clarity, breathing hotly into his end of the phone. "As you will be needing to share bathroom."

"Bogdan." I try to sound as stern as possible, so he'll know I'm Not Messing Around. "What have you done with the bathroom?"

"Is only across hallway. Have put it all in new. Is what girls like, yes? New bathroom suite for pampering? For shaving the legs, for taking the bubble bath, for putting on the body lotion . . ."

I make a mental note to ask Olly to check this bathroom out for hidden cameras before I so much as brush my teeth in there.

"But the thing is, Bogdan, I'm paying rent for a flat twice the size of this one."

"But you are getting brand-new bathroom suite."

"A brand-new *shared* bathroom suite! Across the hallway from a flat you've cut in two!"

"Is chic studio," he counters. "Is minimalist lifestyle."

"But I don't *want* a studio!" I ignore the fact that this place, with its wonky partition wall and its general aroma of sawdust, isn't even in the region of chic. "I wanted a proper flat, Bogdan! With a bedroom and a bathroom."

"In Moldova," Bogdan tells me, sternly, "whole families, with ten children, are living in less than half space than you are getting now."

Which — if it's true — makes me feel like the worst kind of spoilt brat.

On the other hand, he would say that, wouldn't he? He's the one trying to fob me off with a divvied-up flat.

I mean, look at this place. I'm never going to be able to do any of those things I planned here. Those cosy stew parties, for example: how am I (or how is Olly) going to cook when the kitchen space has been reduced to a tiny corner with a single wall-hung cabinet, a two-ring hob and a mini-fridge? And where are my friends going to fit when they pop round for the evening with bottles of red wine? I may not have *hundreds* of friends, but right now I'm worried that even letting Nora bring Mark with her is going to be an issue, And it's even worse than this! I'd almost forgotten about the furniture Olly is bringing round any minute now. Yes, I was very careful about choosing only small pieces, but obviously there was nothing in the props storeroom that was actually *doll*-sized. The lovely leather armchair I picked out will fit in OK, but only if I abandon any hope of also fitting in the little gate-legged table. And I'd chosen this really nice walnut-wood coffee table, and a small but incredibly useful chest of drawers, and Olly is bringing me an old futon from his own flat . . .

Where the hell is it all going to go?

"Bogdan. Look . . ."

The buzzer goes.

That'll be Olly. With all my furniture.

I can't leave him to wait, because he'll probably be pulled up on a yellow line on the main road, with traffic wardens circling like vultures.

"I have to go. My friend Olly's just arrived with my furniture."

"Dolly?" Bogdan asks, excitedly. "She is good girlfriend of yours . . .?

"*Olly*. Short for Oliver. A *boy* friend. Well, not like a boyfriend, but . . ." Actually, there's no harm in Bogdan thinking I have a boyfriend. The buzzer goes again. "I'll call to discuss this again tomorrow," I say, in the firmest tone of voice I can summon.

"I will be looking forward to it, Libby. You can be telling me what you are thinking of new bathroom suite."

I press the entry-phone buzzer to let Olly up, and open my front door just as he turns the landing onto the fourth floor.

"Lib." He takes the last three steps in one and envelops me in an enormous hug. "I haven't been able to get hold of you all afternoon. Are you OK?"

"Well, the flat's half the size I thought it was going to be," I say, into his chest, "and the landlord seems to have a college dorm fetish, but I suppose it could be . . ."

"I meant what happened on location today. The fire thing." He pulls back and looks down at me, wincing, as if he hardly dares peek under the straw sunhat I'm still wearing. "I wasn't sure how much to believe of what the crew were saying, but have you actually burnt off all your hair?"

"No, no, only half. Do you promise not to laugh?"

"Of course."

I wouldn't do this for many people — in fact, Olly and Nora are pretty much the only ones I can think of — but, with a bit of a flourish, I take off my sunhat.

Olly presses his lips together, hard, but he can't disguise the fact they're curling upwards.

"You promised," I remind him, "not to laugh."

"I'm not laughing. I'm absolutely not. Honestly, Lib, it's not even that bad . . ."

"Liar." I open the front door further so he can come in. "Anyway, believe it or not, losing half my hair — oh, and my job, by the way — is only the second worst thing that's happened to me today . . . Ta-da!"

With another flourish, I display my chopped-in-half flatlet.

"You lost your *job?*" Olly says. He's staring at me, and not at the flatlet.

I nod.

"But . . . that *sucks.*"

I nod, again.

"Well, do you want me to speak to Vanessa for you? Threaten to put the catering truck on strike if you're not reinstated as . . . hang on, what was the part you were meant to be playing today?"

"Extra-terrestrial Spaceship Technician."

". . . reinstated as Extra-terrestrial Spaceship Technician? I'm serious, Libby, I'll do it. And Vanessa would have to listen to me, because if there aren't any bacon sandwiches ready at six in the morning the next time that crew is on location, she'll have a riot on her hands."

"That's really nice of you, Ol, but I don't want that." I don't add the obvious — that wild horses couldn't drag me back to work on *The Time Guardians* after my toe-curling humiliation this morning — but there's no need to, because I can see that Olly gets it without me having to say anything. "I'll be fine. Job-wise, I mean. I've pre-paid the first month's rent to Bogdan, and I'll find something new in time to cover next month's."

"Sorry — Bogdan?"

"Oh, yeah, he's my new landlord. In fact, that reminds me, Olly, you don't happen to know what a secret camera in a bathroom might be hidden behind, by any chance?"

"*What?*"

"It's just that Bogdan seems to have a bit of a thing about girls taking showers and putting on body lotion . . ."

"OK, that's it." Looking more than just a little alarmed, now, Olly picks up my jacket from where I've hung it on the back of the door, and holds it out for me to put on. "You're coming back to my flat tonight."

"No, Olly, seriously, it's fine. He thinks I've got a boyfriend now, anyway."

"Who?"

"Bogdan."

"No, I mean, who does he think your boyfriend is?"

"Oh, well, you, of course. So apologies, Ol, but you've just accidentally got stuck with me as an unwanted girlfriend!" This is getting dangerously close to Mistaken Thing territory, I realise, so I add, hastily, "But don't worry, you can dump me as soon as I'm sure there really aren't any hidden cameras in the bathroom. Or anywhere else, for that matter."

Olly turns round for a moment to hang my coat back up on the door, which takes him a lot longer than you'd think, because he keeps fumbling with the loop on the inside of the collar and almost dropping it on the floor,

"Well, anyway," he says, as he eventually succeeds in getting the coat hung and turns back to me, "I'm a little bit worried about getting all your furniture in here. The place is quite a bit smaller than I thought it would be."

"Yes, that's what I was trying to tell you earlier. Bogdan's put that bloody wall up and made one flat into two!"

Olly gazes around the flat for the first time — well, *gazes* is a bit inaccurate, given that it only takes about three-quarters of a second to look at the place in its tiny entirety — and lets out a whistle.

"You know, I *really* don't think the furniture is going to fit."

"Look, can't we start bringing it up before I start panicking about that?"

"Lib, there's no way we can get all that heavy stuff up here by ourselves. Which is why I asked Jesse to meet me here . . . ah, hang on. That could be a text from him right now." He fishes in his jacket pocket, takes out his phone, and nods. "Yep. That's him, on his way from the tube. Look, I'll go down and meet him, and you can crack . . ." He produces, from the paper carrier I've only just noticed he brought with him, a bottle of champagne. ". . . this open!"

"Oh, Olly you shouldn't have."

"Well, you don't move into a new flat every day. Not even a chopped-in-half one with a pervert for a landlord."

I laugh. I can't help it.

"My wine glasses are all in the boxes you picked up from Mum's yesterday, though."

"Ah, well, that's precisely why I brought a few of those boxes in already and left them at the bottom of the stairs. I'll get Jesse to start bringing them up while I get the van open."

66

"No, no, don't worry. I'll come down and get them."

We tramp all the way down the four flights of stairs together, then he heads off to his van, parked just round the corner apparently, and I start lugging one of my cardboard boxes up to my flat . . . then go back down to get another . . . then another . . .

The last thing I want to do is criticize Olly, not when he's being so lovely and so helpful, but he and Jesse are taking a bloody long time to start getting this furniture in, aren't they? I mean, seriously, it's only a small armchair, a coffee table and a three-drawer plywood chest. If it weren't for the bulk, I'm sure I'd be able to bring them up by myself.

Still, at least I've had the time to get all these boxes up, and I ought to be able to find the glasses in one of them. This one, most likely, that I've labelled *NESPRESSO MACHINE AND MISC*: sounds like it's where I might have packed my kitchen bits and bobs. I open it up just as I hear a rather out-of-breath voice behind me.

"I'm telling you, Lib. This isn't going to fit."

It's Olly, who's coming through the doorway. He's purple in the face with exertion, his shoulders are straining underneath his T-shirt, and he's gripping one end of the most enormous sofa I've ever seen.

Not only enormous, in fact, but upholstered in some truly terrible apricot-hued rose-patterned fabric that makes it look like a bomb has gone off in the world's most twee garden centre.

"Well, it might *technically* fit," an equally purple-faced Jesse grunts, inching through the door with the other end of the sofa, "but there's not going to be much room for anything else."

"But this isn't the sofa I put aside!"

"What do you mean?" Olly cranes his head round to look at me.

"I mean, this isn't the sofa I put aside! I didn't put aside a sofa at all, in fact! It was meant to be a leather armchair."

"Well, this is the stuff Uncle Brian told us you'd chosen."

Uncle Brian has made, it appears, a terrible, terrible error.

"And there isn't a leather armchair in the van," Olly adds. "There's this sofa, and the oak blanket box, and the big mahogany chest of drawers, and . . ."

"But I didn't choose any of those things either! I chose an armchair, and a little walnut coffee table, and a *small* chest for my clothes."

"Walnut coffee table?" Olly turns back to Jesse. "Hang on — where have I seen a walnut coffee table recently?"

"There was one in the stuff we dropped off with your mum last night, for the Woking Players," Jesse says, scratching his head in a manner that suggests he's not quite cottoned on to what's happened.

Whereas it's becoming fairly clear to me that the Woking Players are getting my furniture, and that I am getting the Woking Players' set-dressing for whatever Noël Coward play or Stephen Sondheim musical they're performing for the next couple of weeks.

"I'm really sorry, Lib." Olly bends his knees to lower the sofa to the floor, and indicates that Jesse should do the same. I can hardly blame them; it must weigh a tonne. "Do you want us just to take it back to the van?"

"Yes . . . well, no . . . I mean, did you bring that futon you mentioned?"

"Futon . . ." Olly looks blank-eyed for a moment, until recognition dawns. He slaps a hand to his head. "Shit. I forgot about that."

"It's all right. But you'd better leave the sofa here. I've not got anything else to sleep on."

"Are you sure? I mean, apart from anything else, it's a bit . . . well, up close, it's pretty pongy."

"Sort of —" Jesse leans down and inhales one of the overstuffed cushions — "doggy-smelling."

He's right, in one sense: the smell coming up out of the sofa cushions, now that they mention it, is distinctly doggy More specifically the smell of a dog that's been out in the rain all morning and is now drying by a warm radiator, whilst letting out the occasional contented fart. Quite a lot like Olly and Nora's ancient Labrador, Tilly, who farted her way to the grand old age of seventeen; she died five or six years ago but I can still remember her musty pong. Not to mention that there are deep grooves scratched into the wooden part of the arm on one side, as if the rain-dampened dog had a good old go with its claws on there before heading off to dry.

I stare up at Olly, despair taking hold. "Did you *really* think this was the sofa I'd chosen? You didn't stop to question it at any point?"

"Well, I don't know your precise taste in soft furnishings!" Olly says, indignantly. "You make vintage-style jewellery. I thought maybe you wanted a vintage-style living room."

"This sofa isn't *vintage style*, it's . . ." I glower down at the sofa, blaming it, in all its apricot-hued vileness, for everything that's gone wrong for me today.

I mean, let's not beat around the bush: it's been a torrent of crap ever since I got out of bed this morning. Losing half my hair, losing my job, getting short-changed out of a proper flat, Cass riding off into the sunset with Dillon . . .

"I'm sorry," I say, plopping myself down, wearily, on the sofa, whereupon a cloud of doggy-smelling dust billows out. It actually makes my eyes water, which obviously makes it look like I'm crying. The irony being that, actually, that's exactly what I feel like doing. If it were just Olly here, and not Jesse, whom I barely know, I'd probably be bawling my eyes out right now. "You've been so lovely," I sniff. "You, too, Jesse, for lugging the bloody thing all the way up here. I'm sorry."

There's a short, slightly awkward silence, ended by Olly folding his six-foot-three bulk onto, the cushion next to me and putting a brotherly arm around my shoulders.

"Look, Lib. Why don't we leave the rest of the furniture in the van to take away with us, and then go and find your new local? Save you worrying about wine glasses."

Much as a drink at the pub — even the inauspicious surroundings of the dodgy-looking one (no doubt owned by Bogdan) down the road — would probably do me good right now, I just don't have any energy left to make a positive out of the evening. Honestly, all I want to do right now is stick to Plan A: dig my pyjamas out of one of the boxes, pop open the champagne so I can scoff the lot myself without having to worry about finding any glasses, and — oh, heavenly bliss, after the day I've endured — curl up in front of *Breakfast at Tiffany's* (or *Tea at Tesco's* as Olly calls it, in honour of our first meeting) on my iPad.

"Thanks, Olly, but I'm really tired. I think the best thing is to get an early night."

"Ooops, sorry." Jesse makes a beeline in the direction of the front door. "You don't want a third wheel around at this time of night. I'll leave you two to it."

"Us two?" I blink up at him. "God, no, no, me and Olly aren't —"

"We're not together, mate," Olly interrupts, firmly. "I'm fairly sure Libby meant an early night on her own."

"Ohhhhh . . . OK, I just thought . . . still, I'll be on my way, anyway."

"Thanks again, Jesse. You really must let me buy you a drink, I'm really grateful . . ."

But he's already gone.

"Sorry about that," says Olly not meeting my eye. Which is understandable, because the Mistaken Thing is rearing its mortifying head for the second time tonight — twice more than it normally does in the space of months or even years — and I know he'd like to put it back in its box as fast and definitively as possible. "I'm not sure where he got that idea. But in all seriousness, are you sure you're going to be OK here tonight? I mean, you don't even have anything to sleep on."

"Yes, I do. What's the point of having a colossal sofa if it can't double up as a bed for the night?"

"Well, if you're sure . . . look, why don't I come over tomorrow night and help you unpack, then we can talk more about what you're going to do next? I'll even cook you a slap-up dinner, how about that?"

"In *this* kitchen?"

"Oh, ye of little faith. Have you forgotten that time I cooked an entire three-course meal in Nora's student bedsit? With only a clapped-out old microwave and a single-ring electric hob?" He casts an eye over my minuscule "kitchen". "This is professional-standard by comparison. I'll do you a nice roast chicken. Easy as pie. Oh, and I'll even *make* a pie, come to think of it. A pie of your choosing. Lemon meringue, apple and blackberry . . . your pie wish is my command."

"That's lovely of you, Ol, but let me cook for you, for a change. As a thank you for all your help."

"Er . . ."

"Oh, come on! I'm not that bad a cook! I can rustle up a tasty stew."

"*Can* you?"

I give him a Look.

"OK, OK . . . well, that would be lovely, if you're sure, Libby," he says, looking pretty *un*-sure himself. "And I'll bring that pie for dessert."

"Thank you. For everything, I mean."

72

"Any time." He leans over and gives me a swift — very swift — kiss on the top of my head as he gets to his feet. "You know that."

I can't help but feel a bit empty, when I've closed the door on him and have the flatlet to myself again.

Well, to myself and the Chesterfield.

Which, now that we're alone together — me and the Chesterfield, that is — is just making me feel sadder than ever. I mean, look at it: after its moment of glory on screen, whenever that was, it's done nothing but moulder away in Uncle Brian's storeroom ever since.

"Well," I say to the sofa. "Everything's all turned to shit, hasn't it?"

The sofa, unsurprisingly, has nothing to say in reply to this.

"I mean, let's just look at my life, shall we?" I go on, squeezing round the sofa's bulky back and picking up my wine bottle from the melamine counter (because if I'm starting to chat to the furniture, then I really, *really* must be in need of a drink). "Because it's not as if things were exactly terrific this morning, *before* I lost my job, half of my flat and half of my hair." My voice has gone rather small, and very wobbly, so I'm extremely glad that I'm only talking to the sofa, even if it might also be an early sign of impending madness. I hate getting upset in front of real people. No: not just hate it: I just don't do it. Won't do it. Haven't done it, I'm stupidly proud to say, since I blubbed in front of Olly and Nora the first day I met them, at the New Wimbledon Theatre, when my waster of a father cancelled my birthday plans at the last minute. "It's not as if I was making a big success of myself."

I unscrew the cap, take a large swig, and then another, and then I squeeze my way round the back of the Chesterfield so that I can plonk myself down on one of its doggy-smelling cushions. Then I reach for my bag and dig around to find my iPad. I balance it on one of the sofa's wide arms — one thing its bulk is useful for, I suppose — and then I go to my stored movies, and tap on *Breakfast at Tiffany's*.

Because the only way I'm ever going to make it through tonight without drinking all this wine on my own, ordering the largest pizza I can find at Bogdan's takeaway, scoffing down the entire lot and then — inevitably — drunk-dialling my horrible ex-boyfriend Daniel, who will be just as distantly condescending as he was for the majority of our short relationship, is if I've got Audrey to get me through.

I suppose it's one (and only one) thing I have to be grateful to my father for: the movies. For the way the movies make me feel. For the rush of mingled excitement and serenity that I feel when I settle into the sofa, now, to the orchestral strains of *Moon River*. And look at Audrey: just *look* at her. Gliding onto the screen, her beautiful face impassive behind those iconic Oliver Goldsmith tortoiseshell sunglasses, her body moving with dancer's grace in that black dress. And then there's that offbeat pearl-and-diamanté necklace and matching tiara, which look precisely like the kind of thing a little girl would pick out of their grandmother's jewellery box to play dressing-up with, and which —

despite Dad's irritation — were precisely the things *I* was most dazzled by, when I first watched the movie with him, as a nine-year-old. Those glittering jewels made me think, back then, that this otherwordly being must surely be some sort of princess, and they've not lost any of their magic now that I'm two decades older.

Which reminds me: Nora's bridal necklace.

I haul myself up from the Chesterfield — no mean feat when you could lose a double-decker bus or two down the back of these cushions — and s-q-u-e-e-z-e my way back round it to get to the "kitchen", where most of my boxes are sitting, waiting for me to unpack them. My bead-box will be at the top of one of them, somewhere . . . yep, here it is, with Nora's necklace neatly folded inside. In my mind's eye it was always meant to look like something Holly Golightly might window-shop on one of her jaunts to Tiffany's, but I don't know if it's quite there yet. I've strung some gorgeous vintage beads along a plain necklace cord — mostly faux pearl, with the occasional randomly dotted silver filigree — either side of this delicate but dazzling diamanté orchid I found in a retro clothing store in Bermondsey one rainy Saturday when I'd accompanied Olly over there to a food market. The orchid was a brooch, originally, but I've used a brooch converter on the back pin to make it a charm suitable for a necklace. I've already finished it off with a silver clasp at the back, but I think I might dig out my chain-nosed pliers, remove the clasp, then really Audrey-fy the whole thing up by adding another row of pearls and random filigree beads either side of the orchid, thereby turning a pretty pendant into a dramatic layered show-stopper . . .

A little way behind me, somebody says, "Good evening."

I spin round, wondering, for a split second, if madness really is setting in, and if — seeing as I was talking to the sofa a few moments ago — I'm starting to hear the sofa talk back to me.

But it's not the sofa. It's someone perched, in fact, on the arm of the sofa.

And that someone is Audrey Hepburn.

CHAPTER
THREE

OK, first things first: obviously it's not *actually* Audrey Hepburn.

I mean, I may just have been chatting to my new sofa, but I'm not 100 per cent crackers, not yet. Obviously there's no way this is the real, bona-fide, sadly long-dead Hollywood legend Audrey.

But second things second and third things third: if she's a lookalike, she's a bloody good one (she's dressed exactly, but I mean, *exactly* the same as the Audrey Hepburn I've just been watching on screen: black dress, sunglasses, triple-strand pearls and all); but, more to the point, *what the hell is an Audrey Hepburn lookalike doing in my flat in Colliers Wood at eight thirty on a Wednesday evening?*

Before I can ask this question — while, in fact, I'm still doing a good impression of a goldfish — she gets to her feet, leans slightly over the melamine worktop and extends a gloved hand.

"I very much hope," she says, "that I'm not barging in."

Wow.

She's got the voice down absolutely pat, I have to say. The elongated vowels, the crisp, elocution-perfect consonants, all adding up to that mysterious not-quite-English-not-quite-European accent. Exactly the way Audrey Hepburn sounds when you hear her in the movies.

"But how did you *get* in?" I glance over at the door, which I'm sure I locked when Olly and Jesse left. There's no way she can have come in that way . . . Unless she has a key, of course . . . "Oh, God. Did Bogdan send you?"

Her eyebrows (perfectly arched and realistically thick) lift up over the top rim of her sunglasses.

"Bogdan?"

"The man who owns this block. Owns most of Colliers Wood, by the looks of it."

"Colliers Wood?" she repeats, as though they're words from a foreign language. "What a magical-sounding place!"

"It's really, really not."

"Where is it?"

"You're joking, right?"

She stares at me, impassively, from behind the sunglasses. (Oliver Goldsmith sunglasses, I can't help but notice, in brown tortoiseshell, so she's certainly done a thorough job of sourcing a fantastic replica pair from some vintage store or other. Or some shop that sells exact-replica Audrey Hepburn gear, because that necklace she's wearing is an absolute ringer for the one the real Audrey was wearing on my iPad screen a few minutes ago.)

"It's in London. Zone Three. Halfway between Tooting and —"

"How wonderful!" She claps her hands in delight. "I adore London! I lived here just after the war, you know. The tiniest little flat, you wouldn't believe how small, right in the middle of Mayfair. South Audley Street — do you know it at all?"

"Yes. I mean, no. I know South Audley Street, but I don't know where you . . . rather, where Audrey . . . look, I don't mean to be rude, but you have just sort of . . . *showed up*. And I'm not sure I'm happy about other people having keys to the flat, so perhaps you could tell Bogdan . . ."

"Darling, I'm awfully sorry, but I really don't know this Bogdan fellow at all. In fact, it's just occurred to me that you and I haven't introduced ourselves properly! I'm Audrey." She extends a gracious hand, emitting a waft, as she does so, of perfume from her wrist: an oddly familiar scent of jasmine and violets. "Audrey Hepburn."

"Right," I snort. "And I'm Princess Diana."

"Oh, my goodness!" She bows her head and drops into an impressively low curtsey. "I had no idea I was in the presence of royalty!"

"No! I mean, obviously I'm not . . ."

"I should have realized, Your Highness. I mean, only a princess would have jewels like that."

I'm confused (make that *even more* confused) until I realize that I'm still holding Nora's half-finished diamanté and pearl-bead necklace in my hand.

"No, no, this isn't real." I shove the necklace back into the bead-box. "And I'm not Your Highness. I'm not a princess."

She glances up, still balanced in her curtsey. "But you said . . ."

"Yes, because you said you were Audrey Hepburn. Now, don't get me wrong, you're doing a fantastic job . . ."

Which she really, really is, I have to admit, the longer I stare at her.

I mean, I know *anyone* can recreate the *Breakfast at Tiffany's* look without too much trouble — the dress, the sunglasses, the beehive — but she's really cracked the finer points, too. Her hair isn't just beehived, it's exactly the right shade of chestnut brown; her lips are precisely the right shape and fullness; her complexion is Hollywood-lustrous and oyster-pale.

Oh, and it's just occurred to me that I can pin down that familiar jasmine-y violet-y scent, after all: it's L'Interdit, the Givenchy perfume created specially for Audrey Hepburn, of course. Mum and Cass gave me a bottle of it several Christmases back.

"Does it take a really long time?" I suddenly blurt out.

"I beg your pardon?"

"The whole Audrey look. The hair. The make-up. Does it take a really long time?"

"Oh, well, I have dressers to help me when I'm working, if that's what you're asking about. And of course I have darling Hubert to make me the most perfect frocks — this is one of his that I'm wearing right now, in fact! Do you like it? He's such a brilliant designer — and, trust me, it takes some brilliance to

80

put me in a long dress and not make me look like an ironing board! — and such a dear friend, too!"

As she talks, a second possibility is starting to dawn on me.

Which is that she's not an extremely good professional lookalike but is, in fact, an escaped lunatic.

Because she really seems to believe that she *is* Audrey Hepburn. In the way that you hear about people really believing that they *are* (usually) Napoleon, or Jesus Christ. Or Princess Diana, come to that.

"Look," I say, more gently than I've been speaking for the past couple of minutes. "Perhaps it would be best if you tell me who I can call. A friend? Boyfriend? A . . . well, a nurse?"

"Nurse?" She laughs, musically. "But I'm not ill!"

"Well, of course! Absolutely you're not ill!" I'm nowhere near well enough versed in psychology to know whether someone who thinks they're Audrey Hepburn could become dangerous if confronted with the fact that they're *not*. "But it's getting late, and I've got quite a lot of unpacking to do. So if you'd rather I just called you a taxi . . ."

"I can help you with the unpacking!"

"God, no, that's not what I meant!"

But she's not listening. She's tripping daintily over to my boxes, kneeling down beside them and starting to pull off the masking tape.

"I adore unpacking," she says. "Making a house a home! Well, in your case, a flat. And this one is simply delightful!"

Now I *know* she's suffering from delusions.

"Though I must say, darling, you've not done yourself any favours by putting this huge sofa in here. You'd be far better off with some sort of lovely leather armchair . . . Goodness! What on earth is this?"

She's pulled the Nespresso machine out of the top of the box she's kneeling beside, and is gazing at it, from behind her sunglasses, in awe and wonderment.

"Is it a camera? A microwave oven?"

"It's a Nespresso machine," I say, rather irritably because whether it's an act or whether it's a delusion, this whole thing is starting to get a bit much. I'm even starting to wonder if putting in a quick call to Bogdan might be just the thing. After all, if your dodgy landlord can't get rid of Audrey Hepburn lookalikes who won't leave your flat, what is he good for? "You must have seen the adverts, with George Clooney."

"Is he any relation to Rosemary?" she asks, brightly.

"Rosemary Clooney? I don't know, might be a nephew or something. Now, I'm really sorry, but I'm going to have to ask you to —"

"Oh, no, darling, he can't be a nephew! Rosemary would have *told* me if she had a nephew!" She turns back to look at the Nespresso machine, taking her sunglasses off so that she can gaze at it more closely. She puts the sunglasses down on the melamine. "Nespresso, you say? It sounds as though it's the sort of thing that might make you a cup of coffee?"

"Yes, that's exactly what it does, but you already . . ."

I stop.

She's looking right at me, without the sunglasses.

And I feel a bit funny, all of a sudden.

Because — and this is going to sound certifiably insane, I have to warn you — now that I can see her eyes, I'm not so sure that she's an escaped lunatic after all. Or a professional lookalike, for that matter.

I think that, maybe ... well, that maybe she *is* Audrey Hepburn.

I warned you I'd sound crazy.

I mean, what am I actually saying here? That Audrey Hepburn is miraculously, Lazarus-like, back from the dead? And that instead of coming back from the dead to visit her beloved family, or continue her charity work for UNICEF, she's dropped by my titchy little flat in Colliers Wood instead?

No: of course I'm not saying that. Nobody comes back from the dead, to Colliers Wood or anywhere else, for that matter.

But the way those eyes are looking at me ... and you can't fake eyes. Yes, you can buy coloured contact lenses to make them the right shade of chocolate brown; yes, you can bung on a shedload of false eyelashes; yes, you can master the art of the perfectly feline kohl flick.

But you can't, you absolutely *cannot*, fake the way your eyes look at people. You can't fake the light in them, the *life* in them. Nobody could fake that expression she's fixing on me right now, the expression with which Audrey Hepburn has stared out at me from the screen the countless times I've watched her movies.

So really, there are only two explanations, as far as I can see it.

Either this is the *ghost* of Audrey Hepburn, paying me a visit like something out of a Charles Dickens novel; or I'm the one suffering, for some worrying reason, from borderline-psychotic delusions, and this whole encounter is nothing more than a vivid product of my own imagination.

Thing is, I don't believe in ghosts.

"I suppose . . . I mean, I have had a very stressful day . . ."

"Have you, darling?" She pats me kindly on the shoulder, although her full attention is still being held by the Nespresso machine. "Ooooh, I tell you what — we could make ourselves a delicious coffee and you could tell me all about it!"

"A coffee . . . actually, that's a good idea."

In fact, it occurs to me now that — seeing as I haven't eaten or drunk anything (except those swigs of wine) since this morning — a hot, sugary cup of coffee would actually be a very good idea. I never did get that cup of tea Dillon was going on about.

So this is probably all just delayed shock! Combined, possibly, with some seriously low blood sugar. As soon as I've got something into my system, I'll be as right as rain! This (admittedly incredibly vivid) hallucination will fade away, and I can go back to watching a celluloid Audrey on my iPad again. Instead of watching this real-looking Audrey, standing in my flat, surreally oohing and aahing over a Nespresso machine.

"I'll just find the pods." I head for the box she's just been rootling in and start to look for the complimentary box of coffee pods that came with the machine.

"Pods?"

"Yes, the machine needs pods. They should be in here somewhere . . . a whole box of them . . ."

But they're not. There are lots of other things — three boxes of energy-saving light bulbs: what on earth am I doing with those?; an old leather-covered Roberts radio that I'm fairly sure has been broken since my horrible ex-boyfriend Daniel spilled red wine all over it whilst lecturing me on post-structuralist philosophy; a few random espresso cups and saucers that aren't going to be much use to us unless we can actually make any espressos, and a pair of (what I think must be Mum's) orange kitchen scissors — but no coffee pods.

"I don't understand it. I must have packed them when I packed the machine!"

"Diana, really, it's quite all right, we can just —"

"My name's not Diana," I say, tersely, pulling another box towards me, ripping off the masking tape, and delving in. "I know I already said I wasn't a princess, but my name's not Diana either. It's Libby. Libby Lomax."

"I see," Audrey Hepburn says, though in a rather confused voice, as if she doesn't see at all. "Well . . . *Libby* — let's not trouble ourselves with coffee after all, shall we? It does seem to be . . . upsetting you rather."

"It's not upsetting me!" Though as I say this I realize, to my surprise, that I've got warm tears spilling out of my eyes and down my cheeks. "Sorry," I sniffle, wiping my nose with the back of my hand, which drags a long line of damp snot, attractively, from my nostrils to my jawline. *This*, you see, is why I haven't cried in front of anyone for the past sixteen years. "This is all just a bit overwhelming."

"Oh, but of course it is!" she cries. "Unpacking is awfully stressful at the best of times, especially when one can't find the . . . what did you call them? Coffee *pods?*"

"That's not what I meant. It's *you*. Chatting with you like this . . . It's exactly the sort of thing I've always dreamed about, and now that it's actually happening — even if it isn't, really, not outside my own head, I mean — it's all going wrong."

Audrey Hepburn doesn't say anything; she simply takes me by one elbow, pulls me gently to my feet, and helps me over to the Chesterfield. Then she settles me down amongst the voluminous cushions, plumping them around me rather expertly, and managing only the merest wrinkle of the nose when the doggy smell hits her full in her beautiful face.

"There!" she says, as delightfully as ever. "Now, isn't that already a bit better?"

"Of course it fucking isn't!"

OK, I didn't mean to actually *yell*. Or swear. You don't shout obscenities at *Audrey Hepburn*, for Christ's sake. Not even one you've accidentally hallucinated.

But I don't seem to be able to stop myself, now that the floodgates have opened.

"How can anything possibly be a *bit better*, sitting on this joke of a sofa? In this joke of a flat? After my joke of a day?" I stop myself before I can add *in the middle of my joke of a life*, because that feels way, way too close to the bone, and will almost certainly result in

86

me starting to sob uncontrollably, quite possibly whilst also rocking back and forth and hugging my knees. "And now even my subconscious is playing jokes on me!"

"Your subconscious?"

"You and I were supposed to window-shop on Fifth Avenue! We were supposed to drink champagne in Paris! But oh, no — we're here in my horrible little flat, sitting on a sofa that smells like a mouldering Alsatian, and with nothing to sustain us but a Nespresso machine. Unless we pop down the stairs to one of Bogdan's takeaways, that is, for some chicken and ribs and deep-pan pizza."

Audrey Hepburn turns rather pale. "Actually darling, I'm perfectly happy without anything to eat."

"It's just that nothing is going anything like it was supposed to."

"Oh, darling. Nothing ever goes how it was supposed to go." She sits down on the cushion next to mine and — seemingly from nowhere — produces a lit cigarette. She pops it into her cigarette holder and takes an extremely elegant little draw on it before continuing. "You know, the first time I met Cary Grant, I spilled an entire bottle of wine all over him,"

"You didn't."

"I did. *Red* wine. And he was wearing a cream suit."

Even though I'm fairly convinced that she — that my subconscious, I mean — is making this up in order to make me feel better, I still think I can top this one. I point at her cigarette.

"I set fire to my own hair with one of those today. While I was talking to the best-looking man on the planet. Who, by the way, is probably making wild, passionate, gravity-defying love to my sister right at this very moment."

Audrey Hepburn almost drops her cigarette. Her feline eyes widen in horror. "Your sister is in bed with *Gregory Peck?*"

"What? No, no! Jesus, no! The best-looking man I've ever met in real life, I mean."

"Oh, thank heavens!" She looks weak with relief. "I wouldn't have known *what* to say to Veronique the next time I see her!"

"Yes, well, I'm talking about Dillon O'Hara. He's an actor too, as it happens." Though actually, this makes me feel a tiny bit better about my disastrous encounter with Dillon: I mean, sure, he's good-looking and talented and all that, but he's no Gregory Peck, is he?

"Well, I've never heard of him," Audrey declares. "And he can't be so very wonderful if he broke up with you to go out with your sister instead!"

I snort so loudly at the ludicrousness of this that more of that damp snot billows out of my nose.

"God, no! That's not what happened. I only met Dillon this morning. And, anyway, Dillon would never give a second glance to a girl like me, even if he didn't have a thing for pneumatic blondes. Like my curvier, blonder, prettier little sister."

"Darling, that's a ridiculous thing to say. You're extremely pretty!" She doesn't, I can't help but notice, comment on the curvy and blonde thing. "Now, if you'd just stop hiding yourself away underneath that hat . . ."

I take off my sunhat.

Audrey Hepburn stares at my hair.

"Well, *that's* perfectly easily solved!" she says, after a long moment's silence. She springs to her feet and — with the hand that's not clasping the cigarette-holder — grabs the kitchen scissors from the kitchen worktop. "I'm jolly good with hair. I used to cut all my friends' hair in London after the war, when we were too poor to go to the hairdressers!" She puts her head on one side, still smoking, and considers me for a moment. "You know, a fringe would look marvellous on you."

I have my doubts about this, because although it's been roughly two decades since I last had a fringe, the memories (and the photographic evidence) are still with me. And it didn't, by any stretch of the imagination, look marvellous. It made me look like an oversized hobbit. On a Bad Hair Day.

"Oh, yes . . ." Audrey Hepburn is saying, happily, as she takes one of the huge loose covers off the arm of the Chesterfield and starts to tuck it in around my neck. "A fringe will be impossibly chic! Not to mention the way it will bring out your cheekbones."

Memories of oversized hobbit-dom are fading, to be replaced with a vision of that moment in *Roman Holiday* where Audrey Hepburn has all her hair lopped off by the barber, rocketing from gauche schoolgirl to international beauty in the time it takes to fade out and fade back in again. Not that I'm suggesting I possess the other advantages Audrey has (elfin features, incredible bone structure), but if she really thinks a fringe would make me chic . . .

. . . not to mention that Getting a Makeover was one of the things I always used to do in my Audrey Hepburn dream-world. Admittedly that was in the serene surroundings of an old-fashioned beauty parlour, and not in a cramped flat surrounded by boxes. But Still . . .

"Could you really make me look chic?" I ask, wistfully. "And a bit . . . well, a little bit like you?"

"Oh, Libby!" She rests her cigarette holder on the kitchen worktop, and leans towards me in a cloud of L'Interdit. Then she takes a huge hank of my hair in one still-gloved hand, and starts to slice through it with the scissors. "I'm nothing so terribly special."

I stare up at her. "You *are* joking. Right?"

"Not at all." Her scissors are working quickly, confidently. "I mean, think about it, darling: put any of us in a fabulous dress like this one, throw in some Tiffany diamonds to wear, and we'd *all* look breathtaking."

"Hmm. It helps, of course, if you really *are* breathtaking."

It's her turn to let out a snort, though obviously she manages to do so in an elegant and Gallic sort of way (i.e. without damp snot frothing out of her nostrils).

"Breathtaking is as breathtaking does, Libby Lomax. Here you are getting all hung up on not being blonde or curvy enough . . . I mean, just look at *me!*"

I do. I do look at her. And she's every bit as flawless as she's looked in every movie and photograph I've ever seen of her.

90

"When I started out in Hollywood, all anybody wanted was the pneumatic blondes. Jayne Mansfield, Doris Day, poor darling Marilyn . . . I couldn't possibly compete with them! So do you know what I did?"

"Er — carried on looking exactly like you do now, got a starring role in a major movie opposite Gregory Peck, won an Oscar and got every girl on the planet wearing Capri pants and ballet flats for the next fifty years to try to look like you?"

She stops snipping for a moment to give me a rather sharp look.

"I played to my strengths."

"Which is all very well, when you've *got* strengths . . ."

"Everybody has strengths," she says, gently. "Even you. *Especially* you. And it would do you no end of good, Libby Lomax, if you started to believe it. Now hush, and let me concentrate on this fringe."

I do what I'm told, and hush, while she moves the scissors round to the front of my head and starts to snip, daintily, with the tip of her tongue resting in concentration on her lower lip.

She's probably right, if I really think about it. That it *would* do me good if I played to my strengths a bit more. If I stopped comparing myself to the sort of blonde bombshells that attract men like Dillon O'Hara and made the most of myself, instead of grunging about the place in jeans and a grey hoodie. If I stopped trailing in the wake of my little sister and did something — *well* — that I actually want to do, instead of doing something badly that I couldn't give two hoots about . . .

"Done!" she suddenly sings out, and then steps back to admire her handiwork.

Her face fails a moment later.

"*Oh.*"

This is not the tone of someone admiring their handiwork.

"What do you mean, *oh?*"

"Nothing! It looks . . ."

"Chic?"

There's another long moment of worrying silence.

She picks up her cigarette holder from the counter and takes a hasty, rather anxious draw.

Then she says, "Perhaps if we found you a slightly larger hat . . ."

"Oh, *God.*"

I grab my bag, root about for the little foundation compact I know is in there, flip it open and gaze at my reflection in the little mirror.

It's not good.

At all.

The compact mirror may be small, but it's big enough for me to see the extent of the disaster zone. The fringe makes my forehead look like a tombstone. It highlights the length of my nose. It does not bring out my cheekbones; if anything, in fact, my face is more pancake-like than ever before. And it's not even as if the fringe is the only problem: the rest of my hair has been horribly mangled, too; cut in an uneven crop that makes me look like a startled toilet brush.

"I thought you said you knew how to cut hair!" I yell at Audrey Hepburn, who is at least having the decency to look sheepish, while busying herself picking the stray hairs off the Chesterfield. "That I'd look chic! With cheekbones!"

"Admittedly, your cheekbones have rather . . . vanished." She puts her sunglasses back on, avoiding my glare. "But honestly, it isn't that bad! In fact . . ." She puts her own (perfectly-coiffed) head on one side, doing a performance of Woman Appreciating Other Woman's Haircut that wouldn't win her so much as a *TV Quick* award, let alone a Best Actress Oscar. "Mmm . . . yes . . . do you know, now that I'm growing used to it, I think it's actually quite fetching!"

"You said I needed a bigger hat!"

"Yes, but I *always* think there's no look that can't be improved with a lovely big hat! Hubert," she adds, meaningfully, "would agree with me."

"Oh, no. You can't just fob me off with bloody Hubert again. And I can't wear a hat every day for the next two months, until this grows out!"

"Well, then you can wear that fabulous necklace you were holding earlier. That would soon draw attention away from your hair! Maybe with a headscarf at the same time, though, for good measure. Headscarves are simply wonderful! Terribly ch . . ." She stops, obviously realizing that I might not be too keen to hear the word "chic" again any time in, say, the next fifty years. "I wear them all the time!"

"Yes, but if I wear one, I won't look like you, I'll look like ET in that scene on the flying bicycle . . ."

And then I stop.

Because it's just occurred to me.

I'm hallucinating this whole thing, aren't I?

And if I'm hallucinating Audrey Hepburn, then I'm also hallucinating the havoc she's just wreaked on my hair.

I feel relief flood through me — relief that after all the shitty things that have happened to me today, at least I don't *really* look like a startled toilet brush.

And instantly, hallucination or no hallucination, I feel bad for shouting at Audrey.

"I'm sorry," I say.

"Oh, darling, I'm sorry, too. My hairdressing skills might be a little rustier than I thought."

"It's fine. There's no need to apologize." I crouch down to pick up my hat from where I've dropped it on the floor beside the sofa. "I'll get a proper hairdresser to cut it for real tomorrow and at least now I'll know to ignore them if they start trying to talk me into a fringe . . ."

I straighten up with the hat in my hand.

But Audrey Hepburn isn't standing across the other side of the Chesterfield any more.

I'm alone in my apartment, once again.

CHAPTER
FOUR

Bright daylight streaming in through the skylight is the first thing that wakes me up.

The second thing is the most appalling smell.

It's not the Chesterfield.

What I mean is, it's not *only* the Chesterfield, despite the fact I've been asleep with my head wedged into the back of one of its doggy-smelling cushions all night. It's something even worse, something pungent and eye-watering . . .

Yesterday's cheese.

Oh, God, yesterday's cheese.

The Brie de Meaux, the Fourme d'Ambert, and the specially aged Comté. Oh, and the mystery goat's cheese from Le Marathon. I forgot to give them to Olly and I've left them, by mistake, out of the fridge all night. Sitting in that broad shaft of sunlight that woke me up, and that's probably been pouring through the skylight for at least an hour now.

I scramble off the sofa, pull my T-shirt up over my nose and mouth in the fruitless hope that it might take the edge off the pong, and delve into one of my boxes for a plastic bag I can scrape the cheeses into.

God, what an awful shame. All that gorgeous cheese, gone to waste. And I didn't even get to see Olly's face when I gave him the mystery cheese. Didn't get to try it with him, our eyes closed in fierce concentration, as we tried to work out whether or not it was exactly the same taste and texture as the one we devoured on the Eurostar ten years ago.

I press the bag down to get the air out of it, knot it tightly (to discourage the Brie from making a break for freedom) and head for the door. There must be a rubbish bin area round the back of Bogdan's takeaway where I can dispose of it.

As I open the door, though, I'm distracted from the smell of the cheese by the fact that there's an enormous builder's bum on the landing.

Attached to an enormous builder, that is: a man in low-slung paint-spattered jeans and — slightly unusually — a fuchsia-pink T-shirt, kneeling on the landing with his head in the bathroom doorway, fiddling with the plumbing at the back of the bidet.

He turns round when he hears me (or, more likely, when he smells me).

"Good morning," he says, in a heavy Russian (Moldovan?) accent. "Am Bogdan."

"You're not Bogdan."

Because Bogdan is fiftyish, and moustachioed, and more than just a little sinister. Whereas this bloke is twentyish, and clean-shaven, and looks as if he wouldn't say boo to a goose. As well as the whole fuchsia T-shirt thing, which sets him apart from the besuited Bogdan in more ways than one.

96

"Bogdan is my father."

"Ohhhhhh . . . so you're Bogdan, Son of Bogdan," I say, aware that I'm talking like one of the space crew from *The Time Guardians* when they encounter yet another episode's worth of aliens.

"Am Bogdan, Son of Bogdan," he agrees. "Am here for finishing off bathroom. Have fitted extracting fan. Will be putting up mirror" — he nods at a full-length mirror, propped against the wall beside him — "on back of door. Right now am fixing bidet."

"Right. The thing is, um, Bogdan, that I don't really need the bidet fixing. What I'd really, really like — and I have already mentioned this to your father, in fact — is for the partition wall in my flat to be taken down."

"Am not able to do this," he says, with a mournful shake of the head. "Am however happy," he adds (which is interesting as he doesn't look "happy" to be doing anything at all) "to be looking at problem with drain."

"I don't think there is a problem with drain."

"Then what is smell?"

"Oh, that!" I wave the cheese bag at him. "I stupidly left some cheese out overnight, and . . . shit, sorry!"

My waving arm has caught the full-length mirror by the corner, tipping it sideways for a moment, until Bogdan, Son of Bogdan, with surprisingly lightning reflexes for one so large, shoves out a hand to stop it.

Which is when I get a look at my reflection.

"Oh, my God!"

I put a hand to my hair.

My unevenly cropped hair, with a fringe at the front.

"Something is wrong?" Bogdan asks.

"Yes! My hair!"

"Is looking bit strange, is true."

"That's not what I —"

"As if you are madwoman. Who is cutting own hair. With breadknife."

Bogdan's (slightly brutal) opinion of my appearance is the least of my concerns.

Because it's all coming back to me now . . . Audrey Hepburn appearing in my flat last night, before my very eyes . . . all that stuff with the Nespresso machine . . . me losing it a bit when I couldn't find the pods . . . Audrey Hepburn suggesting a haircut . . .

But it was all a hallucination. I mean, I *know* that.

Which means that not only did I vividly imagine an evening in with Audrey Hepburn last night, but at some point during the course of this hallucination, I set about my own head with a pair of scissors.

Or, if Bogdan Son of Bogdan's opinion is to be trusted, a breadknife.

Either way, it doesn't sound the safest thing I've ever done.

And might just mean that the "madwoman" description isn't far off, after all.

"Are you needing to be getting that?"

"What?"

He's pointing into the flat, where — I've just heard it, too — my phone is ringing.

"Oh, yes . . . I suppose . . ." I stumble back inside the flat and pick up the phone without checking who's calling. Which is a huge mistake, because it's my mother.

"Libby?"

"Mum, hi . . . look, this isn't a very good time, actually."

"What the hell is going on?"

The even-more-than-usually-hectoring tone of her voice makes me think, for a moment, that she must somehow know about everything that's gone on in (and to) my head in the last twelve hours.

"I don't know, Mum . . ." My voice wobbles. I put a hand to my hair and pull fretfully at the disastrous fringe. "I guess it has to be the stress of the move, and what happened at work yesterday . . ."

"*What* happened at work yesterday?"

So she doesn't know. Well, right now, when I'm feeling this shaky, is not the time to tell her.

"Right now is not the time to tell me," she snaps, as though she's implanted some sort of device into my iPhone that allows her to read my mind (she couldn't have done, could she?). "Are you on your way, at least?"

"On my way . . .?"

"To my flat! Have you forgotten what day it is?"

I have to rack my brains here . . . it's June, so it can't be her birthday . . . or Cass's birthday . . .

"Cass's big night! The *Made Man's Hundred Hottest* party! Aren't you going to come and help get her ready?"

I sink into the smelly Chesterfield, where I'd rather spend every single minute of today rather than subject myself to Mum. Even the excitement of Cass's Big

Night won't be enough to distract from the hysteria that will ensue when I show up, with my hair looking like this, to break the news about my unceremonious sacking.

"The thing is, Mum, I'm not feeling all that well."

"So take a painkiller."

"It's not pain, really, so much as something . . . viral." Yes! The perfect solution. I cough, loudly. "And obviously I can't possibly risk giving anything to Cass, not before her big night."

"Rubbish. If it's a virus it'll take twenty-four hours for her to catch it," Mum says, briskly (and without, as far as I can see, the slightest bit of medical knowledge to back up this view). "Now, get a move on and get over here. We need someone to pop and get some lunch, and Cass's dress needs picking up . . ."

"Well, can't you do all of that?"

"Liberty!" she hisses into the phone. "Don't be ridiculous. You know I need to stay with her while she has her extensions done, otherwise she'll get carried away and end up looking like Lindsay Lohan on a bad hair day."

"Better that than a hobbit," I mutter.

"What?"

"Nothing."

"Just get here," Mum says. "Now." And hangs up.

"I am able to be fixing for you."

Bogdan Son of Bogdan is hovering in the doorway. (I think he'd have come in, but there might not actually be room for him in the flat.)

100

"It's all right, Bogdan. I've got to go out. I'll worry about the partition wall later."

"Am talking about hair. I am able to be fixing."

I grab my grey hoodie from the heap it's in on the floor and pull it on. "Thanks, Bogdan, but I only got into this mess in the first place because I didn't wait for a professional to sort it out."

"Am professional." He reaches round into his back pocket, the one displaying the builder's bum a few moments ago, and pulls out a little black leather case. This he opens to display a couple of pairs of shiny silver scissors and a small comb. "Please," he adds, in a low voice, "do not be telling father."

"That you ... er ... carry a little grooming kit wherever you go?"

"That am trainee in hair salon. Evenings and weekends. In West End. Am good enough for West End. Also, West End is further from Colliers Wood. Is safer," he adds, meaningfully, and in a way that suggests he's just as intimidated by Bogdan Senior as I am. Then he puts his huge head on one side and studies me for a moment. "Cannot be promising miracle," he says. "But can certainly be making look less like brush from toilet."

I suppose I don't really have anything else to lose.

A bit more hair, is all. But frankly even a Number One buzz-cut all over might be less of a disaster than my self-imposed do. At least it would look like a deliberate style statement, and not like I've gone loopy and set about myself with the breadknife.

Resignedly, I slump back down onto the Chesterfield. "All right. Give it a go."

He slips one of the pairs of scissors out of the leather case. "Is not quite Mayfair salon. Try not to be thinking about smell."

"Oh, God, the cheese . . ."

"Will be working fast, do not worry." He's already started to snip. "Then you can be getting rid of cheese."

"Thank you, Bogdan, Son of . . . actually, I'll just call you Bogdan, if that's OK with you."

"Is fine. And is no need to be thanking. Is good practice. Besides this," he adds, scissors starting to fly, "am thinking you are having decent bone structure, if am able to find it."

He found it.

Look, I'm not going to claim Audrey cheekbones. But Bogdan (Son of, etc) was right: I *do* have decent bone structure, and his super-short pixie crop has brought it out.

His genius scissors have done something feathery and choppy with all those dreadful wonky ends, and he's shaped the disastro-fringe so that it makes my face look heart-shaped instead of hobbit-shaped.

It's no mean achievement.

Honestly, if I were Bogdan Senior, I wouldn't be banning a career in hairdressing and casting all kinds of aspersions (including some frankly unpleasant homophobic ones; Son Of told me quite a lot about his dad while he was snipping away), I'd be using my property empire to set Son Of up in a swanky salon all of his own as soon as possible, sit back and watch the satisfied customers roll out and the money roll in.

But disapproving parents are hard to deal with. And mine may not be a minor Moldovan crime lord, but I'm heartily glad that I'm able to arrive at Mum's flat, now looking a lot less like brush from toilet than I did an hour ago.

Well, I say I'm arriving at her flat; actually I'm arriving at the sprawling new property development, taking up almost an entire block behind Baker Street, where Mum's flat is located. It's all very swanky and all very "Mum": not just residential buildings but also several chichi shops, a couple of Hot New bars and restaurants, plus an über-hip day spa and gym — FitLondon — that's already attracting an eager celebrity clientele to its acro-yoga classes and chakra-balancing massage treatments.

It takes me several minutes to wend my way past all of this, and the most expensive townhouses and apartments, to reach the small studio flats right at the back of the development, but I find number 710 without too much difficulty, having helped Mum move in here a few nights ago, and ring the bell.

Mum opens the door a moment later.

At least, I think it's Mum.

Unless I'm seeing Hollywood legends again. Because the creature standing in front of me looks, thanks to the bizarre amount of hair covering it from head to waistline, an awful lot like Chewbacca.

"What do you think?"

It's Mum's voice coming out from under all the hair, not Chewbacca's plaintive roar, thank goodness.

"I got Stella to do some extensions for me too, while she's here!" she adds. "Freshen myself up before summer school starts!"

(I should explain: Mum is using the proceeds from the sale of the house in Kensal Rise — the part she didn't spend on a titchy studio apartment just off Baker Street — to buy a "Gonna Make U a Star" franchise. They're stage schools with after-school, Saturday morning and holiday-time acting, singing and dancing classes for children, exactly the sort of thing Cass (and I, somewhat less enthusiastically) used to attend. Mum's new branch will be up and running, in a primary school back in Kensal Rise, a couple of weeks from now.

"It looks . . . er . . ."

"Cass says it makes me look ten years younger."

This means that Cass has simply nodded, without bothering to listen, and whilst simultaneously texting, flipping through *OK!* and watching back episodes of *Keeping Up with the Kardashians* on her iPad.

But still, I'll fib and agree, because life's just easier that way.

"They're great, Mum. Really very —"

"Oh, my *God*, Libby." She's swept back a hank of extension and is now able to see out. "What have you done to *your* hair?

So much for my freshly discovered cheekbones. So much, in fact, for the fact that after Bogdan trimmed my hair, I felt so good that I even braved a slight change from my usual jeans and grey hoodie, rooted around in my wardrobe boxes and dug out the black Burberry trenchcoat I bought in a designer discount sale when I was feeling unusually flush with money having done a radio voiceover ad a few years ago. And which has remained unworn ever since, because I never felt chic enough to pull it off until now. I mean, I've still got my jeans and a grey hoodie on underneath, to be fair. Which is probably stupid of me because, I've only just realized, the hood will be bulging at the back and making me look less like Audrey Hepburn and more like the Hunchback of Notre-Dame.

"Don't you like it?" I ask Mum.

"That's not the point." She stands back as I go through the door into the flat, folds her arms and gives me a long, disapproving once-over. "Long hair is so much more versatile! What if you want to audition for a period drama? RTE have just started casting one on the lives and loves of the Brontë sisters, as it happens."

"Oh, Mum, I'm not sure if I'm really cut out to play a Brontë, no matter what my hair —"

"No, darling, I was going to suggest you try out for a part as one of the servants. I was talking to the casting director yesterday — I mean, don't you think Cass would just be *perfect* as Emily Brontë? — and my radar went on for you when she mentioned that they're going to need loads of non-speaking actors to play the housemaids and the village yokels. Stuff like that."

I'm not sure what I'm more depressed by: Mum's certainty that the very highest I can possibly rise in my career is playing a non-speaking housemaid-slash-village yokel, or the (frankly horrifying) image of Cass murdering the role of Emily Brontë.

"But they won't look twice at you if you turn up looking like that!" Mum complains. "Wigs are way too expensive to bother wasting them on the extras!"

"Well, it's done now. And, in all honesty, Mum, I'm not sure I really want to go up for another non-speaking role in anything. In fact, I've been thinking that it might be time to look for another job. A non-acting job, I mean. I'm not sure exactly what, right now, but . . ."

"I suppose they might be able to put you in a mob cap, or something," she muses. "Perhaps if you wore one when you went to the audition . . . or a straw bonnet, maybe, like a yokel might wear . . ."

"Muuuuuum! Is that Libby? Is she finally here?"

I'm actually grateful for Cass bellowing for me, for once, before Mum can suggest any more Ye Olde Country Bumpkin regalia for me to wear to an audition I don't want to go to.

"Yep, Cass, I'm right here."

I slip past Mum and up the stairs to the bedroom, where Cass is currently sitting on the bed like Lady Muck, while her usual hairdresser, make-up artist, and maid of all work, Stella, is hanging plastic sheeting all over the en-suite shower room.

I'd be a bit concerned that something right out of an episode of *Dexter* is going to happen if it weren't for the fact that Stella is surrounded by spray-tan equipment, and that Cass is lazily scooping her freshly extended hair up into the huge polka-dot shower cap she only ever uses when she's about to be St-Tropez'd to within an inch of her life.

"Oooooooh, *Libby*!" Stella stops what she's doing and stares at me out of the en-suite door. "I *love* your hair!"

I've always liked Stella, who's an old friend of Cass's from stage-school days (before sensibly deciding to opt out of show business and start up her own mobile-beautician business instead) but I like her now more than ever.

"Thank you!" I beam at her.

"Are you nuts, Stell?" Cass, still fiddling with her shower hat (and yes, she does indeed have her phone in the other hand, and her iPad, plus a copy of *OK!*, open on the bed in front of her). "She burnt half of it off yesterday."

"*Burnt* it?" Stella — and Mum, coming up the stairs behind me — ask, in unison.

"Muuu-*uuuum*!" Cass rolls her eyes. "I *told* you that already!"

"You did no such thing!" Mum says.

"Oh. Well, I meant to. Libby burnt half her hair off yesterday and got fired. Hi, Lib," she adds, "can you go straight out to Starbucks and get me a . . . oh!" She's glanced up at me for the first time. She frowns. Then she scowls. "Your *hair*! You look . . . you look like . . ."

"She looks just like Audrey Hepburn!" Stella declares.

There's no time for me to be thrilled by the comparison, because Mum is staring at me with her arms folded and her mouth pinched.

"*Fired*, Libby?" she says.

"Yes, but it wasn't my fault. Well, not completely. I had this little accident with a lit cigarette . . ."

"And when were you going to mention it to me? Your mother. Your *agent*."

"It only happened yesterday," I say, in my most practised not-a-big-drama voice, so as to bring about a modicum of calm (growing up in a house with Mum and Cass, it's a tactic I've used a lot over the years). "Anyway, I didn't think it was worth bothering you with, when you've got so much on. You know, with Gonna Make U a Star, and everything."

(This is another tactic I've used a lot over the years — changing the subject, mostly back to something Mum or Cass really want to talk about: themselves.)

"She looks nothing like Audrey Hepburn," Cass is pouting, staring at me in the mirror, then looking at herself, then back at me again. "Maybe *I* should go short. What do you think, Stella?"

"After three hundred quid's worth of hair extensions?" Stella asks.

"Well, if Libby looks that good, I'd look *amazing*."

"You are *not* cutting your hair!" Mum barks at her. "It's bad enough I have one daughter who looks like a lesbian!"

"Honestly, Marilyn," Stella says, "you need to chill. Libby looks great!"

"Stella, please." Mum is icy. "Can you just get on with Cass's tan, please, and leave the serious family matters to us?"

"Mum, for God's sake, it isn't a serious family matter. I mean, it *might* have been, if the accident with the cigarette had been any worse," I add, pointedly, because it occurs to me that Mum hasn't expressed the slightest concern about this part of it. "But really, it's not a huge deal. In fact, it might even be an opportunity for me to —"

"Not a huge deal? It was your first speaking part in five years! Do you have any idea how hard it was for me to get you that job?"

"Oh, come on, Mum, it was only a shitty little one line part." Cass is getting off the bed, taking her robe off to display her pertly naked body, and heading for the shower room. "Vanessa found another random extra to do it about two minutes after she kicked Libby off the set."

"Thank you, Cass," I say.

"You're welcome," she says, completely missing my sarcastic tone.

I'm not so distracted by Mum's growing histrionics, by the way, that it doesn't occur to me to think: if Cass knows that my role was filled two minutes after I was thrown off the set, maybe she *wasn't* otherwise occupied with Dillon O'Hara after all.

"After all the work I've put into your career!" Mum is saying, sinking onto the bed in a soap-opera-worthy display of grief. "I just don't know how you could *do* this to me, Libby."

This is the point, normally, at which my patience would run thin and I'd fling myself out of Mum's apartment in a red-faced whirl of silent fury, slamming doors and muttering expletives, making 1) absolutely no headway with my mother, and 2) a bit of a fool of myself into the bargain.

But today is different.

It's not just because of my new haircut, and the confidence it's given me.

Actually, do you know what: it's nothing to do with my new haircut, or the confidence it's given me.

It's because of last night, and my all-too-vivid encounter with Imaginary Audrey.

Just because I hallucinated her (and just because I hallucinated her being weird about my Nespresso machine and wrecking my hair with a pair of kitchen scissors; though mind you, the wrecked hair turned out not to be a hallucination after all) it doesn't mean that her legendary poise and grace and loveliness felt any less poised and graceful and lovely. And though I'll never have her cheekbones, her waistline, or her ineffable style, I feel like I might just be able to achieve a bit of her poise and grace, if I really make the effort.

So instead of flinging and slamming and muttering, I take a very, very deep breath, and say, in a voice of poised, graceful loveliness (well, not a sweary mutter, anyway), "Mum, come on. I haven't done anything *to* you. It was all just a silly accident."

"Oh, really? Because right now, Liberty, I have to ask myself: *how much of an accident could this possibly have been?*"

Poised. Graceful. Lovely.

"Mum. Seriously. Do you really think I'd have set my head alight on purpose?"

"Well, I'm sure you didn't do it *actually* on purpose. But you may have done it *unconsciously* on purpose."

Poised. Graceful. Lovely.

"I mean, I just find it interesting," Mum goes on, as if she's garnered some sort of psychological expertise from a first-class degree at Oxford University, rather than a monthly subscription to *Top Santé* magazine and a secret addiction to Gwyneth Paltrow's lifestyle website, "that this *so-called accident* happens the *very first time* you get a speaking part in years. A speaking part *I* arranged for you."

"Mum . . ."

"*Or*," she goes on, "it could have been because you subconsciously wanted to sabotage the whole thing before you had a chance to fail."

"Oh, for crying out loud!" I snap, my poise and grace wobbling in the face of Mum's torrent of psychobabble nonsense.

Unless . . . well, *was* I subconsciously sabotaging myself?

It has just the tiniest ring of truth about it, I have to admit.

"You used to do it all the time when you were a little girl." Mum is on a roll now. "That time you accidentally-on-purpose stubbed your toe the day before the *Cinderella* audition, do you remember? I put it down to jealousy of your sister, because she was up for the part of Cinders and you were only trying out for the chorus, but now I'm wondering if it was nothing to do with Cass, and simply because you couldn't handle the pressure . . ."

"It was an am-dram panto! In Hounslow! There wasn't any pressure!"

"Well, of course there wasn't, because you couldn't audition and you never got the part! And what about your Year Five carol concert, when you had a solo line in *Twelve Days of Christmas?* You came down with a so-called sore throat half an hour before curtain-up."

The way I recall this event, I still managed to croak my way, half a dozen times, through the "Six Geese A-Laying" verse before collapsing straight after the concert with a fever of 103 degrees and then being in bed with tonsillitis for a week.

"And what about that day when the Royal Ballet scouts were coming to Miss Pauline's, and you slipped getting out of the shower and knocked yourself out on the towel rail . . ."

"Mum, for the last time, *it was an accident!*" All attempts at Audrey-esque poise have vanished. "And I didn't come all the way over here this morning for a psychiatric evaluation!"

"Yeah, Mum, there's loads of stuff we need Libby to do!" Cass calls from the bathroom, where Stella has started to blast her with fake-tan spray. "I need my dress picking up from the dry-cleaner's and I need some Spanx picking up from the Selfridges lingerie department and I need my ruby pendant altering — so it highlights my boobs better, Lib, remember?"

"I remember."

". . . and I need my I'm Not Really a Waitress for my pedicure — that's an OPI nail polish, Libby, by the way — and I need . . ."

"I know it's an OPI nail polish, Cass, thank you."

"Well, they'll have it in the spa at FitLondon. And can you go there first, please, or my toenails will never be dry in time?"

I'll be dispatched on any menial errand, to be honest, if it gets me away from Mum's amateur-psychology codswallop.

"Fine. I'll go there first."

"This discussion is not over, Libby!" Mum calls after me as I start to head down the stairs. "As soon as Cass's big night is over . . ."

But I'm closing the front door behind me.

The worst is over, at least.

Because that's the thing: as soon as Cass's Big Night is over . . . what? Mum will just move onto the next project she's earmarked for Cass — Emily Brontë, a *Made Man* magazine cover, *Strictly Come Dancing*; neither she nor Cass will care that much as long as it keeps her in the public eye — and my embarrassing sacking will be forgotten.

And when Mum *does* find three minutes to think about it again, and book me in for another extras job on whatever TV drama is particularly desperate right now, I'm just going to decline. Summon back a soupçon more of that Audrey poise and tell Mum politely, but categorically, No.

Of course, I do need to crack on with finding another job in the meantime. The rent on my new flat — even if I can persuade Bogdan Senior to halve it, which I doubt — isn't going to grow on trees.

Rent money that, it only occurs to me as I approach the entrance to FitLondon, I'm just about to blow on OPI nail polishes and Spanx pants for Cass, because she didn't give me any money to pay for it all and she's notoriously bad at paying me back.

Obviously this isn't going to fly, not now that I'm dealing with a minor Moldovan crime lord. I need to go back to Mum's and get some cash from her, or I'll be easily forty quid out of pocket before I know it.

As I turn away from FitLondon's entrance doors, back towards the flat, my phone suddenly bleeps with a text.

It's Olly:

Any decision on pie yet? The pie world is your oyster. Suggest, however, not oyster.

I smile, and start to text back:

Am willing to be guided by you on all matters pertaining to pies. Always enjoy that banof —

Before I can finish typing fee, I bump into a woman hurrying towards the doors. Literally bump into her, I mean: our arms tangle and we'd probably have bumped noses if it weren't for the fact that she's about a foot taller than me.

"Sorry!" I say.

"For fuck's sake, stop texting and watch where you're bloody going!" she barks.

This is slightly unfair — not to mention rude — because her head was down and she's wearing a baseball cap pulled right over her eyes, which themselves are shaded in huge crystal-encrusted sunglasses, so I'd be surprised if she could see where she was going either.

But I don't expect much else from an A-list model, which I'm assuming she is. A-list because of the baseball cap and shades; model because she's practically six foot tall in her gym shoes, with perfect melons of breasts jutting out of her skimpy cropped top. Familiar-looking breasts, if it doesn't sound too weird to say that . . . I've seen them somewhere before — and recently at that. She pushes past me to the FitLondon entrance, jabs a few times at the entry pad, and then strides through the sliding doors as they open.

It's her rear view that clinches my suspicions. Her bum is pert, perfect, clad in tiny hot-pink yoga shorts and belongs, I'm pretty certain, to the girl I recently saw in the pages of *Grazia*, coming out of a nightclub with Dillon O'Hara: Rhea Haverstock-Harley, Victoria's Secret model and assaulter of hairdressers.

And a moment later I'm absolutely certain, because about ten leather-jacketed paparazzi seem to appear out of nowhere, flashing their cameras in the direction of the doors and yelling, "Rhea! Rhea!" after her as she vanishes inside and the doors close behind her.

Which is pretty definitive, let's face it.

"Stuck-up bitch," one of them mutters, charmingly, as they give up taking dozens of photos of a blank set of sliding glass doors and mooch back, en masse, to wherever it was they came from. One of the coffee bars in the piazza, I expect, because there's no entry pad there, and nobody can stop them going in.

My phone pings, again, from inside my jeans pocket.

This time it's not Olly — to whom I *must* send the pie reply, now I think of it — but Mum.

Tell spa to put nail polish on my account. Also u need entry code for FitLondon entrance. Is Cass's birthday.

Of course it is. Mum's code for pretty much everything is Cass's birthday.

And it's nothing to do with the fact that Cass's birthday is the first of January, and so therefore a memorable date. My birthday is 14 February, as it happens, which is a pretty memorable date, too; but, as far as I know, Mum has never used that for anything.

Well, 0101 it is, then.

I turn back to the FitLondon entrance and key this in on the entry pad that Rhea Haverstock-Harley has just used. The doors slide open and I step through.

"Sorry, sorry . . . coming through!"

This is from a short, rather podgy man, hurrying through the doors behind me. Extremely podgy, actually, given that he's wearing a tracksuit and trainers and carrying a squash racket: isn't squash meant to burn about a zillion calories each time you play? And are you even *allowed* to be this podgy (borderline obese, in fact) if you're a member of a celeb gym, frequented by Victoria's Secret models in bright pink hot pants? I feel scruffy enough as it is — and unwelcome, too, given the hatchet-faced receptionist bearing down on me as I take a few steps further into FitLondon's hallowed halls.

"What the hell are you doing?" she yells — actually *yells* — at me.

"I'm just here to get some nail polish," I say, completely astonished and — I have to say — already

116

composing the complaint email to the FitLondon customer services team in my mind. "My mum's a member here, so . . ."

"Where did he go?"

"Who?"

"The man who came in with you!" She glances, frantically, in all directions, before practically sprinting back along the hallway, an impressive feat in four-inch heels. Reaching a glass reception desk at the far end, she grabs a phone, dials a number, and then says into the receiver: "This is Pippa, on reception. Can you send one of the personal trainers out here, please? Some idiot member of the public let a paparazzo in!"

It takes me a moment to realize that the paparazzo must have been the plump man with the squash racket.

And that the idiot member of the public must be me.

"Send Willi, if he's around," Pippa the receptionist is going on. "I need one of the bigger guys like him, in case things get . . . well, where *is* Willi?" There's a short silence, while she listens to the reply on the other end and continues to glower at me. "Teaching a private yoga class? But I don't see anyone booked in for private yoga on the system . . ."

Suddenly, a flicker of understanding passes across her face, and she turns rather pale beneath her perfectly sprayed-on tan.

"Oh," she says. "*That* sort of private class."

Then she bangs the phone down and heads for a door, right next to where I'm still standing, marked *YOGA STUDIO 1*.

"Willi?" she calls, knocking hard on the door. "Just to warn you and your — er — client . . . we've had a security breach, so just be . . ."

Before she can add *careful*, the door is flung wide open and the squash-racket-holding paparazzo is literally carried out, WWF-style, by a very tall, very wide blond man who looks as if he's been hewn out of marble and who's wearing nothing — and I mean nothing — except a tubular bandage on one knee.

Behind them, her crop top askew, and hoiking her pink hot pants back up from mid-thigh, is a purple-faced and *livid-looking* Rhea Haverstock-Harley.

"The camera, Willi!" she's yelling at the large naked blond man. (Willi, evidently. Which, as it happens, is exactly where I'm trying not to look.) "Don't throw him out until you've got his camera!"

"You can't take that!" the paparazzo wheezes, as Willi grabs the Nikon strap around his neck — *that* was why he looked clinically obese; the huge camera hidden under his hoodie — and pulls it off. "That's my property!"

"And this is *private* property," Pippa the receptionist barks, scurrying to the sliding doors to press the Exit button. "You're trespassing!"

"She let me in!" the paparazzo says, jabbing a finger in my direction. "If a member invites you in, it's not trespassing!"

"She's not a member," Rhea Haverstock-Harley says. (Actually, more like *asks*. In an incredulous tone of voice. As in, "*She's* not a *member?*")

"No, she's not," Pippa confirms, crisply, as Willi finally wrests the Nikon from the paparazzo's grasp, bends down and dumps him on the paving slabs outside the door.

I have time to feel a brief stab of sympathy for the prone paparazzo — not because of his unceremonious exit, but because nobody deserves *that* view of Willi (so to speak) — before I feel a sharp tap on my shoulder. It's Rhea, towering over me like a semi-clad, platinum-blonde Gorgon.

"What the fuck did you let him in for?" she screams. "Who do you work for? The *Sun?* The *Mail? Popbitch?*"

I'm tempted, for one insane moment, to reply, "MI5, actually", but decide against it. This is, after all, a woman with previous form for assault. Christ only knows what it was that the poor hairdresser did to deserve being smacked in the chops with a flying smartphone, but it couldn't possibly have been as bad as accidentally outing her as a cheating strumpet.

"No one," I say. "I don't work for anyone. Though, actually, I did work *with* your boyfriend — Dillon, I mean — ever so briefly . . ."

"*He's* behind this?" she spits. "I swear to God, if you tell him what you saw here today . . . well, you didn't see anything, OK?"

"Just a private yoga lesson?" Willi suggests, his voice much more polite — and Swedish-sounding — than I was expecting.

"A naked yoga lesson?" I can't help saying.

"Nobody's naked," Pippa says, soothingly, grabbing a towel from the stack on her desk and — thank God — handing one to Willi.

He folds it neatly in two and hangs it around his neck.

"For fuck's *sake*, Willi!" Rhea yells, as Pippa grabs another towel and actually puts this one around his waist herself. "I'm serious," she adds, fixing her ocean-green eyes on me again with much the same expression as a Tyrannosaurus Rex probably used on whatever unfortunate herbivore crossed its path at lunchtime. "You didn't see *anything*. So there's nothing to report back to Dillon. Got it?"

"Look, I don't really know him, even. And I'm certainly not —"

She's already spun round, and with a brisk, "Willi!" over her shoulder, is marching back in the direction of Yoga Studio 1. To do whatever it is they were up to when the photographer caught them. Whatever it is that has Willi scampering after her like an eager bloodhound.

"Naked yoga," I mutter, as the door closes behind them.

"Yes." Pippa folds her arms and stares me down. "Naked. Yoga."

"Fine. Whatever." Because really, it's no skin off my nose if Rhea Haverstock-Harley is getting naked with anyone, for yoga purposes or otherwise, beyond the fact that I think she's certifiably insane for cheating on Dillon O'Hara with Big Blond Willi. "Can I go to the spa and buy some nail polish now, please?"

"I'm sorry, this isn't the entrance to the spa."

"Oh. Could you tell me how to get to the spa entrance, then?"

"The spa is closed."

It's clear from her tone of voice that she means the spa is closed *to me*.

I'm not about to stand around and argue. Cass's toenails aren't worth the indignity.

"OK, well, thanks anyway." I press the Exit button, relieved to feel the cool, unscented air on my cheeks, and almost equally relieved to see that the paparazzo has got up, dusted himself down and is walking back across the piazza, presumably to moan about his confiscated Nikon to his comrades.

And I need to go back to Mum's and tell Cass she'll have to send Stella out for her nail polish instead.

I'm halfway across the piazza when I see Dillon O'Hara walking towards me.

He's talking into his iPhone.

". . . fourth message I've left for you this morning," he's saying, tersely, into it. "I thought you might have gone to your yoga class, so I'm heading to your stupid bloody gym now. We need to talk about this, Rhea. Call me when you get this message . . ."

There's a flicker of recognition in his eyes when he glances up from his phone, a moment later, and sees me a few feet away from him. He's about to pass me by, I think, with the merest of polite smiles. Which would be fine by me, because I'm not sure I can look him in the eye after hearing him leave that message, and having just seen what Rhea is doing in her "yoga class".

But the flicker of recognition has turned into — no pun intended — more of a spark.

"Do I . . ." He stops. "Sorry, do I *know* you from somewhere?"

"Yes. From yesterday."

"Sorry, love, but I can barely remember what I had for breakfast this morning." He does look a bit rough, it's true: unshaven and slightly bleary-eyed (albeit still simmeringly gorgeous). "You'll have to remind me."

"I'm Libby. From *The Time Guardians*. Remember, with the, er, unfortunate cigarette incident?"

"Oh, yeah! Of course! Fire Girl!"

Which is a much better nickname than I thought anyone would come up with. Quite charming, in fact. Makes me sound a bit dangerous, a bit sexy.

"Did you do something different," he goes on, "to your hair?"

"You mean apart from burning half of it off yesterday?"

He grins. "Apart from that, yeah."

"Well, I had to go bit shorter," I say, putting a hand to it, suddenly self-conscious. "You know, to even it out."

He puts his own (perfect) head on one side and looks at me, hard, for a long, long moment.

"It suits you."

I'm unable to reply anything other than a mumbled, "Really?"

"Absolutely. I'm liking the little . . ." He wafts a hand near the top of my face. "This bit. The fringey thing."

And then his phone bleeps.

While he reads the text that's just come through on his phone, I digest (no, I *savour*) the last nine words he's just said.

When he looks up again, his face is frozen.

He doesn't say anything at all for a moment.

Then he says, "You know, I don't know why more girls don't get their hair cut really short. I mean, it makes a bit of a change, doesn't it? You know, from all those long, swooshy *manes*."

Rhea. He's talking about Rhea.

Or, I suppose, any one of the fifteen bazillion other leggy Amazonian models he's dated.

But, most likely, given the text message and the icy look on his face when he read it, Rhea.

I get this sudden twist, deep in my gut, on Dillon's behalf. It's sort of horrible to be standing right here with him knowing exactly what I've just seen Rhea doing with Big Blond Willi, and knowing that Dillon doesn't have a clue.

He shoves his phone back into his jacket pocket. "So!" he says, in a dangerously light-hearted tone of voice. "Looks like I've got a spare hour or two on my hands."

"Oh?"

"Well, I thought I might be able to meet my sort-of girlfriend here — you know, that one you've been doing all that reading about in the gossip magazines, during your once-every-five-years trip to the dentist — but that's not happening. Needs a massage. Pulled something in her yoga class."

You have to give Rhea credit. *Pulled something in my yoga class* isn't, technically, lying.

"So I can get stuffed, apparently. Even if I blew off a big meeting with my agent to find her this morning."

"I'm really, *really* sorry, Dillon."

He gives me a distinctly funny look. "Jesus, there's no need to sound so devastated. My agent will forgive me."

"Of course. I just . . . feel bad. That you went to all the trouble. Cancelled your plans, and all that."

The funny look softens. "That's really sweet of you, darling."

Darlin'.

I actually feel my heart jump up into my throat. And then stay there, so that I'm incapable of saying anything in reply

"Tell you what, Fire Girl. Why don't you come and say more nice things to me while I eat my lunch?"

"Hhnh?"

"I've got a couple of hours on my hands, didn't you hear?"

"Yes, but . . ."

"So I need someone to come with me while I eat my lunch. I mean, I don't know if you've noticed, but I'm terribly, terribly famous. If I eat lunch alone, I'll get pestered the entire time by people wanting their picture taken, wanting me to sign their bras, women shoving their phone numbers into my pocket . . ."

"How awful for you."

"I know. It's a burden," He glances over his shoulder at the coffee bars in the piazza and lets out a little shudder, though whether because he knows they're full of paparazzi or because he just thinks they look a bit snooty and pretentious, I couldn't say. "I know a great little sandwich bar not too far away from here. What say

I treat you to a tuna baguette. Throw in a packet of Wotsits, too, if you like."

The trouble with all this charming banter is that I don't know if he's serious, or joking.

And, let's face it, the most embarrassing thing in the world right now would be for me to assume he's being serious, stride out towards this sandwich bar with a spring in my step and a song in my heart, only for him to call out after me that he was just kidding. The best strategy, probably, is just to banter back.

"Well, if you're really serious about those Wotsits . . ."

"Oh, I am. Deadly serious. Though, I warn you, you'll have to spring for a can of Fanta out of your own pocket."

"That's only reasonable."

"I'm glad you think so." He sticks an arm out into the road to hail a black cab that's just trundling by, opens the door and jerks his head for me to climb in. "Hop in, then, Fire Girl. Your tuna baguette awaits."

CHAPTER
FIVE

We haven't come to a sandwich bar, and we aren't eating tuna baguettes. Or Wotsits, for that matter. And there's not a can of Fanta in sight.

We're in a posh hamburger joint in Clerkenwell, in the cosiest, most private booth available, eating huge and absurdly delicious hamburgers with perfect crunchy fries, and drinking — as you do with hamburgers, apparently, in Dillon World — a bottle of perfectly chilled Sauvignon.

And the best bit of all is that Dillon is flirting with me.

Of course, this sounds slightly more exciting than the reality, because in actual fact, he seems incapable of *not* flirting. He's flirted with every single female we've encountered since we got out of the taxi: a pretty blonde walking her tiny dog past us on the street; the gorgeous redhead who greeted us as we entered the diner; the curvy Brazilian waitress who keeps finding excuses to come to our table and refill Dillon's water glass, or offer more condiments, or find out if the burgers/fries/side salads/blobs of coleslaw have been prepared to our satisfaction.

And he's only flirting in a ponytail-pulling sort of way. I'm not imagining that I'm about to become his One True Love, or anything. Or even one of his Many True Lusts, nice though this would be.

"You see?" he's saying now, reaching over and swiping the largest and crunchiest-looking of the fries off my plate. "I told you I needed your protection from the slavering hordes so I could eat my lunch in peace. And look," he waves a chip-holding hand around the almost-empty restaurant, "nobody has bothered us."

"That's because it's gone three o'clock and everyone has finished their lunch already and gone home."

"Don't underestimate yourself, Fire Girl." He swipes another chip, and waggles it at me before popping it into his mouth. "I've been in empty restaurants in the past and, before you know it, word gets out, there's a Twitter alert and people come running. But something about you is clearly keeping the peace." He sits back, folds his arms, and studies me intently for a moment. "You've got a sort of . . . *air* about you."

"Air?"

"Mm. Cool. Elegant."

I snort wine out of my nose.

"Less so when you're doing *that*, obviously," he adds.

I grab my napkin and attempt to dab away the worst of the wine in a ladylike fashion, just like Audrey Hepburn would do in the infinitesimally small likelihood that she ever did this herself. (And I don't count the whole spilling-wine-over-Cary-Grant thing. *Spilling* is delightfully kooky; *snorting* is . . . well, not.)

But the compliment has knocked me for six. Because I'm not sure that anybody, in the history of the entire world, has ever called me either cool or elegant before.

"Admittedly it also helps when you're not running around with flames leaping out of your head." Dillon picks up the Sauvignon bottle. "More wine?"

"God, yes. I mean, yes," I say, trying to sound cool and elegant instead of borderline alcoholic. "That would be lovely."

He pours the dregs of the bottle into my glass (Christ, we got through that quickly) and turns round to grab the waitress's attention. "Could you bring us another of the same, darling?"

Oh, dear. A light haze of alcohol is one thing, but if I plough into a second bottle, I risk getting giggly and silly, which isn't going to do very much for this air of cool elegance that Dillon has mistakenly identified about me.

"I'd better not," I say. "I don't normally drink at lunchtime."

"Then I recommend that you start. It improves the afternoon no end. Now, isn't this nicer," he says, settling back into the depths of his half of the booth and sending a dazzling smile across the table, "than that miserable tuna baguette you wanted for lunch?"

"Weren't you the one promising tuna baguettes?"

"No, no, my dear Libby, that can't have been me. When I take a lady out to lunch, I take her in style."

Just for a moment, I remember that the lady he was hoping to take out to lunch today is Rhea Haverstock-Harley.

128

And I think he remembers, too, because he frowns for a moment and grabs the bottle of wine the Brazilian waitress has just brought over without bothering to smile flirtatiously up at her and say thank you.

"So," he says, grabbing my glass and sloshing some wine into it before doing the same with his own, "tell me. What's the plan, Libby?"

"Plan?"

"For you. Now that you're freed from that piffling little job on . . . sorry, what's the show called again?"

"*The Time Guardians*. Seriously," I add, made bold by the Sauvignon, "don't you think you should try to watch an episode or two before someone asks you about it in an interview, or something?"

It's his turn to snort, though less unattractively. "That'll be the day. All anybody ever wants to know when they interview me is who I'm shagging." He drains his glass and sloshes in some more wine. "Anyway, we were talking about you, weren't we? About your big plans to set the acting world ablaze. No pun intended."

"But — er — I don't have any plans to set the acting world ablaze."

"Oh, come on. Aren't all you actresses consumed with ambition? Happy to stab your own grandmother in the back as long as it gets you the big part you want?"

I blame Big Blond Willi for the image that the words "big part" have just conjured up in my head. Well, that and the Sauvignon. Well, that and the fact that it's difficult to sit opposite Dillon and *not* have pretty much all your thoughts turn into naughty, bedroom-related ones. I shove in a couple more chips — at the very least, I can try to absorb some of the Sauvignon — and try, again, to summon up some more of that cool elegance Dillon mentioned earlier. All I have to do, really, is emulate my hallucination of Audrey from last night; it's probably a good idea to stop shovelling these chips into my mouth, then, come to think of it.

"The thing is," I say, "I'm not really an actress."

"If you're not really an actress, darling, then what were you doing covered in zit-covered latex on the set of a TV show?"

"No, I mean, I've just sort of . . . fallen into it." This sounds, I realize, a bit like I'm talking about a heap of dung. Though, come to think of it, a heap of dung isn't a bad description of my entire acting career. "My sister is the real actress. Oh, shit!" I clap a hand to my mouth. "Her nail polish! Her dry cleaning!"

"Oh, Jesus, don't tell me you've taken on a job as her assistant, or something?"

"No, I'm just helping her out for this evening . . . or *not* helping her out, more like . . ." I rootle frantically in my bag for my phone to see . . . ugh — *seventeen missed calls*. Ten are from Cass, the rest from Mum (obviously on Cass's behalf) and as a coda to the whole thing there's a CAPITAL LETTERS text message from Cass telling me, in misspelled text-speak, that Mum is going to have to go out and run all the errands instead and that I am no longer her sister.

I feel guilty now, not because Mum is running the errands (because if there's a role Mum loves *even more* than armchair psychologist, it's put-upon martyr), but because I love Cass, in spite of everything, and I want her to have a nice evening with all the gawping lechers at her party. But I've run errands for Cass a million times before, and no doubt will do again. Whereas this lunch with Dillon is a total one-off. If I abandon it early, just to get back in her good books with my sister, I'll regret it for the rest of my life.

"Everything all right?"

"Yes." I put the phone back in my bag. "She'll live."

"She seems a bit . . . high-maintenance, your sister."

"Mm." It would be disloyal to Cass to say any more. But I can't help adding, "Did you have a nice . . . chat with her? Yesterday, I mean?"

"Nice enough." He shrugs, looking slightly confused by the question. "I meet quite a lot of girls like her when I'm out and about, that's all."

"Maybe you should go out and about a bit less, then."

A cheeky grin breaks across his face, as if he hasn't expected it. "Maybe I should, Fire Girl." He tops both our glasses up with wine, again. "You do seem like chalk and cheese, though. You and your sister. Mind you, I'm nothing like a single one of my eleven brothers, so I can understand —"

"You have *eleven* brothers?"

"To be sure. There's Paddy, and Seamus, and Brian, and Diarmuid, and Paddy . . . wait, have I already said Paddy?"

"You don't have eleven brothers," I say, "do you?"

"Well, of course I don't." He looks straight at me, eyebrows raised. "Does it work, though?"

"Does what work?"

"The whole *Angela's Ashes* schtick. I'm up for a few acting jobs in the States, and my agent is desperate for me to get them. Wants me to big up my Irish background."

"There's a bit of a difference," I feel compelled to point out, "between Bigging Up and Outright Lies."

"D'you know, that's exactly what Our Paddy said when I mentioned it to him."

"Paddy the First or Paddy The Second?"

He laughs. "I do have a brother called Patrick, as it happens. But just the one. And I don't think he'll really help the *Angela's Ashes* image. He's a chartered accountant. In Clondalkin."

"That sounds nice," I say, even though I've never heard of Clondalkin.

"Yeah, it's all right. A bit light on the old amenities. Not like the urban thrills of Angel, where I live now. You can get a bit bored in Clondalkin, if you're a jet-setting model type. You know, the kind of person with no appreciation for a quiet country pub, or a good old family Sunday roast. The kind of person," he adds, with sudden savagery, "who because they spend their entire life down the gym and the spa, primping and preening for their next *photoshoot* or ridiculous showbiz *party*, has forgotten that it's never going to be *real life*."

There's a rather long silence, during which Dillon empties a good third of the new bottle of wine into his glass and drinks it, and I try to work out how to steer the conversation away from Angry Thoughts About — I can only assume — Rhea and back to Flirty Banter With Libby.

"On second thoughts," I say, "maybe you should spin the American casting agents the whole *Angela's Ashes* thing after all. It's a little bit more juicy than accountants in Clonmel."

"Clondalkin."

"There too."

Dillon smiles. This time, it's a big, genuine, warm smile, not his usual naughty grin or sexy smirk, and it makes him look, all of a sudden, very young and sweet and . . . actually, a little bit vulnerable.

"What are you up to tonight?" he suddenly asks.

"Sorry?"

"Tonight. What are you up to?"

"Um, nothing much. Just hanging out with my friend Olly. Cooking stew."

"Call him." Dillon — cheeky so-and-so, actually reaches over the table and into my bag, to grab my phone. "And tell him you can't, tonight."

I fix him with a Look, as much for the instruction as for the handbag invasion. "Why would I tell him that?"

"Because you're going to a party with me instead."

I blink at him.

"Party?"

"Yes. You see, what sometimes happens is that people gather together in a pre-arranged location, usually between roughly the hours of eight p.m. and midnight. Then food and beverages are served, often — but not necessarily — alcoholic ones, and quite often there's also some music . . ."

"I do know what a party is, thanks."

My heart is hammering nineteen to the dozen in my chest, but I'm trying very, very hard to hang onto my Inner Audrey. And in this situation, I think we all know that Audrey wouldn't be falling over herself to agree (yes, yes, Dillon, I'll ditch my oldest friend to go to a party with you! Anything you ask for! And I do mean anything!). She'd remain soignée and refined, and let the man feel he was lucky even to be asking her.

Of course, if I were Audrey Hepburn, Dillon would be lucky just to be asking me, but I can't get hung up on those kinds of details just now.

"I might be able to rearrange my friend, I guess." I feel bad, even as I'm saying this, about letting down Olly which is what makes me add, just so Dillon knows I'm not always such a rotten friend, "I mean, he has these really early-morning starts for work, so it's a massive faff for him to come all the way to my flat on a weekday evening anyway, and I'm a rubbish cook . . ."

Dillon suddenly reaches over the table a second time, but this time he grabs my hand.

I let out a brief — but audible, and ever-so-slightly orgasmic — gasp.

"The address," he says, producing a biro from his pocket with his other hand and scribbling on my palm.

"Of course," I say, feeling like an idiot and hoping against hope that he'll forget the gasp. (It's exactly, come to think of it, what I did during the first conversation I ever had with Olly at the Wimbledon

Theatre, when he grabbed my hand, I thought he was about to kiss me, and all he did was shove a cheese sandwich into it. Though it feels bizarre, now, thinking that I ever could have thought *Olly*, of all people, was going to kiss me at all.) "I'll need that. So I know where I'm going."

"Yeah, that's kind of the point of addresses." He's picking up my phone now — honestly, does the man have no boundaries whatsoever? — and tapping at the screen. "Here's my number as well, so you can call if you're late, or lost, or something. Or if you need any further information about the way parties work."

"Ha, ha," I say, not very impressively, before realizing that actually, I do need one very important piece of information about this particular party. "Is there a dress code?"

"A dress what?"

"Code. You know . . ." I feel hopelessly, embarrassingly uncool, and wish I'd never asked the question. "Black tie . . . er . . . white tie . . .?"

"Well, that's up to you, but if you do insist on showing up in a tie you might feel a tiny bit overdressed."

"No, no, I meant —"

"I know what you meant. For Christ's sake, woman, you really do think I grew up in a peat bog, don't you? I should get you to come with me to my auditions, spin the whole begorrah leprechaun crap without me having to say a word." He snaps the lid back on the biro. "And no, there's no dress code. Wear whatever the hell you like. You'll look good in anything."

The Brazilian waitress, who's just come to our table (to refresh our napkins? to dust for crumbs?) shoots me a look that says, simultaneously, *You lucky, lucky cow* and, *Good in anything? He's being a bit generous, isn't he?*

"More wine?" she asks. "Dessert? We have an amazing raspberry-jam tart and fresh custard."

"Oh, well, I'm always partial to a bit of tart . . ." Dillon is interrupted by a ping from his phone. He glances down at it and his eyes narrow. He gets to his feet. "I need to go. Can you bring us the bill, darling?"

"I'm not sure I've got cash on me . . ." I start to ferret for my wallet. "Can we split it between two cards?"

He stares at me. "You're joking."

"Oh, God, I'm really sorry, would you prefer the cash?" I'm mortified. "I can probably dash to a cashpoint, there must be one nearby . . ."

He stops me talking by, quite suddenly, leaning down and planting a very soft, very tender kiss right on the very top of my head.

"Girls don't usually offer to split the bill with me these days," he says, gently. His forehead puckers, as if he's truly perplexed by what I've just done. "That's . . . well, it's extremely sweet of you, Fire Girl."

Sweet? No!! Quarter of an hour ago, he thought I was cool and elegant! Sweet is *all* wrong!

(And what the hell was I thinking, anyway, blithering on about splitting the bill like that? *That* wasn't very Audrey Hepburn.)

136

Dillon is taking three crisp fifties from his wallet and putting them down on the table.

"That should cover it. So eight thirty tonight, yeah?" he says, slipping his wallet and phone back into his jacket pocket.

"Eight thirty it is! And I promise, I won't be wearing a tie!"

"What? Oh, yeah . . . right . . ."

And he's off, heading for the door without turning back.

I watch him leave, and then I just sit for a moment or two, slightly stunned and woozily marinating in my Sauvignon fug.

Sauvignon that I now deeply, deeply regret. Because, let's be honest, if I'm going out with Dillon O'Hara tonight, I should have started a detox diet and fitness regime . . . ooooh, let's think . . . about ten years ago.

In fact, let's just recap the most important part of that sentence: *I'm going out with Dillon O'Hara tonight.*

Unless I've just hallucinated the past two hours — I *can't* have, can I? — then this is, without a shadow of a doubt, the most exciting thing to happen to me since . . . well, pretty much since the dawn of time.

And now I've only got three or four hours to make myself presentable enough to go out for the evening with a man who usually goes out for the evening with Victoria's Secret models.

Thank God my hair is all right now, but I'm going to need to put in some *serious* effort on the make-up front, and find something to wear . . . Which is a minefield, because the sort of outfits that make me feel my most confident and pretty are probably not at all the sort of outfits that are going to make me fit in at . . .

Let's just see where this party's taking place, according to Dillon's biro scrawl on my right hand.

Depot. 106 Shoreditch High Street.

"Shit," I say, out loud.

It's the *Made Man* party that Cass is going to.

"Here's your tart." This is the Brazilian waitress, coming over with a large bowl and plonking it down in front of me with a bit less ceremony than she was doing when Dillon was still at the table. "That was Dillon O'Hara, wasn't it?"

"Yes."

"He's *lovely*."

"Yes."

"So do you work for him, or something?" she asks, with the confused expression of someone who's just spent the last hour trying to work out how someone like me (non-Amazonian, non-lingerie model) could possibly fit into the life of someone like Dillon O'Hara.

"No. We're just —"

"Ooooh, are you going to Depot with him tonight?" She's caught sight of the scribble on my hand. "I'm *dying* to go there. It's meant to be *amazing*."

"Really?"

"Well, *yeah*. It's impossible to get into, you know." She gives me the faintest hint of an up-and-down. "I hope you've got something good to wear."

OK, that puts the tin lid on it.

I can't go.

I mean, I just can't, can I? It's not just the lack of a decade's worth of health and fitness. Or the fact that I have nothing — *nothing* — anywhere near good enough to wear. Or the fact that Cass is going to be there, and that it's her big night, and that if I turn up, on her big night, with Dillon O'Hara, she's going to kill me.

It's all of these, combined.

Plus the fact that, now that the Sauvignon haze is starting to wear off a little bit, I've realized the truth of the matter: that me going out for the evening with *Dillon O'Hara* is just . . . well, it's just as unreal as Audrey Hepburn was last night. It's a hologram. A desert mirage. The idea can never, really, become reality.

I pick up my phone and scroll through to find where Dillon has put his number. I'm going to text him, immediately to say I can't go. Rip off the plaster cleanly and quickly, then just stop thinking about it.

Here it is, under D for Dillon.

He's saved it, though, under the name *Dillon Seamus Finlan Patrick Eoghan Diarmuid Patrick (again) Malachy O'Hara*.

I let out a laugh. Followed, briefly by a little, longing whimper.

But I can't do it. I just can't. Better, all round, for me to keep the memory of this perfect, albeit slightly bizarre, hamburger and wine lunch, and leave it there. Before sullying the golden perfection of this afternoon by turning up to the party badly dressed, poorly groomed, and slightly flabby.

And let's face it, Dillon isn't asking me there as his *date*. He has a sort-of-girlfriend (albeit one who cheats on him with huge naked Scandinavians). I'll probably spend half the night trying to find him in a crowded sea of supermodels, before bankrupting myself with a taxi home and crying piteously into the doggy Chesterfield for the rest of the night.

I'm already reaching for my phone. I'll be vague, but firm, and bow out of the invitation.

Really sorry, I text Dillon, can't make this evening after all. Thanks anyway, would have been nice.

There. Vague, but firm. No spurious long-winded excuses or white lies.

It does sound a bit chilly, though.

PS, I add, if your middle names really are Seamus Finlan Patrick Eoghan Diarmuid Patrick (again) Malachy then you really don't need my help *Angela's-Ashing* yourself up for the US market.

Before I can change my mind, I press Send.

If Dillon texts immediately back, saying, Don't be ridiculous, you're coming out with me, and that's final.

Well, then I'd reconsider, obviously.

He doesn't text immediately back.

By the time I've nibbled a little bit of the jam tart and custard, put on my jacket, popped to the Ladies, come back and polished off the entire remaining bowl of jam tart and custard, he hasn't texted back either.

CHAPTER
SIX

My phone bleeps as I open the door to my flat, but it's still not Dillon. It's a text from Olly.

That's a shame. So sorry you're feeling ill. Anything I can do?

This is because I texted him, on the walk from the tube, to cancel our stew-eating plans for this evening.

I know. I shouldn't be lying. Especially not to one of my best friends.

And I shouldn't be cancelling, either, not now that I'm not going to the Depot party. I've only done it because I'm feeling so furious with myself for being such a pathetic scaredy-cat about Dillon that, masochistically, I want the punishment of not having a nice evening at all.

I feel even worse about it now that he's texted so sweetly.

In fact, there goes another ping from my phone now — Olly again.

If is flu-like can bring chicken soap?

A third text comes through a few seconds later.

Obv that should have said soup.

And another one about ten seconds after that.

However will do best to track down novelty soap fashioned in shape of chicken if any chance would help?

He's such a sweetheart.

I'm a fool to have rejected a nice cosy evening with him, for an evening alone instead.

Though I'll only be alone, of course, if I don't hallucinate myself a little bit more Audrey for the evening.

It won't happen again, though. It was just a one-off. And, by the way, I don't *want* it to happen again. When it happens just the once, you can put it down to stress. Twice . . . well, you'd be forgiven for starting to think that it might be something a bit more . . .

. . . sinister?

Neurologically, I mean.

So let's really, really hope it *doesn't* happen again. Tonight or any other night.

The thing is, though, that now that I'm back here on my own, I can't help thinking that it might be quite nice to hallucinate Audrey Hepburn again.

Because it was sort of fun, last night, when all's said and done. It might not have been Fifth Avenue or the Tuileries, but it was still *Audrey*. And if my overwrought synapses *did* conjure her up again this evening, I'd be able to tell her about my afternoon with Dillon. And she'd listen carefully and thoughtfully, the way she always did in my Audrey dreamworld, and then she'd say something perfectly incisive and understanding that would make me feel better, instantly, about being too much of a wimp to go to the party with him tonight.

142

But I suppose then we might be getting into scary territory, with those worrying neurological implications I can't quite bring myself to dwell on. Like . . . well, like schizophrenia. Or a brain tumour.

Though I suppose I could . . .

No. That would be weird.

Well, I was just going to say, I suppose what I *could* do is get Audrey Hepburn up *on screen*, press pause and quickly run through the details of my extraordinary afternoon with her on my iPad.

That *would* be weird, wouldn't it?

But it's not like I'd actually think she was really *there*. Not like I'd really believe she could hear me, or anything. All I'd really be doing is popping on one of my favourite Audrey Hepburn films. Nothing weird about settling down to watch *Breakfast at Tiffany's*, is there, after a long and frankly peculiar day in which I've been psychoanalysed by Mum, yelled at by a supermodel, seen parts of a stranger's anatomy that I'd really have been absolutely fine *not* seeing . . .

Yes. I think I'll fire up the iPad again, take off my trenchcoat, settle down on the sofa, and see if I can go to my happy place.

Three minutes later, I know it's been the right thing to do. I'm not bothered about the unpacking mess, about the doggy sofa I'm sitting on, or about the fact that I should be getting ready to go to a party with Dillon O'Hara right now. I start to relax the moment I see Audrey Hepburn amble down Fifth Avenue with her little cup of coffee and her Danish pastry. She's just so exquisite, and her dress and jewellery so beautiful, and you can almost catch the faintest violet-and-jasmine hint of the L'Interdit perfume she was probably wearing when she filmed it . . .

"You haven't seen my sunglasses, have you?"

I let out an actual shriek.

"Gosh, I'm awfully sorry, did I startle you?"

It's her. It's Audrey Hepburn. Again.

Sitting three inches away from me on the other half of the Chesterfield sofa.

But this time she's not, actually, in black-dress-and-beehive *Tiffany's* mode. Her hair is in her trademark elfin crop and she's wearing the rose-embroidered ball gown she deploys to dazzle William Holden in *Sabrina*.

There are no words to describe how beautiful this dress is, up close.

Even if it does clash, a bit, with the apricot roses on the sofa.

The sofa she's suddenly delving down between the cushions of, her brow furrowed.

"I thought maybe they might have dropped down between the cushions . . . my sunglasses, I mean . . . I don't suppose you've come across them, and put them somewhere safe? It's just that they are rather a special pair . . ."

She glances back up at me, her eyes looking almost absurdly huge in that perfectly framed face. In fact, she looks even more beautiful than she did yesterday, although I've always preferred *Sabrina* Audrey to *Tiffany's* Audrey. Her cropped hair highlights her perfect collarbones, her skin looks as if it's been coated in a fine spray of crushed pearls, and the scent of

144

L'Interdit is stronger now, so I wasn't imagining it at all . . .

Except that I *was*, of course. Because I'm hallucinating this whole thing again, aren't I?

"Oh, shit."

"Libby!"

"Sorry . . . it's just . . ." It's a brain tumour, isn't it? It has to be. "Or schizophrenia," I blurt out. "It could be schizophrenia."

"What could be schizophrenia, darling?" But her attention is only half focused on me; she's gazing at the iPad screen. "How terribly sweet!"

"You mean — er — the Danish pastry?"

"No, no, I meant your darling little television screen. Though that horrible Danish *was* sweet, actually. Cloyingly so. I can't bear the things. I begged them to let me eat an ice cream in that scene instead, but no such luck . . . I can't see an aerial."

"Er . . .?"

"For your little television." She points a long, gloved finger at the iPad. "An aerial. Doesn't it need one?"

"It's not a television. It's an iPad." I rub my eyes, fiercely, but when I pull my hands away I can still see her. "I think I need a drink."

"Another difficult day, darling?" Audrey Hepburn asks, as she picks up the iPad and studies it, admiringly. "Exquisite! What did you call it? A padlet?"

"It's an iPad. You use it for the internet, for email . . ."

She blinks at me as if I'm speaking a foreign language she's never even heard before.

"You know what?" I say, "just have a play around with it while I get myself a drink. It's easy. You'll get the hang."

"Ooooh, thank you, darling!" She takes me at my word and starts tapping and pressing at the iPad with her long, elegant fingertips. "Golly it's ever so clever," she marvels, as random stuff — the weather forecast; photos of me and Nora at her engagement party; the Net-a-Porter app I muck around with when I fancy a bit of lush designer window-shopping — pop up and down again. "Honestly darling, you do own the most marvellous gadgets. Oh! That reminds me. Your lovely coffee machine! I've been talking about it to everyone I know!"

Great: now I'm not only imagining that *I'm chatting to Audrey Hepburn*, but that *she's chatting to other people as well*. The mind boggles as to who it is she could be referring to: a spectral Marilyn? A phantasmagoric Cary Grant? A virtual Liz Taylor?

"I wonder," she asks, clasping her hands in a girlish manner, "did you manage to find your pods yet?"

"The coffee pods? Uh, actually, no . . ."

"Well, I'm sure they're in one of these boxes. Why don't I take a look?".

Before I can reply, she springs off the Chesterfield and kneels down in front of the biggest heap of boxes, not seeming to care that she's getting Olly's van dust all over the hem of her ethereal ball gown.

"*This* looks a good place to start." She's opening the box at the top of the pile. "Oh, this could be useful, actually. It's your cleaning rags."

146

"I don't have a box of cleaning rags . . ." I get up, too, and peer into the box she's just opened. "That's my clothes!"

"Gosh, I'm so sorry, darling!"

I snatch the box away from her, wishing, more than ever, that I were actually able to afford the things I drool over on that Net-a-Porter app from time to time. "We can't all own wardrobes full of exquisite designer ball gowns, you know."

"Well, of course, I simply thought . . . well, everything in there looked so very *grey* . . ."

I stamp off to my mini-fridge for that open bottle from last night.

"If it helps at all," she says, in a contrite tone, "your hair looks absolutely marvellous."

"You really think?"

"I do! And I told you all it needed was a good wash and blow-dry."

"Actually this was done by a hairdresser," I say, pointedly, as I get the wine from the fridge and head back to the sofa. "It didn't need a wash and blow-dry, it needed a trained professional with a proper pair of scissors."

"And didn't I tell you" — I think she's ignoring me, because she's turning back to the boxes and opening another — "that a little fringe would suit . . . oh! I think I've found them!"

She turns, brandishing a small wooden box with a Nespresso label.

"Yes, that's the pods."

She lets out a little shriek of delight, gets to her feet and practically falls over the dusty hem of the ball gown trying to get round the Chesterfield and to the coffee machine on the counter.

"Ooooooohhhhh," she breathes, a moment later, opening the box and gazing in awe at the little guide on the inside of the lid. "Ethiopian *Sidamo* . . ."

This is not what I was hoping for when I thought I might like to chat to Audrey about the events of today: me on the sofa mainlining wine from the bottle while she fires up the Nespresso machine. But it looks like even my own subconscious isn't that interested in the details of my day.

"Not even," I mutter at my subconscious, "when I got asked out *on a proper date* this evening."

"A date?" Audrey Hepburn spins round, ball gown swishing, Ethiopian Sidamo forgotten. "Libby that's so *exciting*!"

OK, so my subconscious is forgiven. I even feel a bit embarrassed, now, about making a big deal of it.

"It wasn't really a date . . ."

"Who is he? When is it?"

"Well, sort of now."

"What do you mean, now?"

"That's when the date should be happening. Tonight."

"And you're not *going?*"

I shake my head firmly and take a drink from the wine bottle.

"Libby why ever not?" Audrey's huge eyes are open even wider, in genuine dismay. "Don't you like him? This gentleman that asked you out?"

"No, no, that's not it. I mean, I like him a lot . . . the gentleman, that is . . ." Though the thought of Dillon-as-gentleman is distinctly amusing. (Not to mention the fact that not a single one of the things he's been doing, in my head, ever since I first met him yesterday morning, has been in the least bit gentlemanly.) "I just decided against going. And it wasn't really a date, anyway. Not in the true sense of the word."

"Did he ask you to dinner? Drinks?"

"God, no, nothing like that. Though we did have lunch together today, as it happens . . ."

"Libby!" she gasps. "You had lunch *and* he asked you out the same night? He must be awfully keen on you!"

"Er — honestly, it's not like that. He has a girlfriend, for one thing. Well, sort of. Rhea Haverstock-Harley. Though I did catch her cheating on him today, with a very large Swede."

"The *vegetable?*"

"The nationality."

"Oh, thank heavens," she says, rather faintly. "Though not terribly nice, either way, for your poor gentleman friend. And probably why he'd much rather take you out for the evening instead of her."

"But he's not asking me out *romantically.* I think he just enjoys chatting to a normal person, for a change. He's used to dating Victoria's Secret models, you see . . . lingerie models," I clarify when her forehead furrows in confusion. "They're all gorgeous and leggy and Amazonian and they strut up and down the catwalk in nothing but a bikini and a set of angel wings."

"That all sounds dreadfully vulgar. No wonder he prefers talking to you." She considers me for a moment. "Which is not to say you wouldn't benefit from revealing a tiny bit more skin yourself when you go out with him this evening."

"But I'm *not* going out with him this evening."

"But you simply must."

"But I simply won't."

"But. You. Simply. Will."

I'm rather startled when, as she says this, she fixes me with a distinctly steely look. A distinctly un-doe-eyed, not-at-all Audrey look.

"I'm not taking no for an answer on this, Libby," she goes on. "Because — and do correct me if I'm wrong — it's not as if you're beating off male admirers with a big stick, now, is it?"

"There's no need to put it *quite* like that," I mumble.

"My point is, Libby," — she squeezes round the Chesterfield; it takes a few moments — "that you oughtn't be sitting around here with me." She kneels down beside me, grabs both my hands and looks deep into my eyes. "You ought to be out! Having a wonderful evening! With a man who adores you!"

"He really, really doesn't *adore* me. Anyway, I can't." My throat is going dry and feels a bit like it's seizing up. "Honestly," I manage to say, after a sip of wine, "I just can't. You haven't seen the sort of girl he usually goes out with."

"I'll bet my bottom dollar," Audrey cries, "they're not a patch on you!"

150

I reach for the iPad, Google "Rhea Haverstock-Harley" and shove the resulting images in her direction: Rhea draped seductively over a lucky rock by the sea in an itsy-bitsy bikini; Rhea striding along a catwalk wearing a diamanté bra, matching thong, and glittery angel wings; Rhea posing in nothing but a pair of high heels on a backwards-facing chair a la Christine Keeler . . .

"Well!" Audrey says, a little too brightly, after a long, silent moment. "We'll just have to find you something really, *really* lovely and flattering to wear tonight, won't we?"

"No, we won't, because — as I think I've already said — I'm not going."

"Darling. Far be it from me to pull rank." She stands up, folds her skinny arms, and eyeballs me again. "But I *am* Audrey Hepburn, you know."

Hallucination or otherwise, it's just a little harder than it was, a moment ago, to disagree with her.

"And do you know the one thing I'm most proud of?" she goes on. "It's that I don't let anything scare me. I wasn't qualified to act opposite Gregory Peck. I wasn't good enough to dance with Fred Astaire. But I damn well got on with it and gave it my all, because that's the only way a girl is going to find her place in this world."

It's stirring stuff, I have to admit.

And, quite suddenly, she's less the elfin style queen I've always imagined myself being shopping buddies with. Standing here, right now, she's a warrior princess. She's a Givenchy-clad Boudicca, a kohl-rimmed Joan of Arc . . .

"All right." I get to my feet, too. "I *will* go out this evening! After all, if you can dance with Fred Astaire, I can get on the tube and —"

"My Nespresso!" she suddenly shrieks, as the machine bleeps its readiness to make her coffee. She practically knocks me over as she squeezes round the sofa to get to the kitchen. "Now, where does the little pod go?"

"Look, can we worry about that later? I need to get ready for this party before I change my mind."

"Yes, yes, you're absolutely right." Audrey abandons the coffee machine a second time. "Now, we were going to find you something spectacular to wear, weren't we?"

"No, no, no," I say, hastily, as she heads, in a flurry of couture satin and taffeta, for the clothes box that she discarded earlier. "You said something lovely and flattering. Not spectacular. I don't want spectacular. My sister's going to be at the same party, and it's a really big night for her. And she's going to be pissed off enough that. I'm even there in the first place. So I really want to wear something . . . well, perfectly nice but inoffensive."

"A little black dress!"

"Well, I suppose that would probably be all right . . ."

"Darling, a little black dress is *always* all right." She's already delving into the clothes in the box, shoving aside marl grey hoodie after marl grey hoodie. "Do you have one by Hubert, by any chance?"

"Do I have a little black dress by Hubert *de Givenchy?* No. No, I don't."

"Well, there's no need to worry about that; I'm sure we'll find something else lovely . . ." Though her elegant bare shoulders sag, visibly, as she casts aside yet another (when did I *buy* all these?) grey hoodie. "You do *own* a dress, darling? One is all we need."

"Yes, I own a dress! Look, I obviously need a bit of a wardrobe update, OK?" But fortunately I've just spotted a different sort of grey fabric in the heap of grey fabric, and I pull it out — it's the Whistles slate-grey silky wrap dress I've worn on several Big Occasions over the past few years: my first date with Daniel; my last birthday drinks; the after-party when Cass was nominated (but didn't win) for a National Reality Television Award for her appearance on *Mary Berry's Celebrity Cupcake-Off*. "Ha! A dress!" I declare, waving it at her in triumph.

Audrey Hepburn stares at the wrap dress. "*Is* it?"

"Yes! It's a wrap dress!"

"But darling . . ." She's looking appalled. "It's just a piece of material. It has no *line*. No *structure*."

"It doesn't need to! It's universally flattering! It skims over your curves. It creates a waist."

I realize that I'm simply parroting everything I've ever read about wrap dresses, which is why I spent a small fortune on it in the first place. And now I come to remember it, this dress didn't skim over my curves *or* create a waist; all it did was hang rather limply off my negligible chest and threaten to expose unflattering amounts of upper thigh every time I took more than three steps in succession. But it's the most expensive dress I've ever owned, which is why I've hung onto it instead of consigning it to the charity bin.

From the expression on Audrey's face right now, it really needs to be consigned to the charity bin. Or, more likely, the rubbish bin.

"Fine," I say, putting the wrap dress down. "You win. I won't wear this one."

"I think," she says kindly, "that would best."

And then she practically disappears into the box, head down like a dabbling duck, leaving nothing much of herself visible except for the embroidered train of her ball gown. It's a moment later when she pops back up again with a triumphant look on her face and a black dress in one hand.

"Now, this looks *much* more the sort of thing!"

The dress she's holding is a rather sober shift with a boat neckline and a tricky-to-pull-off hemline that sits, if I recall, at mid-calf. I bought it from Primark without bothering to try it on, in the futile hope — funnily enough — that it would make me look like Audrey Hepburn.

Needless to say, it didn't, and, even more needless to say, it's never seen the light of day since the depressing trying-on session when I got home and took it out of its carrier bag.

"Are you sure?" I look at the dress with a lot less enthusiasm than she's displaying. "It's just a cheapo thing from Primark."

"Well, I can't say I'm familiar with Mr Primark's work . . ."

"No, no, it's not a Mr, it's just a —"

"But I think this will do *very* nicely indeed!" She holds the dress up against me. "All you need is that rather smart trenchcoat of yours, slung over your shoulders, and a few well-chosen accessories. That neckline, for example, is simply crying out for a sweet little diamond pendant, or an elegant string of pearls."

"Right, well, I'll call my bank in Zurich, then get them to crack open the largest of my safety deposit boxes and have a selection flown over to me by private jet."

"Unfortunately I don't think there's going to be time for that," she says, in deadly earnest. "But didn't I see you with a pearl and diamond necklace when I first met you?"

"I highly doubt that . . . oh, you mean Nora's wedding pendant?"

"All I know is that you put it in your little box over here." Audrey is swooshing over to the kitchen counter, where my bead-box is still sitting, and opening it up. "Oh, this will be wonderful on you!"

"I don't know. It's for my best friend, on her wedding day. And I'm not even sure I've quite finished it yet."

She's ignoring me, placing the necklace around my neck and doing up the clasp. "Like I thought," she says. "Wonderful."

It does *feel* rather nice, I have to admit, with the cool weight of the diamanté charm against my skin, and the silky smoothness of the vintage pearl beads . . . Well, I'll just have to justify it as a trial run for Nora's special present: helping me decide whether the necklace should stay as it is, or if it needs that double layer of pearl beads after all.

"Now, the right shoes, of course, always make or break any outfit. Do you have a nice simple pump?" Audrey asks me. "Something with a kitten heel, perhaps?"

"Oh, no. I'm not wearing a kitten heel. Not when I'm going to spend the evening with a bunch of six-foot-in-their-bare-feet models." I haven't forgotten the way Rhea towered over me at FitLondon this morning; there might be all kinds of reasons why I feel small and insignificant at this party tonight, but I'm not about to let my shoes be one of them. "I'm wearing *these*," I say, delving back into the box and rooting around for the only pair of really glamorous shoes I own, a pair of silvery sandals with an ankle strap and a teetering platform heel.

This time Audrey actually looks ill.

"But you could break your ankle in those! And surely . . . well, a kitten heel would be so much more *chic* . . ."

"That's what you said before you mangled my fringe last night," I tell her, glad of the fact that she only exists in my imagination, because I'm not sure this is an argument I'd feel confident having if I really *were* talking to one of the most ineffably stylish women that has ever existed. "Anyway, I couldn't care less if they're chic or not — they make me look five inches taller and half a stone lighter. I'm wearing them. Now, do you think I need any Spanx?"

"Oh!" Her hands fly to her cheeks, which are burning red all of a sudden. "I'm sorry, but that's going to be entirely up to the proclivities of the gentleman you're going out with this evening! And really, Libby,

156

what you want to do in the privacy of the bedroom is really none of my —"

"Spanx *knickers!*" I say, even more mortified by the misunderstanding than she is. "It's a kind of underwear . . . look, never mind. I really need to start getting ready."

"Of course." She looks relieved by the change of subject. "What time is he picking you up?"

"He's not. I'll meet him at the party."

"Why on earth isn't he coming to collect you?"

"For one thing, because I told him I wasn't coming. And for another thing, because it's London. In the twenty-first century."

"That's no excuse!" She looks genuinely upset. "When a man takes you out for the evening, he should come to collect you at your door! With a bouquet of your favourite flowers!"

Again, I'm starting to see what life really is like if you're a beautiful movie star.

"Libby . . ." She's peering at me, curious now. "Has a man *never* brought you flowers before a date?"

"No."

I don't add — because she's a figment of my subconscious, and my subconscious already knows this — that I've never really been on a *date* before. That all my so-called relationships (Horrible Daniel, Unreliable Iain, Brief-but-Mistaken Martin) have started in the same fuzzy ill-defined way that they went on and the same fuzzy, ill-defined way they all finally ended. A few too many drinks and a bit of a snog, followed by a few months (or in Martin's case, thank heavens, only weeks) of not-that-satisfactory sex and introducing each other, uncomfortably, to our respective friends as "the person I've been seeing". No dates. No flowers. No *fun*.

"Then you've been treated very badly." Audrey Hepburn sounds quite cross. "And frankly, this Dillon fellow is going to have to wake his ideas up a bit if he's lucky enough to be in with a chance of dating you."

Now, this, right here, is why I always wanted Audrey Hepburn to be my best friend.

I know she's a figment of my imagination; I know, therefore, that what she's just "said" is actually the equivalent of a positively affirming Post-it Note stuck on a bathroom mirror ('You Look Thin And Beautiful Today!'). But still, the warm glow that's spreading through me is no figment of my imagination. And it's good, even if only for a moment, to believe that what she's just said is true.

"Now," she goes on, "you'd better be taking a nice long bubble bath, then when you get out I can help you with your make-up."

"Actually, there's only a shower. But some help with my make-up afterwards would be lovely."

Because make-up isn't like a haircut, is it? Getting my hallucinated Audrey to help me put on some nice smoky eye make-up isn't going to involve any setting about my head with a dangerous implement. The very worst that will happen is that, in (what I assume to be) my current dream-state, I jab myself in the eye with the mascara wand or something.

"Then help I shall!" She's already setting off for the coffee machine. "Off you go and perform your ablutions, and I'll make you a nice fortifying espresso to drink while we make you up. Some fluttery eyelashes, elegant red lips . . . we'll pull out all the stops, darling! This Dillon fellow isn't going to recognize you!"

OK, I'm not sure Dillon *is* going to recognize me.

The trouble is that there's a very good chance he's going to mistake me for a drag queen.

"Are you quite sure," I ask Audrey Hepburn, as I look at myself in my little round mirror, "that this looks all right?"

"You think one more layer of mascara? Another strip of eyelashes?"

"No, no, Christ, no!"

"More eyebrow pencil?"

"*Definitely* no more eyebrow pencil."

I'm regretting, in fact, that I ever dug around in the far reaches of my make-up bag to find an eyebrow pencil, an item I've never once used since it came Free With Purchase from No. 7 a few years ago. I was hoping I might be able to emulate Audrey's trademark strong eyebrow, but I'm a little bit concerned that it actually looks like I've superglued two sunburned caterpillars over my eyes instead.

"Well, I've already set your lipstick with powder, darling, so I don't think I can go back and put more of *that* on . . ."

"No, look, I'm not saying I want more of anything. In fact, I think maybe I ought to go with a bit less."

"But you look so glamorous! So ladylike! And really, Libby, that dress is so simple, it won't look *finished* without proper make-up. This *tinted moisturizer* nonsense," she adds, regarding my tube of the stuff with almost as much horror as she looked at my shoes. "And whatever that fruity gloop is that you wanted to put on instead of a nice elegant lipstick . . ."

"Juicy Tube."

She shudders at the mere memory. "Darling, I'm telling you. You look like a proper grown-up *woman*. Doesn't that give you the most wonderful feeling of confidence?"

Given that I'm fairly convinced that what I look like is a proper grown-up *man*, it doesn't give me all that much confidence. But she's so glowy with pride that I don't feel I can just scrub it all off with a flannel and bung on the tinted moisturizer and lip-gloss I'd normally use. Anyway, let's face it, on some level, I must *want* to look like I've run amok at the Estée Lauder counter, because it's obviously really been *me* who's trowelled it all on. Perhaps because the only way I feel brave enough to mingle with the Beautiful People at this showbizzy party is under the protection of a full layer (or four) of war paint.

"All right, I'll keep it on." I get to my feet — tricky, because I'm sitting on the cavernous Chesterfield and wearing these absurdly high heels that (whisper it) I'm already starting to regret — and grab the little Accessorize clutch bag that Audrey located in the bottom of my clothes box. Which is the first time I realize that my hands are shaking. And realize, ridiculous though it sounds, that I'd actually really like it if I could take my imaginary Audrey to the party with me this evening.

"Now, you must have a wonderful time! And don't worry in the slightest about me," she adds. "I'll be perfectly all right here on my own."

"You're . . . er . . . staying here for the evening?"

"Just for a little longer. If it's all right with you?"

"But don't I actually need to *be* here in order for you to . . . You want to stay and play around with the Nespresso machine," I add, with a sigh, as I see her feline eyes wandering in the direction of the kitchen worktop, "don't you?"

Audrey turns a delicate shade of pink. "Well, I did rather fancy trying the cappuccino frother."

"Fine. Whatever." My brain isn't capable of stretching to the limits of understanding this, so if my imaginary Audrey claims she's going to spend a happy evening here with a jet of air and a pint of milk, that's just something I'm going to have to accept. "Froth away all you like."

Looking delighted, she leans forward in a L'Interdit cloud and gives me the lightest, gentlest peck: first on one cheek, and then the other. Then she picks up my trenchcoat from where I've slung it on the arm of the sofa and drapes it, stylishly, over my shoulders.

"I know you'll have the most wonderful evening," she says.

And then somehow she's managed to manhandle me to the door, opened it, given me a little shove out onto the landing, and then closed the door behind me.

I can hear a shriek of frothing-related delight as I tread my way carefully down the four flights of stairs to the bottom.

When I open the door to the street, there's someone standing right outside it, their hand on the buzzer.

It's Olly.

"Sorry," he begins when I jump, "I was just about to ring up to my friend's fl . . ." He stops, and looks at me again. "*Libby?*"

"Hi, Olly I . . ."

"But I thought . . . you look . . . aren't you *ill?*"

Shit — I never should have put on all that face powder, should I?

And then I realize. He's not telling me I look ill because my make-up is so unflattering. He's telling me I'm meant to be ill, because that's why I told him I couldn't do dinner.

"Yes. I am ill. Well, I *was* . . ."

"And now you're . . . off out?"

"Mmm, I suddenly started to feel a lot better. And you know how it is, when you've been feeling ill, sometimes you just need to have a bit of fresh air, a walk around the block . . ."

"You're quite dressed up for a walk around the block."

"What?" I try a laugh. He doesn't join me in it. "This old thing?"

"A cocktail dress and heels. And a pearl necklace."

"Oh, is it a cocktail dress?" I glance down, trying to look surprised, as if I might have imagined myself to be in tracksuit bottoms and one of my myriad grey hoodies. "I just threw on the first thing I could pull out of the boxes . . ."

OK, I give up. I'm a crap liar. And I *hate* lying to Olly.

162

"I'm going out," I admit. "And I'm really sorry, I should have told you the truth. Especially when I know you wouldn't really have minded anyway."

"Who says I wouldn't have minded?"

He looks annoyed. No, scratch that: it's worse. He looks disappointed.

"Come on, Olly, it was only eating badly made stew in my crappy flat. I'm sure you've got about a million better ways to spend an evening than that!"

He presses his lips together for a moment, then says, tightly, "I cancelled other plans with some friends to hang out with you this evening. Actually."

"Ol, you really, really shouldn't have!"

"So where are you off to," he asks, "anyway?"

"Well, you won't believe this, but I'm going to a party with Dillon O'Hara."

"Dillon O'Hara from the show?"

"That's the one!"

"*Seriously?*"

"Yes."

"He asked you out?"

"Thank you," I say, frostily, "for the vote of confidence."

"I'm just . . . *surprised.*"

His surprise hurts, more than I'd have thought it would.

"Well, you know, I did promise him I'd leave the larger of my two heads at home for the evening. And that I'd try to disguise the worst of my hump."

"I didn't mean . . . look, let's just forget it." He turns away. "You have a good night, now."

"Olly . . ."

"Oh." He turns back again, reaches into the huge pocket of his donkey jacket, and takes out a folded-over brown paper bag, one of the kind he serves toasted sandwiches in from his catering van. "Chicken soup," he says, handing it to me. "In a thermos, so it should stay nice and warm. And a banoffee pie. You can offer some to Dillon O'Hara as a late-night snack."

"Olly . . ." I say again.

But he's started walking, fast, down the street, and my shoes are way too high and uncomfortable for me to be able to follow him.

CHAPTER
SEVEN

The row with Olly hasn't exactly put me in the mood for a party.

The thing is that we don't argue, Olly and I. I'm not sure we *ever* have, in all the years we've known each other. We've bickered a fair few times, but never once have we had a proper, serious quarrel, one that ended with him walking off and refusing to answer his phone.

At least, I assume that's what he's doing. Because I've tried him three or four times since I got out of the tube at Liverpool Street — to apologize for lying to him and cancelling at short notice, and, to be honest, to see if he might fancy apologizing to me for implying that I'm far too much of a hideous old crone for Dillon O'Hara to even agree to breathe the same air as me — but it just rings out every time. And Olly *always* answers his phone.

I haven't left a message.

Though if I wasn't exactly in the partying mood when I started my journey this evening, I'm in even less of a partying mood as soon as I reach the end of it, and my destination: Depot, on Shoreditch High Street.

Obviously it doesn't exactly help that it's a giant, windowless concrete bunker, not unlike the one Hitler spent his last days hiding in while Berlin was shelled to smithereens around him. Nor that the door is covered by a steel grille and manned by a stern-looking chap in a black suit and crew cut who could easily be Obelix's larger brother.

Oh, shit, I'm not going to be on the guest list, am I?

And Obelix's brother isn't going to believe that I was invited by Dillon O'Hara, is he? It's probably barely even worth me trying to tell him this, with his don't-mess-with-me expression, and that huge, ham-like hand on the door handle, just waiting to block me from . . .

Actually, the ham-like hand is pressing down on the door handle, and the other hand (also ham-like) is waving me through . . .

"Have a good evening," he tells me, in a surprisingly pleasant voice.

Well, perhaps I look as if I'm here in an official capacity — PR person; party planner — because there's no way that Obelix's brother could possibly have mistaken me for a *Made Man* Hundred Hottest. And this is not just me being modest, by the way. This is a statement of fact. Because the door to Depot has barely shut behind me before I'm struck, head-on, by the sheer amount of toned, tanned flesh on display. It's wall-to-wall boobs and bums, as far as the eye can see, with enough blonde hair extensions to sink a battleship. Not that hair extensions *could* sink a battleship, I'd have thought, but you get my point.

All this blonde hair and kumquat-coloured skin is reminding me that Cass will be here at some point this evening, if she isn't already, and the last thing I want to do is bump into her before I've even got one nerve-steadying drink under my belt. I decide I'd better find a bar to get a cocktail, and then a secluded corner to sit in and drink it.

Mind you, there's probably no real need to worry, because Depot seems to be nothing *but* secluded corners.

Whoever designed the inside was, sensibly enough, trying to avoid the whole "Nazi bunker" look and plumped for an "opium-den-slash-brothel" look instead. It's all been divided up with chunks of retro Seventies glass wall and dimly lit with a slightly eerie red glow, through which I can see low, harem-style sofas and, in an extra-louche touch, several huge beds, most of which are covered with sprawling *Made Man* Hundred Hottest nominees, showing off all those boobs and bums I was talking about. There are even more hotties doing a weird kind of hula-hooping grind around the various poles which have been handily put up at various intervals for anyone who might fancy a light spot of erotic dancing, and small groups of men gathered around both these and the beds, looking like hungry Basset Hounds that haven't eaten in weeks. Anyway, through all these exhaustingly sexy shenanigans, right at the very back of the club, I can just make out a long, long bar, so I put my head down and make a swift beeline for it.

As I get closer, I can see that it's staffed with dozens of barmen who are busily occupied making cocktail after cocktail with — nice touch — glow-in-the-dark

167

cocktail shakers. It's pretty heaving on the customer side of the bar, mostly with more of the hungry-looking men trying to rustle up cocktails for the scantily clad hotties, but — rather sweetly — a couple of them stand back to allow me to go ahead of them. I thank them, politely, before turning my attention to the (absurdly handsome) barman, who's just asked me what I want to drink.

"We're doing fresh fruit Martinis," he adds, "if you want one of those?"

"Oh, yes, that would be lovely."

"So what kind?"

"Er . . ." Every single sort of fresh fruit on the entire planet has suddenly slipped from my mind. "Kumquat?" I blurt, presumably because the tanned flesh has brought it to the front of my mind.

"Kumquat would make a revolting Martini." He looks unimpressed. "Anyway, we're not doing kumquat. You can choose from santol, longan or langsat."

"I beg your pardon?"

Now he sighs, really weary of me. "Santol, longan or langsat."

"I'm sorry, but I've got absolutely no idea what any of those words mean . . ."

"She'll have the santol Martini," a voice behind me says.

Unfortunately, it isn't Dillon.

It's a tall, slightly balding man with a blindingly white smile, an equally blinding wristwatch and — I can't help but note, right away — an even more blinding *wedding ring,* and he is squeezing into the small space at the bar beside me.

"Hi," he says, flashing me another of those Cheshire Cat smiles. "You'll enjoy santol," he adds. "It tastes like really sharp apple. I eat it all the time in Mauritius."

"Oh. OK. Well, yes, I'll try that one, then," I tell the barman, determined to order my own drink rather than have this guy take over and do it for me. "Thanks for the tip," I add, politely, before fishing in my clutch bag for my phone so I can start composing my text to Dillon.

Hey, I type into my phone, I managed to make it tonight after all. BTW this place is insane . . .

"I'm Dave." My unwanted new mate leans in, propping one elbow on the bar. "And you are . . .?"

"Libby," I say, continuing to text Dillon. U around? Yep: that'll do. Short, practical, cool and confident. I press Send.

"Libby. What a beautiful name. Is it short for anything?"

"Liberty," I say, for the sake of politeness.

"Liberty. What a beautiful name." Seeing as, this time, he can't ask if it's short for anything, he moves off the subject of names, beautiful or otherwise, and leans over to get the attention of the handsome barman (who's currently measuring vodka and some sort of pale green juice into shot glasses with the concentration and precision of a Nobel-winning chemist). "I'll have one of those too. And I'll be paying for both."

"Oh, thanks," I say, hastily, "but actually, I'll get my own drink."

Hang on: it's just occurred to me that I didn't sign off that text to Dillon. And unless he's saved my number under my name, he might not realize it's me.

I begin a second text: This is Libby, by the way. Just in case it wasn't clear the first time! Lxx

I press Send.

And then immediately regret it, because it was neither cool nor confident.

And what was I doing signing it with *kisses*, for crying out loud?

"So, Liberty . . . if I can call you that . . ." It's Dave, again, flashing his implausibly white teeth. "What number are you?"

"Sorry?"

"*Made Man's* Hundred Hottest, of course." He laughs, patronizingly, as if I'm a muddled-headed idiot. "I'd put you in the . . ." He looks at me, appraisingly from head to toe. ". . . low eighties."

I'm not sure exactly what to say to this . . . compliment? insult? . . . but luckily I don't need to say anything at all, because I'm distracted by my name suddenly being yelled from a little way along the bar.

"*Libby?*"

It's a woman's voice, and it sounds so angry that for a moment I think it can only be Cass, hurtling towards me in a fury that I'm gate-crashing her big night.

But it isn't Cass, and I realize as I crane round Dave's shiny head, my name isn't actually being yelled *to* me, so much as *about* me.

It's Rhea Haverstock-Harley, who must have just arrived at the bar, five or six hungry Basset Hound-men away. And she's yelling in the direction of a mobile phone. Dillon's mobile phone, I can only assume, because — if I crane around Dave's shiny head, through the crowd of Basset Hound-men — I can see Dillon standing beside her.

"Who the fuck," she goes on, "is *Libby?* And *why* the fuck is she texting you? With *kisses*, for crying out loud."

I knew I'd regret those kisses. I knew it.

"So?" Dave asks. "What are you? Eighty-one? Eighty-two?"

"What? Oh, no, I'm not anything."

"You invited *another girl* here tonight?" I can hear Rhea demanding, in an even louder voice — one that suggests she's so sure that everyone around her is wildly interested in the details of her personal life that there's no need for her to keep a lid on it. Which, to be fair, from the expressions on the face of the Basset Hound-men, is probably true. "When you knew *I'd* be here?"

"Jesus, Rhea." This is Dillon. I can't see him properly at all — *bloody* Dave and his shiny great head — and I have to strain to hear him because, unlike Rhea, he's not raising his voice. (Oh, and also because the barman has finally finished his Nobel-prize-worthy chemistry experiment and has started to shake my Martini in his glow-in-the-dark shaker with what sounds like an entire igloo's worth of ice.) "You said you weren't coming. And anyway, I'm not sure what business it is of yours. I mean, you're the one who dumped me this morning.

171

By text message, charmingly enough. Or don't you remember?"

"Hey! Liberty!" It's Dave, again, snapping his fingers in front of my face. "Did you hear what I just said?"

"What? No, I'm actually just —"

"I asked if you were in it last year."

"In . . . sorry, *what* last year?" I ask, hoping my exasperated tone will make him realize I'm not interested in having this conversation, that I'm far too busy eavesdropping — as is practically everyone else at the bar by now — on the blazing row developing behind him.

"*Made Man*! Weren't you number ninety-four? And have you put on a bit of weight since then? I mean, don't get me wrong, it really suits you, but I'm just asking if . . ."

"Oh, well, forgive me for being the one to do the dumping," Rhea is saying now. "I mean, God forbid I should even things out after *you* broke up with *me* the last eighty-seven million times!"

"You're saying you broke up with me to get your own back?" (Dillon again, slightly louder this time.) "Well, good for you, Rhea. Nice maturity."

"*You're* going to lecture *me*," Rhea shrieks, "about fucking *maturity* . . .?"

"So are you on TV?" Dave — damn him! — is moving ever closer. He's blocking me off so effectively now that I can't even see Rhea any more, despite her towering head and shoulders above most of the Basset Hound-men. "In fact, didn't I see you on the last series of *Celebrity MasterChef*?"

Oh, for fuck's sake.

"No. Look, I'm not on TV . . ."

"In fact, fuck you, Dillon!" This is Rhea, again, tossing her hair and spinning away from the bar towards the dance floor. "I'm going to have a dance."

Now I can see her properly I feel, of course, utterly inadequate. She's wearing a scarlet strapless mini-dress that clings to her every yoga-whittled curve (and Willi-whittled, presumably, thanks to all the exertions she was putting in with him earlier) and her hair looks like she's stepped off the set of a L'Oréal advert. Unsurprisingly, the eyes of every single one of the Basset Hound-men are fixated on her as she reaches the dance floor, struts to the very centre, and starts to dance.

If, that is, you can describe what she's doing as *dancing*.

Because what she's actually doing is . . . well, I'm not sure exactly what to call it.

She's standing rooted to the spot, as if her Louboutins have been fixed to the floor with superglue, gyrating her pelvis and tossing her abundant mane. All of which is making her look less like she's dancing and more like she's having sex with the Invisible Man, standing up, while simultaneously blow-drying her hair with an equally invisible Babyliss and starting to feel desperately in need of a trip to the toilet.

I mean, I'm no Ginger Rogers, but at least I have the decency to realize it, and to stand meekly at the edge of dance floors doing a side-to-side sway and hoping nobody notices.

I can't see Dillon's face because of Dave and his *bloody* head, but I can tell that he's staring towards the dance floor.

Is he looking appalled? Embarrassed?

Turned on?

Is he about to stride up there and join her, so that the two of them can publicly make up after their equally public row, and spend the rest of the night doing that weird, needing-the-toilet dance together, while I'm stuck here with Dave and a bizarrely named fruit Martini that I'm starting to think is almost as mythical as the mystery goat's cheese, seeing as it *still* hasn't actually materialized from the barman's glow-in-the-dark shaker?

"So, do you *want* to be on TV?" Dave is asking. "Because I'm a talent manager, and I have to tell you, there might be an opening for someone like you on reality TV. You've got a great look. I mean, I'm not necessarily talking about anything as big as *Geordie Shore* or *Made in Chelsea*, but I've heard they're looking for people for the next series of *Mary Berry's Cupcake-Off*. You should really come to my office one day soon, and we can talk about it some more. Or, better yet, why don't the two of us get out of here for a while and go and find somewhere a bit more private. You know, for a . . . chat."

OK, this is starting to veer away from Unwelcome and heading firmly in the direction of Positively Creepy. And I'm not quite sure what to do, because I'm a bit stuck in this corner he's backed me into and don't see any way out without making a fuss. A fuss which might attract Dillon's attention, which might in turn attract *Rhea's* attention . . . But fortunately it's a decision I don't have to make, because the Basset Hound-men at the bar are starting to move away (having given up on ever getting a drink in this bloody place, probably) and, for the first time, there's nobody standing in between me and Dillon any more.

Dillon leans sideways to get the barman's attention for a drink (he'll be lucky) . . . and our eyes meet.

"Hi," I mouth at him, with a little, hopefully not-too-desperate-looking, wave.

"Who are you waving at?" Dave turns round, and doesn't look terribly pleased, on turning back to me, to see that it was another man I was greeting. "That's not very nice," he tells me. "I'm the one buying your drink."

I ignore this, and make a move to step around him, but he blocks my way.

"Don't be a fucking bitch," he says, loudly.

Which is when Dillon takes three strides in our direction and taps him on the shoulder.

"D'you want to say that again?" he's asking Dave, in a dangerously pleasant tone of voice. "Or did you mean to say something else?"

"Huh?"

"When you called my friend a fucking bitch just now," Dillon explains. "It just seems a particularly unpleasant thing to say to a young lady. Which is why I suggest that the very next thing out of your mouth is a grovelling apology."

There's silence for a moment, while Dave just stares at him.

"Well!" I say, brightly. "Let's just —"

Dillon doesn't take his eyes off Dave. "I'm not going anywhere until I've heard that grovelling apology."

"Who the fuck do you think you are?" Dave takes a step towards Dillon and jabs him in the chest with a finger. "You're Dillon O'Hara, right?"

"I don't see what that has to do with the price of eggs," Dillon replies, with another of those dangerously pleasant smiles.

"Do you know who I work for?" Dave gives him another jab in the chest. "*Donaldson and fucking Peake*, that's who."

Shit.

Donaldson and Peake is one of the biggest agencies in the business. And, thanks to its size, is not just an agency for Z-list reality TV "stars", but also for bona-fide musicians and actors as well.

They're incredibly well connected; they have huge offices in New York and Los Angeles, and you don't want to piss off anyone who works for them.

Not even Dave.

"And what do you do there?" Dillon enquires. "Are you the window cleaner? The guy who waters the plants in the front lobby? Or have you been brought in to head up their brand-new Slimeball department?"

"Dillon, for Christ's sake . . ." I step away from where I'm still boxed in by the wall, grab Dillon by the shirt sleeve and try pulling him in a non-Dave-erly direction, but he doesn't budge.

"You're a funny guy," Dave tells him. "But you know what I think will be *really* funny? Talking to our LA

176

office *all* about you, and your personality issues. That'll be funny, won't it, the next time you turn up for an audition over there, to find your reputation has preceded you?"

"OK, OK," I say, hoping that, even if I can't actually drag Dillon away, I can take the temperature down a notch or two. Because if things get any more heated over here, there's a good chance that Rhea will stop strutting her stuff and start noticing us. "Dillon didn't mean any of that. He's just . . . he's drunk." This, at least, is a convincing explanation. "Aren't you, Dillon?"

"Not in the slightest."

I give him a Look. "You are. You don't know what you're saying . . ."

But all of a sudden, I've stopped caring about impending fisticuffs between Dave and Dillon.

Because who should be heading towards me but my sister.

I briefly have time to notice that — yep, just as reported — her dress does indeed sport a dangerously plunging neckline, and that she's done something, Christ only knows what, with that pretty pendant so that the garnet cabochon is playing peekaboo from between her breasts. But her DIY job on my handiwork is the least of my worries. Because she's looking absolutely wild, and not just because of the abundant hair extensions.

"Cass, hi," I begin, taking a step towards her. "Look, I know you'll be annoyed that I didn't tell you I was coming tonight, but I didn't get the —"

"I don't give a shit that you're *here*. I give a shit that you're here *having a drink with my boyfriend.*"

For a bizarre moment, I think she's talking about Dillon. And then I get it.

"You mean *Dave?*"

"Yes, I mean Dave!"

"Hi, babe," Dave says to her, looking, it has to be said, more than just a little sheepish. "I thought you were having that networking talk with the features editors . . ."

"Yes, and I'd have been straight over here stopping my *traitor* of a sister from chatting you up when I first saw her five minutes ago if they hadn't started talking about a possible bikini spread."

"Cass, I wasn't chatting him up, for crying out loud . . ."

But my explanation is brought to a swift end by Cass, who reaches over the bar, grabs the glow-in-the-dark cocktail shaker that the barman is *still* mucking about with, yanks the top off and chucks the entire contents smack into my face.

Yes, that's right: *my* face.

It's icy-cold, and there are still several large lumps of actual ice inside, and it bloody *hurts*.

Worse than the pain, though, is the fact that everyone within a ten-metre radius — including Rhea, still strutting her bizarre "stuff" on the dance floor — is staring at me, while vodka, santol-fruit juice and, I can only assume, the majority of my thickly applied mascara and eyebrow pencil, slide slowly down my face, from my soaking-wet hair to my chin.

But then Dillon is taking my hand.

And he's leading me around the side of the bar, past the still-startled-looking barman, towards a narrow exit door, presumably used by the staff, partially hidden amongst all the lined-up drinks bottles.

Except it can't only be used by the staff, because there are a couple of black taxis lurking right outside. It must be a secret way out that only the celebrities know about, for when they're trying to make a discreet exit.

Dillon walks me to the first of them, opens the door, and hands me through it before getting in himself.

"Let's get out of here," he says, either to me or to the driver, before the taxi pulls smoothly away.

CHAPTER
EIGHT

The first thing Dillon does, as the taxi turns out of the side street and onto the main road, is lean forward to speak through the glass partition.

"Can you head towards Angel, please, mate?"

Angel?

Hang on: he *lives* in Angel.

Does this mean he's taking me to his flat?

"There's a nice little pub near my building," he adds, sitting back in the seat beside me. "We can get a proper drink there. One without massive great chunks of ice in it. And safely contained in a glass, not chucked all over your face."

Oh. The pub.

Well, that's still really nice, obviously . . . And it's absurd of me to feel even the smallest bit disappointed.

Not to mention the fact that it would be way, way too perfect an outcome. I mean, isn't it enough that he's just rescued me, like a knight on a white charger, from certain death at the hands of Rhea Haverstock-Harley? Or from more icy missiles being hurled at me by Cass? Or from the appalling — and *married*, and *going out with my sister* — Dave?

And isn't it also enough that — all of a sudden — one of his hands is coming up to cup the side of my face, and turning it to face him . . .?

"That's got to hurt," he says.

"Sorry?"

"All that ice, right in your eye." He's studying my left eye (and not, of course, about to kiss me or anything), before running the tip of one index finger around it. "Sore?"

"Yes. A bit."

Which it is. I'm categorically *not* just saying this so that he'll carry on gently tracing his smooth fingertip over my skin.

Though I think I could be forgiven if I was.

Up this close he smells, by the way, of some sort of citrusy shower gel (with more than merely a hint of peaty whisky in the background) and his own eyes are looking darker and more intense than ever.

"She's a fucking cow," he says, after a moment, "your sister."

"Don't call her that. She's my sister."

"Yes, and she just threw a drink in your face. After her boyfriend assaulted you."

"He didn't assault me."

"Only because I was there to leap in and protect you."

"Yes, and a fine job you did of that," I tell him. "You nearly got beaten up, I got a drink thrown in my face, and your agent's getting a call from someone at Donaldson and Peake tomorrow morning telling him that nobody in LA is going to give you a job from now until Doomsday."

Dillon snorts. "Never gonna happen. That guy is small-time. And FYI, I didn't nearly get beaten up. I could have taken him. Now, take that damp coat off and put this on."

He's slipping my cocktail-soaked trenchcoat off my shoulders, then taking off his own dry jacket and sliding it over me to replace the damp one.

"For the shock," he says.

"I'm not shocked."

"For the cold, then."

"I'm not cold."

"For the love of Christ, Fire Girl, would you just let me be a gentleman for once in my life? Lord knows it's a rare enough occurrence."

And, to be honest, I'm not exactly sure what I'm doing, trying to *stop* him from putting his jacket around me. Not when it's still warm from his body, and even more headily scented with citrus (and whisky) from all those hours against his skin.

"After all," he's going on, "you've come out looking like such a lady tonight, so I think I can at least *try* to be a gentleman."

I make a mental note, if I ever hallucinate her again, to thank Audrey for the makeover. For the advice on the dress and the jewellery. Even if she did go a bit overboard on the eye make-up.

(But I would also point out to her that Dillon has told me I look ladylike *despite me* wearing the Rather Unsuitable shoes. Which is one in the eye for her kitten heels and her elegant pumps. Even if I can't feel any sensation, right now, anywhere below my ankles.)

"In fact, d'you know what? I don't want to take you to the pub."

I'm not quite sure how this has happened . . . but is he ditching me already?

"Look at you, in your lovely dress and those beautiful pearls. No, you're way too nicely dressed and elegant for my crummy local." He leans forward again and says to the driver, "Slight change of plan, mate, can you drop us on Owen Street? Just round the corner from Angel tube station? Will you come back to my flat?" he asks me. "And we can have a drink there?"

I blink at him.

"I promise," Dillon adds, "no funny business!"

How can I indicate (without sounding an awful lot less ladylike than he's mistakenly taken me for) that I'd be extremely happy if there *were* funny business? The funnier the better, in fact.

"That would be . . . lovely," I say, in the sort of prim tone you might use to accept an invitation to the vicar's garden party.

"Good. That's settled, then."

We both fall silent for another moment or two, while the taxi continues its way through the still-busy streets.

Dillon is staring out of the window. I don't know what he's thinking.

I'm staring out of the other window. And this is what I'm thinking:

Shiiiiiiiiiiiiiiiiiiiiiiit.

I mean, this is all a very, very bad idea indeed, isn't it?

I could really do with a quiet moment to hallucinate Audrey Hepburn right now, to be perfectly honest, because it wouldn't hurt to have someone — even an unreal someone — to talk a bit of sense into me. Because Dillon is quite obviously on the rebound; he's just had a very public bust-up with his extremely recent ex; and he's fairly obviously more than just a bit drunk.

And as for me, I haven't had sex for so long that I may, actually, have completely forgotten how to do it.

But maybe I'm being ridiculous. Because Dillon has, let's face it, quite clearly stated that no funny business is to be had. And I'm absolutely not under the illusion that — despite his very lovely compliments this evening — he's going to find himself unable to keep his hands off me the moment we step through his front door.

Though it would be nice, obviously.

And I think I'd probably *remember* how to do it, as soon as Dillon, you know . . . reminded me.

"You can pull over right here, mate," Dillon is telling the driver just before the taxi stops at the side of the road. "And keep the change," he says, shoving a twenty-pound note through the little opening in the partition, even though the fare is only £8.50.

I think I'm starting to realize why his agent is so desperate for some Los Angeles TV work to come his way; what with this and the generous tip he left for the Brazilian waitress earlier, he's almost spent more in gratuities today than my entire week's rent for Bogdan Senior.

"Come on," he tells me, holding the taxi door open for me to climb out.

Spine-tinglingly, he puts a guiding hand in the small of my back as we cross over the road towards a huge converted warehouse on the opposite side.

This one is less Nazi bunker, though, and more . . . Dickensian poorhouse.

"They used to make jam here. Way back in . . ." — he waves a hand, vaguely — "olden times. Victorian, perhaps. I think it was jam, anyway. It might have been breakfast cereal."

"I don't think the Victorians ate breakfast cereal."

"Then you already know far more about them than I do, and henceforth I shall consider you my go-to expert on all matters pertaining to Victorian groceries. Expect a call, my dearest Fire Girl, if I ever end up on *Celebrity Who Wants To Be a Millionaire*, with only a question about Victorian jam standing between me and a million quid for a charity of my choice."

I laugh, which makes him smile, and then all of a sudden his hand is sliding around my waist, and down towards the outer regions of my left thigh . . . oh, God, this is it it's happening . . . I'd have thought he'd be a *touch* less, well, ham-fisted is the word that springs to mind, but it's still marvellous, obviously . . .

"Just finding my keys," he says. "Left them in my inside jacket pocket."

His keys. Of course. Don't know why I thought otherwise.

"Got them." Dillon removes his hand from his inside pocket and waggles a set of keys at me. "Come on up," he adds, using one of the keys to open the big double doors at the front of the old jam factory, and ushering me through, "and we can see about that drink I promised you."

First we're in a huge, airy lobby area, full of exposed brick and cast-iron beams; next we're in a see-through elevator, riding smoothly past several more floors' worth of exposed brick and cast-iron beams, and now we've reached the very top of the building and the elevator doors are opening straight into the penthouse apartment that I assume Dillon calls home.

"Well?" he says, before I've actually stepped out of the elevator. "What do you think?"

It's pretty spectacular, is what I think.

It's absolutely huge, for one thing: one ginormous room that must have the dimensions of the entire jam-making factory floor, and with at least twenty feet of airy height between the stripped-wood floor and the sloping rafters. There's a living-room area, complete with leather sofas and what must be a contender for the World's Largest TV mounted against the wall; there's a boys' toys zone in the middle of the room (pool table, Xbox, ping pong); there's a glossy open-plan kitchen running almost the length of one wall, complete with high-shine granite worktops and — oooh, lovely — one of those gorgeous 1950s-style fridges, in eye-catching pillar-box red; and then *aaaalllll* the way down at the far end there are cast-iron spiral stairs leading up to a big mezzanine level, upon which — and I get a tingle up my spine as I see this — is absolutely nothing at all except a colossal, unmade bed.

186

"You think it's too much of a bachelor pad," Dillon says, "don't you?"

"No, no, not at all . . . though obviously if that was the look you were trying to avoid, it might have been sensible to go with a pool table *or* a ping-pong table, rather than both."

"That's only because ever since I was seven years old, all I ever wanted was a pool table *and* a table-tennis table."

"Well, then I stand corrected. You're living the dream."

He grins at me. "I knew you'd get it. I mean, you may be looking all beautiful and ladylike tonight, but underneath it all, I think you're just a seven-year-old kid at heart, too. It's one of the things I like about you."

It's possible that I misheard. But did he just say I looked beautiful?

If you ignore the second part, the slightly concerning bit about him liking seven-year-old kids, it's the most amazing thing anyone's ever said to me.

"OK, sorry, that sounded weird," he's going on, hastily. "I didn't mean that I like little kids. All I mean is that you're kind of . . . innocent. Uncluttered by bullshit. *That* kind of childlike. I don't mean that you sit around all day playing with Lego and chatting to your imaginary friend."

I let out a sudden bark of nervous laughter.

"Imaginary friend? Of course not! What makes you think I have one?"

"Libby, I *don't* think you have one. That was my point."

"Well, exactly! Because they don't exist. Anybody who *thought* they had an imaginary friend . . . even if they *knew* that it was actually imaginary . . . well, they'd be completely crackers, wouldn't they? Or suffering from post-traumatic stress. Or perhaps in the early stages of . . . of some sort of unpleasant neurological illness . . ."

"OK, we *really* need to get you that drink," says Dillon, taking one of my hands and leading me in the direction of the kitchen. "And I'm starting to think we should put something on that eye of yours."

"You mean like a patch?"

"Yes, Libby, an eye-patch. And a skull-and-crossbones hat and a parrot on your shoulder, while we're at it. Of course I wasn't talking about a patch. I was meaning . . . I don't know . . . some ice, or something."

"But I was just injured *by* ice."

"I know, but . . . hang on." He's reaching into the bright red fridge-freezer with one hand, and using the other hand to reach for a Bang & Olufsen phone, sitting on the black granite counter-top. He removes an ice-cold bottle of Stolichnaya from the freezer — selecting merely one, I can't help noticing, from the four or five that are in there — and gestures at me to take it from him as he uses one thumb to dial a number. "If you don't mind pouring the drinks while I just . . . Mum!" he suddenly says, into the phone.

He's calling his *mother?*

Don't get me wrong, it's nice that he's close to his mum. But I think it's safe to say that he was being honest when he said there wasn't going to be any funny business.

Unless a phone call to his mother happens to be his customary mode of foreplay.

And I'm not sure that even Dillon is gorgeous enough to get away with that.

"I know it's late, Mum . . . yeah, I'm sorry . . . yeah, I know it's the only time in the week you can watch your Sky-Plussed *Great British Bake-Off . . . shot glasses in the cupboard to the left of the fridge*," he mouths over at me, not remotely with the sheepish air of a man who's brought a girl back to his über-bachelor pad and suddenly felt the need for a call home to Mummy. In fact, if anything, he's looking more than usually pleased with himself. ". . . Well, what kind of topping *did* she put on her carrot cake? . . . Yes, I think that sounds a bit too clever by half too, Mum . . ."

Charming though this all is, I'm not quite sure what I'm meant to be doing while he has a good old chin-wag with his mother about *The Great British Bake-Off*. Because even though he's told me to pour us both a shot, this doesn't feel much like the sort of atmosphere, any more, in which you can sit around drinking vodka. It feels more like I ought to be putting on the kettle and suggesting a couple of rounds of warm buttered toast.

Though maybe there's one advantage of Dillon nattering away about carrot cake (believe me, there's only one): I guess it gives me a moment to pop off to the loo, or something, and see if I can rustle up a quick Audrey moment just as well here as I can at my flat.

I mean, obviously a normal person, one without Hollywood legends hanging around in their subconscious, would be texting their closest friends for advice right now. But Nora is far too busy treating the sick and injured of central Glasgow, and Olly is in a perfectly justifiable sulk with me, and obviously I *do* happen to have a Hollywood legend hanging around in my subconscious . . .

"*Bathroom?*" I mouth at Dillon, doing a sort of pointy-finger mime to indicate that I need directions, and he responds with a pointy finger towards the very back of the flat, behind the spiral stairs.

"Oh, she's got a nose piercing, has she? . . . Well, no, Mum, I don't think it *is* a hygiene issue, probably. Unless she's stirring the cake batter with her nose, that is . . ."

I reach the bathroom — which is, although obviously just a little guest bathroom, with a loo and a basin, not that much smaller than my flat — and close the door. Then, because I don't want to be too long in here for obvious reasons (if you want to conjure up even more of a passion-killer than a chat with your mum about *The Great British Bake-Off*, I think heading for the loo and not emerging for ten minutes would be a pretty good bet), I sit down on the closed toilet seat, shut my eyes, and . . . well, what?

I've no idea what it is I've done to make the Audrey hallucinations materialize before now. She's just sort of popped up, right when I wasn't expecting it.

I keep my eyes tight shut and whisper, "Audrey?"

But nothing happens. Apart from me feeling a lot more like the village idiot than I did a moment ago, that is.

Still, this doesn't stop me from trying again.

"*Audrey*," I hiss, just in case I need to be more intense to make it work. "Look, I really need to talk. I'm here at Dillon's flat, and I'm getting all these mixed signals, and I really don't know if he's about to kiss me or suggest we bake a nice Genoise sponge cake."

Tentatively, I open one eye. But all I can see is the basin, nicely stocked with posh Molton Brown handwash and lotion, and my own reflection in the mirror above it.

"I'm really serious," I go on, heading closer to the mirror to sort out my eye make-up whilst simultaneously trying to persuade my brain to produce one nice clear mirage of Audrey Hepburn to order, please. (Though actually the thick layers of shadow, liner and eyebrow pencil have stayed remarkably intact, given Cass's liquid assault on them back at Depot, so obviously going out looking like I'd raided a kohl factory was a good idea after all.) "I never expected to be asked back to his flat, and now it's all getting weird and I can't tell what I'm doing here."

There's a line, I suddenly notice, of very fine white powder scattered over the marble surface of the vanity unit beneath this mirror.

For a moment I think it's the crystalline stuff you mix in when you're using Jolen facial hair bleach.

But pretty quickly — because I'm not a total idiot — I realize that it's nothing to do with Jolen at all.

Well, it's the guest bathroom, isn't it? I'm sure Dillon's held some pretty wild parties here, some of them fairly recently. The white powder doesn't necessarily have to be anything *he's* shoving up his nose, does it?

I clear my throat and carry on, hastily, talking to Audrey. Not mentioning a word about the white powder, because I don't think Audrey would approve, for one thing, and I'd just rather forget all about it, for another.

"Do you think he just wants to talk? Do you think maybe he's lonely?"

But Imaginary Audrey has nothing to say on the subject. At least, nothing important enough to say that she's prepared to shimmer into view and tell me so.

"Well, thanks a fucking bunch," I whisper, huffily, already walking to the door, because I've already been in here slightly longer than what I'd consider to be an average peeing time. (I don't want Dillon to think *I'm* the kind of guest to vanish to the loo and shovel suspicious white powder into my nostrils. Just in case, you know, he suggests doing it with me, or something.) "You're oh-so-present when I'm quite looking forward to a quiet evening on the sofa, but when it actually comes to needing some serious advice, you're not around for dust! And, by the way," I add, pulling the door open, "I've been perfectly comfortable in these shoes *all night. And* I haven't broken my ankle, so put that in your cigarette holder and smoke it!"

This might have been a bit soon to boast, though, because I stumble on my way out of the guest loo, turn my ankle on one side, and feel a sharp, painful *click* that doesn't, fortunately, become *a crack*.

"Are you sure you've got that right, Mum . . .?" Dillon is saying into the phone as I limp, slightly, back towards him. "It's just that I don't see how they can have the *entire* episode devoted to flapjacks next week . . . OK, well, look Mum, I'm actually just calling with a quick question. I just wanted to ask what you'd do to treat someone who'd been hit in the eye by flying chunks of ice."

Ohhhhh. I get it now.

He's calling his mum for *advice about my eye*.

That's actually ridiculously sweet.

And makes me want him, at this very moment, more than ever.

"From a cocktail shaker," he says into the phone again. "No, Mum, it wasn't me . . . yes, I know I promised you I wouldn't get involved in any more fights . . . it's a girl . . . no, Mum, don't worry, it's not her . . . I know . . . I know . . . yes, I know . . . I didn't promise you that, actually . . . her name's Libby . . . no, not at all . . ."

Not at all what? I'm not at all *what?*

Something *good* (not at all fat and ugly?) or something very, very *bad* (not at all attractive?)

"Right . . . right . . . even though it was ice that hit her in the eye in the first place? . . . All right . . . we'll talk in the morning, Mum, Love you. Yeah," he says, reaching for the fridge-freezer again. "I was right first time. She says we have to put ice on it."

"Oh. Right."

"And she's the woman to listen to," he adds, pressing a button on the outside of the fridge-freezer, putting his hand underneath the ice dispenser and catching a handful of ice as it tumbles out. "Seeing as she successfully brought me and all nineteen of my brothers through adolescence without visible or lasting damage to any of our major organs."

"I thought it was eleven brothers."

"Oh, no, I assure you, it was nineteen. I might have forgotten to mention Brendan, and Lorcan, and Cormac . . ."

He puts his handful of ice into a nearby tea towel, wraps it tightly, and then lifts it up to the side of my face.

He holds it there.

Neither of us says anything for a moment.

My heart is pounding.

Not only this, but it seems to have climbed upwards, into my throat, and is doing a pretty decent job of hampering my breathing.

"I love your eyebrows," Dillon says, suddenly

"Sorry?"

"Your eyebrows." He clears his throat; it makes me wonder if he's having a bit of trouble breathing easily, too. "I really like them. They're different from everyone else's."

"Thanks. I haven't had them waxed in a while."

Dear Lord, why? Why, why *why* have I tainted this moment with the image of me head-to-toe in verdantly sprouting eyebrow, like Captain Caveman after an unusually long time between grooming sessions?

"Not that I need them waxed!" I practically yell, before he can say anything. "I only meant . . . the reason for all the pencil . . . we were just trying to make a positive out of the situation."

"We?"

"Yes, me and Audrey. She's my . . ." What is an acceptable end to this sentence? "Eyebrow technician."

Which is sort of true, if you think about it.

"Well, they're certainly eyebrows well worthy of their very own technician. Does it hurt?"

"Er — using eyebrow pencil? It might if it were really sharp, I suppose . . ."

"I meant the ice," he clarifies. "The cold. Is it hurting?"

It's only now that I realize the ice is, in fact, making my eye area hurt quite a lot. It's been so nice having his hand there that I hadn't noticed.

"It is hurting a bit."

"I guess I should start calling you Ice Girl now," he says, taking away the tea towel and, regrettably, his hand, and reaching for his shot glass. He chinks it against mine. "So . . . here's to Audrey."

"Huh?"

"Your eyebrow technician."

"Oh. Right. Yes. Here's to . . . um . . . Audrey."

Even if she did let me down in the guest loo just now.

"It's not just your eyebrows, though," Dillon adds.

"What's not just my eyebrows?"

"Whatever it is about you that's different this evening."

"*Am* I different this evening?"

"Mm. I mean, don't get me wrong, I thought you were cute the first time I met you . . ."

He puts down his shot glass and takes a small step closer.

". . . but right now . . . I don't know what to tell you, except . . . well, you're really, really sexy, Fire Girl."

I just about manage to stop the word *seriously?* coming out of my mouth.

But to be fair, even if I hadn't been able to do anything of the sort, it would have been stopped by Dillon's lips. Because, quite out of the blue, he's pressed me back against the fridge-freezer and started to kiss me.

CHAPTER
NINE

As Walks of Shame go, this is a pretty bad one.

It's eight in the morning, the height of the rush hour, and I've just endured a tube ride all the way from Angel to Kennington, still wearing my little black dress, cocktail-smelling trench, pearl necklace, can't-walk-in-them heels and smudged eye make-up from last night.

Oh, and a pair of Ray-Bans I grabbed from Dillon's bedside table before I left, because my left eye, courtesy of Cass, now looks as if I've gone a couple of rounds with a world champion heavyweight boxer. Or, more likely, that I got myself into a horribly messy situation with whatever random man I went home with last night, showing poor judgement as well as some seriously loose morals. And the sidelong glances from my fellow Northern Line passengers have been quite judgey and pitying enough as it is, thank you very much.

(Well, the female passengers' sidelong glances have been judgey and pitying; the pinstriped City Boys, on their way in to testosterone-fuelled jobs, yelling at each other across the trading floor, are giving me longer, more lingering looks from behind their copies of the *Financial Times*, presumably spicing up their morning commute with fetid imaginings of exactly what I might have got up to before the Walk of Shame.)

I've never been more relieved to get off a tube train, let me tell you. Even the agonizing totter from the station to Olly's flat is a picnic in comparison, no matter how much the soles of my feet are burning, or my ankle aching, or how furiously my toes are screaming at me to put on a pair of sheepskin moccasins and *give them a break*.

I didn't actually *plan* to head to Olly's flat, by the way, when I got on the tube back at Angel. I just realized (whilst staring *very intently* at the tube map on the wall of the train in an attempt to ignore all the staring) that my route back home was about to take me through Kennington station, only a five-minute walk (or ten-minute agonizing totter) from Olly's place just off Kennington Park Road. And once I'd twigged that, I also twigged that there's nothing, right now, that I want to do more than sit at Olly's kitchen table, drink a nice, hot cup of tea, and try to let the cosiness wash over me.

Besides, I hate leaving things the way they are between us, and I'll feel even shittier all day unless I can actually speak to him face to face and apologize, again, for lying to him last night.

As I head round the corner to the side-street his flat is on, I finally give up torturing myself and stop to take off my shoes for the last few steps along the pavement.

Ahhhhhhhhhhhhhhhh.

It's bliss. Sheer, mind-blowing bliss.

Almost as blissful as the things I was doing with Dillon in that rumpled, enormous bed, until the wee small hours of this morning.

Oh dear God, it was good.

No, it was more than good. It was incredible. He was incredible. *I*, for the first time in my life, was incredible. I don't know whether it was the vodka, or the game-raising effect of having sex with a man who is a) very, very, very good at it and b) accustomed to being very, very, very good at it with lithe, lissom lingerie models. Either way, I pulled out all the stops last night. There seemed to be nothing I couldn't (and, admittedly, *wouldn't*) do. I mean, seriously. I was athletic, I was resourceful, I was intrepid . . .

And yet, despite it all, I was alone in the bed when I woke up this morning.

I don't know what feels worst this morning, actually: the hangover, the burning feet or the humiliation.

Actually, that's a lie. I know exactly what's worst.

It only occurs to me that Olly might not be in — that he's surely already headed off to work, given the hours he generally keeps — about three seconds after I buzz up to his flat. So I'm pretty amazed when I hear, just before I'm about to slink away again, a slightly bleary, "Hello?"

"God, Olly, I'm so sorry, it sounds like I've woken you up."

"*Libby?* Are you . . . what time is it?"

"Um, eight fifteen."

"In the *morning?*"

"Yes . . ." Oh, God, please don't tell me I'm about to discover that Olly's a casual coke user too — he sounds completely out of it. "Look, it was stupid of me to stop off without warning you, I'll just head home and —"

"No, no, absolutely not. Sorry, I'm just a bit . . . things are a bit chaotic."

A disturbing thought — even more disturbing than the coke thing — has suddenly occurred to me.

"Oh! You've got a girl here! Shit, sorry, let me leave you to it . . ."

"No, no, Lib, I haven't got a girl here! Just . . . just give me a couple of minutes and I'll come down and let you in."

Which is a major relief.

Not that there would be anything at all *wrong* with him having a girl here. In fact, I'm not sure why I even used the word *disturbing*, because obviously it would be lovely if he were to get himself a girlfriend. Heaven knows, he deserves someone amazing in his life. It's been years since he split up with Alison, and . . . well, I just meant, really, that it would be awkward if I'd accidentally interrupted . . . whatever he might have been doing, if he'd had a girl here.

But I don't want to think about it in practice, lovely though it would be in theory. I don't know why, exactly, but the mere thought is giving me this sort of uncomfortable, gritty feeling, as if I've got a pebble in my shoe. At the same time as a grain of sand has flown into my eye.

Now Olly is opening the door, looking as bleary as he sounded. He's obviously hastily thrown on a T-shirt and a pair of trackie bottoms, because the T-shirt is on back to front and the trackie bottoms are inside out.

"Are you OK?" he asks, having the nerve to look at me as if *I'm* the one who looks a total wreck.

Oh. To be fair, he's got a point on that one.

"Yes. Well, yes and no. It's just been a —"

"*Fucking hell.* Your *eye.*"

"What? Oh, God, my eye, yes . . . can you still see the bruising behind the sunglasses, because I was hoping . . ."

"Was it him? Was it Dillon O'Hara? Because I swear to God, Libby, I'll smash his fucking skull to pieces with . . . with the biggest Le Creuset pan I own . . ."

"Olly, Olly, calm down." I sort of bustle him backwards into the communal hallway of his flat before any passing stranger should overhear this worryingly specific threat to beat in somebody's head with a large piece of cast-iron kitchenware, then I take off my Ray-Bans. "This wasn't Dillon. It was my sister."

"*Cass* thumped you?"

"No, she didn't thump me, nobody thumped me, she just threw a drink with a load of ice-cubes in my face. Now, look, I think both of us are in need of a strong cup of tea, so shall we go up and put the kettle on?"

Looking fractionally mollified (and, I suspect, a little bit embarrassed about the whole Le Creuset thing), Olly nods and leads the way up the stairs to his front door, on the first landing.

"Wow," I say, as soon as we get inside, because his flat, which is usually cosy and pretty tidy, looks as if a small bomb's gone off in it. A small bomb containing

Chinese takeaway boxes, a few dozen Stella Artois cans, and . . . oh! two large and rather hairy-looking men, sleeping in their boxers and T-shirts on the sofa and the armchair, respectively.

Definitely not an evening *a deux* with a girl, then.

"Better come in here. I don't want to wake Charlie and Adam," Olly says, *pulling* me in the direction of the kitchen and *pulling* to the sliding door that separates it off from the sitting room.

"Oh, that's Charlie and Adam." These are old friends of Olly's, one from school and one from catering college. I sink into one of the kitchen chairs and start massaging my bruised and battered feet. "I didn't recognize them in their . . . er . . . pants."

"Yeah. Sorry about that. Bit of a heavy night last night." Olly is putting the kettle on and reaching up to a high shelf — just above a shelf of Le Creuset pans, I can't help noticing — for a teapot. "Charlie's just split up with his girlfriend, so he's sleeping on the sofa for a while, and then Adam dropped round and we all ended up having a few too many beers . . ."

"So I see."

"Come on, Lib, you sound like my mum."

"How?"

"Disapproving."

"I'm not disapproving! It's just . . . not like you." I mean, bleary-eyed hangovers and a late start to work sounds a lot more like a Dillon O'Hara start to the day than an Olly Walker one. Except in Dillon's case, the people sleeping on the sofa *would* be girls. Lingerie-clad, blonde ones, I have no doubt.

202

"Well, everyone does something they don't usually do once in a while." His voice is muffled and slightly echoey for a moment, as he reaches far back into his fridge. "Like getting so annoyed with you last night," he adds, as he emerges. "I shouldn't have been like that. I'm really sorry, Lib. Peace offering?"

He puts a waxed-paper packet down on the wooden table.

"I can't be sure," he says, "so don't get your hopes up. But I think . . . drum roll, and all that . . . it might just be the mystery cheese."

"From Le Grand Fromage? I bought one there the other day, too! It was meant to be a surprise for you, but then I forgot about it and left it out of the fridge and had to chuck the whole thing away."

"Oh." He looks a bit crushed. "So you know about it already, then."

"Yes, but I didn't get around to actually trying it, or anything . . . shall we have a taste now? If you can face it before you've even had a cup of tea, that is."

"Actually, cheese is a pretty good hangover cure, I always find. Nice and savoury and salty . . . Wait a minute and I'll toast a bit of walnut bread — we can have it with that."

I already feel about fifty times better than I did ten minutes ago. It's so reassuringly homely here in Olly's kitchen, just like it always is, with the kettle on, and him bustling around with loaves of bread and the toaster, that all the unpleasantness of the morning is receding. Well, *most* of the unpleasantness. I still feel a bit queasy every time I remember lifting my head up off the pillow to see the other side of the bed empty beside me . . . but maybe it's just as much vodka-related queasiness as anything else.

"So what happened with your sister?" Olly asks, as he starts getting knives and plates from a cupboard. "Throwing a drink in your face is a new one, even for her, isn't it?"

"Oh, it was just some silly misunderstanding about this man she's seeing. She thought I was chatting him up . . . you know how dramatic she likes to make everything."

Olly pulls a surprised face. "She thought you were chatting up her bloke, threw a drink at you, but still let you stay the night at her place? I'll never understand your sister and her moods, Lib, I have to say."

"God, no, I didn't stay the night at her place! Are you crazy?"

"Oh, right . . ." Now he just looks a bit confused. "Then where did you stay? I mean, I'm assuming you didn't go home last night, unless you got up this morning and put on an identical version of what you were wearing last night!"

It's my turn to look a bit confused. Because I'd have thought he'd have worked this out by now, given that he knows I went out to a party with Dillon last night, and that he's already come close to throwing one over-protective wobbly, Le Creuset-style, about the black eye he assumed Dillon gave me.

But evidently — awkwardly — I have to spell it out for him.

"Er . . . I spent the night at Dillon's," I mumble.

204

Olly stares at me. "Oh," he says, after a moment. "Right."

Over in the toaster, the walnut bread pops up. Olly gets to his feet, goes over to the toaster, and pops it back down again to get a bit browner.

"I don't really know what I was thinking," I say, talking much faster than I'd have thought I was capable of, with this hangover. "I mean, you know me, Olly. I don't do things like this. Sleep with men on first dates, that is. Not that this was even a proper date at *all*, really."

But Olly is very busy with the toaster, and doesn't say anything.

"And obviously it's backfired on me," I go on, miserably, "because he wasn't there when I woke up this morning. Which anyone with half a brain could have seen coming a mile off."

No reply from Olly, who is *still* faffing with the toaster; I know he's a perfectionist when it comes to his food, but you'd think he was creating a Michelin-starred three-course meal, for all the effort with a bit of walnut bread.

"I just feel really stupid," I say in a very small voice, to match the very small way I'm feeling right now, "Ol. I wish I'd never done it. I wish I could turn back time and never even have gone to that party in the first place."

"Yeah, but you did." The toast is evidently done now, to Olly's exacting standards, because he's coming back over to the table with it. He puts a piece on each of our plates. "Look, don't feel too bad about it, Libby" he

205

says, rather briskly. "What's done is done. As long as you were careful . . ."

"Careful?"

"Yeah, with, you know . . ." He's turning puce. "*Stuff.*"

"Oh, God, *Olly!*" I don't want to talk about safe sex with him! I don't want to talk about *any* sex with him! It just feels too weird. Just like the gritty, pebbly, uncomfortable feeling I had, down on the street just now, when I thought he had a girl in his flat. "Yes," I croak, when I can formulate words again, "but can you do me a huge favour, Ol, and never, *ever* bring the subject up again?"

"The subject of your one-night stand with Dillon O'Hara?" he says, even more briskly than before. Downright *abruptly*, in fact. "Yes, Libby, not talking about it ever again would suit me just fine."

I watch him for a moment as he starts to unwrap the cheese from its waxed paper. Then I take a deep breath.

"Olly, look, if I've let you down in some way . . ."

"You haven't, Lib." He stops unwrapping the cheese and looks at me. "Sorry. You've just caught me in a bad mood this morning. The hangover and all that. And I'm livid with old Goldenballs O'Hara for treating you that way."

"Don't be. It's like being angry with the Pope, surely, for being Catholic."

"Libby, don't even get me *started* with all the things I could be angry with the Pope about, given half a chance."

It's good that he's made a joke — even a not-terribly good one — because it feels as if we're back to normal again.

"I'm sorry too," I say, "by the way. About lying to you yesterday. And ditching you at such short notice. Not that it would've been OK to ditch you with *longer* notice, but . . . well, you know what I mean."

"I know what you mean. It's OK, Lib. Honestly. Let's just forget about the whole thing and try out this cheese, yeah?"

"Absolutely!" I say. "Cut me a little piece and I'll try it on its own first."

"Here goes," Olly says, cutting two slices out of the cheese, handing one to me and keeping one for himself.

We both bite into the cheese.

And chew, solemnly, for a couple of moments.

"It's not it," we both say, simultaneously.

"The one we had in Paris was sort of . . . creamier . . ."

"Fluffier, almost . . ."

"Oh, yeah, fluffy's a good description, actually. Whereas this one . . ."

"I mean, it's really good, Olly don't get me wrong . . ."

"But it's not the same one."

"It's not. No."

"So the search continues."

"The search," I agree, "continues."

And then we sit in companionable silence for a minute, nibbling at some more of the cheese from the waxed paper, and trying it with the walnut toast, too.

At least, I *hope* it's a companionable silence. I *think* everything's OK between us now — certainly I know

Olly's not remotely the sort to bear grudges — and I'm still glad I managed to apologize to him face-to-face.

I just have a suspicion that the mystery cheese-tasting would have been a bit more fun if we hadn't decided to do it on a day when we're both hungover and when I'm still smarting with the humiliation of having been so blatantly dismissed from Dillon's orbit.

Air-brushed out of his mind, too, most likely.

For all my Olympian efforts.

Or perhaps *because* of my Olympian efforts. Perhaps — oh, God — all those gung-ho positions I was trying out, and all that flinging myself about the bed, perhaps it . . . emphasized my wobbly bits in an off-putting manner. Perhaps if I'd just *lain* there, doing my level best to suck my stomach in and making sure Dillon wasn't in danger of getting the slightest glimpse of my derrière . . .

"Lib? You OK there?"

"Yes, sorry, Olly, I just . . ."

The kitchen door opens and in shuffles Charlie. Or Adam. I've only ever met them both when they're together so — especially when I'm trying not to stare too hard at all the hairy leg on display — I can't be sure exactly which of them it is.

"Oh, hey, Libby," Charlie/Adam says, doing an impressive job of recognizing *me*, given that we've probably only met four or five times over the course of fifteen-odd years, and usually when one or both of us were drunk. "Jesus, that's some black eye you've got there. You didn't get that on your date last night, did you?"

"I cancelled my plans with Adam when I thought I was going to be seeing you, and then I called and told him you had a date so we could have some beers after all," Olly starts saying, clearly feeling the need to explain how Adam (*not* Charlie) even knew I *had* a date last night. "Hey, why don't you jump in the shower, mate, and then throw some clothes on, so that Libby doesn't have to sit here assaulted by an eyeful of knobbly knees and hairy feet . . ."

"It's all right. I mean, not that I'm saying you have knobbly knees and hairy feet!" I assure Adam, as I get up. "I should be getting home anyway."

"But Lib, you haven't even had your cup of tea yet. And come on, don't go home to an empty flat when you can stay here for a bit. I'll cook us all some breakfast."

"Oh, don't worry, it won't be an empty flat." Hmm — possibly an error to admit this, given that I can't actually say *why* my flat won't be empty. "What I mean is, it won't *feel* empty, what with that great big Chesterfield hogging all the space! And I should catch up on some sleep anyway, I'm absolutely knackered . . ." Again, possibly an error, given that it sails us perilously close to the whole sex-with-Dillon thing we agreed never to discuss again. "Bye, Adam. Bye, Ol. Thanks for the cheese. And everything. I'll call you later."

I shove the borrowed Ray-Bans back on and, with a wince, the mistaken shoes, give them both a somewhat falsely cheery wave, and head out of the flat, tottering back towards Kennington tube station even more painfully than I tottered out of it.

CHAPTER
TEN

Back in Colliers Wood, I barely make it past Bogdan's Pizza Piz . . . oh, no, hang on, since I went out last night a new sign has gone up. It's Bogdan's Fish 'n' Chipz now, with one of the threatening-looking Moldovans hacking heads off glassy-eyed plaice just the other side of the shop window. Anyway, I barely make it past Bogdan's before giving up with, the shoes again and whipping them off just before I get to my own front doorstep.

I don't know what it is — the eerie quiet; the scent (imagined?) of l'Interdit that trails all the way up the stairs with me — but I'm not remotely surprised, the moment I step through my front door, to see that Audrey Hepburn is reclining on the Chesterfield sofa.

Of course. Of *course*.

I couldn't hallucinate her for love nor money last night, when I could have really done with a hasty chat. But now that all I want to do is curl up in a ball, right where I stand, and sleep and sleep and sleep for all eternity, Imaginary Audrey has made a reappearance.

She's lying on her back, wearing — exactly as she does in *Breakfast at Tiffany's* — nothing but a man's white shirt and duck-egg-blue satin sleep-mask.

210

I don't know why I'm reassured to notice that she's had a change of clothes since I last saw her, except for the fact that otherwise it might suggest that she'd been *here all night* . . . which, given that she only exists in my head, is *way* too complex a concept for my addled brain to compute, quite frankly.

"No, no, just tea and toast for me, please . . ." she murmurs, stirring from an elegant slumber as I shut — OK, bang — the door behind me. "I drank far too much coffee last night, I'm afraid. I'm not sure I ever want to *see* a cappuccino again, darling."

I get up all the way, walk over to the sofa and lift up the edge of her eye-mask.

"Morning," I say, flatly.

She sits bolt upright.

"Darling!" She pulls off her eye-mask completely and gazes at me, eyes wide in horror. "Your eye!"

"Oh, that." I take the Ray-Bans off again and put my hand up to touch the throbbing skin around my eye; Dillon's mother's advice may have prevented it from being any worse than this, but it still feels sore and battered. "Does it look really awful?"

"Dreadful, but that's not the point!" Audrey is on her feet, her hands on my shoulders. "What made him *do* this to you?"

"No, no . . ." She'll be threatening violence with a piece of kitchenware next. "It wasn't Dillon."

"Was there something he wanted you to do in bed, darling, and you didn't?"

"God, no, there was nothing he wanted to do in bed that I didn't . . . I mean, the black eye is nothing to do

211

with him. This was my sister. She threw a drink filled with ice-cubes in my face."

"Why on earth did she do that?"

"Why on earth does my sister do any of the things she does?" I ask, wearily, sinking onto the Chesterfield in a cloud of dog-scented dust. "Anyway, I'm fine. I put ice on it last night. I'm not sure there's anything else I can do about it right now."

"All right, then let me make you a nice cappuccino . . ."

"I thought you couldn't face a cappuccino ever again."

"*Drinking* one, darling. I'm perfectly happy to make one for you! Actually, I got rather good at it last night. Would you like me to make you one with the chocolate on top in the shape of a little heart? Or your initial? Or a lovely —"

"Thanks, but I'm fine."

"Oh, dear, Libby, you do look all in." She sits down and pulls her feet up onto the sofa cushion, clasping her hands around her bare, slightly scrawny knees. "But it must have been a *wonderful* night, darling, if you're only getting back at this time of the morning."

In my old fantasy, the one where Audrey Hepburn was my best friend, and we tripped around Fifth Avenue and the Tuileries together, knocking back champagne and looking fabulous, this is the point at which I'd girlishly confide in her about just how wonderful the night was. In fact, I'm getting a little shiver all along the length of my spine again, remembering all the sheer heavenliness of it: all that snogging up against the vintage fridge-freezer, and then even more delicious snogging on top of the pool table onto which — thanks to his impressive upper body strength — Dillon somehow managed to hoist me up without the use of a small crane, and then this unbelievably sexy retreat up the spiral staircase, shedding various items of our clothing on the way, Dillon's smooth, soft lips nuzzling my neck, and his back muscles *actually rippling* as he picked me up again and carried me up the last few stairs to his bed . . .

But at no point in my Fifth Avenue fantasy did I ever envisage having to tell Audrey Hepburn the distinctly less marvellous aspects of my love life. The depressing, shameful parts where you wake up in an empty bed at six thirty in the morning, without even so much as a one-line note to say goodbye.

I mean, I'm not asking for much. I wasn't exactly expecting to find an epic poem — *For Thee, Fire Girl* — propped against the toaster, or even to find a cheeky text on my phone explaining that he'd had to pop out for milk/bread/pool-table reinforcing equipment, but that he'd be back shortly for another round of filthy sex and I should make myself ready.

And, let's face it, Audrey Hepburn is never going to understand how it feels to end up mortifyingly ditched after an ill-advised one-night stand. In the extremely unlikely event that she ever had a one-night-stand in the first place, she'd doubtless have woken up to a little tray of breakfast, a bouquet of fresh flowers, and quite likely a Tiffany's diamond or three, all showered upon her by the lucky recipient of her affections.

"Libby?"

"What? Oh, yes, it was wonderful. But I don't think anything further is going to come of it."

Audrey pulls a sympathetic face. "Oh, darling, I'm sorry. Though with a man like that, I'm not sure what more you could expect. I mean, Bella, Gina, Maggie, Courtney . . ."

"Who are all these women?"

"This Dillon fellow's previous girlfriends, of course." She leans over the side of the Chesterfield and picks up my iPad. "I read about them on here. Models, most of them, but then what would you expect from a serial modelizer?"

"A serial what?"

"Modelizer. A man who only dates models. At least, that's what it said when I looked up the word on Wikipedia."

"Why . . . *how*, more to the point, were you on Wikipedia?"

"With your lovely padlet, darling. It's terribly easy to use, once you get the hang of it. And Wikipedia is simply marvellous. I'd never have known the slightest thing about your Dillon without it. Or Kim Kardashian, for that matter."

My head is spinning. "Sorry: what made you want to know anything at *all* about Kim Kardashian?"

"Well, I was absolutely intrigued, darling. I mean, I assumed she was terribly important, because you can hardly spend two minutes on this thing without reading *something* about her . . ."

214

She has, I now notice, the slightly glazed look of a person who's spent *way* too long jumping from link to link to link on Wikipedia.

"Right, but you were just saying something about Dillon's exes . . .?"

"Only that there are rather a lot of them. And the most recent one — Rhea, is it? — well, I wouldn't like to get on the wrong side of *her*. Did you know she was once given a police caution for throwing a raspberry at her hairdresser?"

"Er — do you mean *blowing* a raspberry at her hairdresser?"

"No, no, it was definitely *throwing*. And it must have been an awfully hard throw, for it to end up involving a police caution."

I think I've worked out the source of the confusion.

"BlackBerry. Not a raspberry. You mean a BlackBerry."

"Well, it was definitely *some* kind of berry, anyway . . . Oh!" Audrey suddenly jumps to her feet as the front-door buzzer sounds. "I wonder if that's my order."

"Your order?"

"Yes, darling, I've got an absolutely tremendous surprise for you!" She actually claps her hands in gleeful anticipation. "I couldn't help noticing how eager you seemed to freshen up your wardrobe . . ."

The buzzer goes, again.

"And I must say I think Net-a-Porter is the *cleverest* name. It's a play, presumably, on *prêt-à-porter*? And some of their things are just exquisite! Their styling leaves a little to be desired, and obviously the less said about their selection of shoes, the better, but even so . . ."

The buzzer goes a third time.

With a growing sense of dread, I get up and pick up the entry phone. "Hello?"

"This is Ravinder," a polite man's voice comes through the receiver, as the Colliers Wood High Street traffic rumbles by below. "Your Net-a-Porter delivery driver. Can you come down to sign for your delivery, please?"

"But I didn't . . ." I put the entry phone down and turn to glance back at Audrey, who's practically leaping around with excitement, like a child on Christmas morning. "Did you *order stuff* on Net-a-Porter?" I hiss at her.

"Yes! I ordered you your wish list! Well, I took off a few things that I'm fairly sure must have been placed on it by mistake — some dreadful jeans with legs like drainpipes, and one or two rather unattractive blouses — and put on a couple of beautiful evening gowns that I'm sure you'll get *years* of wear out of —"

"There was two grand's worth of stuff on there!"

"Oh, no, no, I didn't have to pay any money for it at all! I just clicked on Order and it all seemed to just happen."

"Because they had my credit card details from the one and only time I ordered anything from them!"

"Ah, well, I just assumed they must send you things for free, darling, because you're an actress. That seems to be the way it works nowadays, no? I always made sure I paid dear Hubert for all the things he sent me,

216

but according to your padlet, actresses are given most of their clothes without having to pay for them."

"Huge celebrities like Kim Kardashian, yes! Not redundant nobodies like me!"

"Darling, I won't have you calling yourself a nobody . . ."

The buzzer goes for a third time.

"I'm really sorry to be a pain," Ravinder goes on, when I pick up, "but the faster you could come down, the better. I'm going to have to go back to the van at least three times to bring you all your stuff, so . . ."

"Go away!" I yell down the entry phone at Ravinder, before somehow clawing back what's left of my manners. "Sorry, sorry, Ravinder, but what I mean is that there's been a mistake. I didn't place any order. Or rather . . ." My head is spinning. "I don't know . . . I must have accidentally placed the order in my sleep, or something . . ."

I mean, this is the only explanation, isn't it? People do all kinds of things in their sleep, don't they: walk, talk . . . place orders for two thousand pounds' worth of designer ball gowns on upmarket internet fashion sites . . . ?

Because unlike the recent occasion when I cut my own hair (while hallucinating it was Audrey who was doing so) or overdid my own eye make-up (while hallucinating it was Audrey doing so), this time I didn't *have* a hallucination of Audrey sitting there with my iPad, ordering up half my Net-a-Porter wish list.

This time I'm just hallucinating her *telling me about it*, as something she did *all by herself*.

But there's just no way that my hallucination of Audrey Hepburn can have *spilled over* into real life. She only exists in my head, for fuck's sake.

The only way that this order could actually have ended up being placed — and it clearly *has* been placed; Ravinder, waiting downstairs with his overspilling van, is the proof of that — is if *I* was the one who placed it. In my sleep. Or while drunk at Dillon's last night, perhaps. Maybe — although I have no memory of doing anything of the sort — I took out my iPhone in between Mind-Blowing Sex Session Two and Mind-Blowing Sex Session Three, and totted up a little online clothes order, just for kicks.

I'd ask Dillon about it, if there were the slightest chance of me ever seeing him again.

Whatever the (worrying, neurologically sinister?) explanation, I'm not going to sign for thousands of pounds' worth of designer togs I can't possibly afford.

"Thanks, Ravinder, but I'm not going to accept the order. I'm really, really sorry," I add, before hanging up the entry phone.

When I turn back to face Audrey again, she's gazing at me, absolutely aghast.

"But Libby, weren't you saying only last night that you urgently needed a wardrobe update?"

"Yes, but I meant clothes to wear to . . . to job interviews, and drinks with friends! Not exquisite ball gowns! From Net-a-Porter! When am I ever supposed to get the chance to wear anything like that, even supposing I could possibly afford it?"

218

"Oh, well, if you'd *seen* them, darling, you wouldn't be asking that question! They were so versatile! One a ravishing black silk, by my darling old friend Oscar de la Renta, and the other a rather elegant chiffon column by somebody called Victoria Beckham. I hadn't heard of her before, so I looked her up on Wikipedia. Her dressmaking credentials may leave something to be desired, but I must say she does seem to have an extraordinarily handsome husband . . ."

I sit down, heavily, on the Chesterfield, and place my head deep into my hands.

"If I just close my eyes and relax," I mutter, "all this will go away . . . close my eyes and relax . . . close my eyes and relax . . ."

There's silence.

I lift my head and open my eyes.

"Darling?" says Audrey Hepburn. "Are you feeling all right? Because if you've changed your mind about that cappuccino, it's ever so easy for me to rustle one up."

"No!" I yell, taking myself by surprise, as well as her. "I don't want a bloody cappuccino! I want five minutes — just *five minutes* — to be left in peace in my flat! Without cappuccinos, or online orders, or ridiculous haircuts! Without *you*," I add, though in a slightly calmer voice, because she's looking so startled by all the shouting, "whatever you are."

"Darling, I'm not a what, I'm a who! I'm Audrey Hep —"

"Stop saying that! You're not! You're not *real*. You're post-traumatic stress, or you're a brain tumour, but whatever the hell you are, I really just wish you'd leave me alone!"

There's another silence. It's longer than the last one, and a lot less comfortable.

"Well," Audrey says, after a moment. Her huge dark eyes are filling with tears, but her voice is steady. "I know you've had a late night, darling, and you're upset about your Dillon fellow leaving you in the lurch. But it's awfully bad manners, you know, to call somebody a brain tumour."

"I'm sorry." I look up at her, despairingly. "But I've no idea why else I keep seeing you like this. Or how I could possibly have ended up placing a massive internet order without even realizing."

"But you *didn't* place the order, Libby. I've told you, it was me! Now, I know you're rather cross with me about it, for some reason, but I was only trying to do something I thought might make you happy. You always seem so stressed out, and . . ."

"I'm stressed out because I keep hallucinating you! Because you keep popping up out of nowhere! This wasn't what it was supposed to be like, when I fantasized about you."

"You *fantasized* about me?"

"Yes, but not in the way it sounds . . . I just used to have this dream that you and I were friends. Actually, come to think of it, you were more like a fairy godmother. And we'd hang out in New York, and Paris, not in my crummy flat, and we'd drink champagne, and go window-shopping, and on the way I'd tell you all the things that were bothering me. I mean, I actually used

220

to have these imaginary conversations with you, where I'd tell you stuff about boys I liked, and my annoying mother, and . . . well, sometimes about my father. My stupid, selfish shit-bag of a father. But I was always imagining *your* side of the conversation as well, and you used to give me such good advice, or sometimes you'd just listen . . . but now I'm actually *seeing* you and *hearing* you, and you're not giving me any advice at all! You don't even appear at the right time, for crying out loud! I mean, where were you last night, when I wanted to ask your advice about the Dillon situation?"

"Well, darling, I was here, of course . . . I'm so sorry I wasn't around if you needed me, but next time you could just email! I've set up a little address on something called Gmail — the instructions were ever so easy to follow, and —"

"You can't have an email address! You're not *real*!"

But I'm prevented from saying any more by a sudden and extremely loud knocking on the other side of the partition wall.

"Libby?" comes Bogdan Son of Bogdan's voice. "You are home?"

"Yes, I'm home, Bogdan, but . . ."

"You are standing next to wall?"

"No, I'm on the sofa, but . . ."

"Please be staying there for moment. Thank you," he adds.

And then there's a loud crash as, first, the business end of a sledgehammer and second, Bogdan Son of Bogdan's face comes through the plasterboard.

"Jesus Christ!" I shriek.

"Am shocking you? Am apologies."

"Yes, you're shocking me!"

I'm not quite shocked enough, however, to notice that Audrey Hepburn has disappeared. Or rather that, now Bogdan is here, the hallucination has been shattered, and I can't see her any more.

Well, either that, or she's just cowering behind the back of the sofa.

I do a hasty check . . .

No cowering. No more Audrey.

"What the hell," I ask Bogdan, as I come up from peering down the back of the sofa, "are you doing?"

"Am standing up to father!"

The fact that he's saying this while still brandishing his sledgehammer is more than just a little alarming.

"Am taking down," he declares, striking his chest with his non-hammer-wielding hand, in the manner of a freedom-fighting Berliner, "partition wall."

"Bogdan, that's really nice of you, but I'm actually getting used to the size of the apartment. And I don't want you getting in any trouble with your father."

"Am not caring. Am not wanting life as a fib."

"Well, good for you!" I'd sort of rather, though, that Bogdan Son of Bogdan's desire not to live a lie didn't look as if it had anything to do with me. "But it might have been a good idea to have checked with me first, Bogdan, before you just set about my wall with a sledgehammer."

"Am not thinking you are in until am hearing voices. Am assuming you are out because you are not signing for delivery. But don't worry, Libby, am doing that for you."

My heart sinks as he holds up, through the hole in the wall, the largest carrier bag I've ever seen. With *Net-a-Porter* written on the side of it.

"Are four more down in hallway. Am only bringing smallest one up."

"Oh, dear lord . . ."

"You are suddenly winning lottery or something, Libby?"

"No! It was a mistake." I'm already grabbing my phone from my bag on the worktop so that I can call the store straight back and tell them Ravinder needs to return and collect the clothes, pronto.

"Is pretty expensive mistake." Bogdan peers at me. "Libby, am not meaning to be personal, but you are not looking the greatest."

"Oh. Well, the black eye probably isn't helping . . ."

"Is not just black eye. Is whole of you. Eye make-up is very smudged. Is making you look like raccoon. On way to fancy-dress party. Dressed as Marilyn Manson."

He reconsiders this for a moment. "Or more likely, come to be thinking of it, Marilyn Manson on way to fancy-dress party dressed as raccoon . . ."

"Yes, thank you, Bogdan, you've made your point . . ."

Wait a moment.

Something has just popped into my head.

Something Bogdan said, shortly after he burst through the plasterboard wall a few moments ago.

"Bogdan, did you say . . . *voices?*"

"Begging pardon?"

"Voices. You said you signed for the order because you didn't think I was in. And you only knew I was in when you heard voices."

"Is true."

"*Plural?*"

"What is this plural?"

"More than one. More than one voice. *Voices.* Is that what you heard?"

"But of course. Am hearing two voices, Libby. Your voice and friend's voice. Friend is telling you about new Gmail address and you are telling her she is unreal. Am not dropping the eaves, Libby, you and friend are speaking loudly and wall is only plaster . . . What is problem, Libby? You are looking beyond the pale."

I'm sure I *have* turned pale.

Because if Bogdan heard two voices, then there's only one logical explanation.

"Multiple personality disorder," I croak.

"Begging pardon?"

"I've read about it online . . . it's like in *Fight Club* . . . or that creepy horror movie set in the motel . . ."

"*Psycho?*"

I was actually thinking of something significantly less classic: a slightly crappy John Cusack vehicle called *Identity*, as far as I remember, where one of the characters ends up bumping off all the other characters — who all turn out to be his alter egos — at a rain-soaked motel in Nevada.

I feel as if I might throw up any second.

"Bogdan," I croak, "I think you'd better stay away from me. I'm serious. There's . . . there's something very wrong with me. I'm not well. I'm not well at all."

"You are needing doctor?"

"I don't know. Actually, yes. Yes, I think I am needing doctor."

He's already reaching into his dungarees pocket for his phone. "Don't panic, Libby. Am calling six six six."

"Nine nine nine. But don't do that, Bogdan!" I yelp. "It's not an emergency. I just think that maybe . . . well, my best friend is a doctor. I just really need to speak to her about this." Now I'm scrabbling for my phone. "I'll be fine, Bogdan . . . but please, I think I need to be alone right now. I mean, I *hope* I can be alone right now . . ."

Because I swear, if Audrey Hepburn pops up the minute Bogdan leaves, I'm going to lose it.

"I am not wanting to be leaving you . . ."

"I'm OK, Bogdan, I promise. I just need to get through to my friend on the phone."

"All right." He looks reluctant, but disappears from the hole, only to return a moment later. "Am able to get you anything from down the stairs? Takeaway coffee? Fish and chips? Chicken and ribs?"

"Thanks, I'm really fine."

Except that I'm not.

I press Nora's name on my phone with a slightly shaking index finger, and am not at all surprised when it cuts straight to voicemail a moment later.

"Nora. Hi. It's me . . . look, I know you're ridiculously busy, but there's something very important

I need to talk to you about. Well, quite a few important things, actually, because I've been doing all sorts of stupid things lately, like setting my head on fire, and sleeping with someone I think is called a modelizer, and . . . and falling out with Olly . . . and the only real live person I've got to talk to about any of this is this Moldovan hairdresser-slash-handyman, who's ever so sweet, but who really isn't medically equipped to deal with it all . . . anyway, I'm rambling," I say, hastily, as I realize that I'm rambling, "but if you have a moment to call me back, I'd really, really appreciate it. Oh, and if you have the chance to read up on multiple personality disorder, at all, before you call me, then that would probably be the most efficient use of your time. Thanks, Nora. Lots of love."

That might, I realize as I end the call, have been a slightly worrying message.

But there's no way I can delete it now.

And anyway, I suddenly feel so very, very tired that all I want to do is lie down on the Chesterfield and close my eyes, and hope that I'm left in peace, by what now looks like my scary alter ego, to have a little sleep . . .

CHAPTER
ELEVEN

I'm woken by a shrill, sharp buzzing noise.

I roll over to the far edge of the Chesterfield and scrabble around in the dark — when did it get *dark*, for crying out loud? — for my phone.

It's only when I grab it, try to answer the call and realize that the buzzing noise is still buzzing that I cotton on: it's not my phone ringing, it's the front door.

I stumble the three small steps to the entry phone and pick it up.

"Hello?" I mumble. (Actually it comes out sounding more like just *lo*, because my throat is too Sahara-dry to make an *h* sound.) "Who's there?" (Which comes out sounding more like *zzzaaair*.)

"Libby?" The voice sounds alarmed. "Is that you?"

"It's me." *(Smee.)*

"It's Nora! God, Libby, you sound awful! Let me up!"

"*Nora?*" I press the button to let her in, then just stand and stare through the confusing darkness at the entry phone for a few moments.

I'm not exactly sure what the hell is going on.

I was literally just talking to Nora on the phone . . . well, leaving that message on her voicemail, that is . . .

and now all of a sudden she's *here?* All the way down from *Glasgow?* And banging on my front door as though the Great Fire of Colliers Wood has just started to rage outside, and she's my only chance of escaping alive . . .?

I pull the door open.

"Nora! What the hell are you doing here?"

"Coming to make sure you're bloody all right, that's what!" She looks terrible. Well, she looks wonderful, because she's well groomed and glamorous and very, very pretty. But beneath the neat make-up and the smart blazer and that cloud of fluffy blonde hair, she looks abysmal. Pale and stressed and ever-so-slightly manic. "I mean, what the hell was that message you left me this morning? I got it at the end of my shift this lunchtime and I tried to call you back for two solid hours, until Mark suggested I'd better just get on a plane and come down here."

"You've just *flown down from Glasgow?*"

"Well, there's no need to say it like I took the nearest flying carpet. We do have aeroplanes up there, you know. And airports." She's already undoing the buttons on her blazer, coming through the door and finding the light switch. "OK, let me have a look at you," she says, before shrieking, "*Jesus,* Libby! Who gave you that black eye?"

"Oh, that was just Cass. She threw an icy cocktail in my face because she thought I was chatting up her boyfriend."

Nora, who — like Olly — knows Cass, obviously has an easier time believing this than Audrey Hepburn did.

228

"OK," she says, taking my wrist in one hand to feel my pulse and putting the other on my forehead. "Have you been running a fever? Have you taken any drugs? When was the last time you ate something?"

"No fever, of course no drugs, and . . . you know what, I don't remember." I stare at her. "Oh, my God, Nora! Do you think it's just hunger?"

"Do I think *what's* just hunger?"

"This whole multiple personality thing! The hallucinations."

"OK, this is why I got on a plane." Nora has put her Doctor's Face on now: calm, capable, and concerned on a merely professional level. "Sit down, Libby, and . . . Jesus, what the hell is this monstrosity?"

She's staring at my Chesterfield.

"It's my new sofa."

"But it's taking up most of the space in here. Don't you need, well, a bed and a table, and stuff like that?"

"Yes, I thought so originally, but actually, you can do pretty much everything you need on this Chesterfield! You can eat on here, sleep on here . . ."

"Theoretically, yes, but it doesn't look like you've been doing much of either." She sits down on the sofa and pulls me down next to her, while reaching into the huge handbag she's got slung in the crook of her arm for her case of doctor's instruments. "Now, let me take your temperature, and then I'll look in your eyes, and in the meantime you should just go on telling me about these . . . what did you call them? Hallucinations?"

"Yes. Oh, and did you get a chance to read up on multiple personality disorder? Because really, all I'd like to know is if it's treatable. I don't need to know all the scary details, but if there's some nice easy medication I can take, I'm perfectly happy to do that."

"Libby." She takes a deep breath. "Why on earth have you got it into your head that you've got multiple personality disorder? Which it isn't called any more, by the way. It's called dissociative identity disorder, and it's extremely serious, and I think we'd all know by now if you had it."

"How?" I ask, leaning forward, urgently. "How would we know? Because I'd think I was talking to a person who can't possibly be there? And talking back to myself as that person? And cutting my own hair with a breadknife while hallucinating that she was doing it? Because all those things have been happening, Nora. All of them."

"Hold on. You cut your own hair with a breadknife?"

"Yes. Actually, no. That's just what Bogdan said it looked like, before he trimmed it himself. Actually I think I must have used the kitchen scissors."

"OK . . . and this person you say you're hallucinating . . . he's a hairdresser called Bogdan?"

"No, no!" I feel marginally insulted, for a moment, that Nora thinks my alter ego could possibly be a hairdresser called Bogdan. "Christ, no, Bogdan is real. He's the landlord's son. At least . . ." A horrifying thought has just struck me. "I *think* he's real. Nora, tell me." I grab her arm. "Can you see that huge hole in the wall over there, or is it only me?"

"Yes, I can see it."

230

"Oh, thank God. Because if I was imagining a huge Moldovan with a sledgehammer, that really *would* be scary."

"I think just *knowing* a huge Moldovan with a sledgehammer is fairly scary, Lib." Nora's air of professional coolness is fading, however hard she tries to pretend it isn't. "Now, look. I can't say for absolute certain, of course, but I honestly think it's pretty unlikely you've suddenly developed dissociative identity disorder. There are plenty of much more likely, much less serious explanations if you really believe you're . . . what? . . . seeing things?"

"Not things. *People*." I take a deep breath. "Audrey Hepburn."

"What about her?"

"She's the person I've been seeing. And talking to."

"Audrey Hepburn?"

"Yes!"

"Your all-time favourite movie star?"

"Yes!"

Nora falls silent for a moment, then she says, in an exceptionally gentle tone of voice, "The movie star your dad's been writing a book about for the last twenty years?"

"Yes! I mean . . ."

OK. I'm getting the sense that Nora has just developed A Theory.

And, like quite a lot of Nora's Theories About Libby (my catastrophic track record with men; my half-heartedness about my career) it sounds as if she's decided it's all down to my relationship with my father.

Or, to be more precise, the lack thereof.

"He's been writing a book about *dozens of movie stars* for the last twenty years," I go on, "and *they're* not all popping up on my sofa. I've not been chin-wagging with Humphrey Bogart. I've not had my hair trimmed by Lauren Bacall. Judy Garland hasn't taken a fancy to the milk frother on my Nespresso machine. Though, in fairness, if I *were* hallucinating Judy Garland, she'd probably be far more interested in the contents of my wine rack . . . anyway, the point is, Nora, that this has absolutely nothing to do with my father. I don't even *see* him any more. I don't even *think* about him."

For a moment, I think she's about to carry on expounding this new theory, but she just stays quiet while she picks up her eye-looking-in-thingy (she's told me the technical name a million times, but it escapes me just now) and then holds it up and shines it into first one of my eyes and then, more carefully because of the bruising around it, the other.

"All right, then," she says, after a moment. "There are still plenty of other explanations. You've been under a lot of stress recently, what with moving, and all of that, and you clearly haven't been eating regularly, and your sister gave you a black eye last night, and — if I didn't mishear your message, Lib, you've somehow ended up involved with a modelizer . . ."

"So you know what a modelizer is, too?"

"Of course." She looks surprised. "A man who only dates models. I think it was from *Sex and the City*. You could look it up on Wikipedia, to find out —"

"No! I don't want to look it up on Wikipedia. And you're wrong, anyway, because I'm not *involved* with Dillon at all."

"Dillon . . . wait, not the Dillon who was coming to work on your show? Not . . ." Nora's mouth falls open. "Not *Dillon O'Hara?*"

"OK, why does everybody seem to find it so mind-blowingly impossible that I could have slept with him? I mean, you . . . Olly . . ."

"*Olly* knows you slept with him?"

"Yes, and there's a conversation I never want to have with your brother again, Nora, I'm telling you. I mean, when you started going out with Mark, did Olly threaten to beat his head in with a Le Creuset saucepan?"

"No, but . . ." Nora looks a bit flustered. "Look, I'm obviously not saying it's mind-blowingly impossible that you slept with Dillon O'Hara, but you *are* saying you've been hallucinating entire conversations with Audrey Hepburn."

"And you think I might have hallucinated having sex with Dillon O'Hara, too?" I gaze at her. *Et tu, Nora.* "Well, thanks for the show of faith, Nor. If you'd been the one in bed with him, you'd have known you weren't hallucinating, I can tell you that."

"Really?" Nora leans forward on the sofa, my best friend for a moment rather than a concerned medic. "He was that good?"

"Oh, Nora. There are no words."

"*Really?* Well, I suppose from all the stuff you read about him in the gossip mags, he's obviously had a fair amount of practice . . ."

"So you do believe me?"

"Well, of course I believe you, Lib. This is all just quite a lot to take in. And I was in such a flap when I got your message earlier, and rushing to the airport to get on the first available flight . . ."

"I'm sorry." I take her hand. "I wasn't thinking. You're an amazing friend, Nora. Getting on a plane like that, especially after a long shift at the hospital. You must be knackered."

"I am a bit. Starving, mostly. And you must be, too. Look, why don't we grab a takeaway, maybe have a nice relaxing glass of wine, and you can tell me a bit more about these hallucinations. Because honestly, Libby," she puts a hand on mine, "I don't think there's all that much to worry about. There are all kinds of perfectly simple explanations, without having to panic about serious mental disorders or — well — brain tumours."

Great. So the fully qualified doctor amongst us hasn't completely dismissed the notion of a brain tumour, either.

And we still haven't actually discussed the fact that I'm evidently not simply hallucinating Audrey Hepburn, I'm talking to myself *as her*, too.

But there's no reason that all of this can't be dissected over some nice, freshly decapitated plaice from Bogdan's Fish 'n' Chipz, or a hefty order of fried chicken and ribs, and — even though I'm a tiny bit worried that some of Dillon's excesses with alcohol might have rubbed off on me recently — a glass or two of that soothing wine Nora mentioned.

234

"No, no, don't worry, I'll go," Nora says, gently pushing me back down as I start to get up off the sofa. "I've still got my coat and shoes on, and you're . . . well, it looks like you might still be wearing the same clothes you had on yesterday?" She peers more closely at my cocktail dress. "You weren't trying to *look* like Audrey Hepburn, were you? I mean, the dress, and your hair, and that pearl necklace . . .?"

Oh, shit. On top of everything else, Nora has now seen her bridal gift, the necklace I was going to present to her as a Big Surprise on the morning of her wedding. So it'll be back to the drawing board on that one, then. Mind you, the delicate beads could well have been permanently ruined by the layer of santol Martini that's probably still coating them and, anyway, I'm not at all sure I could have given the necklace to Nora to be worn with virginal, bridal white on her wedding day: not after I was wearing it (and, if I recall correctly, *absolutely nothing else*) when I was getting up to all kinds of naughtiness with Dillon last night.

"No," I sigh, wearily, "I wasn't trying to look like her, as such, she was just giving me styling advice . . . look, I'll tell you more when you're back with the food, OK? I'd just pop to one of the takeaways downstairs, if I were you," I add, grabbing my bag, pulling out my wallet and handing her the only note I have in there, which is — depressingly — just a fiver. "Tell them you're a friend of Bogdan Senior's. He's their Moldovan crime-lord boss, so they should be terrified enough into giving you a fairly hefty discount."

Nora just stares at me for a moment.

"Honestly, Libby, you and I really do have a lot of catching up to do when I come back with this food."

"I know. Believe me."

I sink back into the cushions of the Chesterfield as Nora heads out of the flat.

My mobile phone is telling me that it's 8.36p.m., so I slept for . . . God, can that be right? . . . almost ten hours. And it doesn't even seem to have helped, because I still feel as though I could doze off to sleep again at a moment's notice. In fact, while I'm waiting for Nora to get back with the takeaway, I might just close my eyes again. Just for a few minutes. I'd quite like to be able to enjoy an evening with my best friend, now that we've got all the neurological stuff out of the way, without yawning every five minutes and dropping off into my dinner. I mean, it's not like there isn't months of chitchat for us to catch up on: the plans she must surely be starting to make for her wedding, and how things are going with Mark now that they're engaged, and . . .

"I'm sorry."

It's — who else? — Audrey Hepburn, sitting beside me on the sofa. She's fully dressed now, instead of just wearing the man's shirt like she was earlier, and in her iconic *Roman Holiday* get-up: white puff-sleeve blouse, full skirt, and a little scarf knotted, stylishly, around her neck.

"I'm ever so, ever so sorry, darling," she repeats, putting a cool hand on one of mine. "I've been thinking about what you said earlier, and I feel absolutely rotten about it."

236

I have to ransack my addled brain to work out exactly what she's talking about.

"You said you wanted advice from me. You said you wanted to talk things through. And you're quite right: I *have* spent too long playing around with your Nespresso machine, and I *shouldn't* have ordered all those clothes."

Oh, shit, the Net-a-Porter order. I need to do something about that asap, before the credit-card bill wends my way.

"I was terribly touched," Audrey is going on, in the gentlest of gentle voices, "when you said you'd always seen me as a sort of fairy godmother. And I realize that maybe you wanted something else from me, something other than a wonky haircut and firm opinions about your shoes."

I laugh. Well, it's a sort of laugh, in a long, let-out breath. And Audrey smiles — that breathtaking, million-dollar smile that kicked off all my ridiculous Audrey fantasies in the first place, all those years ago.

"I'm not sure what I can possibly have to offer," she says, "but I just wanted you to know that I'm here if you need me."

I'm a bit too overcome to say anything in reply.

"Oh, and by the way, I'm something of an expert on stupid, selfish shit-bags of fathers."

"Audrey!" I'm truly shocked to hear the S-word come out of her mouth.

"Well, I am." She slips off her ballet pumps and curls her feet up beneath her on the sofa. "So if you ever want to compare notes . . ."

"I know. Your dad was having an affair with the nanny, left your mother when you were six, moved home to Ireland and became a Nazi sympathizer. My dad left my mother when I was three, for more time and space to work." Even as I say these words, I can hear Dad's voice in my head; after all, he repeated the phrase often enough over the years. "Though at least he didn't start sympathizing with any Nazis. But that might just be because it was the late Eighties and not the mid-Thirties, and there weren't that many Nazis around. I'm sure if there had been, my dad would have found some sort of way of sympathizing with them, just to cause me maximum annoyance."

"Goodness!" Audrey's mouth is open. "How in heaven's name do you know that about my father?"

"Partly because *my* father's been writing a book on you for the past twenty years. Well, you and a few other Hollywood legends."

"How extraordinary!"

"Well, I suppose it is a bit of a coincidence," I say, wearily, "now I come to think of it."

"No, no, I mean that he should have been writing this book for *twenty years* ... Is he a terribly meticulous researcher?"

"No, he's an irredeemably lazy bastard."

My phone bleeps, suddenly, on the floor beside me.

"Oh!" Audrey gasps. "Could that be your modelizer?"

I should know better than to get excited, but I still feel the lurch in my stomach as I lean down to pick it up and look at the text.

But it isn't Dillon. It's Cass.

So are you still coming to the spa for Mum's bday tomorrow, Lib, or not?

Oh, Christ, this is all I need. The annual Lomax Ladies' spa outing for Mum's upcoming birthday. This year, it's being held — where else? — at FitLondon, where the prices are so astronomical that I could only find a single, solitary treatment costing less than a hundred quid to book for myself, and even that's just some crappy-sounding fifteen-minute steam-room algae jobby that still costs seventy pounds and will probably just be me left to my own devices in an empty room with a kettle, a washing-up bowl and a large tea towel to drape over my head, the way I used to when I was 13 and trying to steam-clean the mucky pores on my nose and forehead.

Yes, I reply to Cass, am coming to spa despite HUGE BLACK EYE that am currently sporting.

"Not your modelizer?" Audrey asks.

"Not my modelizer."

Oh good, comes the reply from Cass. Can I go halves with u on whatever present u bought?

"You know, I ended up getting on well enough with mine."

I glance up at Audrey, confused. "Sorry — you ended up getting on quite well with . . . your modelizer?"

"No, no, darling, I never had a modelizer! Though my second husband in particular did have an eye for the ladies . . . but I was actually talking about my father."

"Oh, sorry, I thought we'd moved off the topic of fathers."

239

She shrugs. "Only if you want to."

"God, yes, I want to." I start composing a reply to Cass — ffs can't you just pick up some . . . And then I stop. It's incredibly rude to sit here texting while I'm having a conversation, for one thing, and for another thing, I want to ask Audrey something, after what she's just said. "You ended up getting on OK with him?"

"My father?" Audrey nods. "Decently enough. We wrote. I visited him, occasionally. It was very healing."

I raise a sceptical eyebrow.

"It was, Libby, honestly. I mean, of course I wish he'd not been —"

"A Nazi sympathizer? Sleeping with the nanny? Your father?"

"The way he was," Audrey finishes, giving me a gently reproachful look that makes me feel about an inch high, and ashamed of myself for being so flippant. "But the good part about being in touch with him again, as an adult, was that I started to see that the way he was had nothing to do with me. That all the things he did weren't done to cause me — what was it you said just now? — maximum annoyance. They were done because he simply wasn't capable of anything else."

I don't say anything.

"Anyhow, you don't have to listen to me. I'm no expert. But I do know how it feels to have everything in the world except a proper father."

She sounds so desperately sad, all of a sudden, that I instinctively reach across the sofa to put an arm around her.

240

But she's gone.

The hallucination is . . . what? Broken?

And this time it didn't even take Bogdan coming through the wall with a sledgehammer to do it.

This time, though, I'd have rather liked it if she'd stuck around a little bit longer. Just until Nora came back. Seeing as I was sort of enjoying our chat about our fathers.

Well, as much as you can ever *enjoy* a chat about two complete wasters who go about either a) waving swastikas or b) telling their daughters they *meant* to phone on their birthday/show up to parent's evening/stick to yet another arrangement to go out for dinner, but that their book about the golden age of Hollywood is a little bit more important right now.

I do recognize, by the way, that the swastika thing is quite a bit worse than the Hollywood book thing.

But then, as Audrey just said, before the hallucination shattered, she had everything in the world except a proper father. And I . . . don't. I'm not a world-class beauty, a style legend or an Oscar-winning movie star. I certainly don't have what it takes to travel to poverty-stricken shantytowns in Central America, or famine-ridden villages in Africa, light up some desperate children's lives and raise a tonne of money for UNICEF into the bargain.

I'm not Audrey Hepburn, dealt the card of the crappy father. I'm Libby Lomax, dealt the card of the crappy father.

Though, right now, I urgently need to stop thinking all about crappy fathers, because Nora is going to be back any minute with the takeaway, and I don't want to dwell on the subject any longer. Partly because I really, really do want to hear about Nora's plans for the wedding, and partly because I don't want to accidentally prove right her theory about the hallucinations.

I haul myself up off the Chesterfield and squeeze my way round to the kitchen, to start getting the crockery out for our supper.

CHAPTER
TWELVE

Nora is taking the Paddington Express out to Heathrow for her flight back to Glasgow this morning, and seeing as she travelled six hundred miles at the drop of a hat to come and see me yesterday evening, I think it's only right and fair that I accompany her to Paddington to see her off.

"Now, promise me you're feeling a bit better this morning, Lib," Nora says, as we head into the station's branch of WH Smith to buy magazines, mints and Minstrels for her journey. "After everything we went through last night?"

Everything we went through last night was Nora's extremely thorough de-bunking, over some woefully under-fried plaice and a bucket of woefully dry fried chicken, of my whole multiple personality theory.

Nora being Nora, she wouldn't rest until she'd presented as much cold, hard, scientific evidence as possible that my hallucinations are most likely caused by the combined stress of moving home, losing my job, and accidentally setting my head on fire in front of an entire TV crew.

Which, let's face it, is pretty much what I thought the first time it happened.

And it has at least made me relax, quite a bit, about the possibility that I'm suffering a rare and terrifying identity disorder; one that might not even exist, anyway, according to Nora's brief but thorough run-down of the most up-to-date psychological research. She was the perfect brisk, no-nonsense medical professional about Bogdan Son of Bogdan's claim to have heard *two* voices the other day, too: "Honestly, Libby, the acoustics up here in this old attic are godawful, you know. It could perfectly easily sound as though two people were talking when in fact it was just one person and the reply of some seriously rickety plumbing."

Which, seeing as the quality of the plumbing isn't exactly up for debate, at least has some ring of truth about it.

"And even though," she's telling me now, as we wander towards the magazine racks in WH Smith, "the chances of any of this being caused by a brain tumour are *extremely* remote, so all you need to do is keep an eye out for any other symptoms — headaches, flashing lights, blurred vision. Give me a call and we'll talk it all through some more. Promise?"

"Promise," I tell her, squeezing her hand.

"The most important thing you need to do to bring the hallucinations to an end is to eat proper food, get proper sleep, and most important of all — *relax*. Which ideally means no gadding about with gorgeous, unreliable actors."

"I don't think gadding about with gorgeous, unreliable actors is an option," I tell her, "even if I wanted it to be."

And then, before I can accidentally blurt out that —
despite everything — I'm not sure I *want* to bring the
hallucinations to an end, I tell her I'll go and find the
Polo mints and meet her at the checkout.

When I meet her at the head of the queue a couple
of minutes later, she's looking a bit peculiar.

"Is everything OK, Nor? Do you need me to dash
to Boots and buy you some emergency Tampax or
something . . .?"

She shakes her head, takes the Polos from me and
pays for them, and the stack of magazines under her
arm, at the next free counter. It's only when we get
outside, onto the main concourse, that she speaks again.

"I think you should probably have a look at this," she
says, reaching into the thin plastic carrier-full of
magazines, taking out this month's copy of *InStyle*, and
handing it over to me.

I stare down at — who else? — Kim Kardashian on
the cover, trying to work out what it is Nora is looking
so meaningful about.

"The New Wedge — How High Can You Go?"

"No."

"Compact Foundation: Tried and Tested?"

"*No!* Here, Libby: look." She points at the strapline
at the bottom left of the cover, nestling in the lower
slopes of Kim Kardashian's cleavage.

"Golden Hollywood Uncovered?"

She nods. "Go to the Contents page."

This is starting to feel a bit like one of those pointless
obstacle courses I remember forever being made to do
at primary school, and I'm half expecting Nora to

chuck a saggy beanbag and a hula-hoop at me when, doing as she's asked, I reach the Contents page.

The *Golden Hollywood* title leaps out again, in the Features section, and catches my eye immediately.

Page 123: Golden Hollywood Uncovered. Edward Lomax, author of the definitive new volume on Hollywood history, writes about the hidden lives of the leading ladies of Tinseltown's golden era, from Ingrid Bergman's complicated love life to Audrey Hepburn's tragic relationship with her father.

Edward Lomax, author of the definitive new volume on Hollywood history — and, apparently, world expert on tragic relationships with fathers — is my dad.

Dad's book has been published, and I didn't even know about it.

"Did you know . . .?"

"No. We're not in touch, Nora, I told you."

"But I just thought, if his book was finally being published . . . and it sounds quite a big deal, if he's writing articles for *InStyle* off the back of it . . . I don't know, maybe there was a launch party, or something . . ."

"Maybe there was, but if so, I wasn't invited."

There's a short, awkward silence.

"Well, maybe if you'd even had the slightest inkling of this, it might have been the thing that triggered —"

"Nora, for the last time, I didn't know Dad's book was out, and it's nothing to do with my hallucinations!"

A passing train driver gives me a seriously funny look, and gives me a wide berth, so I think I'd better keep my voice down.

"Honestly, this is brand-new information for me, Nora," I hiss. "And you're making a bigger deal of it, anyway, than it really is."

"Libby, your dad left your mum in order to write that book . . . He once told you he'd had to make the decision between his life's work and his daughter and that he was certain he'd made the right decision . . ."

"Dad told me a lot of things," I say, abruptly. "Most of them utter crap."

"And now the book is done. And suddenly you're having imaginary conversations with the very Hollywood legends he broke up his family in order to write about?"

"Not Hollywood legends. Just Audrey Hepburn."

Nora lets out a long — a very long — sigh.

"OK. Well, I guess I need to be getting on one of these trains if I'm going to make it to the airport in time." She hoiks her bag up onto her shoulder. "Again, all I can say, Lib, is to call me if you need to talk. I promise, I'll make more time for you than I have done these past few months. Work's been crazy, and the wedding . . ."

"I know. You don't need to explain anything to me, Nora. I still can't believe you flew all the way down here for me."

She reaches over and gives me a short, rather violent hug.

"Say hi to your mum and sister for me, won't you?"

"I will. And give Mark a big kiss from me."

I watch as she walks towards the Heathrow Express platform, and wave goodbye as she gets onto the train, which starts to pull out of the station a moment later.

Right, well, I'm not going to read Dad's article.

I'm certainly not going to read his book.

I'm just going to go and enjoy my spa day with Mum and Cass, through gritted teeth, if I have to, and banish all thought of Edward Lomax. And Hollywood Legends, while we're at it.

I turn and head for the Circle Line, shoving *InStyle* magazine far down into my bag as I go.

The entrance to the FitLondon spa is, thank God, on Baker Street itself rather than in the plaza, so I don't have to run the gauntlet of Pippa the ill-disposed receptionist on the main desk. In fact, the girl on the spa reception is terribly sweet, and all prepared to give me a tour of the facilities, from the steam room where my treatment will take place to the changing rooms where, apparently, a complimentary waffle robe and slippers await me.

As much as I love a waffle robe, the thing I really need right now is caffeine, so I just ask the receptionist to point me in the direction of the café.

"Oh, well, we don't have a café as such . . . we have a fabulous juice bar, serving freshly made raw juices and herbal teas, if you fancy that?"

I don't, much, but it's obviously my best bet, so I follow her directions there in the hope that I might at least persuade someone to bung a couple of extra tea bags into my pot of camomile.

It's actually a little area of tables and chairs by the side of the lavish, Roman-style swimming pool, mostly filled with women in waffle robes, one of whom is Cass.

She's sitting at one of the tables closest to the bar itself, a tall glass of pink-tinged smoothie in front of her. Her waffle robe is merely draped, glamorously, over her shoulders, and beneath it she's wearing nothing but an extremely sexy scarlet cut-out swimsuit that barely contains her ample breasts and, with her messy blonde extensions, makes her look a lot like Pamela Anderson in an old episode of *Baywatch*.

"Oh, hi, Libby," she says, glancing up from her phone as I approach the table. "Why the shades? Are you massively hungover or something?"

I sit down opposite her, take off Dillon's Ray-Bans, and look right at her.

"Oh, right," she says. "That."

"That."

"It looks awful."

"Thanks. In case you're wondering, it feels pretty awful, too."

"I might have some arnica in my bag," she says.

This is the closest she's ever going to get to admitting that she's sorry.

The thing is, though, that although my sister's not the world's greatest at apologies, at least she doesn't generally sulk, or dwell, or brood. Whatever nonsense she might have thought, last night, about me chatting up her dreadful boyfriend, she'll have let go already. Almost as quickly as she let go the cocktail shaker full of ice in my direction, in fact.

"You look really rough, you know, Libby," she goes on, as I sit down at the table and put my bag down.

"What, you mean apart from my black eye?"

She ignores this. "So is your new boyfriend not letting you sleep at all?"

"My new . . .?"

"Dillon O'Hara."

"He's not my new boyfriend!"

"Well, I know *that*, Libby." She rolls her eyes. "I'm *joking*. Obviously."

"Oh. Right. Obviously."

"But everyone saw you leave the party together, by the way And I mean *everyone*, including that annoying model he used to go out with. Regan or Rhesus, or whatever her name is."

"Rhea."

"That's the one. You'd better hope you don't ever run into *her* in a dark alley, Libby. She was spitting blood when she saw he'd left with you."

I let out a laugh that's meant to be devil-may-care and chock-full of bravado, but accidentally comes out sounding high-pitched and slightly unhinged.

"So did he just walk you to the tube or something?"

I make a movement with my head that's neither a nod nor a shake, thereby not committing myself to an answer of any sort. Not that Cass is all that interested; she's already decided that walking me to the tube is all that Dillon could possibly have wanted to do with me, so an actual answer is irrelevant.

"You know, I've decided," she goes on, "that actually there's nothing so very special about Dillon O'Hara. I mean, he's not even that good looking. And now that he's pissed off Dave, by the way, his career is going to be, like, totally down the pan."

"Speaking of Dave," I say quickly, partly to change the subject and partly because it's been on my mind, "I assume you've noticed that he wears a wedding ring?"

Cass flips her hair, with a hefty dose of the devil-may-care attitude I failed to nail a moment or two ago, and ignores the question.

"I like *that*," she says instead, in a rather pointed tone, nodding at the pearl-and-orchid necklace that — having definitely decided against giving to Nora; I'll make a start on a new necklace for her instead — I'm still wearing this morning. "Can you make my ruby one into something like that instead? I sort of messed up the clasp when I had to customize it *all by myself* the other night."

"Cass. Come on. I'm really serious."

"So when I go for my body firming experience," she tries a new topic, "should I ask them to concentrate on my bum and thighs or on my stomach and arms?"

"Cass —"

"Because seeing as I've got my audition for that Emily thing tomorrow morning, I really need to sort out my disgusting flabby bits, super-quick."

"Emily?"

"*You* know, Libby! The thing for RTE. The show about Emily Blunt."

"Emily *Brontë*."

"Yeah, that's the one, I think. Hang on: did she have sisters?"

"A couple of them."

"Yep, it's her then." She thinks for a moment. "So were they a bit like the Kardashians? Like, a medieval version?"

"No! And they weren't medieval, they were . . ." Actually, you know what: I give up. "Look, Cass, please, can we just finish talking about Dave?"

"For fuck's *sake*, Libby, he's not *married*." She rolls her eyes at me as if I've just said the stupidest thing she's ever heard. "Not properly. He and his wife are separated. Well, I mean, they still live in the same house and everything, but that's only because he's too nice a guy to upset the children."

I feel, unexpectedly, a lump in my throat. "Oh, Cass . . ."

"He's an agent," she says, as though this brings an end to my concerns as firmly as if she's just said, *He's a newly-beatified saint with a snazzy line in curing terminal illnesses by the laying-on of hands.* "And I've been thinking, I really need to make the move to a proper agent, now that Mum's going to be distracted by the stage school, and by all this shit with your dad."

"But Cass, if you want a proper agent, you could get one without needing to . . . What shit with my dad?"

"Uh, I'm not really sure? Something to do with the house . . .? Oh, you can ask her yourself. She's on her way back from her anti-ageing facial now. Mum! Over here!"

For someone who's just spent close to two hundred quid on an anti-ageing facial, Mum looks absolutely dreadful.

The wild, slightly matted hair extensions don't help, but the main problem is that her eyes are puffy and her nose is red and shiny.

"Mum?" I half get to my feet and pull out a chair for her to collapse into. "What's wrong?"

"That *bastard*," she gasps.

OK, now I *know* it's got something to do with Dad.

Mum is riffling through the pockets of her waffle robe and produces a slightly crinkled sheet of smart, cream-coloured paper, which she passes to me.

"Read that," she chokes. "I need a bloody drink."

"Have my smoothie," Cass says, generously, pushing her barely touched glass over in Mum's direction. "I'm going to ask them to do me a prune juice instead. It's the only way I can think of to blast a couple of pounds out of me before the audition, if I'm going to look anything at *all* like Kim Kardashian."

I unfold the sheet of paper.

It's a typed, official-looking letter, from a place called Latymer Postlethwaite Karney: a solicitor's firm.

Dear Ms Lomax, the letter reads.

We have been advised by our client, Mr Edward Lomax, that you have recently sold 21 Trevelyan Street, London, the property purchased by you and our client in 1985, and held in your joint names ever since. Mr Lomax has informed us that you have not yet sought to recompense him with his half of the proceeds from the sale of the house.

I glance up at Mum, who is gulping Cass's unwanted smoothie as if it's the strong G&T I know she'd much rather be drinking right now.

"I don't owe him a single fucking proceed from the sale of the house," she says when she puts the glass down. "Let alone half. Do you want to know what he's contributed to the mortgage in the past twenty years? What princely sums he's deigned to cough up? Absolutely fucking *zero*, that's what."

Which is, I know only too well, the truth.

I can remember overhearing enough tense phone calls over the years to know that Mum is accurate when she says Dad didn't pay a penny in mortgage payments. And hardly any child maintenance, for that matter.

We are therefore making contact, the solicitors' letter continues, to request that you transfer Mr Lomax's half of the proceeds of the sale of 21 Trevelyan Street into our client account within five working days of the receipt of this letter, or, regrettably, we will be compelled to take further action.

"I've just spent fifteen grand on a stage-school franchise," Mum is wailing, a huge tear rolling down her cheeks and plopping into Cass's smoothie. "And the lease for the premises is twelve thousand a year, and I've already spent five grand on advertising, and then there's almost three thousand pounds already gone on my stage-school-principal wardrobe . . ."

"Mum, this is ridiculous. You don't have to give him a penny, OK? Now, we just need to get you a solicitor of your own and they can write straight back and tell these Latymer people that you were the only person paying the mortgage for the last twenty years. We'll find you a good lawyer, OK?" I put my hand on hers. "They'll handle it all for you and you won't have to have any contact with Dad at all."

"Oh, no, no, no, no, no. I don't want a lawyer! It'll cost me a fortune. Besides, you can't trust them. They're all scheming back-stabbers, sleeping with their colleagues and embezzling their clients' money."

It's just possible that Mum is basing her opinions of lawyers on John Grisham novels and episodes of *Boston Legal*.

"You know, *you* could talk to him, Libby," she goes on. "Get him to understand that he's being unreasonable. Get him to back off, without me having to use a lawyer at all."

I smile, because I'm so certain she's joking.

Mum doesn't smile back.

"You're kidding," I say.

"No, I'm serious, Libby! He'll listen to you. He's never been able to deny you anything . . ."

Mum breaks off, unable to continue with this absurd claim any longer.

"Well, all right," she goes on, looking just the tiniest bit sheepish, and not quite meeting my eye, "but perhaps he might be in the mood for making it up to you, darling! For being such a terrible father all these years."

"I'm not talking to him, Mum," I say, trying to summon up a bit of that poised graceful loveliness that (almost) worked on her the last time she started to wind me up. "I'll give you all the help I can — I'll find you a lawyer, I'll deal with the lawyer, I'll even *pay* for the lawyer if you want me to." (Though, given that I'm virtually penniless, this would be an interesting conversation with the bank manager.) "But I'm not going to talk to Dad," I add, in a poised and graceful — but pretty bloody firm — manner. "It wouldn't do the slightest bit of good, apart from anything else."

"Oh, Libby." Mum tries one of her favourite tactics for getting me to agree to something: scoffing. "You're being silly. Overly dramatic. It's the teeniest, tiniest little favour —"

"Mum. I said no."

She gazes at me, eyes widening, and I can sense that another of her favourite tactics is heading my way: the guilt-trip.

"On my *birthday* . . ."

I may be looking poised and graceful (at least, I hope I am; the stupid giant shades don't help much) but I can feel my heart starting to race. Confrontation isn't my strong point, but this is something I am not about to budge on, not one single inch.

"I'm sorry, Mum. I really am. But I don't want to see him."

Her eyes light up: she's spotted a loophole. "Oh, but you don't have to *see* him, Libby! You could just call him! Email, even! Or just a quick text. I mean, it's one of the great benefits of living in the twenty-first century, isn't it? All these wonderful ways to communicate with people you can't be bothered to have a face-to-face conversation with?"

(I won't dwell, too much, on the fact that Mum invariably contacts *me* by text message, but always prefers to chat with Cass in person, preferably over a lingering girlie lunch).

"Mum, please. Listen to me. I'm not contacting Dad. Not by phone, or email, or text, or Facebook, or tweet. Or carrier pigeon. Or smoke signals."

Which ought to have covered pretty much everything.

"There's always WhatsApp," Cass suggests.

I shoot her a Look. It's neither poised nor graceful.

"Well, I'm only *saying*, Libby . . . it *is* Mum's birthday, after all. You don't turn sixty every day."

"I'm fifty-six!" Mum snaps.

"Right, so *basically* sixty, then . . ."

"Look, I think we can just end this whole discussion," I say, before Mum completely loses it, "by agreeing that Dad's demands are completely unreasonable, and that we're going to get a nice, understanding, *good-value* lawyer who'll write a letter to Dad's lawyers telling them where to get off. All right?"

Mum just sniffs, and doesn't say anything.

"I'll take that as a yes, then," I say, getting to my feet. "Now, if you don't mind, I've got to go and steam myself for the next twenty minutes. I'll meet you both back here at the pool afterwards."

"Leave it, Mum," I hear Cass say behind me, as — presumably — Mum opens her mouth to call something after me. "Libby's right. You need a lawyer.

You don't need to force her to talk to her stupid father."

Which, far more than anything else Cass could ever do, is enough to make up for the cocktail shaker thrown in my face the other night.

But seriously: what the hell is Mum *thinking*, suggesting that I tackle my father?

And what the hell was she thinking, now we're really getting down to it, not getting some proper advice about the marital finances when she divorced him twenty-five years ago?

And, most importantly of all, what the hell is *Dad* thinking? Why is he coming after Mum for his half of the house? When he's just had the wretched book published, so is bound to have earned some money for it, finally? After three decades of bloody *faffing*?

Feeling less poised with each passing second, I stamp my way out of the pool area and back into the lavender-scented corridor, where I'm almost immediately accosted by a pretty red-headed spa therapist in a futuristic white uniform. The name *BETSY* is printed, in block letters, on her name badge.

"Are you Libby?" she asks, peering into my sunglasses. "The eleven o'clock 'steam experience'?"

I imagine that adding the word "experience" is simply a way of justifying the seventy-quid cost. But this isn't Betsy's fault, so I just say, politely, "Yes, I am."

"Lovely! Well, you're going to really enjoy this treatment, Libby. It's completely heavenly. Have you ever done anything like this before?"

"I . . . er . . . don't know exactly what it is, yet."

"Right. Well, it's terribly simple." Betsy pushes open a nearby treatment room door; we're both almost completely engulfed by a huge rush of swirling steam. "You go in here," she says, wafting the steam away, "get undressed — um, including the sunglasses, I'd suggest — and pop on the paper knickers I've left on the bench. Then you simply cover yourself in mud! There's a big bowl of it next to the paper knickers."

"Mud?" I'm a bit worried about this.

"Well, it's actually more like an algae, really, absolutely brilliant at smoothing out all your cellulite and fatty deposits. I mean, obviously it won't turn you into a supermodel . . ."

"Obviously."

". . . but you'll certainly feel much lighter and tighter afterwards! You just apply the algae to whichever parts you're most concerned about, then lie back on one of the benches and relax for fifteen minutes. You can go and shower it all off right afterwards."

So it is a DIY jobby, then. Seventy quid for fifteen minutes of slopping, steaming and showering. Still, I may as well do my best to enjoy the "experience", now that I'm committed. And, in fairness, as Betsy waves goodbye and closes the treatment room door behind me, it is at least calm, peaceful, and a Mum-free zone. There are pretty twinkly fairy lights, and the steam — after that huge rush of it went out of the door — is gently swirling rather than smog-like, and it really *does* smell quite nice: lavender, I think, and a hint of eucalyptus. All a golden opportunity for a precious few minutes of that relaxation Nora was insisting upon.

I take off the Ray-Bans, hang my bag on a little peg on the door, take off my clothes and hang them beside it, locate the scratchy paper thong on one of the benches lining the wall, put it on, and then head for the large bucketful of Betsy's algae to start applying it all over my . . .

Ugh.

This is not heavenly.

I mean, it *smells* to high heaven, but that's another thing entirely.

I slop a large splodge of the rank, sludgy-brown stuff over my bum and thighs and another splodge on my tummy, then I plonk myself down on the little wooden bench, underneath the brightest section of twinkling fairy lights, and . . . well, what? What am I meant to do now?

Think slimming thoughts?

Am I supposed to be *imagining* that the revolting algae is melting away all my cellulite and fatty deposits (which I think was just Betsy's polite way of saying *flabby bits*, by the way)? Or am I just meant to sit here in the gently swirling steam, ignore the overwhelming pong and try to relax?

Or . . .

No. I said I wasn't going to read Dad's article in *InStyle*, and I meant it.

So I'm not quite sure what it is that possesses me to get up, head towards my bag hanging on the peg, reach into it for the magazine, and open it to page 123.

But look, Dad won't *know* that I've read it. He won't become any *more* insufferably self-important and narcissistic just because I've taken a quick glance in the direction of his wretched article, in the total privacy of this steam room. It's not as if I have to text him saying: Great piece in *InStyle*, Dad, and congrats on publication! Much love from your only daughter (that's Libby, by the way) xxx

I'll only speed-read it, anyway. Skim and get the general gist. Besides, I've got to be quick, as the steam is building up again in here and in a few more minutes I won't be able to see my hand in front of my face.

I skip over the magazine's own bold-type intro, and plough straight into Dad's still-familiar prose.

Icons; goddesses; legends of the silver screen: the leading ladies of 1950s Hollywood were all of these and more. What Kansas housewife didn't shed a tear when Judy Garland yearned for home in *The Wizard of Oz*? What impressionable youth didn't fall in love with Marilyn Monroe when she confessed her lust for saxophone players in *Some Like It Hot*? And was there a mousy schoolgirl in the entire world who didn't dream of donning a Chanel suit, tucking a little dog under one arm and letting William Holden sweep them off their feet, the way Audrey Hepburn did in *Sabrina*?

OK, well this is absolutely bloody typical.

Not just the pompous style (is there anyone on the entire planet, I ask, who enjoys a rhetorical question more than my father?), or the patronizing cliché (*Kansas housewife . . . mousy schoolgirl . . .*), but the careless *mistakes*. It was a Givenchy suit, for fuck's sake! Not Chanel! You don't need to have spent the last few nights hanging out with an imaginary Audrey in order to know that.

But behind the glitz and glamour, the private lives of Hollywood's élite were all too often messy at best, catastrophic at worst.

Right, so it looks as if Dad's book is going to be a rip-roaring best-seller, then, attracting, as I'm sure it will, the attentions of the *only person on the entire planet* who doesn't know about Judy Garland's alcoholism, Marilyn Monroe's overdose, or Audrey Hepburn's failed marriages . . .

Wait a minute.

That picture.

It's in the centre of a montage on the second page of the double-page spread, right in between a black-and-white shot of Marilyn Monroe in a headscarf, picnicking on a beach, and a colour pic of Jayne Mansfield between takes, lolling on a bed smoking a cigarette.

It's Audrey Hepburn, sitting on my Chesterfield sofa.

Or at least, a sofa identical to my Chesterfield. The same apricot-coloured roses. The same overstuffed side cushions. The same . . . hang on, the steam is getting too thick to be absolutely certain, but for a moment there I'm fairly certain I saw a deep, doggy-claw scratch on the wooden part of the right-hand arm . . .

The caption — at least what I can read of it (the print is tiny and the steam is making it almost impossible) — says *Audrey Hepburn something before her something test for Roman something at something Studios.*

262

Pinewood.

Is that last word, obscured by the steam, Pinewood?

Because if it's true — if I'm filling in the blanks correctly, and if Dad hasn't made another fairly important factual error — then the caption is telling me that this is a photo of Audrey Hepburn before her screen test for *Roman Holiday* at Pinewood Studios.

Pinewood, where I got the Chesterfield sofa.

I don't know what this means.

As I think I've already said, I don't believe in ghosts. At least, I *didn't*, until about fifteen seconds ago. And I've certainly never believed that furniture could be . . . haunted?

Right: I need to get another, proper look at this photograph, and I'm not going to be able to do it in this pea-souper. I'll grab a towel and nip out into the corridor for a moment so I can do it out there, where it's light and steam-free.

With shaking hands, I grab one of the white towels from the big pile by the door, wrap it around me, open the door — it takes a surprisingly hefty shove — and step out . . .

. . . Onto Baker Street.

I blink, very very hard, to clear my eyes of any steam-related wateriness — or specks of stinky algae? — that might be blurring my vision.

But when I open my eyes again, I'm still on Baker Street.

Standing on the pavement next to a traffic jam of double-decker buses, a set of temporary lights where some workmen are digging up the road, and a crocodile of extremely startled-looking tourists making their way up the street to visit the Sherlock Holmes Museum at 221b, three blocks north of here.

OK, I'm not quite sure how this has happened.

Though I suspect it may have something to do with the deafening ringing sound that has just struck up behind me. It's FitLondon's fire alarm going off, if I'm not very much mistaken, and must mean that there was a second door in the steam room. A fire-escape door, to be precise, leading out of the building onto the street.

The street on which I'm now standing in nothing more than a patchy layer of smelly algae, my scratchy paper thong, an incongruously glamorous pearl necklace and an extremely small towel.

OK, I need to get off the street, and back inside, before anybody other than the startled tourists notices me. Those workmen, for example, who aren't likely to be anywhere near as polite.

I turn back towards the door I've just come out of . . . Shit. Of course. It's a fire escape. It has slammed shut behind me.

All right, there's no need to panic. I can just go in the main entrance, can't I?

Well, no, as it happens, I can't. Because the main entrance doors have just been flung open by none other than Pippa, the receptionist who took so violently against me the other morning.

She's herding large numbers of FitLondon gym members out through the doors, like a bossy teacher herding six-year-olds.

"This is not a fire drill!" she's shouting. "Please leave the building quickly and calmly, and do not return to fetch your personal possessions . . . I repeat, *this is not a fire drill*."

Given that, as far as any of the gym-bods know, they're fleeing for their lives from a terrifying inferno, you wouldn't think they'd be wasting quite so much time staring at me. Which is, embarrassingly, exactly what they're doing right now.

"Hi," I say nonchalantly to a pair of gawping women as they pass me by, freshly dripping in sweat from their interrupted workouts. "Chilly this afternoon," I add, for want of anything better to say, and because it feels important, under the circumstances, to be British about this and talk about the weather.

They continue to stare at me.

I suppose it's *possible* they're only interested in me because I've got a nasty black eye . . .

Nope. It's almost certainly the tiny-towel thing.

"Though I suppose," I go on, "we're lucky that it doesn't look like rain."

Neither of them says a word.

"Still, they're saying it's due to get warmer again," I continue, a bit desperately, "at the beginning of next week. Spells of pleasant sunshine . . . feeling fresh in the breeze . . ."

"Sorry, do you, like, *present* the weather, or something?" one of them asks.

"No, no, I just . . . take an interest . . ."

I'm interrupted by a tap on the shoulder from — I see when I turn round — Pippa the receptionist.

"*You,*" she says.

I clear my throat. "Is there some sort of problem?"

"Is *this* you?"

"Is what me?"

"The alarm. Did you go out of one of the emergency exits, or something?"

"No, no —"

"Then why were you the first one out? These people," she gestures around at the sweaty hordes continuing to emerge from the doors, "were all in the spinning class closest to the main exit. Were *you?*"

Given that I'm neither a member nor wearing anything that could remotely be described as spinning-appropriate, I don't think it's worth fibbing any more.

"In my defence," I begin, "it's a really, *really* bad idea to put an emergency exit in a room that gets so steamy you can't even see your —"

Pippa rolls her eyes. "Well, congratulations. You've just ruined a hundred and eighty-nine people's morning workouts, and seventy-four people's relaxing spa treatments."

"Look, I'm obviously really sorry, but now that you know there's no actual fire, can't you just get someone to turn off the fire alarm and then we can all go back inside? And — you know — put on a few more clothes?"

"No, as a matter of fact, I can't just *get someone to turn off the fire alarm.* The firemen will do that, when they get here."

"There'll be firemen coming?" I stare at her, appalled. "But surely they have *real* emergencies to attend to!"

266

"Maybe you should have thought of that," she snaps, "before you played your hilarious little joke with the fire-escape door. I'm going to call my manager," she adds, snatching a phone from her trouser pocket, "and see what he can do."

She's only just walked away when I feel a tap on my shoulder.

When I turn round, it's one of the two gawping women I was blithering at about the weather.

"Uh, I don't know if you realize," she says, in an abrupt though not unkind manner, "but your towel's tucked into your thong."

"And you're sort of dripping brown stuff all down your legs," her friend says. "It looks a bit . . . well, like you've had . . . *an accident.*"

"And is that a friend of yours filming you on her camera-phone over there?" the first woman goes on. "Because if it isn't, you might want to ask her to stop."

These are three brand-new pieces of information — that my bum is on display to the entirety of Baker Street; that slodgy brown algae is trickling from the direction of said bum; and that someone is filming the resulting sight on their camera-phone. I barely have time to digest them before Cass, a whirlwind of blonde hair extensions, seems to appear out of nowhere to fling a waffle robe around me.

"And piss off, you!" she yells in the direction of the person filming me with their camera-phone . . .

. . . who, I now see, in all her tiny yoga-wear finery, is none other than Rhea Haverstock-Harley.

"Libby isn't it?" Rhea asks, with an evilly-sweet smile, lowering the phone and giving me a little wave. "Very nice to see . . . well, so *much* of you."

Cass is bundling me along the pavement, away from Rhea and all the crowds, before I can say anything in reply.

Not that I have the faintest clue *what* I'd have said in reply. Indeed, it's perfectly possible that the shock has rendered me mute for all eternity.

"Stupid cow," Cass spits, only to flash a huge smile, moments later, at the lorry-load of scaffolders who are driving past us on Baker Street, honking a horn and cheering.

It takes me a moment to realize that the reason for this — more than just the usual interest Cass gets from lorry-loads of scaffolders — is that the waffle robe she wrapped around me is the one she must have been wearing when she exited the gym. All she's wearing right now is her sexy red swimsuit which — thank the Lord — is doing more than anything else could to finally take all the attention off me.

I'm opening my mouth to croak out a thank you when the fire alarm, mercifully, stops.

It's a bit like that moment when a plane lands: the air hostesses tell people not to use their phones until they've actually stopped the engines, and everyone ignores this and starts up their phones in a frenzied free-for-all. Despite Pippa yelling at everyone *not to return to the building* until the all-clear is given, the entire membership of FitLondon heads for the entrance doors all at once, desperate to return to their interrupted workouts and disrupted spa treatments before any of them gains so much as a millimetre of fat or develops a stray wrinkle.

"God, she's a bitch," Cass says, as we watch Rhea, at the front of the crowd, elbowing a heavily pregnant woman out of the way to get through the entrance first. "She has amazing hair, though. Do you think I could ask her where she gets her extensions done?"

I'm still too speechless to say anything. So I simply reach both my arms around Cass's bare shoulders, and hug her tightly to me.

"Get off," she says, though not unkindly, as she bats me away. "You'll mess up my hair."

I do as she asks, even though I know it's not really about her hair. The thing is that for all her love of the spotlight, the last thing Cass wants, when she's done something like this, is any acknowledgement. It's exactly the same as the night of my sixteenth birthday, when the entire day had come and gone without Dad bothering to call (a new low in a long list of birthday-related failings, even for him). I was silently crying beneath my duvet when I heard my bedroom door open and shut, and a moment later felt Cass creep into bed beside me. She didn't utter a single word, just stroked my hair until I fell asleep, and then, at some point, crept back to her bedroom again. She shut me up when I tried to mention it over breakfast the following morning, and neither of us has ever mentioned it since.

I expect neither of us will ever mention this horrific bum-on-show moment ever again either: from my point of view because I just want to pretend it *never ever happened*, and from Cass's point of view because she's already blowing kisses to the gaggle of workmen digging up the pavement on the other side of the road, and has moved on already.

In fact, she's enjoying all the attention so much that it's a good couple of minutes before — thank God — the chill in the air finally gets to her and she reluctantly agrees to be dragged back indoors.

"Where's Mum?" I ask, just about managing to speak in a normal voice again, as we head towards the spa entrance. Because I've only just realized that she didn't emerge in the exodus the way all the other guests did.

"Oh, she's probably still in the juice bar. She refused to leave. She said she'd rather be burned alive than pay your dad half the money from the house, anyway."

Absurd, narcissistic, vexing beyond belief this may be, but it suddenly fills me with a rush of affection for my mother. Coupled with one of Cass's rare but beautiful moments of sisterliness, it's all a little bit overwhelming.

I'll forget, for now at least, that I only came out here in the first place to get that closer look at the picture in Dad's article. Investigating my (possibly) haunted sofa from (possibly) Pinewood Studios is going to have to wait.

I tuck the now-somewhat-muddied *InStyle* under one arm, and hold the spa door open for Cass.

"Let's go out for a late lunch after your treatment," I suggest. "You, me and Mum. Cheer her up for her birthday."

"Well, OK ..." Cass is already squeezing a nonexistent roll of fat on her swimsuit-clad tummy.

"But nowhere with chips. And you can't let me have any bread. Or dessert. Or booze. *Especially* not champagne, because it bloats me . . ."

She's still listing the long catalogue of pre-audition contraband as we make our way back towards the juice bar to find the birthday girl.

CHAPTER
THIRTEEN

Again, just when you might actually *want* a visit from Audrey Hepburn, ghostly or otherwise, she won't make an appearance.

I made several efforts to "summon" her, if that's what you'd call it, when I got back from our post-spa lunch yesterday evening, and a couple more attempts this morning, but nothing. *Niente. Nada.* Zip. So I haven't managed to discuss the whole haunted-Chesterfield thing with her at all, which is seriously annoying. I mean, if anyone can make some sense of it, it ought to be her, the horse's mouth.

In the absence of the horse's mouth, though, I've decided to speak to another bit of the horse instead: Uncle Brian, the props-store security guard, who was responsible for the mix-up with the furnishings in the first place. After all, if there's anyone who should know about the history of all that stuff in the props store, it'll be him, surely. He's worked here for donkey's years, and when I met him, briefly, the day I went with Olly to pick out my furniture, he seemed a sensible, twinkly-eyed, avuncular old chap. I'm not going to go and ask him straight out if he's ever seen ghosts in his warehouse, obviously, but I'm hoping that he might say something that will make a bit more sense of this whole crazy situation. So I texted Olly late last night to ask if he could meet me at Pinewood this morning, because I really need him for moral support. Just in case everything tumbles out all wrong, and I start sounding like a rambling lunatic, Olly will have my back.

I've made it to Pinewood earlier than our agreed meeting time, though — it's still only eight a.m., and Olly isn't due to meet me outside the main gates until half past — and the young, bored-looking guy on duty at the security cabin this morning must recognize me, because I've only been loitering outside for about fifteen seconds before he glances up from his newspaper and waves me through.

I make my way through the gates and towards (yes, it really is called this) Goldfinger Avenue, where the props store is to be found. I might as well head straight there, and text Olly to let him know where I am. After all, maybe it would actually be a good idea to try to have a quiet word with Uncle Brian about all this stuff alone, before Olly arrives. Because there's a chance, isn't there, that Uncle Brian might know *exactly* what I'm talking about? That when I start gibbering about haunted sofas he'll simply nod sagely, pop on the kettle in his little prefab office and — over a cosy cuppa or two — reassure me that I'm by no means the first person to come to him with a tale of this sort; that he himself has long suspected that the spirit of Alec Guinness inhabits a velvet-upholstered ottoman right at the very back of his warehouse.

It's a bit of a hike, past rows and rows of post-production suites and an entire building's worth of workshops, but eventually I reach the huge corrugated-steel warehouse halfway along Goldfinger Avenue. The door to the little prefab office is ajar, so I wander up and peer round the door . . . but there's nobody here. There is evidence of recent Uncle-Brian-esque activity — a half-drunk cup of tea placed on top of a folded copy of today's *Mirror* — but no sign of the man himself.

"Oi! Gorgeous!"

When I turn round, I see that the person who's just shouted this at me is none other than Dillon O'Hara.

He must have clambered out of the black Lexus that's just pulled up alongside the pavement — one of the fleet of black Lexuses that are used to ferry star actors in and out of Pinewood, while the rest of us schlep here by bus from Gerrard's Cross station — and he's walking towards me.

He's wearing Ray-Bans similar to the ones I borrowed from his bedside table the other morning, jeans and T-shirt, and a sort of chunky cardigan with a belted waist that ought to make him look, ludicrously, as if he's raided his granny's wardrobe, but in fact just makes him look sexier, in a louche sort of way, than ever.

"Well, you're a sight for sore eyes this morning," he says as he reaches me, taking off his Ray-Bans. His own eyes look fresher and brighter than I've seen them before, as if he's had a decent night's sleep with no boozing for once. "And talking of sore eyes . . ." He lifts a hand to touch my left eye which — thanks to the magic of about eight layers of concealer — is actually looking a lot better this morning. "Looks like all that ice did the trick. Either that, or my amazing healing hands."

"What . . . what are you doing here?"

"Well, I'm on my way to work, my darling. I'm needed on set at nine sharp this morning. Due in make-up at eight fifteen, a full morning's shooting ahead of me. And people say acting's not a real job."

He stops, clearly working out, from the stony expression on my face, that I'm not in the mood for his particular brand of banter just now.

"I was just on my way in," he goes on, "when I saw you snooping into this office here, so I asked my very nice driver Steve to stop and let me out."

"I'm not snooping," I say, in a frosty tone I'm actually quite proud of. "I'm just here to meet my friend Olly."

"An early morning assignation with another man?" Dillon says, sliding his arms over my shoulders and walking me backwards, gently, through the door and into the privacy of Brian's little office. "Careful, Fire Girl. You'll make me jealous."

I stare up at him. "Are you kidding me?"

"That I can get jealous? You misunderstand me, Libby. I'm a very jealous kind of person. Yes, it may appear that no other man on the planet can hold a candle to me, but I still have my —"

"That's not what I meant." And, by the way, he obviously *hasn't* worked out that I'm not in the mood for his banter right now. "You've just popped back up and started . . . flirting again."

"And you were hoping for what, exactly?" He looks, for a moment, genuinely confused. "Instead of the flirting, I mean? Because I have to warn you, Libby, that if you're looking for a man with a more serious conversational style, we'll have to take someone like Stephen Hawking with us on our next date. He can satisfy your burning need for in-depth discussion on string theory and quantum mechanics, and I can get the beers in and fill in the awkward silences with dirty jokes. And, if I play my cards right, satisfy a few of your other burning needs after Hawking's trundled off home for the night —"

"Just stop it!" I pull his hands off my shoulders and shove them back towards him. "Seriously Dillon, stop. It's unfair. Actually, you know what, it's cruel. Talking like that. As if you . . . *want* me."

He blinks, more confused than ever; either he's a significantly better actor than his recent TV performances would suggest, or he really has no idea what I'm talking about.

"But I *do* want you. I mean, I'm slightly afraid to say it in case I'm accused of inappropriate flirting again. But I really like you, Libby Lomax."

I actually laugh out loud. "Right. Then I dread to think how you treat people you *don't* like."

He raises a quizzical eyebrow.

"Well, I'm just wondering if you always walk out on people you like the morning after they spend the night with you, without so much as a goodbye. Or a note. Or a phone call, or a text . . ."

I'm starting to sound, I realize to my horror, quite a lot like Mum did yesterday, trying to get me to do her dirty work with Dad. But luckily Dillon interrupts me before I can say any more.

"Christ, I'm a fucking imbecile. I should've known that's what you're upset about."

"I'm not upset!" I say. Which would be more convincing if I didn't sound so, well, upset. "It would just have been, you know, common courtesy. That's all. A one-line note: *Morning, Libby, mugs and tea in the cupboard above the sink and help yourself to toast if you're hungry.*"

"Libby . . ."

"Other than that, I wasn't bothered in the slightest! I mean, obviously you're a free agent, and you're perfectly entitled to go off and sow your wild oats —"

"Woah, woah, woah." He holds up both hands. "Since when do you have me sowing wild oats with anyone else?"

I give him a meaningful look.

"Since I was with you the other night, that is," he adds, with frank (and I suppose sort-of-refreshing) honesty. "OK, look, I don't deny for a minute that I should have left you a note. And if I'm guilty of anything, it's just plain old bad manners. But I promise you, Libby, on my mother's life: there hasn't been any oats-sowing. I left in a hurry in the morning because I had an audition."

"An audition," I repeat, flatly, "at six thirty in the morning?"

"No. At two o'clock in the afternoon. In New York. I just got back last night."

I stare at him.

I'm torn, right now, between two incompatible responses: 1) to snort loudly and derisively, and tell him that I didn't just fall down in the last rain-shower; or 2) to tumble into his arms, weak with relief and sorry I ever doubted him, and suggest nipping through the internal door to the warehouse itself to make up properly on one of Uncle Brian's (non-haunted, preferably non-doggy-smelling) sofas.

"I didn't remember to tell you before we went to sleep," Dillon continues. "And you were so obviously knackered — because you slept right through my alarm, by the way — that I didn't want to wake you."

Despite my vacillations, I must be giving him a pretty suspicious, didn't-fall-down-in-the-last-rain-shower look, because he starts to fumble in his jeans pocket, producing a crumpled piece of A4, which he holds out to me.

It is, indeed, a printed-out plane ticket, in his name, for a Virgin Atlantic flight to JFK at eight-forty-five am the day before yesterday.

"Libby look, if you still don't believe me, I can show you the stamp on my passport . . ."

"No, no, God, no, there's no need for that!" I say, hastily, because he's suddenly made me feel like I'm some harpy of a wife complaining about being stuck at home with our brood of kids while he goes off gallivanting. "I believe you, Dillon. Honestly."

"That's sweet. And rare." His face softens, and he puts one hand to my cheek. "Girls don't usually believe a single word that comes out of my mouth."

I'm tempted to suggest that it would help if he cut back on some of the smart-arse witticisms and cut *out* all the indiscriminate flirting, but I don't.

"And by the way," he adds, little-boy-excited about this now, "it was the best audition I've done in months! And for a part in Martin Scorsese's next movie, would you credit it? Not a massive part — I'd get bumped off halfway through by Ciarán Hinds — but it's what my agent Caroline calls a *pivotal* one. And who the fuck cares how big a part it is — it's a *Martin Scorsese movie*, for Christ's sake!"

"That's fantastic, Dillon," I say, and really mean it.

"Well, it's the first time a movie audition has actually gone my way. With pretty fucking perfect timing, I have to say, because it'd be gutting if I'd blown this one. And you know who I have to thank?"

It sounds like the start of an awards-ceremony acceptance speech. "Er . . . your agent? Your high-school drama teacher?"

He looks at me. "You," he says.

I laugh again. Even louder, this time.

"I'm serious," he says. He puts both hands back on my shoulders, rests one thumb on either side of my neck, and caresses, ever so slightly. "I thought all about it on the plane, on the way home. I mean, look, I've been going on movie auditions for the last six months, and they've all been unmitigated disasters."

"I'm sure they weren't that bad."

"One casting director told my agent I was so wooden she wouldn't even cast me in a kindergarten Nativity play."

"Ah."

"As the stable door."

"Well, OK, that does sound quite bad, actually."

"And now here I am auditioning for the biggest break of my career, exactly the sort of thing I'd usually screw up at the last minute, and . . . well, something *happened* to me in that audition room, Libby. I'm not saying I suddenly turned into Daniel Day-Lewis, or anything. I just felt . . . I don't know . . . actually *good* about myself for once."

"For once?" I ask, not even bothering to keep the scepticism from my voice.

"Hey, come on, just because I'm handsome and charming and successful, not to mention frighteningly gifted in the bedroom department, it doesn't mean I sit around all day feeling like I can walk on water." His tone is odd; it's more of his unstoppable banter, yes, but it's suddenly got a serious edge. More than serious: bitter, in fact. "But after that night with you . . . that *incredible* night with you . . ." he adds, more gently, "I woke up feeling like maybe I could."

This is, by quite some distance, the most amazing thing anyone has ever said to me.

Though, to be fair, he's probably never spent the night before with anyone who was *quite* as enthusiastic as I was. You could be the most insecurity-riddled man on the entire planet, and you'd probably have walked away from that super-king-size bed feeling not only as if you could walk on water, but also, for your next trick, heal the lame, cure the lepers and turn water into wine.

After Rhea, and her particular brand of bitchy indifference . . . after the sort of girls he's become accustomed to . . . well, is he only attracted to me because I make him feel like more than just a pretty face?

I think, perhaps, that's a question best examined when he's *not* standing two inches away from me, his hand gently caressing my cheek and his eyes fixed onto mine as if I possess knowledge of the inner workings of the entire universe.

"You know what I've decided, Fire Girl?" he murmurs. "I've decided that you must be my lucky charm."

Completely carried away by the moment, I murmur, in a sexy throaty voice, "You mean sort of like a leprechaun?"

No. *No!* That wasn't sexy. And it wasn't even what I meant to say. In my head I was going to say something about getting lucky, or being charming . . . I'm not sure, now, exactly what, but certainly I wasn't intending to make a link in Dillon's mind between me and a small elfin man dressed in green with a jaunty hat.

It's obviously not what he was expecting either, because he pulls backwards for a moment, gives me a funny look, and says, "Yes, Libby. That's exactly how I think of you. Because obviously nothing turns me on like a nice jaunty leprechaun."

I open my mouth to say something that will save the moment, but I don't have time to utter another word before he places his lips gently onto mine and starts to kiss me.

Mmmmmmmmmmmmmm.

"Will you come over to mine again tonight?" he breathes, in between kisses. "I'll cook. Well, I can't cook, but I'll order in. And I'll open us up a lovely bottle of wine . . . run us a bath . . ."

It's literally the perfect evening, isn't it?

So I'm not sure what makes me say, instead of *yes, yes, a thousand times, yes,* "Dillon, look, I don't know . . ."

"Please. I want to make it up to you."

"That's nice." As is, by the way, the sensation of his hand sliding around my waist, underneath my hopefully-chic-but-possibly-mime-student sweater, to playfully walk his fingers up and down the small of my back. "But I'm just not sure if . . ."

"Is it because of this . . . what was his name? Olly?"

Dillon's fingers have stopped walking.

I blink at him, confused by the question.

"Is he the reason you don't want to spend the night with me?"

I would laugh long and loud at this, if he weren't looking deadly serious.

Christ, he was right about the jealousy thing, wasn't he?

But before I can explain that Olly is basically like my older brother, that there's no earthly reason to be jealous, and that I'm only here meeting him so early in the morning because I need to get answers about my haunted sofa (actually, it might be best not to bring that last one up at all), Dillon has leaned down and started to nuzzle my neck with soft butterfly kisses.

"God, you're killing me here, Libby Lomax," he groans, between kisses.

I'm not sure I've ever been more turned on in my life.

And it must be working for him, too, because he's suddenly moved his lips onto my lips and is kissing me urgently as he presses me backwards against the wall, just like he pressed me up against the retro fridge-freezer in his apartment before all those pool-table shenanigans kicked off the other night.

Except that it isn't the wall, because walls — unless they're made of plasterboard and put up by Bogdan Son of Bogdan — don't give way when you press against them.

Doors, on the other hand, do. Because it isn't a wall that I'm up against, it's the internal door through to the warehouse.

I'm not having much luck with doors these days, am I?

Dillon, possibly because he's a gentleman (or, equally likely, because this sort of thing has happened to him before) somehow twists himself around as we fall through the door so that he ends up toppling backwards, and beneath me, instead of forwards and on top of me. Which means I get a reasonably soft landing instead of being flattened by six foot of solid muscle;

it's extremely considerate of him and — if it were possible — just makes me fancy him all the more.

"Jesus! Are you all right?"

This isn't coming from Dillon, though, who's quite probably too winded by my weight to say anything at all. It's coming from someone standing amongst the heaps of furniture, just a few feet away.

When I look up from my prone position atop Dillon's chest, I can see straight away that it's Olly.

I scramble off Dillon, doing up shirt buttons as I do so that I had no idea he had managed to undo.

"We weren't doing anything!" Nightmarish visions of Le Creuset-wielding mayhem are filling my head; Olly doesn't walk around with small versions of the pans in his pocket, does he? "I mean, we weren't *about to* do anything . . ."

"Speak for yourself," Dillon says. He's hauling himself to his feet, a little bit the worse for wear, but — thank God — not squashed like Flat Stanley, and still able to stand. "Hey aren't you the guy from the location catering truck? The one with the excellent bacon sandwiches?"

"Yes," Olly says, brusquely. (Brusque is OK, though. Brusque is better than what I was expecting.) "Are you OK, though, Libby? That was quite a fall."

"I'm fine." I'm trying to give him meaningful *God I'm so sorry about this* looks, but he's not meeting my eye. "I meant to text you, actually, Olly, to say I'd meet you here instead of at the gates, but . . ."

"Ohhhhhh," says Dillon. "*You're* Olly."

Oh, shit.

Dillon's eyebrows have arched, dangerously, and he's suddenly wearing a smile that isn't reaching his eyes. In fact, all he needs is an evening's worth of vodkas in him, and he'd look exactly the way he did at Depot the other night, right before he started trying to pick a fight with Cass's horrible married boyfriend.

"Actually, Olly must be pretty busy right now." I try another of those meaningful looks in Olly's direction, but he's still not looking at me, so I take Dillon's hand and try to pull him in the direction of the door we've just tumbled through. "We'll leave you to it for a bit . . ."

"Busy?" Dillon isn't budging one inch. "Isn't the props warehouse a pretty weird place for the catering guy to be hanging out?"

"Olly takes old furniture from here when nobody else wants it," I gabble at Dillon, before realizing that this makes Olly sound like a weird rag-and-bone man. "I mean, to help out his mum and her amateur dramatic society in Watford . . ."

"Woking."

"Woking, of course, sorry . . ."

"Does he now?" Dillon nods, sagely. "Then the amateur dramatists of Berkshire are very lucky to have him."

"Woking isn't in Berkshire," says Olly. "It's in Surrey."

"Ah, well, you'd know better than me, Olly old chap. I can't say I've ever had the pleasure of making my way down one of your finest English motorways to visit."

"I don't take the motorway." Olly's eyes are fixed on Dillon's. "I take the A3."

"Really? Wouldn't it be faster to take the M4 and the M25?"

"Out to junction 10?" Olly snorts. "Past the turn-off for Heathrow? I'll remember your advice the next time I'm stuck in gridlock on the M25, going nowhere."

"Hey, if you're going nowhere, it might not be anything to do with the traffic on the M25 . . ."

Right, I have to stop this . . . this . . . well, this slightly bizarre squaring-up to each other about over-populated motorway junctions.

Dillon is looking ready to start swinging punches and Olly looks as if he's prepared to risk a broken jaw to defend his staunch position on the optimal route to Woking.

Which is bizarre, because I wouldn't have thought that Olly (that anyone, come to think of it) could possibly get this worked up about the optimal route to Woking. The right sort of onion marmalade to serve with a tangy Irish Cheddar, yes. The merits of good old English Stilton over poncy French Roquefort, quite likely. Transport options to medium-sized commuter towns, no. I know he might be nursing some lingering anger towards Dillon for leaving me alone in his flat after our one-night stand, but I wouldn't have thought he could get *this* pissed off about it.

Anyway, all I know is that, Olly being my oldest friend and Dillon being my . . . well, whatever the hell he is, it feels like it's my responsibility to end this peculiar disagreement between them before there *are* any punches swung or jaws broken.

"Do you know, I think I just heard someone in the office!" I fib. "Must be Brian!"

"He's gone to get his breakfast fry-up in the canteen," Olly says, darkly. "He'll be ages."

"No, no, I'm almost sure I heard him. And it was lovely catching up with you, Olly but I'm sure you've got to be getting on with picking stuff up for the Woking Players . . ."

"That's not what I was doing, actually." Olly's eyes swivel off Dillon's to meet mine, for the first time since I fell through the door, *in flagrante* with Dillon, and landed at his feet. "I assumed we were meeting here to find you a replacement sofa, so I got here early to start moving stuff out of the way for you to get a proper look."

"Oh, Olly, that's really nice of you. But actually, I don't want to get rid of the Chesterfield."

"Really? But it's such a monstrosity, taking up most of your flat . . ."

"I don't think Libby needs your advice on what to do with her flat —" Dillon begins, only to be interrupted by Olly.

"Yeah, well, I'm just trying to be a good friend and cheer her up a bit," he says, in an oddly hard tone of voice I've never heard him use before. "Look after her. Something you've spectacularly failed to do, thanks to all that Twitter crap."

"Oh, yeah." Dillon pulls a face, distracted from needling Olly for a moment. "Sorry darling, I do feel a bit responsible for that. You're all right about it, though, aren't you?"

"All right about what?" This is sounding — and I'm sure you'll forgive my paranoia — ever so slightly ominous. "What Twitter crap?"

Olly blinks at me. "You haven't seen it?"

"Haven't seen *what?*"

"Honestly, Libby, I wouldn't worry too much about it," Dillon says, slipping an arm round my shoulders and giving a comforting squeeze. "I'm sorry, though. I mean, Rhea only took that video in the first place to get back at you. Because of me, that is."

At the mention of Rhea's video, I suddenly feel a horrible, icy feeling in the pit of my stomach.

"She . . . posted it on *Twitter?*"

"Rhea? Yeah. I'm really sorry, darling. Obviously she's just got it in for you because she knows we slept together the other night. Well, she knows we left the party together, so I'm assuming she's put two and two together and worked out that . . ." Dillon's phone buzzes with a text; he reaches into his pocket, glances at it and pulls a face. "Ah, shit. I really do need to get a move on. They're waiting for me in make-up. But listen, Libby, why don't I call you later, and we'll fix up a plan for this evening?"

I just stare at him, mutely.

How can I possibly go and enjoy a night of wine/bath/debauchery with Dillon when I know that . . . *that* video of me is splashed all over the internet?

"OK, OK . . . well, I'll call you anyway." Dillon leans down and plants a soft, more-than-just-a-little-proprietorial kiss on my lips, before sticking a hand out towards Olly. "Good to meet you, mate," he says, in a tone that suggests precisely the opposite. "I'm sure I'll see you around."

Olly just grunts some sort of vaguely affirmative noise, and Dillon turns and leaves the props store via the door we just fell through, out towards Steve the driver in the waiting Lexus.

And as soon as he's gone, I'm diving for my bag, which fell off my shoulder when we tumbled through the door. But Olly, quicker than I'd have thought, gets to it first and snatches it from my grip before I can reach into it for my phone.

"I know you want to look at Twitter, Libby. But I don't think that's a very good idea."

This is exactly what police officers say to people in detective dramas when they don't want them to go into the morgue and see their horribly mangled loved one.

"Oh, God. Is it that bad?"

"It's . . . OK, I'll be honest, it's not great . . ."

"I need to see it."

"Libby, love, again, I really don't think —"

"Olly, please. Give me my phone."

I hold out my hand and, with a sigh, he puts my handbag into it.

It only takes me a few seconds, after fishing out my phone, to find Rhea's Twitter page. Her most recent tweet, at 16.06 yesterday, is simply the words check out this hilarious vid of my new pal Libby Lomax, guys, a little row of laughing faces like this — ☺ ☺ ☺ — and a link to her Instagram site.

I click on the link and steel myself as the video begins to play.

It's worse, if anything, than I could possibly have imagined.

The opening five or six seconds is an unflattering establishing shot of me in my tiny towel, gesticulating rather wildly at the bad-tempered receptionist, before Rhea and her camera-phone sidle round for my rear view. Which is when things get really unflattering. Because yep, just as those two women warned me, my towel is tucked up inside the back of the paper thong, exposing my rounded, dimpled, and not-remotely-pert bottom for all the world to see. And as I stare at this in horror, the worst happens: a trail of brown sludge d-r-i-p-s, slowly from the region of my rounded, dimpled, and not-remotely pert bottom, and runs in a stream down the back of my thigh.

But for maximum Twitter amusement, perhaps the most memorable moment of all is when, immediately after the two women in the video have clearly told me what's going on in the bottom department, I spin round to face the camera with a look of utter horror on my face. It freezes here, a split second before Cass would have appeared and flung her robe around me.

Then the screen fades to black.

I sit down, heavily, on the nearest piece of furniture, which luckily happens to be a sturdy velvet-upholstered ottoman. (Even more luckily, no spectral figure comes bursting out of it, like a genie from a lamp, as I do so.)

"I did tell you," Olly says, gently "not to look."

"How many people have seen it?" I swallow, hard.

"Well, I mean, obviously this Rhea herself seems to have . . ." He takes my phone from my lifeless hand and directs it back to Rhea's Twitter page. "Er, six hundred thousand followers . . ."

"Oh, my God." I hide my face in my hands before peering out at him between two fingers. Now I'm the one who can barely meet his eye, because the mere thought that Olly has seen so very much of my bum is just too horrendous to process right now. "Are you one of them?"

"One of who?"

"Her followers. How did you see the video in the first place?"

"Oh, um, that's because it was re-tweeted by someone else I follow."

"Who?"

"You don't need to know that . . ."

"*Who?*"

"Just a footballer."

"A *famous* footballer?"

"*Well known*, really, is all I'd —"

"With how many Twitter followers?"

Olly pulls a reluctant face. "A couple of million," he admits. "Ish."

"I see." I take what's meant to be a deep, calming breath, but which actually just makes me feel light-headed and slightly sick. "So I've gone viral."

"No, no, not *viral*, as such . . ."

"It stands to reason, really. I mean, if your footballer re-tweets it to a few more of his followers, some of whom will no doubt have a couple of million followers themselves . . . not to mention all the other celebrities who follow Rhea and who'll be gaily tweeting it to *their* millions of followers, too . . . well, I'm no mathematician, but I think we can safely assume that *everybody on the entire planet* will have seen it by, what, three o'clock tomorrow afternoon?"

"Not everybody on the entire planet."

"Fair point. There will probably be a remote tribe in Papua New Guinea who can't watch it because they haven't got broadband yet."

"Come on, Lib. It isn't as bad as you think. I mean, if it helps at all, some people have been really quite complimentary about you. And have said really quite nice things about . . . er . . ." He's suddenly staring fixedly at my phone. ". . . About your bottom."

There's an *extremely* awkward silence.

"Well," I manage to say, "I suppose it's better than people saying *horrible* things about my bottom."

"That's the spirit!" Olly says, finally looking up from the phone. "And look! Someone commenting here has said you're really fit!"

"Really?" I take the phone and search the Twitter page for the comment. "It doesn't say *fit*," I say, a moment later, handing him back the phone. "It says *fat*."

"Oh. Well, don't pay any attention to that sort of thing, Libby. You're not fat. And these people are idiots. I wouldn't waste a single moment of my life worrying about them. Besides, none of this has made dearest Dillon think any less of you, has it?"

"Yes, but Dillon only likes me because he thinks I'm responsible for him maybe getting a Martin Scorsese movie. That I'm his lucky charm. Or something."

"It didn't look like that was what he liked about you when you fell through that doorway a few minutes ago," Olly says, lightly.

Given that we agreed never to speak of anything Dillon and sex-related, I don't understand why he's just brought it all up again.

And clearly Olly remembers this, albeit too late, because he suddenly says, "So! What was it you wanted to meet here for, then, Lib? If it wasn't about finding a different sofa, that is."

In all the highs and lows of the last few minutes, I'd completely forgotten that I'm meant to be asking Olly to help me bring up the subject of haunted furniture with Uncle Brian. That in fact, in order to do this, I need to bring up the subject of haunted furniture with Olly first, too.

If I wasn't feeling vulnerable enough about this prospect before Olly (and, let's face it, probably Uncle Brian too) saw my bum, dripping brown stuff, on Twitter, I certainly do now.

"I don't know. I mean, it's nothing. Let's forget about it for the time being."

"Really? Because your text made it sound pretty important. And Nora . . ." He clears his throat. "Well, she called me yesterday and told me she'd popped down to see you. That she was worried about you."

"Nora!" I yelp, which is pretty stupid, seeing as she's all the way up in Glasgow right now, and can't possibly hear me. "You two always told me you never talked about me to each other!"

"We don't. I swear, Libby we never mention you. Ever." He says this very emphatically. "She was just concerned. Asked me — no, actually, *told me* — to look after you a bit more."

"Oh, God, so she told you all about the multiple personality disorder thing?"

"Er — no." Olly's eyebrows shoot upwards. "Libby you don't have . . . multiple personality disorder. *Do* you?"

"No, I'm sure of that now. In fact, I wanted to ask you, Ol, whether or not you . . . well . . . do you believe in ghosts?" I suddenly blurt.

He doesn't say anything for a moment. He just stares at me.

"Bloody hell, Olly, it's only a *question* . . ."

"All right, all right. Ghosts. OK. You mean things that float around in a white sheet, with holes for the eyes?"

"That's a Halloween costume. I mean proper ghosts. Spectral beings. Dead people seeming to come back to life to, you know, hang out in your living room and stuff."

"Right. I see."

He doesn't, in fact, see. This much is clear from his bewildered, still-uneasy tone. Which is why I wasn't wild about telling him in the first place. Because if Olly, of all people, doesn't "see", then nobody else in my life is going to. I can be certain of that. Nobody is going to be Bruce Willis to my Haley Joel Osment. Well, until I talk about it with Audrey Hepburn herself, I suppose.

294

"For what it's worth, Lib, no, I don't believe in ghosts. At all"

"No," I say. "Neither did I."

"Look, if you're hearing noises in your flat, or something . . ."

"I'm not. It's fine. Everything's fine. Well, as fine as it can be, when the entire world and its mother is gathering around a water-cooler right now to mock me."

"Libby, it's not the entire world."

"Sorry, I keep forgetting about that tribe in Papua New Guinea."

"Not just them. Me."

I manage a wobbly smile.

"Besides, I hear Papua New Guinea is pretty spectacular. If you end up having to move there on a permanent basis, that is."

I love him for trying to cheer me up, but if he tries any harder I'm going to cry.

"I should get going," I say, "and let you go and get on with work. Aren't you on location today?"

"Yeah, but Jesse can handle it till I get there. If you want to hang on for a bit to speak to Uncle Brian about . . . what was it, exactly, you wanted to speak to him about?"

"A historical matter," I say, reaching for my bag and slinging it over my shoulder. "I'll do it another time."

"Well, can I give you a lift anywhere? I'm working all the way over in Wapping today, but I can drop you somewhere if it would help?" He jerks his head towards his van which, I can now see, is parked out behind the warehouse, beside the corrugated-iron doors. "We can talk more about this . . . ghost stuff, if you like, on the way?"

"I'd love a lift," I say, feeling wearier than ever, "please, Olly. But let's not talk about ghosts. In fact," and there's nobody else in the entire world, maybe not even Nora, I'd feel comfortable saying this to, "can we not talk about anything at all? I just feel like I need to switch everything off, right now."

And Olly nods, and doesn't say a word, but just slings a kindly arm around my shoulders as we walk towards his van together.

CHAPTER
FOURTEEN

From the waft of L'Interdit that greets me the moment the moment I open my front door, I know that Audrey has come back.

She's sitting on the Chesterfield — black cocktail dress and wide-brimmed hat, I note, another of her iconic looks from *Breakfast at Tiffany's* — and she's holding my iPad in one hand and an espresso cup in the other.

"Oh, darling," she says, in a stricken tone, as soon as she sees me. "I'm so terribly, terribly sorry."

I'm not exactly sure what it is she's terribly, terribly sorry about until she swivels the iPad towards me and I see that she's on Twitter.

"But mostly I'm just so *angry* on your behalf!" she adds, putting her espresso cup down, with a sharp clatter, on the floor beside the sofa. "This Rhea woman is quite obviously unhinged. Though, given her track record, you were lucky, darling, that she didn't pelt you with soft fruit into the bargain!"

I drop, wearily, into the cushion beside hers, pick up her espresso cup and drain what's left of the contents. All the questions I've had in my mind since yesterday, my plans to ask her if she really is a ghost, and if she really has — what? — *manifested* out of the ancient Chesterfield . . . I just don't feel like asking them right now. Even the blissful silence Olly treated me to, in his van on the way to the station just now, wasn't enough to re-energize me after the trials of the morning.

"The sheer vulgarity of invading your privacy like that! And for what? Simply because a man has turned his attentions to you instead of her?"

"Well, apparently the fact that she's richer than me, thinner than me and prettier than me isn't enough for her. She wants to destroy my life as well."

"This hasn't destroyed your life."

"You've never seen what happens," I tell her, "when a video like this goes viral."

"Viral?"

"All over the world. So that everybody sees it. So that people gather round someone's computer in the office to laugh at it. Here, and in America, and in Australia, and in France, and Germany . . . I'll be a laughing stock for the rest of my days."

"Darling, you won't be a laughing stock for the rest of your days. These things blow over. Today's gossip is tomorrow's chip paper. And I'm doing everything I can to help, by the way," she adds. "Fighting your corner as hard as I'm jolly well able."

"Fighting my corner?"

"On Twitter. Oh, Libby, if I thought Gmail was fun, its got nothing on Twitter! And so easy, once you get the hang of it. I've just created my own account — you see?"

Audrey pushes the iPad in my direction and points, excitedly at the top of the Twitter page she's on.

@LittleBlackDressAndPearls, I read.

"That's my user name," she explains, with a little wink. "Good, isn't it?"

"It is, actually."

"And I've got three hundred and fifty two followers already! In only two hours! Can you believe it? Unfortunately, several of them are rather unpleasant-sounding men who want to know if I'm wearing undergarments with my little black dress and pearls . . . but the majority of them seem awfully nice. And in complete agreement with my statements about you, by the way."

"What statements?" I grab the iPad from her, a sense of by-now-familiar dread rising in my gullet.

But actually, as I read Audrey's most recent tweets, they're not that bad.

@LibbyLomax is a dear, dear friend of mine and I can confidently say she's not at all overweight., she's written, rather lengthily, in reply to a tweet written by someone called @RheaHaverstockHarleysSparklyBikini. (I don't need to read the original tweet to work out that it probably wasn't all that complimentary about my appearance.) In fact, sir, I suggest you refrain from cas

Here she ran out of characters, and carried on in a second tweet:

asting such ungallant aspersions on an utterly lovely person, such as I know @LibbyLomax to be. The world would be a much better place if it

A third tweet:

had more fundamentally good and decent (and, again, not overweight in the slightest) people like @LibbyLomax in it. If you haven't anything

A fourth:

nice to say about her, please don't say anything at all. Her friends would be enormously grateful. Yours truly, @ LittleBlackDressAndPearls.

My eyes have filled with sudden tears.

"That was really nice of you, Audrey."

"Darling." She squeezes my hand. "You're welcome."

"But I don't have a Twitter account, by the way. Called 'At Libby Lomax' or anything else."

"Oh, but you do now! I started one for you!"

I gaze at her. "What on earth for?"

"Libby. It's the twenty-first century. Besides, you're an actress, aren't you? Don't you think you ought to have some sort of public profile?"

"Well, I've bloody got one now, haven't I, whether I like it or not?" I say, as much in reference to my brand-new unwanted Twitter account as to the fact that millions of people around the world are mocking me even as we speak. "Can't you just close it straight back down again?"

"But you were getting oodles of followers! Five or six hundred, the last time I looked."

"Yes, oodles of people like whatshisname . . . Rhea Haverstock-Harley's Knickers, or whatever he called himself . . . being vile about the way I look! Please, Audrey. Shut it down. I can't deal with any more of this right now."

300

"All right. If that's what you prefer. I'll sign back in as you and close it down." Audrey takes back my iPad. "Have you had a *really* dreadful morning, darling?"

"Yes. Well, no. I don't know. I mean, I saw Dillon again."

Her eyebrows arch beneath the brim of the huge hat. "The modelizer?"

"Mm. He only ditched me the other morning because he had an audition in New York — or so he claims — and now he's saying he wants to see me tonight . . ."

"Darling, you can't possibly!"

"I know, I know, he's frighteningly untrustworthy, and, well, I suppose I can't help suspecting he's got a bit of a substance abuse problem . . ."

"You don't have a thing to wear! Not unless," she goes on, hopefully, "you saw sense and hung onto those lovely things from Net-a-Porter after all?"

Oh, Christ, that wretched order, that I still haven't got round to returning. But I'm not going to mention that to Audrey.

"You really think I should carry on seeing him?" I ask.

"Well, it wouldn't hurt to go on a date or two, darling. With someone who thinks you're spectacular. I mean, obviously I couldn't, in all good conscience, advise you to get *serious* about a man like that, but that shouldn't mean . . . gracious me!"

Her hand has frozen on the iPad screen and her perfect lips have fallen open.

"What? Oh, God, I'm not getting Twitter death threats now, am I?"

"No. You're just . . . well, you seem to have rather more followers than you did when I last looked at your account an hour ago."

"How many more?"

"Eleven thousand."

"Audrey! This is exactly why I wanted you to shut it down! I don't need eleven thousand people being nasty about my bum!"

"I know, I know, I'm awfully sorry, darling . . ." She's peering harder at the screen. "You know, I can't see anyone saying nasty things about your bottom, in fact . . ." Now she starts to scroll down it. "Everybody seems to be asking where you got your necklace."

"My *necklace*?"

For the second time since I sat down on the sofa beside her, she shoves the iPad in my direction.

Hi there @LibbyLomax, I read the first tweet my eyes land on, from someone calling themselves @ MajorFashionista. Totes loving necklace yr wearing n that vid!!!!!!!!! Whr did u get it?????????????????????

"If she'd not used all those question marks and exclamation points," Audrey observes, sounding faintly peeved, "she'd have been able to spell out her words properly instead of resorting to all those horrible abbreviations."

Hey @LibbyLomax, says the tweet directly below, this time from someone called @EmilyTheVintagePrincess. Fab diamanté and pearls, sweetie. Please don't tell me it's a one-off vintage find — I NEED THAT NECKLACE! Xx

A quick scan over the dozen . . . two dozen . . . *three dozen* messages below this reveals requests in an identical vein: loving that necklace . . . want that necklace . . . can you tell us where you got that necklace?

"You see?" Audrey thumps a hand, surprisingly vehemently for a probable ghost, and for Audrey Hepburn's one at that, on her seat cushion — so hard, in fact, that something drops out onto the floor from underneath it. "*There're* my sunglasses!" she cries, reaching down to pick up the Oliver Goldsmith tortoiseshell frames and sliding them on, even though we're indoors. The effect is to make her even more fabulous-looking than ever. "I *told* you," she goes on, "that most people were being awfully nice. Complimenting you on your jewellery rather than being unpleasant about your figure."

"Yes . . . I'm just a bit surprised."

"Don't be, darling! Just enjoy the attention." She raises a fingertip above the iPad screen, poised for action. "Now, we must send out a tweet telling people where the necklace is from. Somewhere called Nora's, I remember you told me? Is that a boutique? A jewellery store?"

"No, it isn't from anywhere called Nora's. It isn't *from* anywhere at all. I made it."

"Goodness!" Audrey tilts her sunglasses downwards and perches them on the tip of her nose for a moment, staring at me. "You *are* talented, Libby."

"I don't know . . . I just muck around with stuff, really . . ."

"Well, we aren't going to tell your followers you *just muck around with stuff.* You need to *own* this, darling!" She tap-tap-taps with her finger on the screen. "*Made it . . .* no, I think we'll say *designed*, that sounds much better *. . . designed it myself*," she says, as she types.

"Audrey, no, don't send that, it makes me sound like . . ."

"Thanks ever so much for all the lovely compliments. Yours sincerely, Libby Lomax. And . . . send . . ."

Now that I'm pretty sure she's a ghost, and not a hallucination — not to mention the very real online order she managed to make on my behalf — I guess this tweet has actually gone out there. Sort of like the civilized, twenty-first-century version of some chain-clanking poltergeist writing words in their own blood on the wall of the house they're currently haunting.

"Audrey, come on, I still want to shut the account down. Responding to anything is just going to fuel the fire."

"Fire isn't always a bad thing. In fact, I think you could do with a little more fire in your life."

"You wouldn't say that if you'd ever set your head alight with a cigarette. Seriously, Audrey. Shut it down."

"Ooooh, look, darling!" She turns the iPad back towards me. "Now people are asking who stocks you!"

"Who *stocks* me?"

"Your jewellery designs."

@LibbyLomax, I read on the screen, where do you sell your stuff? . . . @LibbyLomax, can I get one exactly like that in one of your stores and how much is it? . . . @ LibbyLomax do you have a website and does it use PayPal?

"What shall we reply?" Audrey asks, breathlessly. "Shall we say your website will be up and running soon?"

"Why on earth would we say that?" I'm actually starting to feel a bit sick here. The adrenalin, the shock of everything that's happened over the last couple of hours, the sip of the dregs of Audrey's strong espresso on an empty stomach . . . "I won't have a website up and running soon. *Ever*, in fact."

"Well, we ought to say *something*, Libby. These tweets are coming through thick and fast . . . oh!" She takes her sunglasses fully off, now, and peers down at the screen. "You've just had a private message . . . from someone called Emma Watson. Is she a friend of yours?"

The name is ringing a bell, but I can't quite place it.

"She's asking if you might be able to give her stylist a quick call . . ." Audrey is reading the message. "That she'd love to get hold of one of your necklaces as soon as possible . . . a lovely polite lady, she sounds, I must say. Properly written sentences; it's simply a pleasure to read!"

"Hang on . . ." I've just realized where I recognize the name from. "*Emma Watson?* As in, the famous Harry Potter actress?"

"Harry who?"

"Let me see." My hands are slightly shaking as I grab the iPad and look at the message myself.

Dear Libby, the direct message reads. (Actually, it's a series of several direct messages, but I'm piecing them together.) I'm really sorry to message you out of the blue like this but I've just seen you tweet that you're actually the designer of the necklace I've been coveting ever since I saw it on that viral video yesterday. If you have a moment, might you be able to give my stylist a quick call (details following) and let her know if you could get the necklace (or another one similar from your collection) sent out to us before I fly to LA tomorrow morning? Very many thanks indeed, Em x

There's a phone number at the bottom of the last message.

I'm just about to declare the whole thing a cruel hoax when — just to be certain — I click on the @EmWatson link on the top of her messages.

OK, so she has over fifteen million followers.

This makes the probability that she is, in fact, the real Emma Watson quite a lot stronger, doesn't it?

"What an opportunity!" Audrey is getting to her feet. "And this Emma is well known, you say?"

"Quite well known, yes . . . what are you doing?" I ask, as she stoops down to riffle in my handbag, by the front door. "No, hang on," I add, realizing that she's taking out my mobile phone, "we can't just call her!"

"This stylist lady? But of course we can! We have her telephone number, don't we?"

"Yes, but I've no idea what to . . ." I break off, because Audrey has suddenly handed me my phone, and it's already dialling the number she must have just tapped into it. "For fuck's sake! I can't call this stylist without —"

"Hello, Debbie Lederman speaking."

I stare, mutely, at my iPhone, which has a pleasant-sounding Scots woman's voice coming out of it.

"Answer her!" Audrey whispers. "Go on!"

"Hello?" the Scots voice says, again. "Is anyone there?"

"Um, yes, sorry . . . Debbie? My name's Libby, I don't know if —"

"Oh, Libby, hi! You're the designer Emma's just texted me about, right?"

"I'm . . . er . . ."

"Well, thanks for calling! I've only just had a chance to see this video that's doing the rounds . . ."

"Yes, look, about that . . ."

". . . but I agree with Em, your work is fabulous. Is that particular necklace still available?"

"It's not . . . I mean, *I'm* not . . ." I take a deep breath. "It's not really available, as such."

"Damn. The rest have all sold out, yes?" She tuts. "Well, I'm not surprised. I'm just annoyed with myself for not knowing about you before. So do you have anything similar you could show us? Em's heading to LA for a month tomorrow and she'd really like to be able to take some of your pieces to accessorize with while she's over there."

"Bloody hell."

"Sorry?"

"Nothing. I just . . . I could let you have the necklace, if you — if Emma — really wants it."

"But I thought you said it was all sold out."

"No, no, it's not sold out, because I don't have any to sell."

There's a brief, confused pause on the other end of the phone.

"I don't understand . . ." Debbie Lederman says, after a moment.

"Tell her you'll let them have that one!" Audrey hisses, waving the iPad at me for good measure because — oh, for heaven's sake — she's just been Googling Emma Watson's Wikipedia entry. "Emma Watson is a *huge* star!"

"Libby? Are you still there?"

"Yes, sorry," I tell Debbie. "I can always let you have this one."

"Which one?"

"The one I'm wearing."

"So . . . it is available?"

"Yes. It's available."

"Oh, my God, Libby, that's fantastic. Can I ask how much it is? Emma is so often given these things for free, but if you're a young, new designer I know she'd much prefer to pay."

"No, no, it's free. I mean, no charge."

"So you'll loan it to us?"

"No, she can have it. I'm not giving this one to Nora now, anyway, so . . ." A surprisingly fierce look, from Audrey, silences me on the Nora front. "Look, why don't I pop it in the post this afternoon, special delivery or something? If you just give me your address?"

"Heavens, don't do that! I'll send a bike messenger to pick it up from your studio. Unless . . . well, is there any way you'd have the time to pop to my office this afternoon and drop it off yourself? It's just that I'd really like to meet and have a quick chat. I'm always keen to forge links with new designers. Or I could come to you, if it's easier?"

"God, no, don't do that. Er — yes, I could easily come to you this afternoon. But Debbie, honestly, I'm not really a designer, I only make these necklaces for friends and family, and —"

"Libby, my dear," Debbie says, briskly but not unkindly, "you can fill me in on your life story when we meet later. As long as you've got the necklace Em has asked for, that's all that matters right now, OK?"

"OK."

"Aces. I work in-house at Butterfly PR, Twenty-Two Dover Street. Can you get here for about three?"

"Yes. Absolutely."

"Good, well, just ask for me at reception when you get here, and we'll go and grab a quick coffee together, OK? Thanks so much, by the way, Libby. I'm going to give Emma a call right now. She'll be thrilled."

It's only when I put my iPhone down that I realize my hands have gone from shaky to juddery, and that I'm feeling sicker than ever.

"Oh, my God," is all I manage to say.

"Oh, Libby! This is just . . ." Audrey Hepburn flings her thin arms around me, bashing me slightly with her huge hat as she does so. For a hug from a ghost, it's surprisingly sturdy. "It must be like a dream come true!"

Which isn't exactly the case.

Because I've never dreamed about this before. Designing jewellery for movie stars to wear. Designing jewellery for *anyone* to wear, apart from my sister and my friends, that is.

Though I'm not sure *why* I've never dreamed about it, because it's apparently something I'm a bit better at than I've ever really thought.

Wow.

Is this what it feels like to actually be good at something, for a change?

Because (now that the shaking and the sick feeling are slowly wearing off, that is) it feels pretty great.

"And there are still more tweets coming through," Audrey says, gleefully returning to the iPad, "with people asking where to get hold of your necklaces . . . and another private message just in, too. The lovely Emma, I expect, thanking you for . . ." She stops, as she reads the new message. Then she looks up at me. "Is your father called Edward?"

"Yes. Why?"

"He's just sent you a message, darling."

I look at the iPad screen she's — again — holding out towards me.

It's another private message. This time from @Edward LomaxBiographerAndFilmHistorian.

Hi, Libby. I didn't know you were on Twitter. Give me a call sometime? Dad.

Everything seems to go very still around me.

I read the message again, all fifteen words of it.

Hi, Libby. I didn't know you were on Twitter. Give me a call sometime? Dad.

It's the most I've heard from him in half a decade.

"What are you going to reply?" asks Audrey, in a soft voice, sitting down on the Chesterfield beside me.

I shake my head.

"You can't just ignore him, darling."

"Oh, but I can." No sooner has she sat down than I get to my feet. "It's a talent I must have inherited from him, actually. Ignoring your closest relatives."

"Libby. Don't you think . . .?"

"No, I don't. I've just had a pretty bloody fantastic thing happen to me, for a very refreshing change, and I've absolutely no intention of letting a random tweet from my father ruin this moment for me."

"It was a private message, actually, darling, not a . . ."

I silence Audrey Hepburn with a look.

"So can we just delete it, or at the very least stop talking about it? Because I've got a very important meeting to get to and I really need you to help me glam up a bit."

"Of course!" She takes off her hat in a business-like manner and places it next to her sunglasses on the sofa. "It will be my pleasure. Though it really is a shame you didn't keep those Net-a-Porter things, because there were quite a few bits and pieces in there that would have been perfect for this occasion. A smart pencil skirt, a nice Breton jersey . . . it wasn't just formalwear, you know."

"Well, I didn't keep them," I fib, "so we're just going to have to make do with what we've got."

Even Audrey's not quite enough of an actress to hide her visible disappointment at this prospect, but she's uncomplaining as she heads over to my still-unpacked wardrobe boxes to begin the sift-through.

"And you're absolutely sure," she says, after a moment, "that you don't want to reply anything at all to your father?"

"I'm absolutely sure, Audrey, thank you."

She seems, finally, to get the message, because she simply nods, gives me one of her beautiful, heart-melting smiles, and returns to my boxes without saying another word.

Given that I'm probably going to be meeting Dillon tonight, it really, really wasn't a good idea to pack away a selection of finger sandwiches, two clotted-cream-and-jam scones, a slice of carrot cake with cream-cheese icing and a mini lemon tart when I had tea with Debbie Lederman just now.

But she was *sooooooo* incredibly nice, introducing me to the other girls in her office as "this fabulous new young jewellery designer I want to cultivate", and not at all like the bitchy, appearance-obsessed fashion stylists I'd always assumed celebrities must hire, that when she suggested we pop over the road to the Wolseley for a spot of afternoon tea while we chatted, I wasn't exactly going to say no.

And my error over all that calorie-laden food aside, it was a pretty fantastic meeting. If I was nervous, handing over Nora's necklace for her to see up close, I needn't have been, because she oohed and aahed and said she loved it even more. Then she asked all about me, and wasn't at all bothered by the fact — impressed upon her once again — that I'm *not* a proper jewellery designer, fabulous or otherwise. She just said that I was missing a trick, not making a career out of this, and that she'd love to see any more examples of jewellery I've made recently, and that if I make anything else she'd love to see that, too . . .

Like I say, pretty fantastic.

And even though I should probably scurry along a packed Piccadilly on my way back to the tube, now, with my head down, just in case anyone recognizes me as the bottom-revealer from That Video, I don't. I don't care, really, if anyone *does*. Because I feel like I'm walking on air, fifteen feet above the crowds, buoyed up by the incredible thing that's just happened to me.

I mean, *could* I do this? Make a career out of my jewellery bits and bobs?

Potentially succeed at something I might actually be good at, instead of failing at something I was never really supposed to be doing in the first place?

Because I'm not saying that, if I made a career from jewellery-making, I *definitely wouldn't* set my head on fire, or get locked out of spas semi-naked with my towel tucked into my thong, or have unflattering Instagram videos of me posted for all the world (except possibly a few dozen tribes-people in Papua New Guinea) to see. Obviously those things *could* happen, whether I was a failed actress, or a successful jewellery designer, or a bus driver, or the head of the Bank of England, for all I know.

But the point is that even if those things did happen, at least they'd be happening to a person who was going somewhere in life. To a person who was *doing something*, rather than just sitting on the sidelines watching Hollywood fantasy on her iPad and watching real life happen to everybody else.

I'm absolutely bursting to tell somebody about this, and the person I'm bursting to tell is Olly.

These days, it occurs to me, since Nora's been working in Scotland, he's pretty much the first to hear all my big news, good and bad, the moment I get it. He was the first person I called after I found my new flat. The first person I called after Daniel dumped me. And vice versa: I was the first person Olly called right after he got the loan to start his own catering company a couple of years ago; the first person he called when he was awarded the big contract with Pinewood Studios; the first person he called when he and Alison split up, only a few months after getting a flat together. He'll let out one of his big shouts of delight when I tell him, and insist that we book a nice meal out, as soon as possible, to celebrate.

But as I get my phone out of my bag to call him, I see that I've had a missed call from Dillon — almost an hour ago, while I was scoffing scones with Debbie Lederman. He didn't leave a message.

Well, I'll give him a call back and find out if he really meant what he said, earlier, about us spending the evening together.

And *then* I'll call Olly and tell him my good news.

(And then, after that, if I really am going to be seeing Dillon tonight, I'd better hurry to M&S on Oxford Street and buy the strongest pair of control knickers I

314

can find. Preferably some that are reinforced with titanium, the better to rein in the clotted-cream-scone-induced bloat.)

I call Dillon's number.

His phone rings and rings, and is almost certainly just about to go to voicemail when he picks up.

"Hey," he says.

"Hi! I was just calling to see if you're still up for it tonight?" Then, because I realize how that sounded, I add, hastily, "Dinner, I mean. If you're still up for dinner. Because I know I wasn't sure before, but if you're still free, I'd really love to . . ."

"Dinner?"

"Yep. I don't know if you've heard of it. It's this meal that people often eat some time between the hours of six and nine p.m. If you're posh, you call it supper, and if you're not so posh, you call it tea . . ." I pause, feeling rather pleased with myself for turning one of his favourite kinds of jokes back on him for a change, and waiting for him to laugh. But there's just a bit of a silence. "Um . . . Dillon?"

The silence continues.

"Are you still there?"

"Yes, sorry, I was just . . ." He must have turned away from the phone for a moment, because his voice fades, briefly, before coming back as normal. "Look, I can't do dinner tonight, actually. My apologies."

While it's obviously a bit concerning that he's changed his mind, what's more concerning is the clipped, distant tone he's using.

"I've got to catch a flight to Rome," he adds, curtly, "in six hours."

"Rome?"

I'm hoping that he's going to say, *Yeah, it's this major European capital city, in a country called Italy . . . maybe you've heard of it . . .*

He doesn't. He just says, "Yeah, so that's why I can't do dinner. But, like I say, my apologies."

"It's just . . . well, that's quite short notice. To have to . . . go to Rome."

Even as I say it, it sounds ludicrous. I mean, I was prepared to buy the whole New York story, but such a random travelogue, in the space of just a few days, is starting to seem more than a little bit fishy.

"That's why I'm busy. I'm getting a few things packed. I'm meeting Martin Scorsese over there."

"Oh, wow, Dillon, that's —"

"Anyway, I'll call you when I'm back, yeah?"

"Sure." I try (and pretty much fail) to sound causal. "Whenever. No hurry."

"Great."

"I mean, I'm sure you'll be back in a couple of days . . ."

"OK, well, good talking to you."

"*Baby,*" a voice suddenly calls in the background. "*Who are you talking to . . .?*"

It's Rhea's voice.

I freeze. Which isn't the best timing, as I've just stepped out into Piccadilly and narrowly miss being sent flying by a motorbike that has to swerve into the middle of the road to avoid hitting me.

"Stupid cow!" the rider of the motorbike screams at me as he rides off, for which I can't really blame him.

"No one," I hear Dillon reply in a muffled voice, as if he's covering the mouthpiece of his phone with one hand.

"*Then come back to bed . . .*"

I pull the phone away from my ear and press the End Call button.

"You all right, love?" A woman with a buggy and a toddler on reins asks me, as she somehow manages to find a spare hand to pull me back onto the pavement beside her. "That could have been messy!"

"It already is . . ."

"Right. Look, you should probably go and get yourself a nice cup of tea, or something. Or — hang on a minute — have one of these." She rifles around in the back of the buggy and produces, a couple of seconds later, a bright purple pouch of toddler's fruit smoothie. "This'll get your blood sugar back up," she adds, pressing it into my hand.

"Thank you . . . I'm just a bit . . . I mean, he was with *her* . . . She told him to come back to bed . . ."

The woman glances down at her toddler for a moment, presumably checking he hasn't understood what I'm saying, and then she leans a bit closer to me.

"Men," she says, in a low voice. "They're all the bloody same."

Then the green man lights up and the beeps sound, and she crosses over the pedestrian crossing with her buggy and toddler safely in tow. From the other side of the road she turns and makes a "drinking" motion with one of her other spare hands, though whether it's to remind me to drink the toddler's smoothie or to go and find the nearest stiff drink, I don't know.

I don't know *what* to do with myself, to be honest with you.

This is so, so much worse than simply waking up in the morning and finding that Dillon had gone.

After everything Rhea has done to me . . . after all those things he was saying to me only this morning . . . he was in bed with her?

I feel so terribly, terribly stupid.

Cretinously humiliatingly, and — worst of all — *predictably* stupid.

And I genuinely don't understand why I'm doing what I'm doing at this very moment. Which is reaching into my jacket pocket for my iPhone, and calling the very last person I ever thought I'd call in a situation like this.

The very last person I thought I'd ever call, in any situation, ever.

I'm calling my father.

CHAPTER
FIFTEEN

Right, well, I blame Audrey for this. Bloody Audrey, with all her talk about mending fences with her father, and not expecting him to be anything different, and — I now realize — sowing the seeds in my head that maybe this Happy-enough Families situation is one I could achieve, too.

If (*when*) this all goes horribly wrong when (*if*) Dad gets here in a few minutes, I'm going to give Audrey a piece of my mind when I get back home to my flat, I can tell you.

Here, by the way, is The Jade Dragon, in Chinatown, Dad's favourite restaurant. It's the place he *didn't* bring me sixteen years ago for my belated thirteenth birthday celebration, and it was the place I suggested to him when, just an hour ago, we spoke on the phone.

Spoke pretty briefly on the phone, by the way; it wasn't all that promising. He sounded astounded when he answered (though I suppose, at least, he did answer), with a bemused "*Libby?*"

"Yep. It's me."

"Yes. Why are you . . . is everything all right? Nothing wrong with your mother?"

(I'm not sure what was more depressing: the fact that he immediately assumed that the only reason I'd be calling him was to announce dire news about Mum, or the fact that I detected more than a mere hint of hope in his voice as he asked the question.)

"No," I said, "Mum's fine. I'm just calling because . . . well, I thought you might like, maybe, to meet up."

"Meet up?"

"Yes. For a . . . a bite."

There was a short silence on the other end of the phone.

"Uh . . . yeah, sure. A bite. Why not? When's good for you?"

"Now? Tonight?" I blurted, only just managing to stop myself before adding, as my teenage self would have done: *Actually don't worry about it I'm sure you're working or busy doing something else so really I'm fine let's just do it another time no problem.*

"Er . . . yeah. I could do tonight, I guess."

"OK. Shall we go to . . ." I went blank.

Because this meeting with Dad, unlike the many meetings I held with Audrey over the years, hasn't been endlessly replayed over and over in my head, with a different script and in a different and exciting location. I deliberately haven't given my father one last thought for most of the past decade; I certainly haven't ever given a single minute over to thinking where we might meet, if I decided to have it out with him.

". . . The Jade Dragon?" was the only place that popped into my mind.

320

"In Chinatown? I haven't been there for ages, but . . . sure. The Jade Dragon. If it's still there. Why not?"

"Right. Good. An hour from now? Six thirty-ish?"

"Sure. Six thirty-ish. I'll see you there, Libby."

Though there must have been quite a lot more *ish* about the six thirty, in Dad's mind, than there was in mine.

Because I've been here since bang on the dot of half six, and it's now just gone twenty past seven.

And there's no sign of him.

I'm on my second plate of salt-and-pepper squid (I feel self-conscious just sitting here alone, obviously waiting for someone, and the chopsticks give me something to do with my hands) when my phone bleeps.

It's not Dad, texting to cancel. It's Olly.

Has he showed up yet?

This is because I texted Olly on my way into the restaurant fifty minutes ago, to tell him I was about to have dinner with my dad.

Not yet, I text back.

Then, a moment or so later, because I'm worried he'll be concerned about me sitting here all alone, I text a cheery, Squid quite nice, though! and follow this with a ridiculous winking face.

"Oh, Libby."

I practically jump out of my skin, a nanosecond after sending this text, to look up and see Olly standing at my table.

"That was . . . how on earth . . .?"

"I got on the tube to come here as soon as you texted me earlier," he says, sliding into the seat opposite me. "You know. Just in case."

My heart, which has rapidly been freezing over for the past three-quarters of an hour that I've been sitting here waiting for Dad, thaws, instantly, into a mushy puddle.

I'm sorely tempted to get to my feet, clamber over the table with no regard whatsoever for the plate of salt-and-pepper squid on it, climb onto Olly's lap, put my arms around his neck and kiss him.

Hang on, did I say *kiss him?*

No, no, no. I meant, obviously *hug him*.

"You mean," I say, carefully, "in case he couldn't be arsed to show up."

"Well, you know, it's quite a journey from . . . remind me where he lives these days?"

"Holloway Road. Four stops on the Piccadilly Line."

"Ah. Right." Olly looks a bit defeated. "How late is he?"

"Forty-five minutes. So far."

"I'm sorry," is all he says.

"That's OK. It was so nice of you to come."

"You'd do the same for me."

"What, if your dad had stood you up at the last minute once again?" I say, with a snort, because Olly and Nora's dad, Archie, is the sort of dad I'd once have thought only existed in teatime sitcoms made for children: a golden-hearted dispenser of cups of tea and rounds of toast, present for every single one of his (many) offspring's milestones.

"You've been there for me through all *my* crap, is what I mean. When Mum was so ill right before my exams. When I couldn't get a loan from anywhere to set up the business. When Tilly died — do you remember?"

"Oh, God, Olly." This is the last thing I need right now; a reminder of Olly's faithful old Labrador, Tilly, or of how devastated he was when she was put down. I can feel tears pricking my eyes. "Please don't talk about that right now!"

"OK, but all I'm saying is that I'm always here for you, Lib."

I manage to choke back an unwanted sob. "Like Tilly?"

"Yes . . ." He seems to stop, suddenly, even though he's sitting down. "Actually," he says, "no."

"No?"

"No! Not like Tilly! I'm not a bloody Labrador!"

"Well, yes, I know that, Olly, obviously, I just meant . . ." And then *I* stop.

Because my father has just come into The Jade Dragon and is walking across the floor to join us.

"My dad," I croak at Olly "Here. Now."

He looks five years older than the last time I saw him, which isn't exactly a surprise because it's roughly five years since the last time I saw him, at his mother's funeral. He's wearing his usual garb of skinny jeans, leather jacket and David Bowie T-shirt (which he should probably start rethinking, given that he must have been fifty-eight on his last birthday), and when he realizes I've seen him, his lips draw back in the weird forced smile he always pulls when he sees me, as though I'm a slightly tiresome next-door neighbour who's going to keep him chatting about the weather for half an hour.

I get to my feet as he reaches the table, and Olly does the same, sticking a hand out towards my dad in a flustered sort of manner. It's a bit odd, but at least it deals with the thorny issue of whether Dad and I are going to hug or kiss each other in greeting.

"Olly Walker," he tells Dad, before adding, "I'm not staying."

"Oh, right . . . you're Libby's boyfriend?"

"No. Just a friend," Olly says. "But good to meet you anyway, Mr Lomax."

I love Olly for the fact that he manages to hover on the edge of politeness while saying this, and yet still somehow make it clear that he thinks my father is a bit of a shit.

"Will you give me a call later, Libby?" he asks. "Doesn't matter how late."

"Will do," I tell him. "Thanks again, Ol."

If it weren't for the fact it would sound really, really odd, I'd call — *and I really, really don't think you're a Labrador* after him.

"Nice bloke," Dad says, as Olly walks away from our table, and out of the restaurant.

"He is." I sit back down in my seat and pick up my chopsticks, to have something to do with my hands again. "The best, in fact. The squid's good. Sorry there's not much left. I didn't know if you were going to make it or not."

"Yeah. I got held up." There's a slight pause which, with anybody other than my father, would almost certainly be filled with the words, *I'm really sorry I kept you waiting.* He sits down opposite me, and helps himself to a piece of squid. "So. It's been ages."

"Five years."

"That long?"

"Gran's funeral."

"Was *that* five years ago?"

"Yep."

"Oh. Right. Well."

Once again, I remind myself to give Audrey a piece of my mind when I get back to my flat tonight. Because this is going even worse than I thought. I'd forgotten, somehow, just how flat and unenthusiastic my dad can be. How it's not just the way he smiles at me that makes me feel like that tiresome neighbour: it's the way he talks to me as well. The way he's always talked to me, in fact.

As if I'm a necessary evil.

Well, all right, I'm going to try to do what Audrey advised so that, if nothing else, I'll be in an even greater position to Have A Go when I see her later. I'm not going to let Dad's old habits get to me. After all, it's not like it's personal to me, this air of detached, world-weary boredom. He does it — has always done it — with everyone.

"So," I say in a shaky voice, "you tweeted me."

"Yeah. I saw that video of you doing the rounds . . ."

"Oh, God," I moan, because the thought that *my estranged father* has seen my naked, dripping bottom on Twitter is just . . . horrifying.

"Don't worry, I only saw the first few seconds." He looks almost as uncomfortable as I do. "But it made me search to see if you were on Twitter, and there you were."

"Yes." Thanks again, Audrey. "There I was."

"Quite a lot of followers, you've got!"

"Well, you know . . ."

"I've got about ten or eleven thousand myself."

This is why he agreed to see me? To make it clear he's got plenty of Twitter followers himself?

"And I'm expecting more and more, now that the book is coming out."

"Oh, yes. I'd heard."

"Oh, you did?" This, at least, brightens him up considerably. "Yeah, it hit the shelves last Thursday. So I've been pretty busy with signings and all that . . . a book tour coming up. I'm due to record something at the BBC first thing tomorrow morning, in fact, a segment for *Woman's Hour* on Radio Four, so I'd better not be too late tonight. Got to be fresh for that."

I note, dully, that his age-old reason (OK, excuse) for always being too busy to spend any time with me has morphed, seamlessly, from Busy Writing the Book to Busy Promoting the Book.

Honestly, right now, I'd actually rather appreciate it if he took a leaf out of Audrey Hepburn's father's book, produced a little paper swastika from the pocket of his leather jacket and goose-stepped around The Jade Dragon, because at least that would make me disappointed in him in a fresh, original way.

". . . and there's been a lot of interest from *Newsnight Review*," Dad is going on, "and there might be some serialization in the *Mail on Sunday*, and I'm

326

writing a piece about Cary Grant for the *Sunday Times* magazine . . ."

"Did you know," I say, conversationally, "that Audrey Hepburn once spilled wine all over him?"

"Who?"

"Cary Grant. Red wine. All over his cream linen suit."

There's a flicker of something in Dad's eyes.

"No," he says, in a tone that hints at interest rather than disbelief.

"Yep."

"Where did you hear that?"

"Just . . . you know. I read it somewhere."

He leans forward. "When they were filming *Charade*?"

I can't help wondering, as he asks this, if Dad happens to recall — as I'm doing, right now — the occasion we watched *Charade*, together, when I was nine or ten. It was at a time, a rare and brief time, if only I'd realised it back then, when he was making sufficiently good progress with the book to mean that he wasn't cancelling our one weekend a month at the last minute, and that he was in a relaxed mood when I went to stay with him. That *Charade* night was a Friday, with an entire cold winter's weekend of movie-watching stretched out before us, and Dad had bought me a bottle of sparkling Shloer and arranged posh deli meats and olives on a wooden platter for us to nibble at, which made me feel as if I'd reached some impossible acme of adult sophistication. He set it all out on his battered little coffee table, and chinked his own glass (of real wine) against mine, and before we settled onto his battered leather sofa to watch the movie, he told me about how he'd first watched the movie with *his* dad, one damp Sunday afternoon, thirty years ago. Which made me feel simultaneously safe and cosy, and strangely proud, as if I was the newest in a long and noble line of Lomaxes to discover the later works of Cary Grant, and that Dad was . . . handing me a torch, somehow. And I think he might have felt the same way, too, because he reached over, a few moments after Walter Matthau appeared on the screen, and rested one hand on my head for a full half-minute. Thirty-two seconds. I know, because I stopped concentrating on the movie so I could count them.

But now Dad sits back in his seat again, with a curt shake of the head. "Actually, come to think of it, I don't think that ever happened."

"It did, Dad. I'm sure of it."

"Well, it's a nice little story. But apocryphal, I'm sure."

You know what? I think he's just remembered *exactly* that Friday night at his flat. And I think he was enjoying my Cary Grant/Audrey Hepburn gossip, despite himself, until he felt the dangerous possibility that he might reconnect with me in some way Be forced, against his will, to acknowledge that we're more than merely polite acquaintances. That I'm someone he might actually owe a commitment to.

"I don't think," he goes on, lofty again now, "there's much you can tell me about Audrey Hepburn that I don't know already."

"Givenchy," I mutter. "Not Chanel."

328

"What?"

"Nothing," I say, because I'm feeling sullen, and furious, and prickly with acute misery, exactly the way I did the last time I saw him, when I decided I couldn't stand to feel that way any more, and pretty much cut him — without any resistance from his side, I have to point out — out of my life.

I mean, it's just not working, is it? For all Audrey's pep talk, for all her own claims of success at building bridges with a terrible father, I'm not having the remotest hint of success myself. If anything, I'm feeling even worse about it all than I did before he sat down opposite me. It's this visceral, deep-down-buried *ickiness*, and I don't think there's anything I can possibly do to make it any better.

Audrey Hepburn was obviously a much stronger woman than I am. As if I didn't already know that.

"And you're still in the extras game, yeah?"

"Sorry?"

"You're still an extra, on TV shows? At least, that's what you were up to the last time I saw you."

"Oh . . . yes. Well, actually, no. I'm stopping all that, I think."

"Oh?"

"Well, I'm thinking of going into something else . . . jewellery design, maybe."

"Oh, yeah, I saw all those people tweeting you about a necklace, or something." He reaches for a piece of squid. "So your mother's finally letting one of her daughters step off the stage, then, is she?"

I don't like — I've never liked — his tone when he talks about Mum.

"And she's still in the agenting game, I take it?" he adds.

The extras game . . . the agenting game . . . could he make it any more obvious that he regards these jobs as a bit of a joke, compared to his high-faluting academic one?

"Not really. She's setting up a stage school franchise, in fact."

"Oh, Christ, she's finally got around to inflicting that on the world, has she?" He rolls his eyes. "She was going on about that even back when I was married to her. And that's where my profits from the house are ending up, presumably?"

"Dad." I don't often call him this. Even when I was much younger, he always preferred it when I called him "Eddie", which I used to think was a sign of how cool and chilled he was, but I eventually came to realize was just another way of him avoiding being a father to me. In fact, there's a small chance I'm calling him "Dad" now just to get back at him for being so rude about Mum. "You don't seriously think you ought to be getting half of the money from the house, do you?"

"That's between your mother and me."

"Well, no, it's not, actually. You were the one that brought it up, just now. And you're the one who brought in the lawyers. So really, at the very least, it's between Mum and you and your solicitors."

He presses his lips together so tightly that they become a thin line of displeasure, but he doesn't say anything.

I take a deep breath. "I mean, don't you think it's a bit unfair, Dad, after all these years when you didn't so much as pay a single month's worth of —"

"So, jewellery, eh?" he interrupts, in a voice that makes it clear he has absolutely no intention of discussing the house; that he'll shut down, as he always does, any attempt at discussing anything uncomfortable. "Isn't that a tough career to carve out? Hard to make a living, unless you're really good at it."

"I've just given a necklace to Emma Watson, as it happens," I say, tightly.

"Emma who?"

"*Watson*. You know. The little girl from the Harry Potter films. International mega-star. *Fifteen million followers on Twitter.*"

"Oh, her. Right." He pauses for a moment, seemingly unsure how to respond — or, perhaps, simply incapable of putting the words *that's* and *terrific* together in a two-word sentence, like a normal person would. "Well. It's a start."

Right at this moment, something snaps.

No. *Snaps* is the wrong word. I feel myself *snap*, like an overstretched elastic band, when I'm with Mum, and she's getting on my nerves about my career, or going on and on about me sabotaging all her efforts to find me work, or waxing lyrical about my sister's talent, looks and ambition, in comparison to mine.

This is different, It's not an elastic band, snapping. It's a long, thick, heavy rope, one that wrapped itself around me tighter and tighter over the years, so gradually that I didn't even notice it — and it's uncoiling.

Because for the first time in my life, I can see what an absolute arse he's being *and it's not getting to me*. I can see that he's feeling shit about something himself — what I've just said about the mortgage payments?; the fact I've got more followers than him on Twitter? — and he wants to make himself feel better.

But whatever the reason that's making him behave so charmlessly and childishly, whatever the reason that makes him unable to give me a hug or a kiss when he sees me, whatever the reason he wants to put me down, I suddenly twig that it's his problem.

His failing.

It's sad. It's terribly sad. But I'm not devastated.

Is this what it feels like, I want to run home to my haunted Chesterfield and ask Audrey Hepburn right now, *when you finally get there? When you realize that he just is what he is, and that expecting him to be any better is like expecting the tide to roll back just because you want it to?*

"Oh, and while we're on the subject of Twitter . . ."

"Were we?"

"You just mentioned Emma Watson's fifteen million followers, didn't you?"

"I did, Eddie. Yes."

". . . why don't you maybe tweet a link to my publisher's webpage, whenever you're next on Twitter?

Just mentioning my book. I mean, what with all those people asking about your bracelets, or whatever, I'm sure some of them are going to be interested in reading a book your father's written."

Is he serious?

Is this, then, the real reason he made the effort to contact me for the first time in five years? To leech off my sudden wellspring of Twitter followers?

I should probably be angry, but all this is only making me feel more and more sorry for him. I mean, he hasn't seen me in five years. Hasn't had a conversation, apart from two minutes of funeral-related chitchat, with me for ten. He doesn't know — hasn't asked — where I'm living, or if I'm still single, or if I've had a couple of children of my own. The only thing he wants, apparently, from his only daughter, is help with a sales boost.

Which, just like that, uncoils the final loop of the rope.

"Sure," I say. "I'll do that for you."

And then I start to get to my feet and signal the waiter for the bill.

Dad blinks up at me in amazement, almost as wide-eyed as Ziggy Stardust in the picture on his T-shirt. Because, let's be honest, he's the one that always does the leaving. Anything else makes no sense to him whatsoever.

"Well, you have an early start, as you said," I say, by way of explanation, as I pull on my trenchcoat and belt it at the waist. "But it was nice to see you. We should . . ." The words *do this again sometime* can't quite make their way past my lips; I'm not, and never will be, as huge-hearted and gracious as Audrey Hepburn.". . . keep in touch a bit more," I finish, and surprise myself by finding that I mean it.

"But I'm going on a book tour really soon; it'll be weeks until I'm back in London and . . ."

"It's all right," I tell him, before he feels the need to run through his entire itinerary for the next six months just so he can make it clear that he's the one who's too busy to keep in touch with me and not the other way around. "Just the occasional text message would be nice."

"Oh. Right."

"Advice about a good new movie to go and see, or something," I say, because I guess if there's one thing he's given me — one thing that despite everything, I'll always be grateful for — it's my love of the movies. He might be no real father, but he's a pretty decent film critic. And it feels strangely fulfilling to let him play to the one strength he's ever exhibited.

"I mean, no pressure," I add.

And then, because he suddenly looks so old, sitting there in his teenager's clothing, I lean down and give him a kiss on the cheek.

"Bye, Eddie," I say. "Good luck with the book tour."

I hand two ten-pound notes to the waiter on my way out and — in what I now call, with an unavoidable pang of pain, *Dillon-style* — don't wait around for whatever change is due to come my way.

Then I get my phone out of my bag, and send a quick text to Olly.

Finished dinner. Leaving now. L xx

About fifteen seconds later, he replies.

Are you OK? Was it awful? O xx

I stop outside The Jade Dragon, just for a moment, and look back in through one of the plate-glass windows.

Dad is reaching out with one hand to help himself, absently, to a piece of cold salt-and-pepper squid. With the other hand he's reaching into his jacket pocket to take out a book — something about James Stewart, it looks like from the photo on the cover — and starts to read. He hasn't even noticed the waiter hovering at his shoulder, trying to give him the change from my twenty-pound note.

Not awful at all, really, I reply to Olly's text message. Just Dad.

Then, without looking back, I set off along Gerrard Street towards Leicester Square tube station.

CHAPTER
SIXTEEN

It was stupid of me not to have waited for my change at the restaurant, now I come to think of it, because it's left me too broke to do what I really want to do now, which is to pick up a (cheap) bottle of fizzy wine from the off-licence near Colliers Wood tube station, take it back to my flat, and do my damnedest to get hold of Audrey Hepburn so that I can raise a glass to her and thank her, from the bottom of my heart, for the advice about dealing with my father.

Honestly, I feel like I've drunk an entire bottle of fizz already, and proper, vintage champagne at that, not just some cheapo Cava. I feel free. Light. As if I could break into dance at any moment, walking along this chewing-gum-pocked pavement from the tube to my flat, a bit like Audrey herself in the beatnik nightclub in *Funny Face*.

I don't even care, any more, about the still-fresh wound left by Dillon's betrayal. Because for the first time in my life, at the ripe old age of 29, I actually feel like a grown-up. Like a proper *woman*, not a messed-up little girl.

And though I realize I should probably have got there long ago — put my father, mentally, in a box marked "Simply Incapable," rather than letting that heavy old rope wrap itself around me all my life — it's a pretty momentous occasion for me.

Oh, well, I've probably got a bottle of red stashed away at the bottom of one of my moving boxes, which will do perfectly well for toasting the amazing Audrey.

Not forgetting, of course, that as soon as I've brought her up to speed on what just happened with Dad, I really do need, now, to confront her head-on about the whole ghost thing.

There's a conversation I can't say I'm going to relish.

I mean, how do you broach something like that? To someone's face, especially a beautiful, sensitive, *alive* face like Audrey's? Do you go super-formal: *Sorry to bring this up, but I just wanted to say that I'm not sure you're a figment of my imagination after all, and I was wondering if you'd mind discussing the possibility that you might be some sort of phantom? Or possibly a poltergeist. I'm not sure of the correct terminology.* Or go the opposite way, and just chuck it casually into a conversation about something else: *Another glass of wine, Audrey, or shall we crack open something stronger? Oh, and talking of spirits . . .*

Maybe I'd just be better off not mentioning anything at all.

Because it's not as if it really matters, I guess, whether she came out of my head or out of the ancient Chesterfield sofa. The only thing that matters is that along with the crazy haircut, the Nespresso fixation and the insanely large Net-a-Porter order that . . . *shit* . . . I've *still* got to call them to come and pick up, the advent of Audrey has turned my life around in more ways than one.

After all, if it weren't for her, this Emma Watson stuff would never have happened. And, alright, the Dillon wound is still horribly fresh, but thanks to Audrey, I still got to have that amazing night with him, which — once the wound has healed — I'm sure I'll be able to look back on with more than mere fondness . . .

The odd thing is that I can hear Dillon's voice now.

Not in my head, I mean, saying all the insanely sexy things he was saying to me between his rumpled sheets.

But actually *here*, at the top of the stairs as I climb them up to my flat, right now.

". . . so you'd suggest a little bit off the front? You don't think the floppy fringe is working for me?"

Sweet Jesus. He's not . . . he *can't be* . . . talking to *Audrey?*

"Is what am suggesting, yes. Less floppy, more choppy."

Oh, thank God. It's not Audrey. It's Bogdan Son of Bogdan.

Though my relief (that Dillon hasn't met my house-ghost) is swiftly replaced by unease (that Dillon is chatting to Bogdan) and confusion (that Dillon is here *at all*).

I take the last night of stairs three at a time and hurry through the door to my flat, which is open.

Dillon and Bogdan are sitting on the Chesterfield, passing Bogdan's thermos of tea back and forth between them.

"Can be doing it for you now, if you are liking," Bogdan is saying, "while we are killing the time, before Libby is getting back."

"Libby's here now," I say, and at least get the satisfaction of seeing them both jump, then turn to look at me. "Dillon," I add, as he gets to his feet. "What are you doing here? How do you even know where I live?"

"Detective work. Well, a couple of pestering phone calls to Scary Vanessa, actually. She had your address on file. And I did call on my way here, by the way, but it just went to voicemail."

"I've been on the tube."

"Well, luckily your friend Bogdan here let me in . . ."

"Am here to put back plasterboard wall," Bogdan tells me, sadly, nodding towards the hole in the wall that he must have climbed through to let Dillon into my flat. "Father is going wobbly when am telling him that am taking wall down."

"Throwing a wobbly," I correct him. "I'm really sorry about that, Bogdan. But perhaps you should just put the wall back for now, and then try to work out another way of standing up to him soon. Something a bit less . . . messy."

"I'm with Libby on this one, mate," Dillon tells him, clapping a hand on Bogdan's huge shoulder. "I'd just quietly focus on your hairdressing, if I were you. Play the long game. Maybe try to save up a bit of money and think about opening a salon of your own. Then just invite your dad along to your grand opening — preferably when there are plenty of witnesses around — and that'll say more about your independence than knocking down his walls ever could."

Irritatingly, this is good advice.

But I'm not about to let it sway my low opinion of Dillon. Not one little bit.

"You are amazing," Bogdan tells him. "Libby," he adds, to me, "this is amazing man. At first am thinking he is only good-looker, but we are chatting for last half-hour and he is very lovely, too. Thoughtful and kind. And wonderful. You are lucky to be knowing him, Libby. You are fortunate to —"

"Yes, I get the message, Bogdan, thanks." I give him a look that quite clearly means *can you make yourself scarce for a bit so I can find out exactly what Mr Wonderful is doing here*, but it's possible that this look translates badly into mangled English/Moldovan, because Bogdan just stands there, beaming happily between the pair of us, like a vicar at a Richard Curtis wedding, and doesn't move a muscle.

"Bogdan, mate, I was wondering, could you maybe pop down and offer some of that tea to the taxi driver? Just while I have a word with Libby here?"

Bogdan, eager to do Dillon's bidding, is off out of the door with his thermos so fast he doesn't even have time to stop and tell me more about how amazing Dillon is before he goes.

"He's a sweetheart," says Dillon, as we both hear Bogdan thundering down flight after flight of stairs. "Nasty-sounding father, though."

I can't do this again. Stand around listening to Dillon's charming chitchat until he gets around to

340

realizing that I'm upset about something and then comes up with some fairy tale about New York, and Martin Scorsese auditions ... a fairy tale that I cretinously swallow, just because he's so sexy and gorgeous, and because he (mostly) makes me feel like the warm sun is shining right down on me just because he's asked it to.

"Was any of it true?" I hear myself ask. "I mean, did you really go to New York that morning? Or did you go to Rhea's instead?"

"Yes, I went to New York that morning. No, I didn't go to Rhea's. I'm not with Rhea."

"I see. So that was just a recording of her voice I heard through the phone earlier."

"No. It was her. Messing with you."

I don't react to this right away. Instead I put my bag down on the Chesterfield, then coolly and calmly remove my trenchcoat and drape it over the arm of the sofa. Only then do I look at him — right at him — and speak.

"Messing with me?"

"I went to her flat, after filming yesterday morning, to tell her to take that stupid Instagram video down. I mean, all right, it's probably pretty pointless, seeing as it's been re-tweeted half a million times . . ."

Well, I suppose it's nice to be popular.

". . . but as a gesture, I think it's the least she could do. Though you probably won't be all that surprised to hear that she refused."

"And then you went ahead and slept with her anyway?"

"No! Jesus, Libby, will you stop thinking the absolute worst of me, every five minutes. Of course I didn't bloody sleep with her! We just rowed, the way we always do. And then you called, and she heard me talking to you, and she obviously decided to get her kicks by pretending to call me back to bed. Because she's really not a big fan of yours, Libby, I hate to tell you. She's jealous, which is a pretty new feeling for her."

"Jealous? Of me?"

"Yeah. Because I told her how I feel about you. And even if she doesn't want to be with me enough to *not* be fucking some guy at the gym (which she very charmingly told me all about, in quite some anatomical detail, I might add, this afternoon), she still doesn't want me to fall for somebody else. Especially when she knows I never fell for her the same way. That I've never really fallen for anyone in the same way, to be honest with you."

The poise I've been so proud of ever since we started this conversation has vanished.

I can't speak. I mean, I can't croak out a single, solitary word.

"Fire Girl." He comes towards me and cups my face in his hands. "Look. I don't know what this is. It doesn't make all that much sense to me. I'm not used to feeling like this. But I do know that I'd really like you to stick with me while I work it out."

OK, and that hasn't done much for my powers of speech, either.

Because — and do correct me if I've got completely the wrong end of the stick here — I think Dillon is

342

telling me that he wants me. And not just in bed, either, for my ego-boosting enthusiasm between the sheets, but for something more.

"You'd turn down," I say, "a supermodel, in favour of me?"

"I'd turn down five supermodels, darling, all at the same time, in favour of you." He grins, wickedly but sweetly. "I've *had* five supermodels, all at the same time, and it all gets a bit confusing, I can tell you. Too much hair. Too many limbs. And it didn't make me feel any less like shit when I looked at myself in the mirror the next morning."

Well, you have to admire his honesty, even though — if I'm going to be able to do this with Dillon — I'm going to have to work triple-time to get the image of him with five perfect-ten models out of my head . . .

Hang on, he's reaching into his pocket now, and taking out a folded sheet of paper, which he hands to me.

"What's this?" I ask, without opening it.

"A boarding pass. I want you to come with me for the weekend, Libby Come to Rome."

"*Rome?*"

"Yeah, it's this major European capital city," he says, "in a country called Italy. Maybe you've heard of it? They eat pizza, and pasta, and drive around on Vespas . . ."

"Dillon. Why do you want me to come to Rome?"

"Because you make me laugh. Because you make me comfortable. Because I fancy the pants off you, and because they're putting me up in a nice hotel over-looking the city, and because I want to take you to bed and do extremely un-holy things to you while we watch the sun set over St Peter's. Because you're my lucky charm, so I need you close by when I meet Martin Scorsese. And because no matter what happens in that meeting, I want to go back to that hotel room with you afterwards, and order wine and gelato, and stay up so late talking that we sleep in and miss our flight home the next morning."

Damn him and his way with words.

And that way he has of looking at me that makes me certain, despite everything, that they're not just words, and that he really, truly means it.

"I'd need . . . I mean, there's packing . . . and what time's the flight?"

"Ten forty-five. It's why I've a taxi waiting for us outside. If we leave pretty soon, we'll get there in time. Assuming there's no traffic build-up near junction ten at this time of night, that is."

I wonder what the sudden pointed tone is about, until I remember that peculiar disagreement with Olly.

"Libby?" he adds. "Come on, sweetheart. What's your decision?"

What *is* my decision?

For a moment, I can almost hear Audrey's voice in my head, telling me I need a bit more fire in my life.

But, like I say, Audrey's not the one who's ever been in danger of getting burnt.

And this isn't just being near fire, this is *playing with* fire. There's the modelizing. The drinking. The suspicious white powder on the marble basin-top.

But it's *Dillon*. And it's *Rome*. And he wants to do incredible things to me while we watch the sun set over

St Paul's . . . sorry, I mean St Peter's . . . and the mere thought of the incredible things is making it difficult to keep my head straight . . .

"I'll come."

His face breaks into a broad smile, and he leans down and kisses me.

If it weren't for the fact I have to hastily pack for a weekend in Rome with him, I'd never want this kiss to stop.

But I do have to pack, and locate my passport in one of these unpacked boxes, and I'm quite sure there'll be a few more of these kisses to look forward to as soon as we're Heathrow-bound, so I pull away.

"I need to get some clothes into a bag . . ."

"Sure. Just not too many," he says, with a cheeky wink. "I'll go and tell the taxi we'll be a few more minutes. You know, this is a cute little place, Libby," he adds, as he heads for the door. "Cosy. And that's quite a hunk of sofa."

The Chesterfield. Audrey.

If I wanted to speak to her before this astounding development with Dillon, I want to speak to her more than ever now.

Well, I'm going to have to try to get hold of her while I pack, because there isn't really time to do it any other way.

As soon as Dillon closes the front door behind him, I plonk myself down on the sofa. Because the sofa, as far as I can tell, is where this all emanated from in the first place.

"Audrey? Audrey, it's me. Are you there? Can we talk?"

Nothing.

I close my eyes, in case that might help.

"Audrey, I have to talk to you! The most amazing things have been happening. Are you there?"

I open my eyes, hoping to see a Givenchy-clad vision on the sofa beside me. But still, there's nothing.

All right, well, what's Plan B?

I'll get on and pack, because I really need to hurry up here, and because — now that I think about it — Audrey has always popped up, before now, when I haven't actually been expecting her.

With slightly shaky legs (I still can't quite believe Dillon said all those lovely things to me just now; that he *thinks* them, in fact) I hurry over to my boxes and start looking for the squashed-up holdall that I know will be in there somewhere.

"Am blue with envy," comes a voice behind me.

Nope: not Audrey. Bogdan Son of Bogdan.

It's not that I'm not pleased to see him, it's just that there's no chance of Audrey making an appearance if he's here.

"You are agreeing to go to Rome?"

"Yes, I'm agreeing," I say, finally locating the holdall and shaking it out. "Help me, Bogdan! I don't know what to pack."

"For weekend away with bad-boy actor Dillon O'Hara? Who, by the way Libby, am giving you much kudos for snaggling."

"I think you mean snaring. But thanks anyway Bogdan."

"For weekend away with this man, am thinking naughty knickers and not much alternative."

"Well, sure." My cheeks are flushing and my heart is racing at the mere prospect of this. "But I do need a *few* more bits and bobs, Bogdan. For sightseeing, and meals, and stuff . . ."

"Why not be taking new things from Net-a-Porter order?"

Oh, Christ, that *bloody* order!

"No, Bogdan, I can't do that, in fact I really have to send it all back . . ."

"Oh, Libby, please do not be doing that!" He disappears through his hole in the wall for a moment, and then re-emerges holding several pieces of clothing in his huge hands. "Am loving this pencil skirt. Is perfect with this stripy T. And dress by Victoria Beckham is almost as gorgeous as husband —"

"Bogdan! You shouldn't have got it all out! Oh, God, you haven't taken the labels off, have you?"

"Do not be worrying, Libby am doing no such thing. You are able to be wearing clothes for weekend in Rome and then returning them when back."

"No! I'm not doing that!" (It's not that I'm not tempted, but on the form of the past few days, I'll accidentally set light to the pencil skirt and somehow contrive to stumble upon an open-air paintballing battle the moment I step out of the hotel in the — admittedly absolutely stunning — Victoria Beckham column dress). "Look, I've got enough OK stuff of my own already to be able to pack for a weekend. I just need one dress, and some decent jeans . . . there should be a skinny pair folded up in one of the boxes . . ."

"All right. Am putting some things in bag for you while you are fixing make-up."

"I don't need to fix my make-up."

"You are needing," he tells me, firmly, "to fix make-up."

Seeing as it was seven o'clock this morning when I first put my full face on, he's probably got a point. And anyway, I don't have time to do both — pack *and* glam up a bit — by myself. So we work in companionable silence for two or three minutes, Bogdan holding up bits and bobs of my clothing, regarding them mournfully and then either discarding them or popping them into the holdall, and me putting on fresh blusher and mascara, plus another layer of concealer on my eye, then dashing over to the bathroom across the hallway to do my teeth and grab my wash-bag.

"Am packing black dress, grey skinny jeans, selection tops, nice shoes. Am *not* packing diabolical grey hoodies. And am assuming," Bogdan intones, holding out the full-to-bursting bag as I come back into the flat, "you are preferring to be packing naughty knickers yourself. In handbag, perhaps."

"Yes, you're right. Thanks, Bogdan." I pop my wash-bag and make-up into the holdall and zip it up. "In fact . . ." I see one final opportunity to have a moment of alone-time. ". . . while I do that, can you maybe pop down and tell Dillon I'll be two more minutes?"

"Of course. Will be taking bag and coat down for you," he says, taking the holdall back, picking up my black trench from the arm of the sofa and sloping off out of the door to go down to the street.

OK; this really is the last chance before I go.

"Audrey?" I hiss, while simultaneously rummaging through one of my clothes boxes in search of . . . a lacy black bra and knickers, yep . . . and this sort of see-through floaty nightie thing, perfect . . . I pop both into my handbag before scuttling to the Chesterfield and sitting down. "Please turn up, just for a minute. I'm going away to Rome for the weekend — with Dillon, can you believe it? — and I really, really wanted to tell you something before I go."

Again, nothing happens.

"Can you hear me, at least?"

There's no answer to this question, one way or the other.

"The thing is, I just wanted to say thank you, Audrey. From the bottom of my heart. Because I went to meet my dad tonight, and even though it was awful at first, it ended up going just the way you said. Like this rope was unfurling itself from around me . . . well, I probably don't need to explain it to you, do I? The fact is, it's just . . . *better*."

But still the only sound I can hear is the low traffic rumble from Colliers Wood High Street outside.

"Anyway, I'm off for this weekend away with Dillon now, of all things. I don't know what you'd say about it if you were here. I hope you'd think it's insanely romantic. Maybe you'd just think it's insane. But this

349

sort of thing has never happened to me before —
getting swept off to the airport by a gorgeous modelizer
— so I'm seizing the moment for once in my life. And
it's *Rome*, Audrey! You of all people must understand
why I'm going?"

This time, when there's no reply, I decide it's time to
call it a day.

I'm not sure exactly why, but I'm getting the feeling
that I won't be seeing Audrey Hepburn again. On the
haunted Chesterfield, or anywhere else for that matter.

I just have this sense that she knows I'm going to be
OK.

Or maybe it's just that *I* know I'm going to be OK.

I hastily locate my passport — miraculously exactly
where I hoped it would be, in a large box-file marked
IMPORTANT STUFF — then pop it into my
handbag alongside the naughty knickers, which I'm
going to have to do a better job of stashing in an inside
pocket before we go through security at Heathrow. I
grab my keys and head for the door.

"It was wonderful hanging out with you, Audrey," I
say, to the apricot-coloured Chesterfield. "Drop by for
a Nespresso any time."

And then I close the door behind me.

Dillon's waiting taxi is contributing to something of a
snarl-up on Colliers Wood High Street: a van has pulled
up on the opposite side and is starting to unload huge
crates of (dear God, I hope) dead chickens for delivery
to Bogdan's Chicken 'n' Ribz, which means that larger
vehicles like buses and lorries are struggling to get

through the narrow gap. So I put a bit of speed on and hurry towards it.

Dillon and Bogdan are standing on the pavement, chatting ("you are really thinking I should be opening own salon? You are thinking I am having what it is taking?") and Dillon's handsome face lights up in a smile when he sees me coming.

"Perfect timing," he says, as he opens the taxi door for me; then, before I get in, places my trenchcoat solicitously over my shoulders. "Amazing shades, by the way," he adds. "Just the thing for Rome."

"Shades?"

"They fell out of your coat pocket when Bogdan handed it to me. I hope they're not damaged, or anything."

"Sure, but I don't actually . . ." I slide a hand into the pocket of my trench and pull out a pair of sunglasses.

Oliver Goldsmith sunglasses. In brown tortoiseshell.

I glance over at Bogdan.

"Bogdan, did you . . ." I try to sound more casual, because Dillon is standing right here, after all. "I thought I said I didn't want to bring anything from that Net-a-Porter order."

Because that's where they must have come from, surely?

"You are saying this, Libby, yes."

"But these sunglasses —"

"Are not from order. Am not seeing them at all before now."

"They're pretty fabulous," Dillon says, putting the sexiest of hands in the small of my back and starting to guide me into the taxi. "A lot like the ones Audrey Hepburn wears in *Breakfast at Tiffany's*."

That's because, I know without a shadow of a doubt as I look more closely at them, they *are* the ones Audrey Hepburn wears in *Breakfast at Tiffany's*.

The ones she lost, and then found down the side of the sofa.

But they definitely haven't been in my coat pocket before now. Definitely weren't in my coat pocket when I was coming back from The Jade Dragon, earlier. I had my hands shoved in my pockets for most of the walk home, because of the nip in the air, so I think I'd have noticed.

I think — in fact, somehow, don't ask me how, I *know* — that Audrey has left them behind for me. Deliberately, before she went on her way, as a sort of memento of her existence. A souvenir of our time together.

And if the sunglasses are so real that they're here in my hand now, in the outside world, for Dillon and Bogdan to see as well as me . . . well, does it mean that Audrey, too, was somehow . . . *real*, after all?

"Libby?" Dillon slides an arm around me as the taxi moves off; I hadn't even noticed he'd got in beside me. "Is everything all right?"

"Everything's good. Better than good. Perfect."

"That's exactly what I was hoping you'd say." He leans closer and gently, spine-tinglingly, nuzzles my neck. "I'm really glad I met you, Fire Girl," he murmurs.

"And I'm glad I . . ."

There's a quiet ping, from my iPhone.

". . . met you," I finish.

"Traffic's looking iffy on the A3, mate," the taxi driver is suddenly pulling open his little screen to say. "Happy for me to try the South Circ instead?"

As Dillon leans forward to discuss this with him, I reach for my bag and slide out my iPhone.

It's Olly — a reply to my last text about my dad.

Proud of you, Lib. Speak in the morning. Sleep well O xx

I would reply that sleep might be a bit tricky tonight, seeing as I'm on my way to catch a late-night flight to Rome with Dillon O'Hara, but given how much Olly seems to dislike Dillon — and wary of inciting another Le Creuset threat — I obviously don't do this.

Thanks, Olly, I text back. And if I didn't make this clear enough earlier, you're definitely not a Labrador. Love you loads. L xx

"He's going to take the South Circular," Dillon tells me, sitting back again and sliding that arm back round my shoulders. "But don't you worry; we're going to get ourselves to Rome tonight, even if I have to sprout wings. Or hire a private jet and fly us there myself. That would've sounded a bit cooler if I'd said it first, wouldn't it?"

"Oh, Dillon." I pull him in closer. "When did you ever need to worry about not sounding cool?"

He laughs, and leans down, and starts to kiss me, as our taxi wends its way through the dusk towards the South Circular, and Heathrow, and our Roman holiday.